VALIANT SON

ENGLAND'S LEGENDARY BLACK PRINCE

R. JAY BRENNER

ISBN 979-8-218-76842-3

Published by Royalty Books

Dedicated to
Ami Beatty Johnson Janes

E.  P.

TABLE OF CONTENTS

DRAMATIS PERSONAE

Due to naming customs of the period, many persons portrayed in this novel share the same name. To minimize confusion, name spellings were altered or variations or nicknames were used, if they existed at the time. For the same reason, many are referred to by their titles rather than their names, for example, Warwick vs. Thomas Beauchamp.

English Royal Family

King Edward III — King of England; also grandson of King Philippe IV of France

Queen Philippa — consort of King Edward; daughter of Count William of Hainaut

Edward of Woodstock — eldest son and heir

Isabella — eldest daughter, Countess of Bedford

Johanna — (Joan) second daughter

Lionel of Antwerp — second son, Duke of Clarence

John of Gaunt (Ghent) — third son, Duke of Lancaster

Edmund of Langley — fourth son, Duke of York

Mary — third daughter, Duchess of Brittany

Margaret — youngest daughter, Countess of Pembroke

Thomas of Woodstock — youngest son, Duke of Gloucester

Queen Isabella — Mother of King Edward III; daughter of King Philippe IV of France

Queen Joan — King Edward III's sister; Queen of Scotland

The Kent Family

Jack — (John) future Earl of Kent, first cousin to King Edward III

Joan — daughter of the Earl of Kent, first cousin to King Edward III

Lady Margaret (née Wake) — Countess of Kent; John and Joan's mother

Notables

Henry of Grosmont — cousin, Earl of Derby, later Duke of Lancaster

William Bohun — Earl of Northampton, Constable of England

William Montagu — Earl of Salisbury

Lady Catherine (née Grandison) — Countess of Salisbury

Will Montagu — son and heir, Earl of Salisbury

Thomas Beauchamp — Earl of Warwick, Marshal of England

Robert Ufford — Earl of Suffolk, commander

William Clinton — Earl of Huntingdon, Admiral of the Western Fleet

Hugh de Audley— Earl of Gloucester

John Stratford — Chancellor, Archbishop of Canterbury

Lady Elizabeth de Clare — royal cousin, granddaughter of Edward I

John Chandos — knight/commander, Edward's mentor and companion

William St. Omer — Edward's household steward

Thomas Holland — knight, commander

Roger Mortimer — knight, Edward's companion

Richard FitzAlan —Earl of Arundel, commander

John de Vere — Earl of Oxford, commander

Godfrey de Harcourt — Norman Vicomte, under-marshal

Reginald Cobham — knight, commander

Thomas Hatfield — Bishop of Durham; commander

Bartholomew Burghersh (elder) — 1st Baron Burghersh; tutor, diplomat & commander

Thomas Ughtred — knight/commander, Vanguard's under-marshal

James Audley — knight/commander, Edward's companion

Hugh Despenser — knight/commander

GLOSSARY OF TERMS

Affinity - The following of a lord.

Aketon - A padded jacket with long-sleeves; a simple form of armour either worn under a hauberk or independently.

Aventail - A flexible curtain of mail attached to the skull of a helmet that extends to cover the neck, and often also the throat and shoulders.

Banneret - A knight entitled to bear a banner; of higher status than a bachelor, junior knight.

Baron - A vassal holding land directly from the crown; serves as a member of the king's council.

Barbican - A fortified entrance to a town gate, castle, or bridge, sometimes with towers.

Bascinet - An open-faced, conical-shaped helmet.

Berfois - A tiered viewing stand for spectators.

Bombard - A type of siege cannon.

Buss - A brief kiss, often on the cheek.

Caparison - An ornamental covering spread over a horse.

Centenaur - Commander of 100 archers.

Chamberlain - Officer of the Royal Household responsible for managing the household.

Chancellor - Officer of the Royal Household serving as the monarch's secretary.

Chanfron - Plate armour to protect a horse's face and ears.

Chattel - Humans considered property.

Cog - A flat-bottomed ship a central mast and square sail.

Cortège - A procession; train of attendants.

Constable - Officer in command of the army or important garrison

Cote - Hut or cottage.

Cotehardie - A long-sleeved, closely-fitting garment worn over a smock and often laced.

Courser - A swift and strong horse used in battle or to hunt.

Crenelated - A fortified wall topped with square battlements (notches) from which to fire at attackers.

Crossbow - A ranged weapon utilizing an elastic launching device mounted horizontally.

Demense - Land attached to a manor.

Destrier - A warhorse trained for battle.

Faubourg - A neighborhood or district outside a fortified town's walls.

Fealty - An oath of loyalty sworn by a vassal to his lord.

Galley - A narrow, shallow-draft warship with ramming beaks and carried 6-60 oarsmen.

Gambeson - A tight-fitting, wool-padded garment worn under mail.

Greave - Plate armour to protect shins.

Harness - Protective body armour worn by a soldier

Hastilude - Military games, tournament

Hauberk - A mail shirt covering the neck & shoulders but eventually worn to the knee.

Hobelar - Fast-riding infantryman.

Jesses - Short leather straps attached to a hunting raptor's legs for control

Jupon - A sleeveless, tight-fitting jacket worn over armour typically displaying the wearer's coat of arms.

Kit - A set of equipment for battle including protective gear and weapons.

Lists - An area designated with ropes or barriers which defined a tournament field.

Livery - An identifying design, such as a uniform, ornament, symbol or insignia that designates ownership or affiliation.

Longbow - A powerful, vertically drawn bow, usually six feet in length, with extensive range.

Mangonel - A type of trebuchet that requires manpower vs. the use of counterweight.

Mail/Maile - Small rings of metal interlinked and fashioned into a mesh-like protective garment. The use of chain is a misnomer and derives from a misunderstanding of how mail is made; there are no chains involved, only linked rings of metal.

Maistresse - A woman in service with authority, such as a house-keeper or governess.

Mêlée - Hand-to-hand confused combat.

Natheless - Even so, nevertheless.

Palfrey - A highly-valued, smooth-gaited horse comfortable for riding

Parapet - A low protective wall at the edge of a structure, balustrade.

Pavise - An oblong shield large enough to cover an entire body used by bowmen.

Piaffe - A slow, high-stepping trot without moving forward.

Quintain - A medieval, lance-handling training mechanism consisting of a shield and a dummy suspended from a pole. When the shield was struck by a charging trainee's lance, the apparatus would rotate. If the target were struck accurately, the trainee could avoid being sruck by the rotating arms.

Retinue - A collection of persons retained in service of a noble, often military men.

Ribald - A type of early cannon made from several small-bore barrels strapped together by steel bands and mounted on a cart or wagon.

Routier - A soldier belonging to a free company.

Rufter - A loose-fitting, leather hood worn by birds of prey trained for hunting.

Sangfroid - Composure, equanimity

Scabbard - Sheath for a sword.

Sergeant - One of twenty-four knights in attendance on the king.

Springald - A type of catapult or oversized crossbow to fire bolts or stones.

Sumpter - A pack horse, pony, mule or other animal.

Surcoat - A long outer garment worn by soldiers over mail, often displaying coats of arms.

Tilt - Originally the name given to the barrier between joust combatants; later the term referred to riding with a lance at rings, and later still, a synonym for joust.

Trappings - Long cloth or leather coverings draped over warhorses to deflect projectiles.

Trébuchet - A counter-weighted catapult siege engine to hurl boulders.

Tun - A large barrel or cask for wine.

Vambrace - Plate armour to protect the forearm.

Vassal - A free man holding lands from a lord who owes homage and services.

Ventenar - Commander of twenty archers.

Wardship - A feudal lord's control of a minor heir, lands and income.

Duchy of Aquitaine

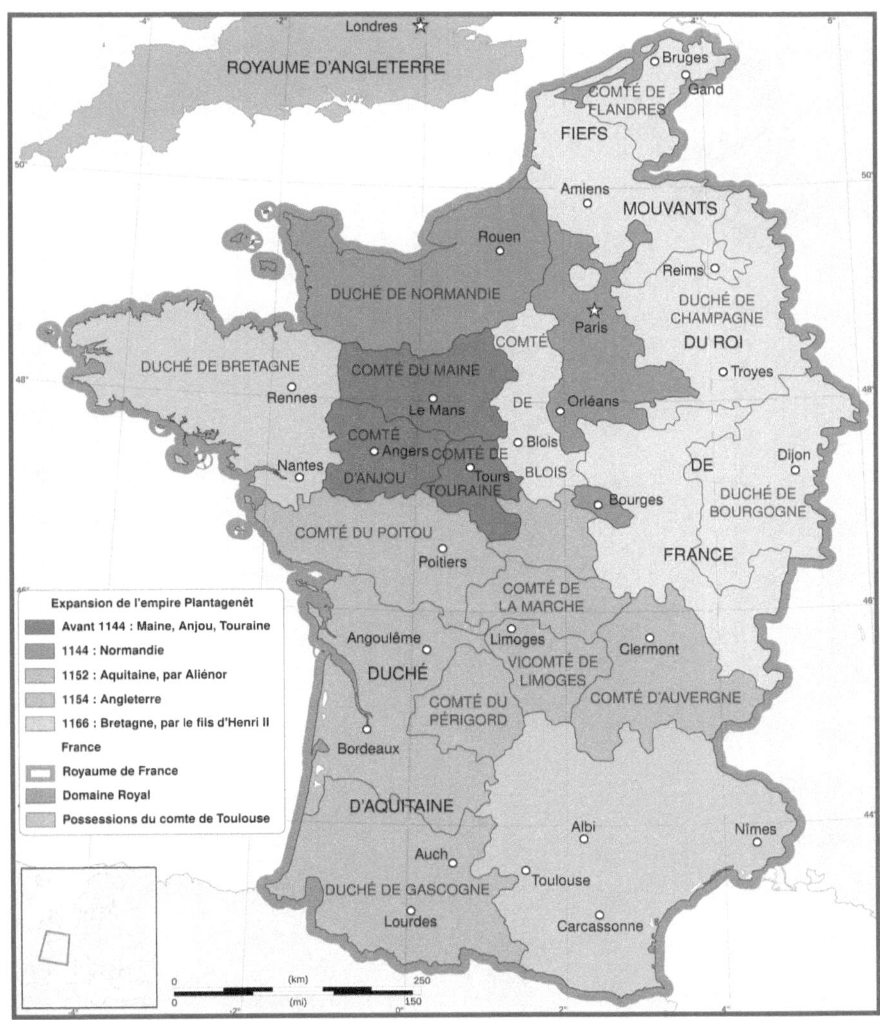

The Duchy of Aquitaine (Gascony) was an English-held territory in what is now southwestern France. The duchy became part of England when Eleanor of Aquitaine married King Henry II in 1189. Technically, Aquitaine was a vassal state of France, and homage was owed to the French king, often causing friction between monarchs.

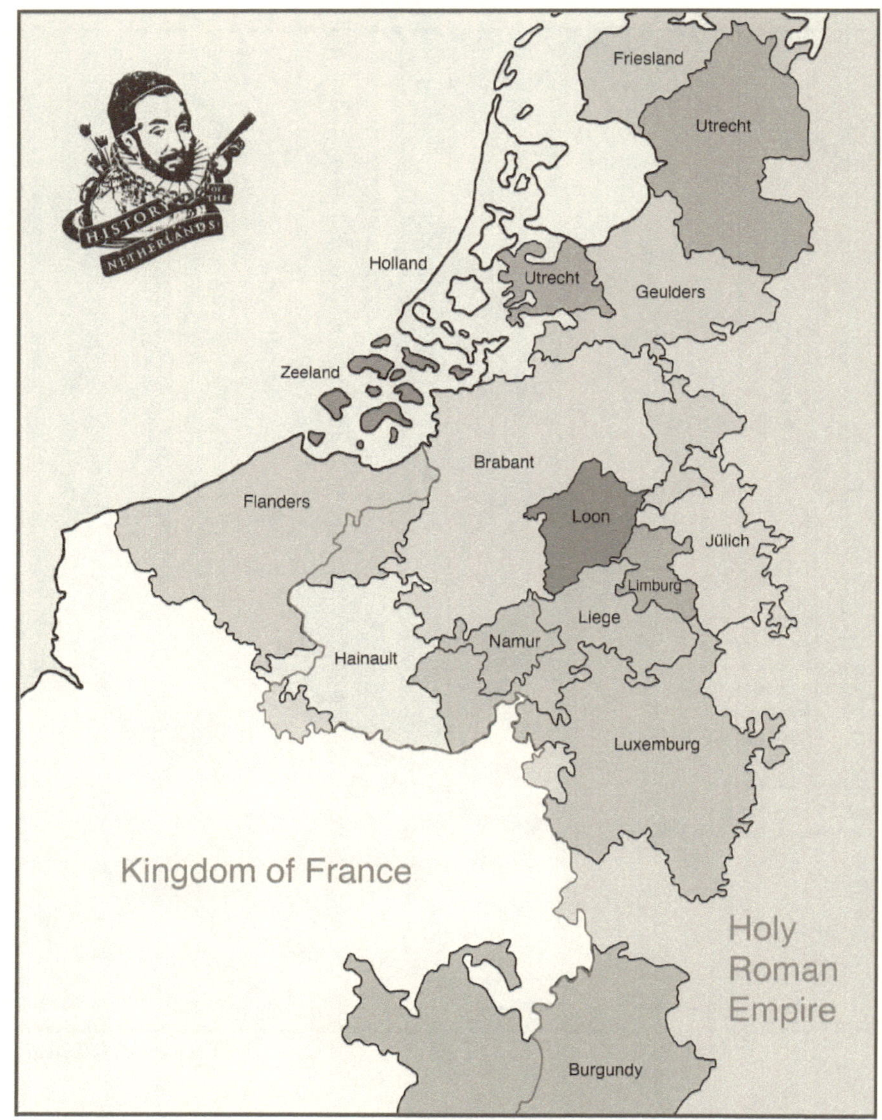

Permission for use courtesy of David Cenzer

The Low Countries encompass modern-day Belgium, the Netherlands, and Luxembourg. In 1330, the politically fragmented region consisted of the counties of Flanders, Holland and Zeeland, Hainault, Guelders, and the duchy of Brabant. The region produced textiles dependent on English wool.

1346 English Army Invasion Route

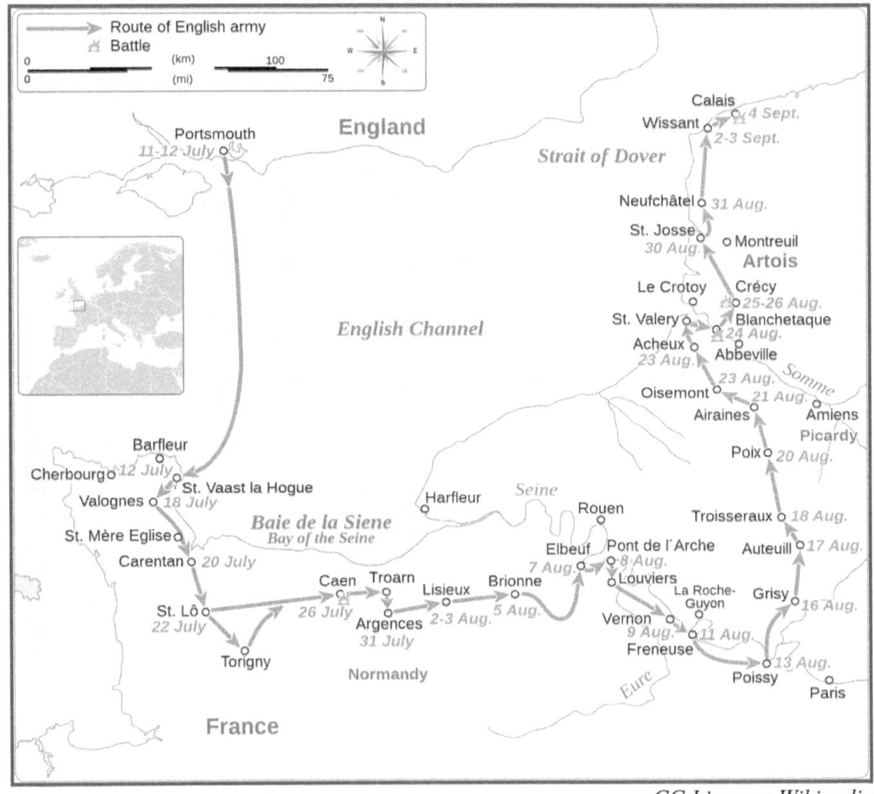

The English fleet landed in Normandy at Sainte Vaast la Hougue on 12 July, 1346. The army marched for almost seven weeks, a distance of approximately 300 miles (480 km), until battling the French at Crécy on 26 August, 1346. The English then laid siege to Calais, lasting from 4 September, 1346, until the garrison surrendered on 3 August, 1347.

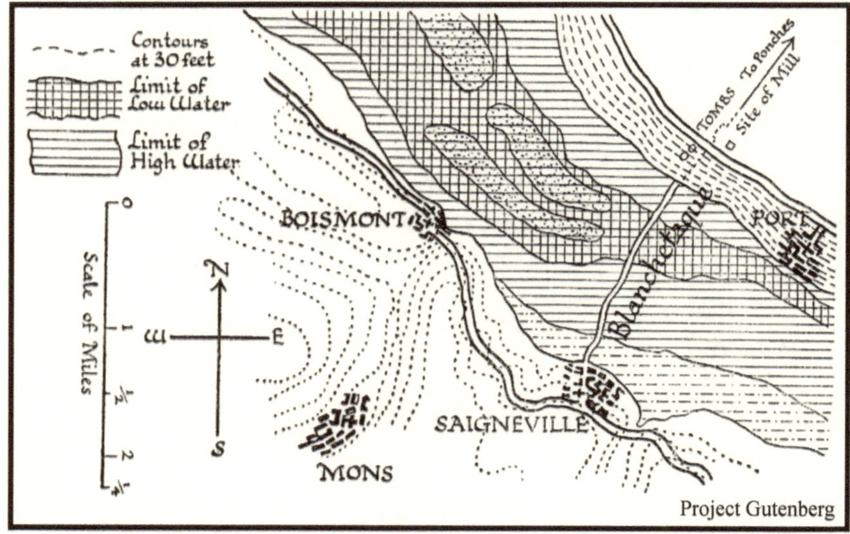

Fording the Somme at Blanchetaque for the English in 1346 was like completing a Hail Mary pass in an NFL game today. The estuary was bounded by steep banks, with a tidal variance of as much as 25 feet. The ford itself was comprised of firm marl, a sedimentary rock mixture of clay and calcite.

Terrain of Crécy

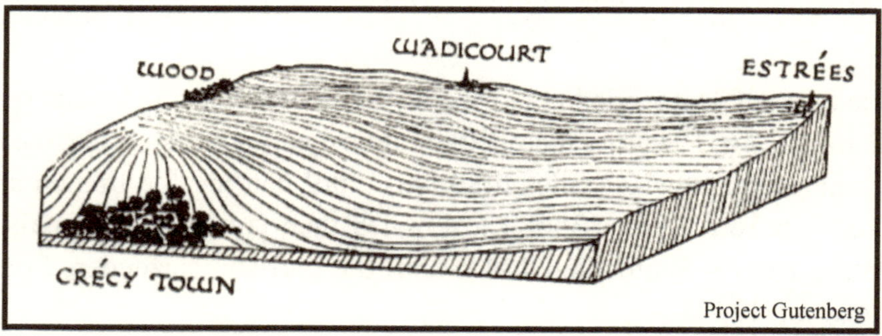

The nature of the terrain at Crecy played a critical role in its value as a defensive position. As shown here, the slope was steeper at the end nearer Crécy and the slope's incline was deceptive, appearing less steep and challenging than it would be for horses attempting to charge uphill in rain-drenched soil.

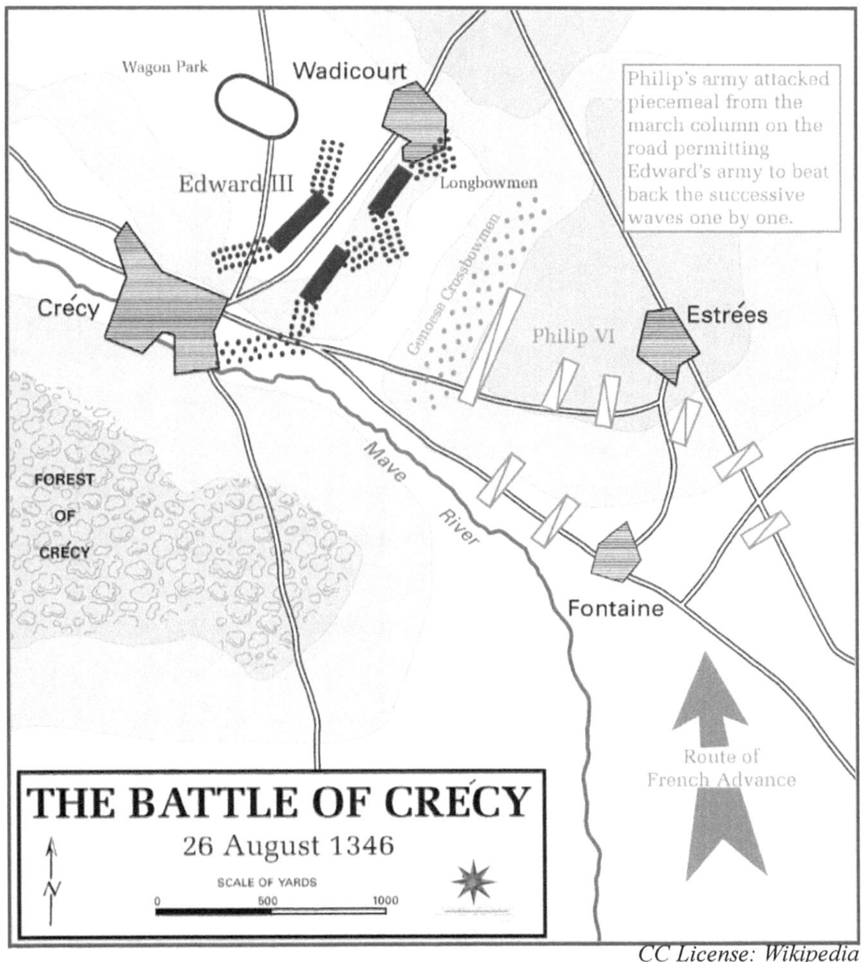

CC License: Wikipedia

The site itself helped even the odds for the English, outnumbered 4:1 by the French. The English arrayed on a ridge with the English army defending the higher ground and using the river gully to the west and farming terraces to the east to protect its flanks. The savvy English prepared the terrain, digging pits and ditches and placing sharpened stakes to disrupt the French cavalry charges.

TASTE OF DUTY

March 1338 – Windsor Castle

Edward tightened the grip on his sword and crept ahead, stealing from tree to tree, shadow to shadow. His heart pumping in his ears, he held his breath, and listened.

Nothing.

Even the birds were silent. The back of his neck prickled.

Edward edged forward again, the musty odor of rotting leaves wafting up with each carefully placed step. Any stray sound might alert the French to his retinue's position. He hunched behind a stump, scanning the grove for enemy movement. A patch of ochre flashed to his left. His heart leapt, then settled. *Jack.* His cousin darted behind a tangle of bushes.

A breeze rattled the branches overhead. Edward held his breath again, trying to catch any sound which did not belong, A branch snapped behind him. He jerked around. *Will.* Advancing from the rear. He shot Will a warning look. His misstep could cost them their lives.

Edward studied the terrain. A rough track cut through the wood about a dozen yards ahead. Huge boulders mounded both sides and tree branches twisted overtop forming a murky tunnel.

Perfect for an ambush.

Edward remained motionless, straining to hear over the thudding of his heart. His father's voice played in his head. *A king leads.* Taking a ragged breath, he half rose, raised his wooden sword above his head and signaled, then dashed forward and ducked behind an outcropping. Will and Jack scurried to the rocks and huddled beside him.

Faint voices and the creak of a saddle drifted from the track. Edward held a finger to his lips, then peeked over the rocks. Two riders approached. He ducked down and gestured for his friends to remain still.

Hoofbeats sounded nearer. A horse snorted.

"Is the rumor true…about the ships?"

"Yesterday's dispatch confirmed it," a second, gruff voice said. "A fleet of galleys flying French colors was spotted off the South Coast."

Edward knew that voice: the Earl of Warwick, an advisor on the king's Council. Why were enemy ships sailing so near shore?

"King Philippe violates the Pope's edicts as if they do not exist," the first man said.

The horses plodded on.

"The French do not belong anywhere near our coast," the Earl said. "Damn that French dog!"

When the riders passed out of sight, Edward climbed to his feet. "Did you hear?"

Jack tapped his sword against a rock. "I wonder why the ships are here?"

Will brushed dirt and leaves from his gold-embroidered tunic. "You can continue playing your silly make believe mission, but I am going to find my father. He will know what is afoot and will not keep it from me."

At Will's implied slight, Edward stiffened. Just because Will was ten, two years older, he thought himself better than them. Edward was fed up with the Earl of Salisbury's pompous heir.

He clenched his fists about to wipe the smirk off Wills face, but Will turned around. Only a coward would punch someone in the back. Edward gritted his teeth. He could hear his father telling him to pick his battles wisely. Edward checked his temper and unclenched his fists. Will would get his comeuppance one day, just not today.

Jack leaned on a boulder. "Should we head back? I could do with something to eat."

"Like always," Will said.

"What say we race back?" Edward glanced from Jack to Will.

"Alright." Jack grinned.

"You take that path." Edward pointed his sword. "Will, you take that one, and I will take this one. Meet at the courtyard's side gate."

"Want to wager who will win?" Will asked, a smug twist to his mouth.

"One, two, three, go!" Jack sprinted away. Will chased behind until Jack cut to the path on the right.

Edward raced downslope, whooping, and running through puddles from the previous day's storm, splashing water and mud onto his hose. Tiny brown dunnocks flitted from the hawthorns covered with white blooms. Thank heaven old Master Burley released them early from lessons. Who could concentrate on Latin on a day as fine as this? He slowed and breathed deep. Could a person actually smell green?

He swished his blade into the plants and bushes lining the trail. A loud splash came from the direction of pond. He walked that way, then stopped short. Jack's sister, Joan, her back to him, stood near the edge of the pond. Rings rippled across the surface.

Joan must have heard him. She turned around and stared, her eyes the same clear blue as Jack's. Tears smeared the dirt on her cheeks and her hair straggled from a blue ribbon. She sniffed and wiped her nose with the sleeve of her kirtle.

"Is something amiss?" He hesitated to ask her.

Joan toed the rotting log at her feet. "M-mother is leaving… again."

"Oh." Edward scratched his nose, not sure what to say. "My father goes away all the time, too."

"At least you have a father!"

Edward cringed for putting his foot in it. "Yes, well—I am sorry about your father, but I am glad you and Jack came to live with us."

Still frowning, Joan brushed at her skirt, smearing the dirt into dark smudges. Joan was in for a scold from her mother. Lady Margaret fussed about such things.

"You know, Jeanette, you are my best friend," he paused a moment, "even if you are a girl!" He stuck his tongue through the gap of his missing tooth.

Joan tried to hide her grin. "So, toothless Edward, what are you doing out here?"

"Fie! I forgot. I have to go…to meet up with your brother and Will." He dashed off, calling over his shoulder, "Come, if you want."

When the castle ramparts finally appeared through the trees, Edward's chest heaved. Joan panted up beside him.

"Ho, Edward!" Will leaned against the upper bars of the gate with Jack sitting cross-legged at his feet. "I might ask what kept you," Will said, his lips twisting in a sneer, "but I see you picked up a barnacle."

Joan's cheeks flushed bright pink.

Edward glared at Will. "How dare you be so rude? Apologize to Joan, right now." The king did not tolerate bad manners. Neither would he.

Will shrugged, a smug look on his face.

Edward crossed his arms. "I cannot believe how ill-mannered you are. What kind of knight do you think you will make with such behavior? Now, apologize."

Will hesitated, looking anywhere but at Edward. Then he mumbled, "Sorry."

"Is that the best you can do? Your apology is as feeble as your sword skill."

Will turned red as a cock's comb. His gaze flew to Joan, a curve at the corners of her mouth. A few moments passed before Will said more in a more humble tone, "Sorry, Joan."

Jack scowled at Will. "Why do you have to be so mean? What has Joan ever done to you?"

Hoofbeats clattered on the other side of the wall. "Ho, you boy, take my mount!" A man said. "Where is the king? You, ginger, take me to him. Now!"

Jack peered through the bars of the stout wooden gate. "A courier," he called over his shoulder. "Od! He is wholly covered with dust and his horse is lathered in a thick, brown slutch."

"Can you make out his colors?" Joan asked.

"Hard to tell. Could be gold lions on a red field. There may be a quartered chequy beneath the mess."

"Those sound like the Earl of Arundel's colors," Edward said, squeezing in front of Jack to look.

Jack whistled. "No wonder his mount looks done in. Covering the distance from Sussex would take at least eight hours."

Edward looked back over his shoulder. "I wonder what is so urgent."

King Edward paced his privy chamber, back and forth, back and forth, wearing a path between his writing desk and the oak table in the center of the room. A roar erupted from the menagerie below, followed by three chest-rumbling harumffs. The king chuckled to himself. He paced just like Tower lions. But, unlike the Barbaries, he was unfettered, free to confront his foe. The faux French king's interference would not go unchallenged, not in Gascony, Scotland, or on English shores. Not when the French crown rightfully belonged to him, not that Valois usurper, his cousin Philippe.

The king stopped in front of a hunt scene hanging on the wall behind his paper-littered desk. He saw it, yet he did not. Arundel's courier pounded more than sixty miles to report the French attack on Portsmouth. Unbelievable. Half the town was torched before Arundel's men drove them off.

God rot Philippe!

He began pacing again, his boots rapping sharply against the planks. *Jesu!* His advisors should have responded to his summons by now. Where were they? His mind seethed anew recalling Philippe's confiscation of Aquitaine the previous summer. That duchy belonged to England, to him! So much for Pope Benedict's peace.

A knock sounded. His chamberlain opened the door and one by one, his advisors filed in, all except Huntingdon. Archbishop Stratford, his Chancellor, hobbled in last. Six decades slowed the archbishop's gait, but his mental acuity remained sharp..

'Huntingdon is on his way, sire." The gems on the archbishop's cincture clicked as he doddered inside.

"*Bon.*" King Edward commanded the head of the table and waved everyone to seats.

Henry, Earl of Derby, his cousin, sat to his right. He and Henry grew up together; he admired the man. Tall and fair, Henry's repute arose from his successful Scottish campaigns as well as his success with the ladies.

"*Mes amis*, nothing remains unknown for long around here, not the way rumors fly through these halls. By now you have all heard of Portsmouth's ruin at Philippe's hands."

"If the reports are true," Derby said, "half the town was burned, including the warehouses. This is not the first time Philippe has trampled the pontiff's truce and not likely his last."

"Derby is right," Robert Ufford, Earl of Suffolk, said. "That dog Philippe can attack us at will. He fears no papal reprisals, not when he hosts the Holy See in Avignon." Suffolk used his hands ebulliently when he talked, a habit which drew much teasing from his friends. The earl accepted the frequent teasing with good grace, one reason the men held him in high esteem. His steadfast support of the king and his reliability in battle were two others.

Suffolk added, "Philippe protects the Church and that toady, Pope Benedict, will do nothing to jeopardize his comfortable position."

Murmurs of agreement rippled around the table, then went silent.

William Clinton, Earl of Huntingdon, appeared in the half-open doorway. "Your pardon, sire." He took to a seat.

"You are aware of the situation?" King Edward asked.

"Indeed. I just came from questioning the courier. He provided details: the number of ships, sizes and estimated number of men-at-arms. This was no small undertaking by the French." Deep lines webbed the corners of the earl's eyes, earned from many hours aboard ship.

"*D'accord.*" King Edward nodded.

The French posed a serious threat and the men around the table felt it. The tension in the chamber became palpable. Men shifted, rubbing jaws and fingering moustasches.

"It is long past time we put an end to the Valois usurper's transgressions," Derby said.

"*Certainment*," King Edward agreed. "What might you suggest?"

"If we are to go against France," Suffolk said, "we need a friendly port for landing troops and supplies."

King Edward steepled his fingers, pleased these men were coming around; the discussion was moving in the direction he desired.

"Gentlemen," Huntingdon tapped the table. "Suffolk is right about securing a friendly port. In fact, we may need more than one. Lord King, might I ask where negotiations stand with your relations in Hainault and Flanders, and your cousin in Brabant?"

"Yes, my relations." King Edward prowled the chamber. Of all his boyhood companions present, Huntingdon was the most clever. His question required an honest explanation, one more candid than the king was inclined to offer today.

"It vexes me no end to report my queen's brother remains uncommitted to my cause."

"Perhaps he does not see the benefit of freeing himself from Philippe's yoke," Derby said.

"Indeed, it may be so. As for my cousin of Brabant," King Edward, pressed his lips together. "I have no doubt my relations choose to believe Philippe's false promises, that he will honour their provincial rights."

Stratford raised a finger. "If I may make a suggestion, my lord?"

King Edward nodded.

"Your emissaries have long toiled to enlist your relations as allies: regrettably sire, they failed."

Heads around the table nodded.

Stratford continued, "Might you achieve greater success should you make the request in person?" The chancellor's lips quivered up at the corners. "You are known to be quite persuasive."

Suffolk grinned. "Indeed, sire, not one of us resists your…er… charm for long."

King Edward allowed himself a chuckle. These men knew him well, though no one possessed a more artful tongue than the wily archbishop.

Stratford rapped the table, ending the levity. "Let us not forget the peril you face should you go abroad."

"Nor the danger here," Derby added. "Should you sail to Flanders, as soon as the Scots catch wind of your absence, they will resume raiding our northern shires."

"The matter has not escaped me," King Edward said. One man at the table remained silent thus far. "What say you, Hugh?"

Deep lines creased the Earl of Gloucester's aged brow. He raised deep-set, hooded eyes. "Go to Flanders, Lord King. My troops are well-armed and well practiced in defeating the northern mongrels."

A smattering of laughter followed Gloucester's remark. Skirmishing with the Scots and chasing them back across the border was second nature to him.

King Edward clapped his hands. "So, are we in accord, *messieurs*? I am to sail to Flanders despite the risks? We set our sights set on France?"

"Aye."

"*Bon.*" King Edward sent silent thanks heavenward for the

loyalty of his stalwart friends. Though they agreed, an uncertainty hovered below the surface.

Derby frowned. "The campaign will require every soldier we can muster."

"Indeed. Stratford, send orders to Salisbury. Break off the siege at Dunbar. The troops are to return to London immediately.."

Stratford tapped his fingers together. "What about the mission in Gascony?"

"Cancel it. We cannot spare the men. For now, the Gascon lords must repel the French attacks on their own."

"Not for long, sire," Derby said. "When Philippe learns of your landing in Flanders, he will recognize the threat, and recall his forces from Gascony."

"You make a good point." King Edward rubbed his jaw, aware of what the men were likely thinking. During his absence, someone must stand in his stead. In the past, his brother John, Earl of Cornwall, acted as Guardian. "Archbishop?"

The chancellor sat up, brows lifted. "Yes, Lord?"

"When I depart my realm, my son will serve as Guardian." The men's faces registered various levels of doubt.

"Young Edward?" Suffolk's voice pitched higher. "With respect, sire, your son is not yet eight and though nimble-witted—"

"There is no one else. Not since my brother's passing." A familiar pang struck. John died just shy of twenty years, the ache of his death remained, though buried. "My heir will serve more as figurehead than monarch, and will catch on quickly enough with Stratford's guidance." The king aimed a pointed look at the archbishop. "As chief counsel to oversee affairs, you will ensure no ill befalls my son."

Stratford stood. "An honour, sire. May I assume the lords gathered here will sail with you, save Gloucester? Who do you appoint to young Edward's Council?"

The question was not unexpected. "Arundel and Neville."

"As you wish." The archbishop rested his hands upon his ample middle. "I shall send out the writs."

"While my heir and his household reside in the Tower, London is to be closed to outsiders. Set the garrison to reinforce the palisade and add twenty men-at-arms and fifty archers to its guard. Huntingdon, how soon can we sail?"

"Requisitions will go out immediately, sire. Admiral Mauny's Northern fleet will sail from Dunbar to join with mine." Huntingdon served as Admiral of the Western Fleet. "Assembling the fleet will take several weeks. Let us aim to sail the week after Easter, from Great Yarmouth?"

"*Bon*. It cannot be soon enough."

Joan perched on a stool in her bedchamber while Lady Margaret stroked a brush through Joan's hair. A small fire crackled in the hearth to chase the early spring chill from the chamber. Joan curled her toes and tucked them under her smock, then closed her eyes, enjoying the feel of the brush against her scalp. She loved when her mother performed the routine chore herself, for it seemed the only time her mother paid her any attention.

Joan's maid hummed softly as she tucked Joan's chemise and kirtle in the wardrobe chest, then drew back the bed curtains.

"Begging your pardon. Shall I fetch your cup of milk now, Lady Joan?"

Joan nodded. Her maid's footsteps padded across the floor and the door latched behind her. Joan crossed her fingers, hidden in the folds of her gown.

"*Maman*, please, let me go with you and Jack. I promise, I shall not be any trouble." She hoped this time her mother would say yes. She hated always being left behind.

Lady Margaret's strokes grew sharper. "However do you get your hair in such dreadful tangles?"

"Ow!" Joan winced.

"Be still! This would not be so painful, if you behaved like a lady instead of running through the woods with Edward and his friends."

Heat rose in Joan's cheeks. Nothing she did seemed to please her mother while her brother could do no wrong. Her mother doted on Jack.

"You have beautiful hair, my dear, when properly dressed. Your flaxen tresses and blue eyes set you apart. You are too young to appreciate them, though one day you will come to see your beauty as an asset and value it."

How many times had Joan listened to her mother's litany of how the Lord blessed Joan with uncommon beauty, hair of palest gold, and eyes the color of cornflowers? At least, her mother described her as such. Her appearance seemed all Lady Margaret found pleasing about Joan. She took a breath and risked asking again, despite a likely no.

"*Maman*, please cannot I go with you?"

"Do not vex me." The brush stopped. "Have I not made myself clear? You are to remain here at court with Queen Philippa and her ladies." Her mother resumed her task, tugging through snarls.

Joan looked over her shoulder. "Why must I?"

"Do not test my patience further, girl!" By the twisted look on her mother's face, Joan was in for another scold.

"Listen to me." Lady Margaret rounded on Joan. "Though you may be ten years, it appears I must lay out all before you. As cousin to the king, you share with him the first King Edward's blood."

"Mother, I know this."

"Yes, you know he is your cousin. However, you have no fortune, nor lands of your own. While the king reversed your father's attainder for treason, his lands were already granted to others. We have nothing unless my appeals in the courts succeed." Lady Margaret put down the brush and installed herself on a stool.

"Your presence here at court reminds King Edward of his obligation to our family. After all, it was he who signed your father's death warrant, though loathe to do it and forced by that wicked Mortimer."

"But *Maman*-"

"The burden falls to me to labour on your brother's behalf to regain the Kent lands. You, young lady, must do your part to keep in your cousin's good graces. The king has been good to us and I believe Queen Philippa favours you, like a daughter."

Joan lowered her eyes. It was not right for her mother to take advantage of the queen's affection. Her mother schemed to influence the king so he would grant lands to Joan. King Edward probably felt guilty about signing his uncle's execution orders.

From what she was told, he brought Joan's family into the royal household as soon as he was free from Mortimer. Joan remembered no other home. Her mother was right about Queen Philippa. The queen did show a fondness for Joan and was so kind, yet Joan longed for her mother's affection.

"Please, *Maman*, I wish to be with you, to g-go with you and Jack."

"Enough!"

Joan flinched. Tears welled and she blinked them back. Crying would only stoke her mother's ire.

Emma returned with a cup of steaming honeyed milk, its aroma somehow calming. She picked up the brush and plaited Joan's hair.

Lady Margaret picked up one of the candles. "You may go," she said, dismissing Emma.

Joan climbed into bed and slid under the coverlet. She cupped her hands around the enticing brew and sipped.

Protecting the candle's flickering flame, her mother made to leave. At the doorway, her stern expression softened. "You and young Edward are thick as thieves. I doubt the pair of you will notice our absence." She offered a thin smile. "Now, that is settled. Go to sleep."

At mid-day, following a meeting with his Chancellor, King Edward dismissed his escort at the entrance to Queen Philippa's solar and rapped on the door. To his surprise, Philippa opened it herself, greeting him in a claret satin gown embroidered with doves of gold and fashioned in the new slim style. He recognized the fabric as one he personally selected, as he often did.

When Philippa rose from her curtsy, he reached for her hand and feathered a kiss upon it."Thank you for attending me so promptly, my lord." Philippa signaled her ladies, embroidering in the outer chamber, to leave.

When the door closed behind them, his wife's eyes met his, her lips lifted at the corners, and widened with genuine warmth. Philippa's smile reached all the way to her dark eyes, her sultry look never failed to stir him and this was no exception. He grinned in response to her smile while raising his brows in question.

"My request has not inconvenienced you?" Philippa gestured for him to sit.

"*Non, ma chérie.*" King Edward lowered himself onto a padded bench alongside the gaming table. He accepted a goblet of wine from his wife, her fingers adorned with four gem-studded rings. One for each child, including their fourth, William, born earlier in the year. Sadly, God claimed him and Philippa mourned his loss still.

His wife offered him an almond and currant cake, his favourite sweet. After he made his selection, she laid the plate on the table and strolled toward the window as if to look out, her satin skirts rustling with her movement. While he savored the confection, he admired Philippa's curves accentuated in the afternoon rays. Noting her gown, her scent, and his favourite sweets, the corners of his mouth curved upward; his artful queen wanted something.

Philippa tilted her head becomingly. "My lord…husband, if you would hear me out?"

With an inkling of her purpose, he nodded.

"Dearest, might you reconsider your decision for the girls to accompany us to Flanders?" Her smile dimmed; a furrow formed between her eyes. "Isabella and Johanna are so very young, susceptible to many ills—"

He held up his hand. "Your motherly concern does you credit, yet you need not distress yourself. Our good doctor will accompany us and attend to the family's well-being, especially yours, *mon coeur*." He dropped his gaze to her waistline, its thickening barely discernable.

Philippa smoothed her hands across the front of her low-waisted gown.

Previously, they discussed the French situation; he explained he could no longer ignore King Philippe's attacks, but he was not fool enough to challenge Philippe alone. He needed allies and those most likely to support him were their relations in the Low Countries. Philippa must accompany him as a reminder to her family of the ties which bound them.

He set aside his refreshment, reached for Philippa's hand, encouraged her closer, and into his lap. Though married ten years, a rosy hue graced her face.

"*Ma chére femme*, you know there are goodly reasons for our girls, and Joan, to accompany us." As he traced each of Philippa's fingers, she trembled.

"Consider, *ma petite*, though only ten years, our *jeune cousine* Joan shows signs of great beauty and, like you, the girls are destined for political unions. What better way to secure alliances? You know the truth in this, *n'est ce pas?*"

"Yes, but the thought of leaving them so far away to be raised by others…" Philippa's lips trembled. Her unfeigned anguish undid him. Raising her hand to his lips, he placed a kiss upon each finger.

"Think on our Edward. At seven he is too young to be left behind without family."

The king smoothed his fingers across his consort's cheek. "While your concern does you honour, *mon coeur*, it must be so."

Young Edward hurried in response to his father's unexpected summons. With each step, his apprehension grew. Did he do something wrong? When he reached the chamber door, he halted facing the carving of a fearsome griffin with its talons extended for a kill.

Edward shuddered a deep breath, then knocked.

The king's chamberlain opened the door, bowed to him, and departed abruptly. Normally a pleasant fellow, his hasty departure added another prickle of fear.

"Ahh, *viens ici,* come." The king rose and waved Edward forward.

"*Bonjour, mon père*...Lord King." Edward bowed. "You wished to see me?"

"*Oui.*" He gestured to a stool. "There is a matter we must discuss."

His father did not appear angry with him so what was this about?

"You heard of the French attack on Portsmouth?" The king crossed his wrists behind him, rocking back on his heels.

Edward gave a shaky nod.

"*Bon.* You should note such things. Be assured, brave men expelled those French dogs and they no longer threaten our shores." The king rested a hand on the mantle; his blue eyes sparked fire.

"What you do not know, Edward, is King Philippe's forces also attacked lands in our duchy of Aquitaine. They seized the towns of Penne and Blaye."

Edward never heard of either place.

"Enough is enough! We must stop King Philippe's attacks on our lands and put an end to his support of the Scots. That faux Valois king must pay the price for his transgressions!"

A vein pulsed in his father's jaw.

"We must show the French imposter this lion of England has teeth!"

Edward flinched.

"My advisors agree, but should we take up arms against France, we need allies. I must therefore go across the sea to persuade your mother's brother, my cousin of Brabant, and other powerful lords to join my cause."

Edward twisted the ruby ring on his thumb. His insides jittered. Was he supposed to say something?

"Your mother will sail with me, as will your sisters, and Joan."

"What?" Edward jumped to his feet. "*Mon père*, you mean to leave me here? Alone?" He cringed at the whine in his voice.

"You are old enough to shoulder more responsibility. Besides, you will not be alone. I will appoint advisors to guide you."

Edward's throat tightened. What if his father never came back?

"You will serve as Guardian of the Realm. It is your duty."

Duty. The word sounded as if from inside a cave.

"Me?"

The king placed a hand on his shoulder, and crouched down to look him in the eyes. "There is no one else, Edward, not since your Uncle John died. Though your memories of him may be few, as Duke of Cornwall, you bear his title. I relied upon him. Now, I rely upon you."

"*Mon père*, I am honoured by your faith in me and I do not wish to displease—"

"You can do this, *mon fis*" His father stood. "You showed me you are ready when you welcomed the Pope's emissaries to London last autumn."

He did? Edward searched his memory. Perhaps it was that time when he rode his pony in a procession with two silver-haired men in red robes.

"The Cardinals were charmed, and during their visit an important truce between our country and France was secured. *Alors*, you are more experienced than you think." The king tousled Edward's hair. "You are gifted with the two most vital traits of good kings."

"I am?" Edward nibbled his bottom lip.

"Authority and leadership. When you play with your friends they listen to you."

Heat crept up Edward's neck.

"Your task is not so formidable, *oui*?" The king pressed

Edward's shoulder. "*Bon*. Never forget, the blood of ancient kings, anointed by God, flows through your veins. You trust me?"

Edward swallowed hard. His father expected so much from him.

In Edward's chamber that night, embers glowed in the hearth. Moonbeams pierced intermittently through a gap in the bed curtains, shifting their color from rose to burgundy and back again. Edward thrashed in his bed coverings, wrestling under a chilling doom since the discussion with his father.

A cool draft slinked through the silence and footsteps whispered the scent of flowers. Edward peeked through the brocade panels framing his bed. "*Maman?*"

"*Oui, mon petit.*" Queen Philippa floated toward him, a wisp of smoke trailing from her fluttering candle. She placed it on the traveling chest and nudged the bed curtain aside. Her blue satin gown rustled as she settled beside him and her unbound hair fell in chestnut waves across her shoulders. As she leaned closer, her scent and hair tickled his nose. "You are troubled?"

How did she always know? Edward choked his next words past the lump his throat. "You are all going to Flanders without me." He did not know how to describe his feelings?

"*Maman…*"

She brushed a lock of hair from his forehead and cupped his cheek. Her brown eyes looked into his. "I want you to listen closely." Her voice tensed like a bowstring. "You have told me many times you dream of becoming a knight, *non?*"

He nodded.

"The duty of a knight is to obey his liege lord without question, is it not?"

He nodded again, his cheek brushing against her silky blue gown.

"Imagine your time as Guardian as a knight's challenge, not a brief contest like a joust but a test of stamina, like a siege."

Edward snuggled against her, comforted by the steady rise and fall of her breathing.

"Trust your father, Edward. Trust your king."

Tears slipped down his cheeks. Above all else, he wanted to make his father proud. "How shall I know what to do?"

She brushed his tears away and settled back against the tester. "Ahh, *mon fis*, Honourable men, like Archbishop Stratford, will be here to help you." She tucked his head against her shoulder. "As the king's heir, you owe him steadfast loyalty. Your father deserves no less. You must accept his will with unconditional grace. This is your duty."

Duty. That word again.

They sat in stillness, save for a few sparks from hearth. Of course, he trusted his father. He was the king. The lump in Edward's throat threatened to choke him. "W-what if you never come b-back?"

She squeezed him tighter and rested her chin on his head.

The wooden cross hanging on his chamber wall appeared through a gap in the bed curtains. The Savior's arms were spread wide and nails pierced His hands and feet. The Holy Ghost hovered above Him. Jesus sacrificed his life for His father.

Edward pulled away from his mother's embrace. "You are right, *Maman*. I owe a duty to my lord, my father."

A Thief in the Night

July 1338 - Port of Orwell

Gulls screeched over Edward's head, adding to the clamour of Orwell's busy port. The sharp wind and drizzle kept many less hardy townsfolk from venturing outside. Coarse seaman and burly porters trudged the slippery ramps, hauling royal chests and stowing them aboard the *Thomas* before the tide turned.

Thwack! Thwack! Thwack!

The banners at the top of the masts beat in an irritating rhythm and only made Edward's miserable mood worse. He worried the inside of his cheek and tasted blood. The banners, England's royal arms and four other saint-inspired banners, were intended to impress potential allies, when the ships docked in Antwerp. The smallest was thirty feet long and the largest seventy-five. According to his father, winning admiration was the first step in gaining support. Yet, the majesty meant nothing to Edward. All he could think about was that his father was going to war, and he might die.

A crowd of local merchants and families gathered on the wharf, all jostling to catch a glimpse of England's sovereign before he sailed. Over a hundred royal household guards lined the port's main street and stationed themselves about the quay. The red and gold royal livery stood out against the grey of the jetty and sky.

Edward leaned against the side of the inn. Merchant ships rocked in the bay, waiting for slips to open. The shriek of a low-flying seagull and the splat of the bird's discharge on the weatherworn planks at his feet broke Edward's reverie. "Cursed birds!" He ducked under the inn's thatched awning. A stream of servants carted supplies to the royal ships..

Edward!"

The wind whipped his name from Joan's lips and her hair across her face as she scurried from the inn. Clutching her traveling cloak tight, she skidded on the wet jetty, catching herself before she fell. He shifted over to make room for her under the eave.

Joan scraped damp strands of hair from her eyes. "What are you doing out here in the rain? Oh, look!" She pointed to the banners streaming above the ships. "Saint Edmund, Saint George, Saint Edward, and Saint Thomas. They are ever so grand."

Edward huddled deeper into his cloak.

Joan tugged his elbow. "Is something amiss, Edward?"

He yanked his arm away.

"What ails you?"

"Od! Need I explain? You are all going away."

Joan nibbled her bottom lip. "Oh." Joan wriggled her hands through the slit in his cloak, and found his hand. Although Joan's fingers were cold, he did not pull away.

"I'm so sorry," Joan said. "I have been so excited about our journey I did not give any thought about how you might feel." She squeezed his fingers.

The scent of salt and fishermen's catch wafted in the wind, rippling the banners and banging the inn's wooden sign. Since learning of his father's mission, Edward prayed every night his family would return safely and his father would not die in the war.

Beyond the harbor's calm, whitecaps frothed in the bay, like the thoughts in his head. Several moments passed before Edward managed to speak. "In the past, my Uncle John acted as Guardian for my father. Now, as my father's heir, the duty falls to me."

Joan edged closer. "What an honour."

He untangled Joan's hand and rested his forearms on the railing. "If I tell you something, you must promise not to tell."

Joan nodded. "I promise."

Edward's throat ached. "I am scared—I am afraid I am not good enough."

Joan nudged his shoulder. "You are being silly and do not credit yourself. Do you not remind me there is more to me than my fair appearance? As Guardian, you are able to show everyone your courage and patience." Joan paused. "And your quick mind. You are more than your father's first-born son."

Edward shook his head.

"Think on it," Joan said. "Even when Will provokes you, you keep your wits about you."

"Well, I suppose you are right, at least about that."

Joan jiggled his elbow. "Believe me, you will do splendidly. Your father will be proud."

Perhaps Joan was right about needing more confidence in himself. After all, his father would not have appointed him Guardian, if he did not think Edward able.

As the drizzle eased, horses hauled wagons up the slope piled high with goods unloaded from the smaller boats moored at the water's edge. A mangy tabby prowled among the stacks of ale barrels waiting to be loaded.

"I shall miss you, Jeanette." Edward's voice cracked.

"I shall miss you, too, but we will return before you know it." Joan removed the small golden brooch, styled in the shape of a deer, from her mantle. "I want you to have this."

"No, your lady mother gave it to you as an Epiphany gift. I remember because you told me your father saw a white hart on the palace lawn the morn of your birth."

Joan pressed his fingers around the brooch. "I want you to have it, so you do not feel alone." She blinked raindrops from her lashes. "Promise to write to me."

"If you write to me." He hugged her, then reached under his cloak and pinned the brooch over his heart.

The inn door thudded open. His mother exited, clutching his sisters' hands. Their nursemaids hovered close behind, thank goodness. Isabella and Johanna squabbled constantly, testing his mother's patience.

"There you are, Edward. We wondered what had become of you." Queen Philippa steered his sisters around the puddles. Her household retainers—butlers, cooks, musicians, maids—trooped from the inn toting the last satchels and hand boxes to the ship.

Releasing the girls' hands, his mother held out her arms and embraced him. "*Mon petit fils.*" She rested her cheek against his damp hair. "You will be fine. You are strong, like your father." She kissed the top of his head. "Do not fret overmuch, for we will all be together again soon."

Edward allowed his mother to hold him for several moments while he swallowed against his tears; he would not cry. He bent down and kissed each sister's cheek.

Queen Philippa readjusted her hood. "Come, Joan, it is time." She clasped her daughters' hands as they walked away. Isabella waved to him while little Johanna skipped, glanced back, and stuck out her tongue.

"*Au revoir,* Edward," Isabella called.

"*À bientôt,*" Joan sang out as they reached the boarding ramp.

He raised his hand, his chest so tight he could barely breathe. "*Bon voyage!*"

Cheers broke from the crowd as King Edward emerged from the inn.

Edward's pulse quickened. The final farewell was upon him.

A customary flurry surrounded the king and harried retainers trailed behind him, pelted with his last-minute instructions. Archbishop Stratford, bearing a saint-like aura, glided beside the king.

Edward hesitated to approach, uncomfortable in the archbishop's company though he would serve as the head of Edward's Council. The chancellor's manner unnerved Edward, as if the cleric could see straight through him.

"Be certain the wool subsidies are sent on time," the king said, his expression and tone one of warning. "I am relying on you to ensure there is no shortage. Do not fail me, Stratford. Much of the funds are already pledged to my allies and my army must be fed."

The archbishop half-bowed. "I shall do all in my power, sire."

The crowd grew more raucous, elbowing one other to gain a better view of the king. Well aware of the impression a king must make, he wore a blue velvet cloak trimmed with the fur of a silver fox.

Edward glanced down at his garment cut of the same fabric but now sodden. Maybe standing in the rain was not such a good idea.

Two other men strode in his father's wake: Richard FitzAlan, Earl of Arundel, and Baron Ralph Neville. Both would serve on Edward's advisory council. He shared some aquaintenance with the Earl, but none with the Baron.

The king signalled Edward it was time for the dockside ceremony they rehearsed. Trumpets sounded and the crowd fell silent.

Edward's heart raced as he knelt at his father's feet. An icy chill seeped through his body like the wet soaking through his hose.

The king placed both hands on Edward's head. "Lord Edward, Earl of Chester, Duke of Cornwall," his voice boomed, "by the grace of God, I, King Edward, the third of that name, proclaim you Guardian of England and all its peoples." The words resounded like a priest's benediction.

Edward rose, standing tall with his shoulders back and concentrated on keeping his legs from wobbling. Raising his chin, he spoke boldly so those gathered should hear him. "My Lord King, I am mindful of the honour you bestow, and the trust you place in me. Faithfully shall I execute my duties to the realm in your esteemed name." His voice did not falter; he breathed a sigh of relief.

His father gripped Edward's shoulders and looked into his eyes.

Edward whipped his arms around his father's waist before realizing what he had done. He shut his eyes and squeezed with his whole heart. *Please, please come back!*

King Edward patted his shoulder. "Do not fret. All will be well."

For a few moments, Edward squeezed tighter.

Barely above a whisper, his father said, "*Je t'aime, mon fis.*"

Edward trembled. He swallowed past the lump in his throat and stepped back. "I love you, too."

Pride shone from his father's eyes.

Edward would do anything to earn that look again.

October 1338 - Tower of London

At the furious pounding on the schoolroom door, Edward's head snapped up. His tutor, Master Burley, winced at the persistent raps. As he rose and straightened, Edward imagined he heard the man's joints creak. With a shake of his balding pate, Master Burley waved Edward back to his lesson. Fie! An interruption —any inter-ruption—was better than Latin declensions.

Master Burley hobbled to the door and opened it, ending the racket.

A flushed-faced page half-bowed, corrected himself, and sank to one knee. "Beggin' your p-pardon, my lords," he said, "Arch-bishop Stratford requests Lord Edward's presence in the hall. He bade me say, it is an urgent matter."

Edward's stomach rolled. These past months he grew accus-tomed to a regular routine. For the Chancellor to send for him, something awful must have happened. To his father? *Please, Lord, no.*

He hurried down the passageway. Were there more guards posted or did he imagine it? When he reached the great hall and saw the number of people gathered there, and heard their rumbling, the sick feeling returned.

He hastened to the dais where Chancellor Stratford and the Earl of Arundel waited, concern etching their faces as they bowed to him. His legs trembled as he lowered himself onto the lone chair. He hoped no one noticed.

Arundel stepped forward and a hush fell. "Lord Edward, please forgive the intrusion but a courier rode in a short while ago with an urgent report. The French raided Southampton and the Isle of Wight."

Outrage rumbled through the hall, palpable and rising in

waves.

Edward's heart thumped. Before his father departed, he warned Edward the French might return and attack again. Knowing this did nothing to ease Edward's mind or his stomach.

The Earl ran a hand through his greying hair, cast an odd glance at Stratford, and continued. "Regrettably, there is more to report, lord."

"Have the French not caused enough damage?" A man shouted. By the manner of his dress, he was likely a London merchant.

"I regret, the French captured two of our ships, the *Edward* and the *Christopher*. Both were sailing off the coast of Flanders carrying supplies and wool for the king."

More angry mutterings swept through the hall.

"Quiet!" Edward called. *Lord help him.* He needed to think.

Deep creases lined Chancellor Stratford's brow. "It appears King Philippe believes we are weak with our king away. I dare say, he might be so bold as to attack London itself."

A restless energy, men shifting and grumbling, spread through the assembly. Edward slid his ruby signet ring on and off his thumb. What should he do? What would his father do? Stratford and Arundel stood silent, waiting. Edward must speak.

"My lords, surely, before the king sailed, he discussed the possibility of another attack with you." Edward surprised himself, his voice was steady and he sounded strong.

"Indeed," Arundel said. The king suggested we offer the French a warm welcome…with piles driven into the Thames. Those filthy curs may sail up the river, but, God's bones, they will not sail back again."

The sounds of fists pounding and men cursing engulfed the hall.

Stratford gestured for calm. When the crowd quieted, he said, "Would it not be a wiser course for our ships to patrol the mouth of the Thames?"

Arundel aimed a dark look at the archbishop.

Edward could almost hear the Earl's thoughts. What did a

churchman know about battling the French? Discord between two of his advisors was to be avoided.

"Peace, my lords. We must fight our enemy not each other." *Rely on your advisors, Edward. Trust their judgment.* "While your opinions differ, I believe both have merit. The threat posed by the French must end and I trust that between you, you will resolve the best course of action to secure our safety."

Over the following days, all London was on edge, expecting an attack at any moment. As often as he could, Edward patrolled the Tower parapets, searching downriver for any sign of the French. Three days passed, each more tense than the one before.

Despite the threat, Edward's morning lessons with Master Burley continued. Edward worked on sums when shuffling footsteps sounded at the schoolroom doorway. Chancellor Stratford entered, his presence as staid as ever.

"Lord Edward, Master Burley, pardon my interruption." He bowed to Edward. "I thought you should be advised of the latest reports." The archbishop folded his hands across his middle. "I have come personally to inform you the French have withdrawn."

Before Edward could respond, footsteps pounded in the passageway outside the chamber. A grave-faced Arundel marched in and paused a mere foot from the archbishop.

"You see? Just as I said, Stratford. I told you the French would not return, not while our king rallies troops on King Philippe's doorstep. You should not have doubted me."

It appeared the discord between them remained. Did his father deliberately pitch them against one another?

November 1338 – Tower of London

As the weeks passed with no sign of the French, one day after morning lessons Edward visited the royal mews with Jack and Will. Roger Mortimer, the king's ward, and new member of Edward's household, joined them. When they filed into the côte, the squawks and kak-kak-kaks from the birds besieged them.

Hugh, the head falconer cautioned, "Keep still 'n mind yer voices." His gruff tone belied a tender heart, though as the keeper of twenty years, he brooked no nonsense. Hugh's word was law.

A hooded falcon perched on his gloved fist. The boys remained quiet while Hugh carefully removed the protective rufter from the raptor's head. The juvenile roused its feathers, blinked several times, and swiveled its head, surveying the boys and surroundings.

Will beamed. "Is he not magnificent? My father gave him to me for my birthday."

Hugh gave Will a piece of raw pheasant and he tried to entice the bird to hop onto his glove. The falcon blinked, ignoring Will's offer.

"Look at his eyes," Roger murmured. "The black ringed with yellow is so piercing." He brushed his unruly mop of red hair out of his eyes, one haloed greenish-purple. Roger, oft times, paid a price for his pranks.

When the falcon showed no interest, Will scowled.

"Be patient," Hugh said.

Much to Edward's surprise, Will showed more tolerance with the bird than he ever did with people. The falcon blinked again and then took the bait, hopping unto Will's fist. He pressed his thumb overtop the leather jesses attached to the bird's anklets.

Edward was envious; he longed for a hawk or falcon of his own. His kestrel was fast and agile, yet he hoped his father would grant him a bird of higher status when he returned. If his father returned. Just the thought scared him.

"Is not King Edward's peregrine larger?" Roger asked.

"Because he hunts a female," Will sneered. "Everyone knows female peregrines are larger than males."

"What shall you call him?" Edward tried to distract Will.

"Majestic."

"'Tis enuff fer one day," Hugh said, extending his hand. "Here, giv 'em t'me."

"Speaking of hunting…is anyone hungry?" Roger's stomach growled.

After raiding the kitchen, they wandered into the hall. Edward moved a stool closer to the hearth near the dozing hounds when Archbishop Stratford's clerk approached. He bowed and extended a rolled parchment bearing the royal seal.

Edward took it and, preferring to read in private, headed to his chamber. The letter, addressed to him, was written in the king's own hand.

> *"For some months we have made it known to you that since our arrival the treasure we expected to aid our endeavors and support our own good people has not arrived. If we had failed to raise a loan we would have been perpetually dishonoured to the peril of ourselves and the realm of England."*

Edward felt punched in his middle. This was not the first time his father complained about the lack of funds, though Edward was unaware the situation was so serious. Did his father have enough money to feed his army? What about his mother and sisters, and Joan? Did they have enough to eat? Since the letter was directed to him, his father must expect Edward to do something. But what? He did not want to let his father down.

He hastened to the chancellery. The door stood ajar and he entered without pause. "Lord Archbishop, my father writes he is in need of money."

Stratford glanced up from his work, his lips pressed tight, while the fingers of his left hand tapped the table. Laying his quill aside, he rose. "Lord Edward." He offered the courtesy of a bow. "Your father would be pleased you seek my counsel."

Heat crept up Edward's neck. The archbishop's tone conveyed a subtle rebuke for Edward's abrupt interruption, but he was not about to back down. "My father seeks aid, Archbishop."

"I regret not much can be done at this time."

Edward pulled out a stool and sat, brows knitted. "Why?"

Stratford returned to his seat and steepled his hands as if praying. "Shall I explain how the funds are raised?"

Edward bobbed his head. No one bothered to tell him before.

"Representatives of the king purchase wool from the shepherds and it is sold to merchants abroad. The difference between what is paid to the shepherds and the price the foreign merchants pay belongs to your father. The arrangement requires Parliament's authorization."

"I see. So, why does father say the funds have not arrived?"

"Ahh…because the wool yields were not as robust, nor the prices of wool sold abroad as high as expected."

"Cannot more wool be purchased and resold?"

"Alas, not until next spring's shearing."

"And no other funds are available?"

"Regrettably, no."

Edward retired to his chamber. The king would be terribly angry, yet his father must be told and it was Edward's duty to do so. After penning the letter he reread it; one line stood out.

"No other aid can be raised by any means."

November 1338 – Antwerp

The river hulk cruised past the low-lying fields flanking the Scheldt River. King Edward stretched his neck and shoulders trying to relieve the tension. He returned to Antwerp after six weeks, traveling from Koblenz to Mechelen, one court to another, using every persuasion, yet his relations resisted committing to his cause. The laughing cries of Herring Gulls echoed across the river's wind-rippled surface as if to remind him of his failure.

He drew his cloak tight. "*Mes amis*, let us get out of this chill." The king removed to his cabin and tossed his mantle to a servant. Derby and Salisbury rested at the table while he stalked the small space.

"God's teeth! This trip has been for naught. What good is my cousin when he cannot be bothered to meet with me? He makes pretty excuses not to leave Brabant, but the truth of it is he is too fearful to proclaim openly for me against the French dog."

"There is at least one bright spot," Salisbury said. "Count Willem committed Hainault to invade with you."

"Yes, yes, though only as far as the Cambresis. He refuses to cross deeper into France."

Derby leaned forward. "You should not blame—"

"Do not humour me. I am in no mood." Scowling, he plucked a mug of ale from the tray left by the serving lad and gulped half down. "My other spineless allies stall for time, all the while my debts mount. The wool exports raised less money than expected and funds suffer delay. Damn Stratford! How can I meet my allies' demands for payment or provide supplies for my troops?"

"Each delay seems to incur another," Derby said, "though we might take heart your allies have agreed, at least, to a start date for the campaign."

King Edward slumped onto a stool, his head in his hands. "Not until May. My coffers will be empty by then."

The sun played chase with the clouds over St. Michael's Abbey where Joan sheltered in the lee of the garden wall. A bitter wind gusted off the river rattling the branches above, causing her to huddle deeper into her woolen mantle.

Closing her eyes, she prayed. "Holy Mary, Mother of God, watch over our queen and protect her during her travail." Joan took a deep breath, made the sign of the cross, and opened her eyes.

The verdant green hues and earthy scents helped soothe her concern for the queen, more of a mother to Joan than her own. Though she pleaded to remain with the queen and her ladies, her request was denied. Maidens were prohibited from the birthing chamber. She mouthed the words of another prayer, this one for this new royal babe's health. The last babe, William, died not long after his birth.

The queen grieved the loss of her second son deeply, as did

Edward. With two younger sisters, he longed for a brother. She missed him and read his infrequent letters over and over again. While Edward wrote little of his duties as Guardian, the pages overflowed with tales of adventures with Roger, Jack and Will.

Like most days since they landed in Antwerp, a thick layer of grey blanketed the sky. Following their arrival, they traveled from one noble court to another as the king sought allies. With each passing week, Joan's dream of adventure mouldered into the bleak reality of jouncing in wagons and slogging through rutted roads deep with mud.

She celebrated her eleventh birthday in September and, losing any interest in playing with Isabella and Johanna, Joan frequently wandered the abbey garden. How she longed to go out riding, like Edward. But here, she was told, no guards could be spared to accompany her.

Raindrops from the morning sprinkle dripped from the trees in a soft, lulling cadence.

"Begging your pardon, my lady."

Joan started. A man wearing the king's livery stood a few feet away.

"Please forgive me. I did not mean to startle you." The mellow tone of his voice resonated in the small, enclosed space. He looked familiar.

Joan whisked several windblown strands of hair from her face and within moments, she placed him as the knight who rode the grey stallion at the king's recent tournament, the gallant causing whispers among the queen's ladies. Strands of copper threaded his dark hair.

Joan folded her hands in her lap. "Your apology is accepted, sir."

Crinkles appeared in the corners of the man's eyes, but as he glanced around the garden, his grin faded. "You are unescorted?"

Joan's cheeks warmed. She lowered her gaze.

"Your pardon, my lady. Might I be so bold as to introduce myself?"

Joan nodded.

"Sir Thomas Holland." He made a stately bow as if greeting the king or queen. How charming. No wonder the ladies chattered about him.

Joan rose and dipped a curtsy. "Sir Thomas." She paused. "You are in the king's service?" How silly she sounded. Why else would he be dressed in royal livery?

He grinned. "Forgive me, Lady Joan, I do not mean to offend, but it is disturbing to find you alone."

"You know who I am?"

Dimples appeared. "It is my duty to know the members of the king's family."

"Hmm…." She fingered a spent leaf clinging to a vine.

"If I am not mistaken, you are the king's young cousin, Lady Joan of Kent, are you not?" He added, "Should you not be with the queen's ladies?"

Joan angled to look at him. "They are attending to our lady." She worried her bottom lip. What might she say without speaking out of turn? "You see, the queen's travail has begun."

"What joyous news!" His eyes, not quite green nor brown, seemed to twinkle.

"Indeed, it is, sir. While we wait, I sought solitude here, taking advantage of the break in the weather." She twisted a fold in her gown. Did he notice her disquiet?

"May the Lord's grace safeguard our lady and her babe." The knight's solemn tone bespoke honourable concern. He extended his arm. "May I offer escort?"

Drawn by his chivalry, Joan rested her hand on his arm and as they wandered the shrub-lined path, her insides jittered. A silence grew, broken only by the crush of pebbles beneath their feet. Why could she think of nothing to say?

"Have you no one to keep you company?"

Sir Thomas sounded sincere. "Only the princesses. They are as dear to me as sis—oh!" She stumbled and grasped hold of the knight's arm.

"Careful," he said, steadying her.

Joan's pulse rose a notch. "Th-thank you."

"Say nothing of it."

Thick lashes framed his eyes. A warmth crept again into her cheeks. The abbey bells tolled, reminding her of time passing. Though this knight of the king's guard showed her courtesy, she dare not remain alone in his company.

"You must excuse me, Sir Thomas. It has been some hours since I left our lady queen. I must return."

He halted his steps. "I must not keep you."

"I pray joyful word awaits me inside and we have cause to celebrate."

Sir Thomas pressed her fingers and bowed. "It has been my pleasure."

"Good day." Joan bobbed a curtsy and as she hastened away, she scanned the garden before passing through the arched portal. Tongues would wag if anyone chanced to see her alone with Sir Thomas. More might be read into the encounter than it warranted. The handsome knight already generated gossip among the ladies.

When Joan passed the queen's chamber she was met by an infant's lusty wail. Would the babe be the brother Edward yearned for or another sister?

December 1338 - Tower of London

A blizzard raged outside the Tower, the sideways-blowing snow so thick the Thames disappeared and the incessant whistling was driving Edward mad. Each time someone entered the hall, a bitter chill blasted in. Edward focused on the chess board, considering his next move.

Roger blew on his fingers, reached for his queen, hesitated, then moved his bishop.

A pair of finely-crafted leather shoes stepped into Edward's line of vision.

"Lord Edward." Archbishop Stratford half-bowed, then held out a folded parchment. "A ship docked before this latest squall and I thought you might be eager to read this."

Edward glanced at the seal. "Thank you, Archbishop." The mighty chancellor did not often deign to deliver letters personally.

"Roger, I should like to read this. Would you mind?"

His friend shrugged. "You were winning."

Edward called to a servant to have a fire lit in the queen's solar. No one would disturb him there. He helped Roger pack up the game pieces and then they wandered to where Jack and Will diced with two storm-idle squires. Edward watched for a while, their play reminding him of games with his mother. She enjoyed a good gamble and, unlike him, she won more often than not.

By the time Edward reached the solar, flames teased the larger logs. He found his mother's lingering floral scent comforting and settled onto a tapestried bench, stretched his boots toward the hearth, and wiggled his toes. Before long, he might feel them again.

After breaking the wax seal, he unfolded the parchment and began to read, though only a scant winter light filtered through the ice-webbed panes. With Jeanette's first words, his gloomy world brightened.

"You have a brother."

Edward bowed his head and made the sign of the cross, thanking God for granting Edward's plea. Joan wrote his brother was named Lionel, the same as Lancelot's brother in the tales of King Arthur.

> *Our lord king hosted a grand tournament in honour of the queen's churching and Lionel's birth. He ordered matching garments fashioned for all of us made of dark blue velvet trimmed with silver braid and pearls. What a spectacle we made as we paraded forth to sit beneath the canopies of dark blue silk strewn with silver stars. Twenty-six honoured knights competed.*

Edward closed his eyes and imagined the bright pennons flying and the trumpets blaring as each knight entered the lists. He heard the galloping hooves and the lances shatter. Oh, how he wished he could be there!

Spring 1339 - Tower of London

The sullen skies and bitter cold which settled over the city at Christmastide lasted well into February. Ice sheeted the Thames, thawed, and froze again, yet between storms, ships docked, bringing reports from abroad. Edward attended daily mass, practiced sums at his lessons, and on Tuesdays, attended Council meetings. To his surprise, he began to enjoy them, especially when the Earl of Arundel explained the shifting relationships among the foreign rulers. Many of the king's allies still hesitated to commit to sending troops into France. The political maneuverings reminded Edward of a game of chess.

The months passed. One misty morning in early June, Edward patrolled the Tower ramparts with the sergeant of the guards. In a week, Edward would celebrate his ninth year. Would his father remember?

A ship skimmed the incoming tide and made for the Tower dock. Royal colors rippled from its mainmast. The *Thomas*. The king's flagship. Edward hastened to the chancellery, eager to learn of the king. As he entered out of breath, the Earl of Arundel was about to sit. Lord Neville, already seated, rose and the men bowed. Archbishop Stratford stood in the corner of the chamber, holding a leather courier pouch.

After everyone settled, he pulled out the parchment and skimmed it. His brow furrowed and his lips firmed in a thin line.

"Lord Chancellor?" Edward's voice cracked.

Stratford cleared his throat and read. *"Trusting in God, I shall invade France with or without allies."*

Edward reached for the parchment. He felt sick.

At the end of his morning ride, Edward reined his pony to a halt outside the Tower stable. He hopped down, loosened the girth, and ran his hands over Jaiet's flanks to check if his pony needed cooling before being put up. Jaiet tugged Edward toward the stable door, eager for the oats waiting in his stall. A voice drifted from inside the stable.

"Yesterday's dispatch confirmed it."

Edward froze in the shadowed entry. The voice belonged to the Earl of Arundel.

"Since King Philippe did not defend the Cambresis, the king presses Count Willem to push deeper into France."

Edward dared a peek. Arundel stood with another man. Though his back was to Edward, he could not mistake the gravelly voice of Baron Neville. Edward remained still. Were his counselors keeping reports from him? He was *not* too young to understand.

Neville ran a hand through his hair. "Our liege is deliberately provoking King Philippe, yet the coward does not take the field."

"Mayhap Philippe conceives a longer game." Arundel wove a blade of straw through his fingers and added, "He plays the pontiff like a puppet."

"You view the pope's recent peace delegation as Philippe's delaying tactic?"

"Indeed. King Edward cannot refuse to meet with the pope's emissaries and while he does, our forces remain idle in the field, depleting his meagre coffers, exactly as Philippe—"

Jaiet stomped a hoof.

Arundel glanced over. "Lord Edward."

Fie! Jaiet gave him away.

The baron spun around, his surprise quelled by a polite mask. He bowed.

"My lords." Edward urged Jaiet forward, his hooves clopping distinctly in the hushed aisle. Though eavesdropping often earned

Edward scolds from his mother, how else would he learn what was happening?

A few days later, Master Burley departed the schoolroom leaving Edward to his studies. As soon as the door closed behind his tutor, Edward retrieved his father's recent letter from beneath the parchments on the table.

On the feast of Saint Denis, we entered Vermandois and received the Pope's cardinals sent to talk peace. While there, much to our joy, the long-awaited word reached us that Philippe agreed to meet in battle setting the date of 20-21 October. On said date, we arrayed in our battle formation only to receive a second message requesting us to wait until the next day. To our deep regret, Philippe failed to appear. With winter approaching and in need of supplies, we withdrew to Hainault.

Edward laid down the parchment. A king's duty bound him to protect his kingdom and its people, yet King Philippe seemed to prefer disgrace to battle. Why would a king choose to bring such shame upon himself? Edward sighed. At least, his father was safe in Hainault. Footsteps sounded in the outer passage. Edward tucked the parchment aside.

"What have you there, Lord Edward? May I see?" Master Burley held out his hand. His tutor missed little and Edward doubted the letter contained anything of which Burley was not privy.

Master Burley skimmed the letter. "Have you questions?"

"Yes, sir." Edward's cheeks warmed. He hated to admit his confusion. "I do not understand. Count Willem hesitates to march deeper into France, the Church sends a peace delegation, and King Philippe refuses to take the field. Why?"

"Ah, my young lord, you need not be embarrassed." Master Burley lowered himself onto the stool beside Edward. "A wise man does not allow pride to prevent him from seeking aid when in need of it." Placing a hand on Edward's shoulder, he added, "Honesty between us is vital if I am to instruct you about the greater world and not just teach sums and Latin."

"Yes." The king held Burley in high esteem for his wide knowledge, and Edward admired him for the same reason and two others— Master Burley did not condescend to him, nor lie. Master Burley was one of only a handful of people Edward trusted. As his tutor said, Edward must be honest if he wished Master Burley to be honest in return.

"If you would explain, please. My father is counting on me."

Burley folded his hands and rested them on the table. "You can rely on me to tell you true, Lord. Where would you like me to begin?"

Edward twirled the ruby ring on his thumb, still too big for him. "My father has withdrawn his troops. Why?"

"A fair question." Burley tugged an ear. "Your father is attempting to force King Philippe into battle, though to achieve a decisive victory, your father needs a greater force than his own. He needs allies to supplement his troops with theirs."

Edward nodded.

"The key lies with Flanders."

"Flanders?"

"Indeed. Flanders relies on English wool for its weaving industry and cannot afford to lose your father's good will for fear he might cut off supply. But Flanders' ruler, Count Louis, owes homage for his lands to King Philippe. The Count must balance his loyalties and seeks to remain neutral."

Edward squeezed his eyes shut to concentrate. When he opened them, Master Burley continued.

"Recently, King Philippe enacted damaging policies against Flanders, and in protest the Flemish people rose up against Count Louis. He fled to Paris for safety."

"Count Louis ran away from his own people?"

"Indeed, he did."

"But if the Flemish are subjects of King Philippe, should not their king protect them rather than causing harm? If a king does not protect his people, why should they be loyal?"

"Ah, Lord Edward, you are a bright young lad." Burley patted Edward's shoulder." King Philippe's sanctions against Flanders have driven the Flemish people from his affinity, toward supporting your father." He paused. "Here is the most important point. Your father needs Flanders to declare *openly* for him against France."

"So, if I understand, for my father to win the war, he needs Flanders to side with him?"

"Precisely." Master Burley rose. "Now, if you have no more questions, let us take up our lessons again."

Edward sat up straighter. "Not quite yet, Master Burley." Though his tutor wore a sharp expression, Edward was determined not to be dismissed. "What must happen for the Flemish to side *openly* with my father?"

Master Burley rubbed his jaw, the semblance of a grin teasing the corners of his mouth. "Another good question. Although I am not privy to our king's intentions, your father is nothing if not clever. I have no doubt he will sway them."

January 1340 - Ghent

Dampness permeated low-lying Ghent. It seeped through walls, including the ones in the chamber provided by Queen Philippa's brother for King Edward's use. He stood before the hearth chafing his hands near the fire to catch its heat. Bishop Burghersh, his emissary, fingered the crucifix attached to his cincture as he reported the results of his diplomatic mission. Dark shadows ringed his eyes, fatigue evidenced in his face, his slumped shoulders, and his every movement.

"It is beyond me, sire, to reason King Philippe's thinking. The sanctions he laid against the Flemish last autumn generated unrest, but nothing compared to the uproar over his recent confiscation of Lille and Douai."

"Philippe is a fool. He seems determined to stoke Van

Artevelde's rebellion against him." Fortunately, Philippe's latest blunders played right into King Edward's hands, as sweet to him as his favourite almond cakes. "Philippe has all but severed the Fleming's allegiance to him and when my plan cleaves it completely, Flanders will not hesitate to join me on the battlefield." He rubbed his jaw. "It is time to take the next step."

The bishop steepled his hands, tapping his fingertips together. "You contemplate a bold step, sire, one that is certain to raise Philippe's ire."

"*Oui*, it is a gamble." He sat down across from Burghersh. "But when I state my claim and the Flemings acknowledge me, the Pope's threat of interdict and any effort to impose his two million florin fine is nullified. Flanders frees itself from the pontiff's sanctions for taking up arms against Philippe, for he will no longer be their liege lord."

A smile hovered on Burghersh's lips. "Just so, sire."

"Next week, then, and not a detail left to chance."

King Edward lingered in Philippa's outer chamber while her ladies made final adjustments to her ensemble. "You know, *mon coeur,* I do not take today's matter lightly."

"Indeed, I do know." Philippa smoothed the folds of her gown, so cleverly designed to conceal her advanced condition.

For the past week, the tailors he commissioned worked feverishly to complete their garments, designed to showcase his royal status. The purple silk brocade tunic and matching hose he wore, overlaid with a purple satin cloak trimmed with ermine, were certain to impress. Atop his head rested his most elaborate gem-studded gold crown.

Philippa's gown and cloak were of similar fabric which draped becomingly over her heavily-rounded form. Motherhood became his wife, though the frequency of her pregnancies, and risk of her labours, caused concern. *O Lord, let this next birth be a safe one.*

His wife's toilette complete, King Edward offered his arm. They left the residence surrounded by their escort dressed in the newly-tailored royal livery.

A watery sun struggled through the clouds, shedding a flat light onto Ghent's thrumming central market. All manner of goods brimmed in the jumble of makeshift stalls: candles, bolts of cloth, ribbons, and other household goods. Merchants bawled the excellence of their wares and gestured in heated barter. The tantalizing aromas of fish stew and freshly-baked bread competed with the pungent odours of wet wool and livestock.

A large wooden stage commanded the center of the square where players and jongleurs performed to the delight of the townsfolk. Dozens of colorful banners flew above them: all bearing golden *fleurs de lis* upon azure fields quartered with flaxen leopards ready to spring from crimson satin.

The milling crowd pointed, with puzzled expressions, at the heraldic devices of England and France oddly quartered on the banners. As they thrashed in the breeze, the sound added to the clamour of voices, lowing cattle, bleating sheep, and squawking fowl.

Trumpets blared. Heads turned and conversations ceased.

Minstrels dressed in bright particolored costumes stepped to the rhythm of drums, flutes, and pipes at the head of King Edward's grand procession into the square.

"Zien daar!"

"Look!"

"De Engelse koning!"

As word spread of the presence of England's king and queen, more Flemings crammed into the square, exactly as King Edward intended. After taking several deep breaths, the unsettled feeling inside him eased, and he strode forward with a beaming Philippa beside him. The most influential of Ghent's ministers walked behind, followed by members of England's highest-ranking nobility. At the base of the stage, the procession halted and the minstrels formed into one line.

King Edward held Philippa's hand and squeezed it gently; she returned his pressure. Philippa's presence meant the world to him. She chose to be at his side, despite her advanced state. He was concerned this pregnancy, so soon after Lionel's birth, and the stress of the occasion, might harm her or the babe. The king helped his queen up the steps and to the center of the stage. He paused a moment, then clasped Philippa's hand, and raised their hands skyward.

Cheers burst from the prominent burghers and English nobles.

"To England!"

"King Edward!"

The magistrates of Bruges, Ypres, and Ghent assumed their honoured places on the platform and addressed remarks to the crowd, expressing grievences against France and encouraging freedom from tyrany.

King Edward's pulse danced. Today, he would free himself from King Philippe's hegemony, setting himself on equal footing with his longtime nemesis.

At the conclusion of the speeches, King Edward stepped centerstage. The crowd shuffled and craned their necks for a better view. He pitched his voice for all to hear.

"*Goede mensen van Gent....*" He waited for the crowd to hush.

"*Waardige* burgers and honourable people...." He spoke his greeting in Flemish, thanks to his wife's tutoring. "The esteemed ministers standing before you champion my cause against France."

A groundswell of disgruntled comments rumbled up from the crowd like a vast wave cresting toward shore.

"I oppose King Philippe and vow to restore your confiscated lands and protect you from all aggressors." King Edward took a breath. "I solemnly pledge to honour the liberties and long-held rights of the citizens of Flanders."

Murmurs of assent rippled through those gathered, while more people, curious about the activity, shouldered in.

He waited; he must get this right. "Most humbly do I beseech you to join the esteemed leaders here today in swearing your fealty and obedience to me." One-by-one, he singled out several of the most prosperous-looking Ghent merchants below him. A few tipped their heads. None avoided his gaze.

"Today, by the grace of God, I, Edward, the third of that name, proclaim my rightful place as King of France, and of England, Lord of Ireland and Scotland, and Duke of Aquitaine."

Many gasped.

He gestured for silence. "As the grandson of France's King Philippe, the fourth of that name, nephew of his sons, the Kings Louis, Philippe, and Charles, and son of their sister, Isabella, daughter of France, I hold forth my hereditary right as the true sovereign of France."

There came several heartbeats of silence, then a thunderous roar and cheers of approval.

King Edward's heart soared.

February 1340 - Ghent

Two weeks later as evening fires were lit, King Edward prowled his chamber. Although Flanders recognized him as the rightful King of France and pledged allegiance to him, his lack of money threatened everything he accomplished.

"This cannot stand, Kilsby. How dare Parliament refuse my request for funds again? Damn my emissaries and damn Stratford. I ask you, what good is his silver tongue if he cannot persuade them?"

His secretary made no response, nor did the king expect one. "Order the ship made ready. We leave tonight."

Kilsby left and returned a short time later.

"Sit and take up your pen," the king said. "Letters must be sent." The fire burned to embers by the time King Edward finished dictating and his secretary penned his orders.

Kilsby dashed a last line and set down his quill. "If you will excuse me, sire, I will take these to our couriers."

King Edward rubbed his eyes. If he were unable to pay his

troops and reimburse his allies, all his efforts over the last eighteen months would be for naught. There was no doubt his allies would abandon him and England's cause lost.

With a heavy sigh, the king settled on the couch and stretched out his legs. Failure loomed under a mountain of debt. His last chance to salvage his campaign—his only chance—meant appealing to Parliament in person. Damn those demons. Bow to their king they would.

On King Edward's last visit to Brabant, Duke Jan warned him. "Do not try to leave." His cousin's threat was clear: England's king and family were not free to leave until his debts were paid.

Yet, leave he must.

He rested his eyes while the matters plaguing him played havoc in mind. Would his commanders and army hold their ground or lose it when he was not on the battlefield with them? Then there were Philippa and the children. Sure to be held hostage for his debts.

Debts, debts, and more debts.

Since his crowning, money was a never-ending concern, and a concern his son would face, too. How could he help Edward to develop the skills needed to leverage Parliament, if he, England's God anointed king, failed in this mission?

"We must leave, sire."

King Edward startled awake.

John Darcy leaned over him holding a flickering taper, offering the only light in the chamber save the glow from a sliver of red embers.

The king threw his legs over and sat up, working the slumber from his brain.

"As you ordered," Darcy said, "we have put it about we will be off on an early morning hunt."

Having dozed in his clothes, the king rose and prepared to leave, the dawn still hours away. Outside, shadows cast by the light of a single lantern shifted as he hastened across the stable yard to the horses, snorting softly as he and his escort mounted.

William Kilsby handed him a black kerchief. "Tie it on, sire." Only his secretary's eyes showed above the cloth masking his face.

Scarf in place, the king gathered his reins.

Kilsby extinguished the lantern. "This way, sire."

King Edward entrusted only a handful of men with his plan to escape, and they now surrounded him: Kilsby and Darcy in front, Northampton and Admiral Mauny flanking him, and the Earl of Warwick's sons, John and Guy Beauchamp, behind.

Clad in all-black, they set off—the escape timed to a moonless night. Little sound signaled their departure, for they rode without spurs and their horses' hooves were wrapped with heavy fabric.

While the column snaked through a shrouded maze of narrow lanes and ramshackle buildings, the king reminded himself to loosen the stranglehold on his reins. Debris scattered in a sudden gust. A shutter banged. The stench of decay and feces from the dank streets made him gag.

His mind raged and his belly seethed with shame; he, England's sovereign, was sneaking away in the night like a common thief. He pushed the thought away. Now was not the time.

Once clear of the city, his entourage heeled their horses into a canter and for several hours they rode without speaking, down country lanes, and through villages. Reaching Sluys, they reined down at the Zwin harbour, their arrival and sailing, timed to the outgoing tide.

Heart in his throat, the king dismounted and sprinted to a stack of crates alongside a warehouse while his companions scouted the quay for signs of betrayal. A few torches belched plumes of rancid smoke as he waited, skulking like a dockyard rat.

Admiral Mauny stole toward the ship, slipping past the slumped sentries snoring peacefully, courtesy of a cask of drugged ale.

"Hist!" Kilsby's signal filtered above the tide lapping against the jetty.

The king edged around the crates, dashed across the weatherworn planks, and up the ramp to the ship tugging at its mooring lines. Above the odour of rotting fish, rain scented the salt breeze. When did he ever cross the narrow sea and it did not storm?

"Cast off," Mauny ordered, his voice muted.

Once aboard, King Edward breathed deeply several times to calm his racing pulse. To his relief, the ship slid undetected through the inky harbor toward open water. He sank to the deck, his back against the forecastle support beam, his thoughts turning to Philippa and his family. He crossed himself, closed his eyes, and silently prayed.

Grant me, O Lord, Your safe deliverance.

No sooner did the cog sail clear of the hithe than it bucked in an off-shore wind, and the sea began to rise. The ship breached a swell and plunged into a deep trough, spouting plumes, drenching the deck, and stinging his face. He clung to the wooden support as if his life depended upon it. Because it did.

"Lower the sail!" Mauny bawled the order, though it could barely be heard above the storm's growing wrath. Seamen dared death as they climbed the rigging, and released the lines. Two burly crewmen below wrestled with the canvas.

The vessel rose and dipped, its timbers groaning in protest. Angry mountains of water crashed over the heaving prow, washing the sailors' feet out from under them, and forcing the pair to scrabble for purchase. One lashed a rope, tied to the mast, around his middle while the other frantically clung to it.

The king dared not remain on deck exposed to the sea's fury, knowing full well *mal de mer* would soon claim him. He rose, legs braced apart, and staggered as the ship crested a saw-toothed swell. Hand over hand, he clawed his way toward shelter and ducked down the hatch. The ship pitched and his head smacked the bulkhead. "God's blood!" Lurching into his cabin, he grabbed a bucket and tied himself to the bunk.

The ship plummeted, twisted in a trough, and hurtled up again. Bile roiled in his gut; he swallowed hard against it, and with each roll, he willed his stomach to obey.

As the wind and sea raged, the ship pitched, rocked and bobbed like a cork.

Wave after gut-wrenching wave, the king's stomach heaved and he spewed into the bucket. When nothing remained, dry heaves racked him, and once thoroughly emptied, he wiped his face and mouth with his sleeve.

Seawater rushed under his cabin door and feet pounded down to the hold.

"Bail, you devils, bail!"

Muted shouts bore through the ship's creaking timbers, drowning out his pitiful moans. Seawater flooded his cabin. He clung white-knuckled to the bunk, flung side to side as the sea battered the wallowing vessel. He lost all track of time, only prayed Mauny's years of experience would see them safe.

Water sloshed. Buckets banged.

"Bail, I say! You turds want to die? Bail!"

The storm thundered and seamen cursed.

Between retches, the king offered prayers to the patron saint of the sea. "Holy Erasmus, I implore Thee to intercede on my behalf, asking God to grant me life that I may reside in the Faith through which Thou didst obtain Thy glory."

Adding to his prayers, he entreated the saint for the safety of those he was forced to leave behind: Philippa, so close to term again, the children, his army and commanders, Salisbury and Suffolk. A merciful God could not wish the king's life to end aboard this stinking hulk and catapult his son into a life for which he was not yet prepared.

For three days, Mauny commanded the ship's battle against the storm; the battered vessel finally floundered to shore at Harwich. Then, the admiral maneuvered it south, hugging the coast and entering the mouth of the Thames. Under his skillful hands, the ship limped up the river to dock at the Tower beneath a moon shrouded by clouds.

King Edward, recovered from his sickness, followed Northampton leaping from the ship onto the empty jetty. "Where is the alarm?" the king railed. "Where are the guards?" Holding his ire barely in check, the king stormed through the water gate, pounded his way to Stratford's chamber, and flung open the door.

"How dare you!" The archbishop shouted from within the cocoon of his bed curtains.

"How dare *I*, your King?"

Stratford thrust out his head, his face lit by the flare of a torch Northampton held up behind the king. The shock on the archbishop's face was almost worth the thrashing the king suffered. *Almost.* He aimed a hawklike glare at his chancellor.

Stratford scrambled out. "Sire, we thought you in Ghent." He bowed, his nightdress catching the light.

The king stepped closer, his face inches from the archbishop's. "Indeed. I was, but as you see, I am *here* now." Menace edged his voice, concealing his mirth.

Dumbstruck, a tick appeared at the corner of Stratford's mouth.

"My dear archbishop, you will summon Parliament to assemble forthwith." He glowered, gesturing to the archbishop's writing implements. "Now. This cannot wait until the morn."

Stratford motioned to his servant to light a candle. "As you command, Lord King."

"And Archbishop?"

"Yes, sire?"

"I will suffer no delays. None. Not by anyone." The king narrowed his eyes to threatening slits. "I trust I have made myself clear?" It was not a question.

Whatever it took, he would redeem his honour and his reputation which were as shredded as the ship's sails. He wheeled and pounded out the door. He would not rest until his kingdom, and his family, were safe.

Victory at Sea

King Edward's footsteps echoed beneath Westminster's hallowed arches as he left the Painted Chamber for the Great Hall where members of Parliament assembled. Debt threatened the life-blood of his kingdom and to save it, he must convince Parliament the war with France was not only in his interest, but theirs.

He rehearsed his arguments while he dressed, donning his most impressive tunic, fashioned of cloth of gold, and his one remaining crown—a thin gold circlet, its stark simplicity a symbol of his impoverished state. The crown he wore when annointed, his most elaborate adorned with gemstones, stood as surety for his debts, as did his beloved Philippa. As he recalled her recent letter, confirming her safety, a lump formed in his throat. *Sweet Jesu!* How did it come to this?

Pausing before the entry doors, he breathed deeply and vowed no one would leave the hall until his needs were met. No one. Whatever promises were required, he would make them. Failure was not an option. He closed his eyes for a moment and envisioned the outcome he sought. When he opened his eyes, he straightened his shoulders, raised his chin, and summoned his not inconsiderable charm. Then, flexing his fists, he nodded to the solemn-faced, liveried guards to open the doors.

Trumpets blared and while those seated rose, the rumble of voices hushed.

The king advanced into the chamber, smiling and inclining his head, acknowledging many of the fashionably dressed noblemen and the wealthiest London merchants and tradesmen cramming the benches and aisles.

Energy coursed through him as he stepped onto the dais, enabling him to see beyond the heads of those closest to him. Troubled faces peered up at him. He breathed deep to quell the rampant flutters within him. Taller than most men, his presence alone commanded attention and he employed the advantage now.

"Noble lords and gentle Englishmen…I, Edward, the third of that name, your God-anointed sovereign, King of England and France, stand before you. As your king, my sworn duty is to protect England from her enemies." He spoke with ceremonial deliberateness, engaging each man in a personal *tête á tête* and weaving an intoxicating aura of intimacy.

Midway in the crowd, several men met his eyes and shouldered their way forward.

He lowered his voice, drawing them in. "Time and again, Philippe, the false Valois king of France, has proven his desire to see England's ruin. He attacks our merchant fleets, encourages our Scottish subjects to rise up against us, and assaults our lands, not only in Gascony but here, on our southern coast."

Disgruntled mutters washed through the crowd.

King Edward breathed, waiting. "Who here does not recall Portsmouth's burning and the sack of Southampton?" He hardened his voice. "Or the horror and dishonour endured by our wives, mothers, and daughters, at the hands of our French enemy?"

A torrent of outrage flooded the room. For several minutes he allowed the outburst to continue. To succeed, he needed these men angry and eager to seek retribution.

"Silence!" A voice rang out. "Let us hear our King!"

Men shuffled. The room stilled.

"Loyal subjects, hear me. I need not remind you of the dangers we face if nothing is done to prevent King Philippe from becoming ever more emboldened, before he strips from us all we own, all we value and hold dear. He must be stopped! As your king, you look to me to stop him. Is it not my duty?"

A low rumbling of voices rippled through the hall.

"Indeed, it is my duty to end France's abuse of our realm. To my mind, protecting you from attack is but a simple matter." He paused. "From your faces, many of you doubt my words. Do not, good sirs, for by doing so you name me a liar and impugn my honour.'

"Heed me, for I know the truth of my words." King Edward searched the crowd for those men known to have spurned his previous entreaties for funds. He met each man's gaze in turn.

"To protect England, our homes and families, we need only accomplish one simple task." He raised and deepened his voice, speaking with conviction. "Simply put, we need only keep our enemy far from our shores."

A sea of baffled, bewildered, confused and puzzled faces gaped at him.

Un… Deux… Trois…Quatre…

Stretching up to his full height, he continued. "We must take the fight to France…force the false king to exhaust *his* resources and treasury to defend *his* lands and *his* people."

A bee-like hum swarmed the room as his message penetrated; the current war in France was more than a private matter between two kings. In Ghent, he deliberately challenged Philippe's right to France's throne, calling into question the legitimacy of Philippe's reign. Now that Flanders recognized King Edward as their rightful monarch, with their support and adequate funding from Parliament, he would wield the power to free England from France's longstanding oppression.

The buzz in the room intensified as comprehension dawned. King Edward's lips twitched upward. Though it might take hours of wrangling yet, and countless concessions, he was certain, in the end, he would win the funding he sought.

King Edward pushed aside the various documents, scraps of parchment and scrolls scattered across his worktable, spilling some onto the floor. He unrolled the map he reviewed earlier to study it more carefully.

After two hours of debate, Parliament granted the necessary subsidies to keep his French campaign from collapse. Yet, an alarming report arrived from France. He must return.

A knock sounded and his chamberlain opened the door.

"Ah, Huntingdon, I need ships."

"Sire?"

"While I have been here seducing those *bouffons* in Parliament, the French retook much of my hard-won Cambresis." He picked up a parchment and thrust it at his admiral. "Here, read this."

The admiral skimmed the first part of the document. A deep crease appeared between his heavy brows. "King Philippe's son, Jean, and Count d'Eu took Valenciennes?"

The admiral's astonishment mirrored the king's. While Huntingdon resumed reading, the king paced back and forth before the window. His shadow seemed to mock him, his movements futile, while his mind raced considering first one course of action and then another.

"God's nails!" The Earl roared. "Salisbury and Suffolk were captured?"

King Edward recoiled just the same when he read the missive. The thought of his two most loyal commanders—two closest friends—imprisoned in Paris, he could not bear it. Their aid all those years ago freed him from Mortimer's crippling grip.

The Admiral's eyes blazed. "We must free them."

"To do that, we must bring Philippe to his knees." The burn in the king's gut matched the fire in Northampton's eyes. "We need not only ships, but men…archers, arrows, horses, supplies."

The admiral strode to the door. "With the muster in Yarmouth?"

"And at the Pool of Orwell. One port will not accommodate all the vessels and provisions we require."

The Earl swung the door wide. "It will take time to assemble." Huntingdon started out of the chamber.

"Admiral?"

Huntingdon paused.

"By all that is holy, Philippe must not take Flanders." King Edward closed his eyes and groaned. "Sweet *Jesu*, Philippa is there!"

April 1340 - Byfleet Manor

Edward searched the Wey's dappled riverbank for the flat round stones, the best ones for skipping. He was released from his duty as Guardian, but the relief warred with regret in having to part from his father so soon after his return. For two joyous weeks, they spent most afternoons riding and hawking together and they often shared meals together, just the two of them. He was mesmerized by his father's tales of the Low Countries and battles in France.

One evening while dining, his father laid down his knife. "I think it is time you and your companions remove to your estate at Byfleet."

"I want to stay with you."

"Yes, I know, I have enjoyed our time together, too, but I must ready for my return to France. Northampton is charged with assembling men, arms, provisions, and ships, but my oversight is essential. You and I, we both have our duties."

Along the riverbank, Edward stooped and picked up a rock.

"Ho, watch this," Jack called, tossing a stone. When it skipped four times before sinking, he whooped and tripped over a root. It would be just like him to fall in.

Roger wandered ahead waving a branch at a pair of mute swans.

"Better leave them be," Edward said. "I think those are the same swans I came upon two days ago. They were wicked mean about their nest.”

“Od!” Roger shouted as the pair hissed and charged him. He scooted backwards just fast enough to avoid their snapping bills.

“Are you three done with dodging swans and skipping rocks?” Will mocked. “I am for the tilting yard.”

Roger sprinted past Will. “Last one back is a white-liver!”

Jack bolted after them. “Not fair! You have a head start!”

Edward pounded down the path to catch up.

Will and Roger raced neck and neck until Roger leaped over a log and caught his toe He stumbled, and Will streaked into the lead. If he won, there would be no end to his boasting.

Edward reached the boathouse where they stored their equipment and grabbed a padded gambeson, helm, and a truncheon. He panted his way to the practice yard where Jack was dragging his boot heel in the ground marking a square, while Will and Roger warmed up. Edward sank onto a nearby log. Jack joined him.

Will and Roger faced off.

“*En garde*!” Edward called.

The pair took each other’s measure, circled, feinted and lunged, with an occasional crack if one of them connected.

Roger made the mistake of dropping his guard. “Ow!”

“Good strike, Will,” Edward said. “One point.”

His friends thrust and spiraled, and within minutes they were red-faced and panting. Will jabbed, his foot slipped, and Roger smacked Will’s helm.

“Fine strike,” a deep voice called.

Will and Roger dropped their arms and all four stared at the intruder. Sandy-haired and stubble-faced, the man sat astride a bay stallion with a white blaze.

“Lord Edward!” St. Omer scurried from the manor. “Pardon my oversight,” his steward panted. “I have been remiss in my duty to inform you of Sir John’s imminent arrival.”

Edward and Jack rose as the knight threw his leg over, slid to the ground, and bent to one knee. “Lord Edward…Sir John Chandos at your service.”

"Sir John." Edward acknowledged, then nodded for the knight to rise.

Will and Roger hurried over not wanting to miss anything.

"Chandos, I anticipated you yesterday," St. Omar said. "Something delayed you?"

The knight's lips twitched and the corners of his eyes crinkled. "A filly caught my eye."

St. Omer smacked the knight's shoulder, sending dust flying. He waived to a stable lad. "Here, boy! Tend to this horse."

Chandos handed off his reins. "Give him a good rub down," he said, with a pat to his mount's neck. "He has earned it."

As the lad walked away, Edward asked, "What brings you to Byfleet, Sir John?"

"By our lord king's orders, I am to join your household." The knight's hazel eyes flicked to St. Omer.

"Again, I beg your indulgence, Lord Edward. "The message arrived a few days ago but slipped my mind."

"Did your manners flee with your memory?" Edward asked. "Sir John must be weary from his travels. Have refreshments brought."

Chandos wiped his brow. "Cool ale or cider would be welcome."

"Enough for all of us," Edward said. "Ale, bread and cheese, if you will."

"As you wish, my lord." St. Omer hastened off.

Will, Roger, and Jack gaped, not uttering a word.

Chandos said, "My young lords, I should very much like to observe your match, if you would be so good as to permit me."

After Edward offered introductions, Will and Roger took up their places. Chandos lowered himself onto the log to watch, with Edward on one side and Jack on the other. When the sparring resumed, Jack called the hits and kept score.

On a closer look, the knight was younger than Edward first thought. He leaned closer.. About the filly you claimed delayed you… she was no horse."

Chandos scratched his nose. "My lord?"

"More likely the filly was a maiden."

"A lass?" Chandos feigned confusion.

"Come, I shall not run tattling to my father."

"Keep your shields up," Chandos called. "Your friends show some skill. Have you similar prowess?"

"The best," Edward said. "I am especially masterful at keeping secrets."

"I wager you are quite accomplished."

Roger hooked his foot around Will's ankle and when Will bobbled, Roger smacked his helm again."

"Point for Roger," Jack said.

"Do you enjoy a good wager Lord Edward or perhaps dicing?"

Edward turned his head. "Me, gamble sir?"

Their eyes met and Chandos grinned. "I thought as much."

Edward laughed.

Will paused, holding up his hand, halting Roger in mid-swing. "Are you laughing at us?"

"No!" Edward put his hand over his mouth to smother a giggle.

"Not at all," Chandos offered, managing to keep a straight face.

Edward, trying to muffle a laugh, snorted.

"What is so funny?" Jack asked.

The dam broke; Edward and Chandos roared.

For two weeks Chandos drilled them daily in the use of weapons. Today, they practiced with lances, aiming to hit the target mounted on the quintain. Edward wiped the sweat from his face with his sleeve. Will straddled the wheeled wooden horse. Edward and Roger prepared to push.

Chandos and Jack watched from a log. "One… two… three… go."

Edward and Roger dug in their heels and heaved. The wheeled horse slowly gained momentum and as the distance to the target closed, Will lowered and couched his lance, aiming at the painted knight on the quintain's arm.

Wham! The arm spun. When the lance struck, it jammed against Will's shoulder and slammed him backward into Edward. He tripped, and as the horse continued forward, Edward fell face first in the dirt.

Chandos chuckled but Jack, knowing better, smothered a laugh.

Edward rolled over, not at all happy, and spat out a mouthful of dirt. After a few momments, Roger offered a hand up. Once on his feet, Edward wiped his mouth and sucked air. Sweat trickled down his dirty face. *Jesu.* If he could only ease off for once, but no, not a chance; the king's expectations were clear.

Hoofbeats thudded at the far end of the courtyard. The rider jumped from his lathered mount and spoke to a stable boy who pointed toward the house.

Chandos held up the water bucket. "Perhaps a drink?"

Will grabbed the ladle and drank first, then they passed the bucket around. After everyone drank their fill, Roger dumped what was left over his head. He shook his ginger mop, sending water everywhere, then threw back his head and bayed like a hound.

Edward laughed. He liked Roger; he never took himself too seriously.

Will rubbed his shoulder and grimaced. "That last go hurt."

"Serves you right," Roger said. "Your aim is rotten."

"Who are you to judge? A whey-faced nobody, grandson of a traitor."

Roger's jaw clenched and he balled his fists, ready to go at Will.

"Enough!" Chandos raised his hand. "You remind me of squabbling hens."

Though the rebuke silenced Will, the tension remained. Although it was true Roger's grandfather was executed for treason, Will's insult breached the bounds of chivalry.

Chandos continued, "The king sent me here to transform you half-grown fopdoodles into battle-ready men-at-arms. So, get up off your lazy arses and—"

Lazy?

"… saddle your horses. Time to *ride* at the quintain."

Roger whooped, jumped to his feet, hauled Edward to his, and looped arms. He twirled them around in a jig and kicked up his heels.

"About time," Will grumbled.

Chandos ignored his grousing.

"Lord Edward!" St. Omer hastened from the manor. Lines creased his brow. "A message from the king." He waved a parchment. "He summons you to join him on pilgrimage before he sails for France."

Edward's joy died.

He snatched the letter from St. Omer and headed to the river where he sat beneath his favourite willow, leaned against its trunk, and read. After the pilgrimage, Edward was to resume his duty as Guardian.

Duty. That word again.

Edward stared between the weeping branches to the river, flowing peacefully to the Thames, to the sea and the ships waiting to take his father to France—to war. Before sailing, they were to visit St. Edmund the Confessor's shrine, to pray for his protection and God's mercy.

Edward would serve as Guardian until the king returned…or serve as England's king, if he did not. Edward closed his eyes. *God help me.*

King Edward rode along the Suffolk track, consumed with thoughts of preparations for his return to France. Parliament had granted the funds, finally, and following the Parliamentary session, he returned to his chamber to find an alarming dispatch. He crumpled the parchment. By all that was holy, how did Salisbury and Suffolk, his most experienced commanders, manage to get themselves captured? If their troops failed to hold, the campaign was in peril of total collapse. No matter what, Flanders *must not* fall to the French. Sweet *Jesu!* Philippa was there.

The king shook himself from his stark thoughts and while his palfrey's rocking gait helped ease his spiraling mind, it was his son riding beside him who changed the course of his thoughts. The boy chattered non-stop, recounting long hacks with his companions, the monstrous fish he caught, and the knight newly installed in his household. 'Sir John this, and Sir John that.'

While Edward prattled, the king listened, smiling and nodding in all the right places. He promised himself his children would grow up in happier surrounds than those he endured, caught between his parents' deadly tug-of-war for power.

"Look, Papa!"

In the distance, the four stately stone towers of Clare Castle soared above the treetops. Whenever his travels brought him near, he made a point of stopping at his cousin's estate. Lady Elizabeth's sage insight impressed him, though it arose, sadly, from her past travails.

"Cousin Elizabeth is different from other ladies," Edward offered.

"Different? In what way?"

"Well, *Maman's* ladies talk mostly about babies, but Cousin Elizabeth speaks of breeding horses and hounds, and hawking."

Such a perceptive observation from one so young. It seemed the boy he left behind eighteen months before, grew in more ways than height. "Is that all?"

Edward grinned. "She does not let me win at chess. I like her."

"Lady de Clare *is* unique. Did you know she once lived in Ireland? Your great-grandfather arranged her first marriage to the Earl of Ulster."

"First? How many times has she been married?"

"Three." King Edward winked. "Our cousin has led an adventurous life. Perhaps, one day she may tell you about it."

Adventurous indeed. Elizabeth buried three husbands before the age of thirty, the last, Roger Damory, one of his father's favoured companions.

The bleating of sheep roused him from woolgathering. The flock grazed within a low stone wall, and Clare Castle's stacked-stone arch rose at the far end. Trumpets blared announcing their arrival. His entourage clattered through Northergate into the cobblestoned inner bailey. King Edward raised a hand in greeting to the dozens of staff gathered to welcome him and his heir.

Lady Elizabeth de Clare stood a prominent and imposing figure on the stone steps of her manor. His cousin was one of the wealthiest women in the realm. She and her two sisters inherited the vast de Clare holdings of the esteemed William, Marshal of England. Through no fault of her own, Elizabeth was cheated by dishonourable men, requiring her to battle in the courts to reclaim what was hers. The fact that she won was proof of the lady's acuity.

"Good day, Lady Cousin," the king hailed, reining to a walk.

"God's blessing upon you, Lord King." Lady Elizabeth smiled.

He dismounted and a groom took his horse.

"Welcome to Clare Castle. Thanks to Our Lord for your safe arrival." She curtsied. "You suffered no ills on your journey?"

"None too trying."

"God's good day to you, too, Lord Edward."

"And to you, Lady Elizabeth." Edward slipped off his pony and bowed to her curtsy.

The king laid a hand on his son's shoulder. "Edward has been keen to call upon you."

"And I to see him, sire." Sincerity rang in her voice, mirrored by a twinkle in her blue-grey eyes. She gestured them to the castle's entry and as they reached the threshold, she said, "My young lord, I believe you have grown at least two inches since I last saw you and, if I am not mistaken, you have a few new teeth as well."

Edward grinned, a pink hue creeping into his cheeks.

In the great hall, Elizabeth bade them sit, and offered a plate of candied dates, a particular favourite of Edward's. While the king and Elizabeth spoke of family, local affairs, and farm yields, young Edward consumed a fair number of sweets, though before long, he began to stir.

"Lord Edward," Elizabeth said, "remember the falcon we spoke of during your last visit? He arrived not long ago. Might you care to escort me to the mews?"

Edward's face lit up. "May I, *mon père*?" Edward licked honey from his lips and wiped his fingers on a damp cloth provided by a servant.

"*Oui*, but mind Lady Elizabeth."

Edward hurled himself off the bench. "I shall, Papa." He grabbed Elizabeth's hand and tugged, urging her to walk faster.

The next evening, King Edward relished the lavish meal of fish, fowl and roast Elizabeth arranged. Not only did his cousin remember young Edward's favourite treat, she made certain this meal ended with King Edward's favourite, the sweet kiss of currant and almond cakes.

After sending his son off to bed, King Edward escorted Elizabeth from the table to more comfortable seating near the hearth. His boots rapped the oak planks in time with the swish of his cousin's satin gown. The sound reminded him of Philippa and his guilt at leaving her bit him.

He settled his cousin onto a tapestried bench and eased into the one across from her. A serving maid entered with a decanter of Elizabeth's personal blend, poured for them, and moved off to clear away the remains of their meal.

Elizabeth raised her cup. "Dearest Cousin, let me express my joy at the birth of your third healthy son. Our Lord blesses you."

"Yes, with another son and my beloved wife's sufferance." He lifted his cup and sipped, enjoying the *uisce's* piquant flame on his tongue. "We named him John, after Philippa's father and my brother." Silently, he prayed for his brother's soul. Only two years separated them; he missed John still.

"Two sons born abroad," Elizabeth said. "What will the gossips make of it?" Her voice crackled in mock censure.

No one save Elizabeth would dare speak so baldly to him, surrounded as he was by many who said only what they thought he wanted to hear. He treasured Elizabeth's discernment, his trust in her deep-seated. "Certes, there will be talk."

She ran her finger around the rim of her cup. "You are too shrewd to be taken in by such."

Momentarily, he closed his eyes and when he opened them, he met Elizabeth's gaze. "My wife and I shall weather the gossip."

"Then you are vexed by another matter?"

"Ah, *oui*, the gossip is not the cause." He sipped. "When I left the Low Countries, my only choice was to leave Philippa behind. She is safe enough in the hands of my allies, for now."

"For now?"

"The French are emboldened by my army's recent losses and reports of the French advancing into Hainault are disturbing." His voice caught. "It is imperative I return. My family must not fall into enemy hands."

Quiet descended like a blanket, the room's only light the blood-red glow of the fire's embers. He sipped again, rolling the *uisce* over his tongue; a hint of mint dueled with the smouldering heat.

"Another royal courier arrived today." Elizabeth's naked comment barely broke a whisper. Her veiled invitation eddied in the room like a spectral mist over a moonlit moor. The lady possessed a penetrating intelligence as well as patience, the same traits for which her grandfather, William Marshal, was known, having served four Plantagenet kings, the last the irascible John.

King Edward succumbed to the lure of her silence. "Yes…a dispatch from abroad."

Elizabeth's gown rustled.

"Philippe has seduced the Genoese shipbuilders. Two dozen new galleys enrich his French fleet and all are reported sailing east from Honfleur."

The *uisce's* subtle fume lingered on his lips. "All poised to bid me welcome."

Elizabeth's faint inward breath pierced the stillness.

May 1340 - Suffolk Coast

The royal entourage rode out from Bury St. Edmunds, England's royal red, gold, and blue pennons flittering against a blue-grey sky. Following the king's stay at Clare Castle, he had progressed to St. Edmund's shrine to seek God's blessing and pray for the soul of the Thomas of Brotherton, his uncle, laid to rest while the king was abroad.

Masses at the holy shrine offered less enjoyable distractions for his young son than Clare Castle. Edward had fingered his rosary piously, and mouthed prayers, half-suffocated by the scent of incense. Did his son believe in the power of prayer or only mirror his father's devotion?

Throughout King Edward's life, he believed God answered his prayers. He implored Him to heed his pleas yet again—for victory in the upcoming battle, as well as for the safety of his wife, and children. His future, theirs, and all of England depended upon it.

The entourage traveled south along the hard-packed track's dips and rises, past undulating pastures and fields rippling with new shoots. Edward trotted his pony, repeatedly circling out and back around. The leisurely pace was too sedate for a boy about to turn ten.

"You sit your pony like you were born to it," the king said. "I believe you and Jaiet have partnered well over the years."

"Yes, he has been a patient schoolmaster." Edward stroked his steed's shiny black coat stippled with white hairs.

His son rode with fluidity but little grace. Edward's legs dangled well past Jaiet's flanks. "Your pony seems to have grown shorter," the king said, maintaining a straight face.

Edward's brow crumpled in thought, then his eyes widened. "*Oui*, Papa. I love Jaiet and always will, though a stallion would be most appropriate now."

The conviction in Edward's voice tickled the king, yet his son said nothing more, a sure sign he was learning the benefit of biding one's time.

"Can we canter now, Father?"

"*Oui*." The king called the order, his heart swelling at the *joie de vivre* beaming from his son's face.

Regrettably, the battles looming on two fronts intruded. Aside from the French fleet awaiting him at sea, the Scots were likely to invade the northern shires again as soon as he left England's shores. Before sailing, he must appoint men to Edward's advisory counsel who were experienced in war as well as governing, for they would need to put down any uprising by the Scots.

As the sun lowered on the horizon, salt scented the air. It would not be long before they reached Holbrook's modest village where the Rivers Stour and Orwell joined.

"What say you, Papa?" Edward's grin revealed the new teeth Elizabeth mentioned.

The question interrupted King Edward's brooding, its meaning unclear until Edward patted his pony's neck.

"We will consider a new mount for you upon my return."

Edward's smile vanished. "Must you go?"

"*Certainement*. My troops in France depend upon my return."

"Yes, but—"

"Your mother is there, your brothers and sisters, and Joan. I must bring them home."

"Certainly, but—"

"Duty demands my return, Edward. You know this." He winced inwardly at the sharp edge in his voice.

Edward's lips trembled as he tried to hold back tears, then he pressed his heels to his pony's flanks and galloped ahead. How his fatherly heart ached for the boy who must grow up too fast. Better to let him go. Better for Edward that his king not see him cry.

Sunlight brushed the landscape in golden, then orange hues. The rolling farmlands levelled, giving way to miles of mudflats lining the estuary. Shorebirds—redshanks, snipes, godwits—cried overhead before alighting to scavenge in the shallows.

The harbour was empty. Where were the ships?

By now, the harbour should be teeming with dozens of vessels preparing to sail. *Jesu!* His gut twisted. More delay.

May 1340 - Port of Orwell

Boots pounded the planked floor at the seaport inn, then stopped. "Lord King, I beg you to listen." Chancellor Stratford's voice sounded more strident than usual. The raps on the floor started again.

Edward leaned in, placing his ear closer to the wall. Eavesdropping again. Yes, if he wanted to know what was happening.

"Sire, the particulars in the report came directly from the Duke of Guelders, made known to him through two trusted shipping merchants, Conrad Clypping and Peter Gildesburgh."

"Never heard of them," his father's voice was clipped.

Edward searched the wall for a crack. Thankfully, he was alone and would not get caught and scolded. No one told him anything, or if they did only half the story. If he were expected to take up his duty as Guardian again, he must know what was going on.

"Please listen, my lord," Stratford continued. "The Duke's communiqué states King Philippe intends to block your return; he has amassed over two hundred ships." The archbishop's pitch rose. "My liege, King Philippe is intent on your capture. You must not sail."

"Enough! You do not tell *me* what I should or should not do, Stratford."

No trouble hearing now.

"*You* do not rule here." *Whack!*

Edward flinched. Whatever his father hit, he gave it a solid smack. The poor Archbishop.

"Most humbly, my liege, I beg forgiveness for any perceived transgression." Stratford lowered his voice. "As your Chancellor and sworn advisor, duty requires me to give good counsel."

Edward quieted his breathing.

"Sire, Philippe's fleet poses too great a risk."

"Bah! As a man of God, what do you know of war?"

Edward imagined the mocking look which accompanied his father's tone. How could his father take the chancellor's warning so lightly?

"You dare suggest I abandon my allies…my wife…and children to my enemies?" A chair grated, and boots scraped the floor.

"My concern is for your safety, sire, should it please you."

"It does not!" *Wham!*

Edward jumped.

"Get out, Stratford. Get out, now!"

Footsteps, then the door rasped open and closed.

"Good counsel, my arse!" his father grumbled.

Edward's hands shook. The king's fury scorched through the wall.

A knock on his father's chamber door..

"Come." More foot shuffling. "Ah, Admiral Morley," the king's voice mellowed. "As expected. *Bon*, Lieutenant Crabbe accompanies you."

"Sire." The door latched shut. Stools scraped the floor.

Edward knew the Admiral and pictured him, his mane of gray hair, weathered face, and his squint-lined dark eyes. His father praised Morley, said the Admiral accomplished more to protect English shipping than any other commander.

"Good of you to attend me. Both of you."

Edward admired his father's ability to recover his calm so quickly.

"What account have you, Admiral?"

"Naught good, my lord," Morley said.

"*De Fransen* sailed *van Honfleur, Mijn Heer.*" Must be Lieutenant Crabbe. "*Ja*, two honderd ships.."

Edward remembered his father telling him Crabbe was once a Flemish pirate. A real pirate! What stories he must tell! Edward spotted a crack near the corner of the wall he missed before. When he peeked through, the Admiral was unrolling a parchment—a map.

"Our scouts spotted the French fleet off the coast of Sluys near the mouth of the Zwin. The sighting was on the eighth, Lord," Morley said.

"The reports are not exaggerated?" King Edward drummed his fingers on the table. His father paid attention and sounded more concerned now. "No matter. We must sail. Our troops, even now, assault Tournai and taking it depends upon my return with reinforcements and supplies."

Edward adjusted his position so he could see better.

Morley scratched his chin. "I agree our troops need help, though to return just now presents a grave danger. May I suggest we assemble a larger, stronger fleet before sailing?"

The king turned on Morley. "Do you and Stratford conspire against me?" His father's tone cut like a blade.

Morley reeled back. "Not at all, sire. It is my opinion; the hazard is too great."

"The greater is to delay. Christ's blood, Morley! You suggest I abandon my troops, my wife and children. By all that is Holy, no!"

Edward no longer needed an ear or an eye to the wall. How could his father sail knowing the French lay in wait with a much larger fleet? Edward squinted through the crack again.

"Hear me, Admiral. I will sail, and if you, and Crabbe here, are too cowardly, I will go alone."

What? Edward's hands shook.

"My liege, never doubt my loyalty, nor my resolve to protect you. Where you lead, I go. Even should I perish, I sail with you." Morley's fierce tone laid bare his determination.

What was his father thinking? Despite all of Morley's warnings, his father still intended to sail? Edward thought he might be sick. He backed away from the wall, hit the bed, and sat down hard. If the French captured his father, would they execute him? What if his father never came back?

June 1340 – Port of Orwell

Edward leaned forward, resting his arms on the wharf rail and his chin on his forearms while seamen loaded supplies onto the few ships which remained in the estuary. Men-at-arms and archers, staves in hand, strode up gangways—more retinues than he ever saw before. Gulls swooped overhead, their cries not nearly as loud as Edward's would be, *if* he were able.

For several weeks, the harbour had resounded with the constant din of saws and hammers refitting the ships. The horse stalls were stripped away to make room for troops— three archers for every two men-at-arms, and wooden platforms constructed, fore, aft, and atop the mainsails, as firing stages for the bowmen.

With each new delay, the king's temper flared hotter. Edward shuddered as he recalled his father turning on one of his closest friends, their cousin Henry of Grosmont.

From across the jetty, a familiar voice interrupted Edward's thoughts. Chandos supervised several broad-shouldered crewmen wrestling a trébuchet on board the largest ship. He already managed the securing of mangonels and springalds aboard other vessels. As Chandos explained, these would be used for hurling bolts, stones, and fireballs toward enemy ships. Edward was not pleased when he learned his friend would sail with the king. One more person important to him to worry about.

"Edward, *ici*, come." The king climbed down into the long-boat ferrying him to his flagship and return Edward to shore.

Edward crossed the jetty, the odour of fish easier to endure than his absolute dread. He tried not to wobble as he stepped into the landing boat, and then perched on its small plank bench. Nearly two years before, he said farewell to his family from this same port. Then, the king headed to war while Edward stood as Guardian. At eight, he was little aware of what the destination meant. Now, at ten, he knew.

Duty.

The longboat cut across the harbour, and each rip of the oars tore at Edward's belly. The *Thomas'* one square sail reflected white onto the grey-green surface of the easy ripples of the bay. England's arms, its lions quartered with France's lilies, fluttered blue, red, and gold from the mainmast. Twin castles topped the mainsail of the cog set to carry the king, his personal men-at-arms, and archers into the fray. Edward leaned against his father's shoulder, praying the king would come home again.

Draping an arm across Edward's shoulders, his father said, "Fret not. All will be well."

Edward's throat ached. "*Mon père*, do not shield me from the truth."

The king's eyebrows raised in question.

"I did not mean to eavesdrop, b-but I heard what Chancellor Stratford and Admiral Morley told you at the inn and heard you shouting at them."

The king chuckled and touseled Edward's hair. "The entire town probably heard me. My temper got the better of me, did it not?" The knot in Edward's stomach drew tighter.

"Please, do not jest. The French have so many more ships."

"But we have God and Saint George on our side. Have faith, *mon fils*. Be strong." He held Edward's gaze. "*Promet moi.*"

Edward's throat was so tight he barely managed to choke out the words. "I promise."

"*Bon.*" His father squeezed his shoulder.

The oarsman slipped his blades and the boat slid alongside the larger vessel. He grabbed the rope ladder dangling down its side, and steadied the boat. With one last squeeze of Edward's shoulders, the king stood.

"Remember, you have given your word."

"Yes, Father." Edward wanted to hug his father, but could not in full view of all the others. After all, he was ten.

The king scaled the ladder and once on deck, he leaned over the rail and touched three fingers to his brow, offering their secret salute.

The Father, Son and Holy Ghost.

Though little reassured, Edward called, *"Reviens bientôt! A la victoire!"*

23 June, 1340 – Zwin Estuary

After saluting his son from the ship's rail, King Edward retired to his cabin. The despair in Edward's eyes tore at the king's heart, and the lump in his throat nearly choked him. Yet, sail he must. The future of England demanded he return and defeat the French. Accompanied by a small flotilla, the *Thomas* would put to sea on the midnight tide and rendezvous with the main fleet off the coast of Harwich before dawn.

Throughout the night, he tossed and rolled in his bunk, dozing on and off. Finally, he gave up, dressed, and went on deck. A brisk wind snatched at him, and he wrapped his mantle tighter. The horizon to the east seamed a milky white below a sky laden with dark clouds. Some might say the heaviness presaged doom in the coming conflict, yet more likely, it hinted at nothing save a latent squall.

While he had tossed in his bunk, the two English fleets merged and now sailed southeastward. The single-sailed, flat-bottomed cogs pitched in the buffeting wind. His commanders' vibrant-coloured banners rippled atop their ships' masts. Above him, England's arms snapped its own tense rhythm.

"We should make the coast off Blankenberge by nightfall, sire," Admiral Mauny called.

"*Bon.*" The king widened his stance against the roll of the ship.

The *Thomas* ploughed into a deep trough drenching the bow. Seawater sluiced off the king's hood while a few runnels dribbled inside, down his neck. He hunched deeper and clutched the rail tighter. With each pitch and roll, his stomach lurched.

Ignoring the sea's icy fingers, he stared ahead, intent on the looming contretemps. Philippe dreamed and boasted of capturing him. The Valois pretender misjudged the lion of England's fangs, and claws.

Dieu et mon droit.

Victory whispered on the wind.

As the day faded, he gazed south where a sandy strip appeared on the horizon, growing ever more prominent as Morley called orders and the *Thomas* maneuvered closer to shore. The deepening dark swallowed a coastal town.

Morley ordered the sail lowered and the ship slowed. "Drop anchor!"

Chains rattled and the captain joined him on deck. The *Thomas* swayed gently in the shallow waters off-shore Blankenberge, the muffled lapping against the hull soothing after the vessel's deeper dance.

"The Zwin estuary lies about fifteen miles east, sire." Morley pointed.

The king half-turned, his left shoulder to the northwest wind. A thick layer of clouds blanketed the stars over the Zwin estuary, the river's gateway into France's interior. Reports confirmed the French fleet was anchored at the river's mouth, effectively blocking the quickest route to unite with England's land forces. Philippe's choice of place to foil his English foe's return was a good one.

The rhythmic slap of oars drifted up, and a longboat scraped alongside the hull. In moments, a mop of windblown russet hair appeared above the rail. Admiral Huntingdon climbed aboard, followed by Admiral Mauny and Lieutenant Crabbe. Mauny hailed from Hainault and knew these waters well. He first arrived in England as a member of Philippa's Hainault household.

In the king's cabin, Morley unrolled a hastily-drawn map and weighted the corners. "The estuary is about three miles wide."

The men gathered closer.

Crabbe jabbed a finger. "We are hier, Mihn Heer."

The king leaned in. Crabbe knew these waters better than anyone. Years before, Mauny captured the former pirate when Crabbe commanded ships for the Scots. The king reimbursed Mauny, paying for Crabbe's ransom. At the pirate's release, he switched his allegiance. His service was worth every florin since, and never more valuable than now.

"The Zwin hier," Crabbe pointed, "and de Fransen ships anker naar Cadzand Island hier." Intent faces followed the lieutenant's fingers across the map.

"Sire," Huntingdon broke in, "any word from young Ufford?"

Mauny edged forward. "Has the lad reported in?"

The king paced at the head of the table. "Not yet." Robert Ufford, the Earl of Suffolk's son, had sailed ahead of the fleet to scout the French position. "While we await his account, pray the blessed northwest wind holds." He did pray, for without it, their cause might be lost.

The men adjourned to their ships to await word. King Edward stretched out on his bunk, his mind wrestled with indecision. Should he fight or sail around Cadzand and march inland from a port further east? Which would be wiser—to stand or withdraw? Philippe avoided battle and in the Cambresis his cowardice worked to King Edward's advantage.

Yet, English troops were eager to make France pay for its attacks on their homeland and the French monarch's boasts of capturing England's king steeled their determination. The French poltroon could ill afford to withdraw this time, as he would humiliate himself. A defeat would prove him inept. Nothing would please the King Edward more.

Muffled voices, scrapes, and bumps at water level interrupted King Edward's musings. He rose from his berth, his pulse keeping time with the rattle of the mast's rigging. He slipped from his cabin to the deck beneath an inky sky stippled with thousands of stars. The locations of the constellations now flickered from altered positions.

Morley joined him near the rail as Reginald Cobham and John Chandos, climbed aboard. Both knelt. "Sire, we come from Lord Ufford," Cobham said.

"*Bon.*" The king motioned the knights to their feet. "Come to my cabin." The king knew Cobham well, a veteran of several Scottish campaigns. Chandos mentored young Edward, demonstrating an astuteness not often seen in one so young. "Morley, send a signal to summon the others and, while we wait, send in my page with food and ale."

Lanterns swayed with the ship's gentle rocking as the four men gathered around the table. Cobham began to recount their sortie. "We rowed to shore with our horses tethered and swimming behind." He broke off a chunk of bread. "The bishop, Henry Burghersh, went with us, sire." He tilted his head toward Chandos. "His idea."

The king fingered his beard. Chandos invited Burghersh, and all three went to shore? "Go on."

The young knight picked up the tale. "Upon landing, we unearthed the Flemish Admiral Lambyn and he suggested scouting with us."

More bumps and voices drifted from water level. One by one, the king's commanders entered the cabin—Derby, Gloucester, Arundel, and Northampton—and settled themselves around the table, the parchment map in its middle.

The king set down his mug and cleared his throat. "*Messieurs,* while there is no need to tell you why we are undertaking this perilous venture, I feel compelled to voice what is in my heart and what I do not say often enough." He took a breath. "To all of you I say, your service and loyalty are beyond price to me." Grave faces stared back at him. He nodded to Cobham. "Let us begin. If you would, Cobham."

"Sire." Cobham stood. "The French fleet anchors at the southeastern end of Cadzand Island and blocks our entry to the Zwin." He tapped the map and then glanced at Chandos.

"The ships are arrayed in three lines, here," Chandos said. "The largest ships, *Black Cock, Saint George,* and *Christopher* hold the front line, along with our enemy's flagship, *Saint Denys.*"

"God's wounds! " Northampton cursed. *"Christopher* is one of ours, stolen by those curs!"

King Edward nodded. "Indeed."

"There is more, sire. Admiral Lambyn noticed a peculiar situation which caught all of us by surprise." Cobham paused, a smug curve to his lips. "The ships are chained together."

"Dit is gud!" Crabbe said. "Da Fransen cannot manoeuvreren."

"Pure lunacy," Mauny said. "Who commands? What idiot?" Cobham's face darkened. "According to Lambyn, the command is split between Hugh Quieret and France's Constable, Nicolas Béhuchet."

"Quieret." The king chuckled. "God favours us with not one fool, but two." In the heat of battle, a duel command could not make quick decisions.

Chandos cleared his throat. "Lords, not only are the French galleys chained together, the current drives them into shallow water near shore."

"God's blood! They cannot navigate." Huntingdon shook his head. "They must be mad!"

King Edward smiled, much as a satisfied cat. "Yet, their foolishness offers advantages, *n'est ce pas?*"

Over the next hour, the men debated a course of action and finally agreed on Morley's recommended order: Huntingdon,

Northampton, and Mauny would command the front line. Morley would position the *Thomas,* with the king aboard, slightly behind. Derby, Arundel, and Gloucester would command the second line of ships, filled to overflowing with fighting men. Captain Crabbe would command the supply ships in the rear.

In the dark before dawn, King Edward balanced on deck. His decision made, he put his trust in God and Saint George, their protection invisible, yet as present as the crimson and white tribute pennon soaring above him. Suddenly, a single bright signal beacon pierced the dark.

England's motley collection of ships weighed anchor and sailed out of the estuary on the outgoing tide, and away from his enemy. He turned his back to the taffrail and peered behind them, toward the mouth of the Zwin. As the eastern horizon paled, a shimmering, opaque haar veiled the sea.

He squinted at the mist. Within it, a forest appeared. He blinked.

C'est impossible.

He blinked again, squinted and stared at the forest jutting out of the water.

He rubbed his eyes. The image cleared. Not a forest, but the countless masts of his enemy's anchored fleet. The haze and morning light tricked him.

The king turned around and faced into the wind, ruffling his hair and blessing his cheeks with salt spray. In every direction, English ships sliced through the swells toward the open sea. What would his enemies, anchored in the estuary, think when they awoke and discovered the English fleet gone?

The sun climbed higher dissolving the haze, while England's makeshift navy skimmed over the frothing swells. It would be hours yet before the tide turned. And with it, his ships would turn to ride the incoming tide, backed by a steady northwest wind. His fleet would soar across the water, like arrows fired from longbows, to bear down on the unsuspecting French.

Gulls swooped and squawked in the ship's wake. Would the unexpected English withdrawal beget the confusion and indecision he desired? He prayed his ploy would work…that it was already working. Pennons snapped the king from his brooding.

Morley swaggered across the deck wearing a wide grin, his beak of a nose casting a long shadow. "My liege, you are indeed a shrewd fellow and it is why we follow you."

The king glanced skyward. During his woolgathering, the sun rose close to its apex. The ship shuddered beneath his feet; its timbers groaned.

The tide turned. The ships turned.

Time to run before the wind.

King Edward's pulse surged with the tide. The blessed wind held.

Glory to You, O Lord

He gripped the rail tight as the *Thomas* tore through the swells.

Arrayed in three lines, each ship's commander adjusted to take full advantage of the heaven-sent Northwest wind. Crews shortened or increased sail, making the minute adjustments keeping the ships in formation. Sparks glinted from the men-at-arms cramming the ships in the first two lines, and archers awaited the signal to scramble into the castles and crows nests.

"Captain Crabbe spoke to me of his disappointment, sire." Morley's words caught on the wind. "Crabbe hoped to captain a ship at the front."

The ship pitched, and the king adjusted his stance. He inclined his head toward Crabbe's rear line. "Do you know what those ships carry?" He paused. "For over a year, I struggled to wrest funds from Parliament. Only a fool would entrust his hard-won treasure to a man of lesser ability. I am no fool."

The king won the clash with Parliament at great cost. Humbling himself did not come easy. He would not forget.

The wind billowed the cogs' single sails, making the ships

appear like cloud puffs scuttling across a peaceful summer sky, in sharp contrast to the deadly fray awaiting them. The king imagined the savagery once the ships closed within firing range. Arrows thick as a hail storm. Grappling hooks hurtled. Vessels wrenched hull-to-hull. The battle cries as men scaled the rails. England's arms run up French mainmasts.

Trumpets sounded far off the bow. The king's heart beat a brisker tempo as the azure and gold of France's colours hove into view above the largest ship. Would his strategy succeed? Would the reappearance of the English fleet catch his foe by surprise? What were Quieret and Béhuchet thinking? Doing?

France's fleet appeared formidable as they drew nearer. Dozens of Genoese galleys dominated the estuary, their sides reinforced with timber panels to repel efforts to board, exactly as Cobham and Chandos reported. One item, small yet significant, that Chandos and Cobham noted portended a boon.

Sailors crewed the galleys, not soldiers.

A seamen's meagre fighting skills were no match for the prowess of England's battle-hardened men-at-arms. Every nerve in the king's body prickled.

As the distance closed, archers shimmied up the cogs' riggings and scrambled into place. They retrieved cords, tucked away, protected from the damp, and restrung their bows. At four hundred yards, perhaps farther with the aid of the wind, the French would come within longbow range. Every arrow finding its mark would help level the field.

Across the English front line, the men-at-arms readied for boarding. The king's fingers trembled as he tied off his leather coif and donned his helm.

English trumpets signalled.

Above the wind, centenaurs shouted. "Nock."

The distance narrowed.

"Draw."

The ships neared.

"Loose!"

Arrows flew. The king's chest vibrated as if filled with a horde of locusts.

"Draw! Loose!"

"Draw! Loose!"

Thousands of arrows thrummed, arched up and over the breastworks of the French galleys. Screams erupted. The king winced as he imagined the barbed points ripping into the tightly-packed sailors.

The *Thomas* crested, plunged and rose again.

The English ships now came into crossbow range. Genoese bolts sheared the air. The king ducked behind a barrel. A bolt thumped into the mast, missing him by mere inches. His heart thudded. Though the Genoese were shooting into the sun, shooting blindly, their bolts struck, and men screamed. A shriek from above cleaved through him. An archer dropped to the deck; his head split like a beet. Bile rose, threatening to overcome him. He forced it down.

Lord have mercy.

Northampton, Huntingdon, and Mauny aimed their ships directly at the French vessels; the chains linking them glinted in the sun. Northampton, in the nearest ship, braced for impact with the *Saint Denys*. Timbers crunched and groaned as his ship rammed the hull of the French galley. Rocks and fire missiles flew. While flames shot up his ship's canvas, Northampton bellowed, "For England!"

Several men-at-arms pitched grapnels at the galleys, exposing themselves as easy targets for the crossbowmen. A knight staggered, a bolt through his forehead. Another stepped bravely into his place, taking a bolt to his thigh. Blood spurted, yet he held firm while a comrade fixed the line.

English horns blared. "Forward!" Northampton roared.

The king prayed and made the sign of the cross.

The *Thomas* shifted beneath him. Morley adjusted course, the *Christopher* lay dead ahead, now within longbow range. Centenars bawled.

"Draw!"

"Loose!"

Bowstrings sang.

The king clung tightly to the rail. With a thunderous yowl the ships collided. Timbers cracked. The archers needed no urging. Bodkin points drilled through French leather and mail to keep the French at bay while English grappling hooks flew and lines were secured.

"Sound the attack," the king commanded.

Horns sounded again.

"Forward!" he roared. "For England!"

Deafened by his men's answering battle cries, he rushed forward, blood racing in his veins. With Cobham on his left, the king threw a leg over *Christopher's* rail. A pock-faced seaman charged. The king kicked out, smashing his boot into the man's chest and he reeled backward onto the deck. In the seconds it bought, the king launched himself onto the deck and his foe, jammed his blade in the gap beneath the man's helmet and jerked it sideways. Blood spurted; the man gurgled a last breath.

At a blur of motion to the king's right, he grabbed his dying foe, and rolled, using the body as a shield. The man's body jerked as a sword pierced his back. The king freed his blade and rammed it into his assailant's unprotected calf. The man staggered and fell, his eyes sightless, his throat ripped through by an arrow.

The king's surcoat wrenched as he was yanked forcefully upward to slam against the chest of a steel-clad giant. Eyes glittered above cheek plates. The king's breath seized.

"Sire." The giant released his grip and grinned, a bloody gap where a tooth once was.

The king shuddered, relieved. "*Merci,* friend. After the battle, search me out—" The man was gone, charging after a seaman attempting to slip over the rail. After a glance around, the king bent over and sucked in air. Cheers erupted behind him, and he spun. The quartered lions of England winged up *Christopher's* ropes.

Thanks to Thee O Lord.

King Edward peered across to the other vessels. From

Huntingdon's ship, springalds launched pots of burning oil at a French galley. Black, acrid smoke enveloped the ships. Breathing must be torturous. Tiny burning embers drifted, igniting canvas from ship to ship.

All along the enemy front line, French colours were struck. *Thy will be done.*

Cobham strode among the horde of cheering men who retook *Christopher*, a gash across his cheek already clotted.

"Cobham," the king shouted to be heard above the din. "Get a message to Mauny to secure these galleys while we take the second line."

Cobham hesitated, his eyes fixed on King Edward's hand.

Blood covered the king's left hand, though he never felt the blade. "Go! Give Mauny my message."

The king brushed away any thought of his injury. "*Á moi!* Here! To me," he rallied his guard. "You fought as bravely as any I have ever commanded, but the battle is not won. What say you, we show these hedge-born French what Englishmen are made of?"

The men cheered, "For England!" Their cry resounded across the bay. English aboard the other ships echoed in triumph. The king squinted east toward the French second line. Canvases were filling. The chains must have been cut.

"Morley!"

"I see them, sire." The admiral set the reclaimed *Christopher's* course to intercept the French. Morley had captained this ship before and was familiar with how it responded to a freshening wind.

The king perched at *Christopher's* rail, his eyes locked on his prey. Oblivious to the dousing of salt spray, he prayed. "*Non nobis, Domine, non nobis,* To Thy name give glory"

The sun blazed behind them as the ship skimmed over the water. Men cleaned weapons while archers scaled the ship's rigging. The ship neared. Horns sounded.

Ventenars called.

"Nock."

"Draw."

"Loose."

Feathered shafts flickered deathly white.

Distant men shrieked.

As *Christopher* bore down on a French galley, crossbow bolts seared into blinding sunlight to splinter *Christopher's* sides and deck. Spalls flew. English screams chorused with those of impaled French. Genoese crossbowmen worked frantically to lever their weapons back into firing position. The time it took allowed each English archer to loose four or five arrows.

"Poltron!" A shout from the galley carried across the water. A soldier booted a crossbowman hunkered behind a breastwork. *"Sans valeur!"*

A boom and crash jolted the king onto the deck. *"Deus vult,"* he yelled, righting himself. "To victory! For God and Saint George!"

Howling like a pack of ravenous wolves, his retinue seethed up and over the sides of the galley. Arrows arched over their heads.

Frenchmen shrieked. Bolts flew.

The English horde propelled the king forward onto the deck already strewn with writhing men and puddled blood, the air tainted with metal. A glancing blow caught his helm. He faltered, and swung his blade, his stroke parried skillfully by a grinning Frenchman. The king leapt back from the bloodied steel slashing his surcoat. He feinted, glimpsed an opening, and lunged. The tip of his sword pierced mail, through leather, into flesh. Blood gushed. He twisted his blade as he wrenched it out; the stench made him gag.

Half-bent, chest heaving, the king jerked sideways, barely avoiding a deadly blow. His counterstrike caught his foe's elbow. Crimson spread. The man's blade clanked on the deck as he slumped, clutching his arm.

Beside the king, a man wailed through blood and bone; a crossbow bolt had shattered his jaw. Across the galley's deck, men grappled with French knights holding their ground, but the seamen, untrained for combat, cowered or clambered over the rail rather than face certain death from the English onslaught.

The king panted, searched his mouth for moisture, and made the mistake of looking down. The rings of his mail hauberk were split, and blood streamed from his thigh. When did he take the cut? He stumbled.

Chandos rushed toward him. "My liege." He shouted into the mêlée, "Here, to the king!" Knights encircled him while Chandos cut a strip from his surcoat. Chandos tightened the binding to stem the blood.

King Edward sucked in a breath. "*Merci,*" he rasped.

"We must get you to safety, sire."

The king scanned the ship, the vermillion-slick deck littered with bodies. Admist the moans of the wounded and dying only a few French remained fighting. "I am safe enough." He swayed and reached out a hand. "Help me to the rail." England's lion would not succumb. On unsteady legs, the king propped upright, shielded his eyes and squinted across the estuary. Battle cries carried from the other ships.

English soldiers swarmed crablike up the side of the nearest ship. Terror struck its French crew, and they flung themselves overboard. The king scanned farther east, where dozens of Flemish flags rippled in the wind. The Sluys garrison was sailing out to attack the ships in the French rear line. God bless them. A few French barges broke away to skirt the east end of Cadzand Island. He prayed Crabbe's ships would intercept them.

Plaintive cries, a deathly keening, sounded near shore. He shivered.

Lord have mercy.

Hundreds of bodies bobbed in the shoals. There, in the pink-tinged shallows, the citizens of Bruges, loyal to England, slaughtered any French who tried to get to shore. Bishop Burghersh's pleas had been heard.

King Edward made the sign of the cross.

Thy will be done.

Relief flooded through him. With God's Grace, victory was theirs.

Dusk settled slowly over the estuary. Under an ascending ivory crescent, the *Thomas* rocked gently in the outgoing tide. His wounds tended, King Edward sat on a makeshift pallet, leaning back against the rail. The stench of black smoke and torn flesh, combined with the distant moans of injured men, made rest all but impossible.

A boat scraped the ship's hull. "Ho, *Thomas*, permission to board." A sweat-matted head of russet hair appeared before Chandos threw a leg over the rail and landed on deck.

"Your pardon, sire." He sank to one knee.

"Chandos." The king motioned the knight to his feet.

"My lord, a crew captured the French commander, Nicholas Béhuchet. The men seek permission for ransom."

King Edward scowled. "Béhuchet. One of Philippe's trained dogs." He pinched the bridge of his nose. "For many years, the dear Constable has done his utmost to cripple English shipping." Pausing, he stared unseeing into the distance.

"Your orders, Lord King?"

The king inhaled and let out his breath slowly. "What of the other?"

"Admiral Quiéret?" Chandos shrugged. "Dead in the fighting, sire."

"A pity." Indeed, for he should have suffered a more inglorious death.

The knight's lips quirked up. "Captain Crabbe took command of *Christopher* and gives chase to ships of the French third line, my lord. They are thought to be under command of Pietro Barbavera."

"Barbavera. The Genoese pirate. Should anyone succeed in bringing the villain back to face English justice, it would be Crabbe."

"About Béhuchet, sire."

The king refocused on Chandos. "We owe the constable a great debt, do we not?" He cast his eyes toward the ship where, in the shrouded moonlight, two men restrained a third. "The men must bear disappointment."

Chandos cocked his head. "Lord?

"No ransom. Hang him."

Chandos swallowed.

"Let him dance from the prow of his own ship."

Chandos retraced his climb down the ladder to the waiting longboat.

King Edward lay back. His leg throbbed. To deny his men a justly deserved ransom did not sit well, however, on this occasion, his choice was clear. He would have Philippe know the pain of losing one of his own, and learn the lion of England's charge was no bluff.

Hours later, as twilight deepened to night and a lantern cast shadows across the deck, King Edward rested with his coterie in companionable silence. Earlier, he knighted several brave men and lauded the archers for their skill and courage. From low origins they might hail, yet he valued them no less.

The sea lapped at the ship's swaying hull. Like the king, Northampton and Huntingdon took their well-earned ease, as did his cousin, Derby. Henry recently returned from his command in Gascony to lend aid to this fight. He admired Henry, and envied him, for he played as hard as he fought and made no apologies. Upon their return to England, he could imagine the celebrations.

The king repositioned his aching leg, thankful his injury was not worse. Philippa would fret, while his heir would be relieved the French did not prevail. The king imagined his family's long-overdue reunion, holding his infant sons, and his daughters. Everyone together, safe on English soil with a better future ahead, one free of Philippe's interference. When he returned to England this time, it would not be as a whimpering dog.

He broke the genial spell. "My friends, most assuredly this victory is owed to you and God's blessing, for *He* blinded the French commanders as the sun did the Genoese bowmen."

"*Amen,*" said Northampton. "The *Christopher*, *Saint George*, and *Black Cock* are back where they belong."

"A great triumph, *mes amies,* though we must not forget the good men who sacrificed their lives this day."

Derby named them. "Butler, de Poynings, de Mouthermere, and de Latimer. I knew them well." All served at one time or another under Derby's command.

"Honourable, loyal men," the king said. Derby would feel their loss most keenly.

The king motioned for aid to rise and balanced precariously on one leg. His throat tight, he spoke humbly. "*Messieurs,* I am in your debt once again." He bowed his head to them and then glanced skyward.

Thanks be to Thee, O Lord. To Thy name give glory.

A star streaked through the glittering tapestry.

"I bid you all a *bonne nuit.*" He hobbled to his cabin.

Although bone-weary, his thoughts did not rest. England achieved a great victory this day. Philippe was humiliated, and his boasts of superiority proven false. A grin spread across the king's face. The route into France now lay open to him. Possibilities raced through his mind. Philippe would feel how deep was the English king's bite.

Homecoming

January 1341 - Shene Palace

Joan stretched within the warmth of the down coverlet, grateful to sleep in a bed which did not rock. After the king's ships docked in London, and the initial fanfare faded, Joan traveled with the royal family to Shene Palace, the king's favourite riverside manor.

The winter sun struggled through the horned-pane window as Joan lazed with a cup of hot cider fetched by her maid. Finished, she slipped from her bed and dressed. Her maid laid a lambswool wrap around Joan's shoulders when her chamber door burst open.

"Dearest daughter, how lovely to have you home again." Lady Margaret strode in, offered Joan a hasty embrace, and bussed her cheeks.

"Mother." Joan smiled weakly. Though she and her mother were never close, two years away now made her mother seem a stranger.

Lady Margaret took Joan's hand and held it to the side. "How you have grown, my dear." She twirled Joan around as if appraising merchant goods. "You have filled out and blossomed, as I knew you would."

Heat flamed Joan's cheeks. "As you see." Of course Joan changed. She was no longer the ten-year-old girl who sailed to the Low Countries with the royal family.

"You may go," Joan said to her maid.

Lady Margaret made herself comfortable on a cushioned bench

near the window and Joan perched on a stool. She anticipated her mother's arrival, just not at this hour. "How are you, Mother? How is Jack? Is he here with you?"

"Your brother does well. His knightly training advances in Lord Edward's household."

"How is Edward? Is he still full of mischief and losing at dice?"

"Mind your tongue! Even in jest, do not speak so of the king's heir."

Joan lowered her eyes. "Your pardon, *Maman*." Though Joan changed, her mother did not. Forever would she find fault with her daughter.

"Lord Edward's household has expanded. Many more young men of noble birth reside with him now. When he is in London he resides across the river at Kennington. From what I hear, he often removes to Berkhamstead Castle in Hertfordshire, or Byfleet Manor in Surrey. I hear he is expected here at Shene on the morrow."

"Yes, Edward wrote to me. I am looking forward to seeing everyone again."

"You and Lord Edward were forever with your heads together." Lady Margaret's eyes flitted over Joan's personal items. "Young William Montagu will be of Edward's party. You remember him?"

"Of course. We all played together."

"Young Montagu has grown into a handsome young man. The Earl of Salisbury is quite proud of his heir." Lady Margaret brushed at an invisible speck on her gown.

"Queen Philippa's homecoming celebration allows for the renewal of many old acquaintances as well as the making of new ones," Joan offered.

"Indeed." Lady Margaret rose. "Well, I shall take my leave and pay my respects to our Lady Queen." At the chamber door, she paused. "You must look your best tomorrow eve. I shall attend you."

What? Joan followed her mother to the door. Her mother wanted Joan to look her best? Offered to help her dress?

Lady Margaret's footsteps sounded in the passageway, then

stopped. Glancing back over her shoulder, she said, "There is a matter I wish to discuss with you."

With a swish of her skirts, her mother was gone. The woman was up to something.

Joan paused in the portal allowing her eyes to adjust to the dew-kissed garden's bright light. Edward waited for her at its far end. He sat on a bench, but jumped up and rubbed his backside. The bench must be damp. He paced to the rose arbor and back. Patience was not one of her cousin's strong suits.

The night before, she and Edward reunited formally at the celebration honouring Queen Philippa's return. Royal protocol prevailed so she and Edward managed only a stiff greeting, not the sort of personal reunion for which she longed.

"Meet me in the garden tomorrow after Terce," he whispered.

Joan welcomed her cousin's invitation—a reunion devoid of the court's prying eyes—where they could be themselves. She stepped across the threshold and Edward turned. When she reached him, she stopped and curtsied deeply, her eyes cast down in demure fashion.

"What is this, Jeanette? You know you need not be so proper with me."

She rose with practiced grace, maintaining a serene expression.

Edward screwed up his face. "Is something amiss?"

For a few moments, she held her pose until a giggle escaped. "Oh, Edward, I missed you so." Neither spoke as they hugged, holding each other close for several moments. Joan broke away, stepped back, and studied her cousin from head to toe. Where was the little boy, the playmate she left behind?

"You have grown taller, Edward. We are about the same height now." She should not be surprised at the changes in him. Not only taller, Edward's face lost its roundness and he carried himself differently, more erect with his chin high.

"I am not the only one, *mon amie*. Look at you, such a proper lady. In this sunshine, you glow in that gold-coloured mantle."

"Thank you," Joan said, pleased he noticed. Edward's regard for lush fabrics and fashion mirrored the king's. He often commissioned elaborate costumes for special occasions.

"Your eyes have not changed. They are as blue as ever." Edward caught her hand and swung their hands while they wandered the garden paths. Chaffinches chirped and flitted in the boxwoods as they passed.

Joan sighed. "I thought of you every day and wondered about your duties." They paused at the rose arbor and as she began to sit on the bench beneath it, Edward stayed her.

"The benches are damp." Instead, he offered his arm in knightly fashion. "I thought of you, too. I hope you never go away again. None of you, ever. Especially my father."

"You must have worried for his safety." Sunlight glinted from the brooch pinned to Edward's cloak—he thought to wear the golden hart she gave him before sailing to Flanders.

"I was so lonely when you left, so unsure of what my duties entailed, but after a few months, I began to enjoy them. When my father first returned, I was so happy, but then he left again." Edward's face clouded. "I knew a fleet of French galleys was waiting to intercept him."

Joan squeezed his arm. "You feared he would be killed." Edward idolized his father and his death would have been unbearable. Even worse, Edward would have been crowned in his father's place. How daunting that would be for Edward, even with Queen Philippa's support.

"You were so eager to go to Flanders," Edward said. "Tell me all about your travels. Do not think to leave anything out, including your secrets."

Joan caught a breath and slid a sideways glance at Edward. His expression showed nothing but curiosity. "I never dreamed we would be gone so long." Nor dreamed so much would happen.

"Everything was so unfamiliar: the language, the manner of people's dress, the food."

"Indeed, it must have seemed strange."

"Your Lord Father progressed from one noble court to another, and more times than not, we journeyed with him. We lived in constant upheaval, and he was so beset by his duties, he could spare little thought for us." She plucked a boxwood leaf and twisted it in her fingers. "Verily, there was not much to do, especially during your lady mother's confinements. Two new brothers!"

A smile lit Edward's face. "I never imagined."

"Indeed. We were filled with joy, and relieved, at the safe delivery of both babes. Of course, your sisters were companions for me, but as you know, Isabella and Johanna squabble all the time. They are not particularly good company." Joan tossed the leaf into the bushes. "Why did not you write more often?"

"I did not think you would be interested in hearing about my duties."

"No, but I loved reading of your exploits with Roger and Jack. I was terribly homesick and lonely until…." Joan caught herself.

"Until what?"

Joan wandered away, ill at the thought of telling Edward. Should she? After her mother's horrifying pronouncement the previous evening, Joan needed to confide in someone. Someone she trusted. Someone who would take her side.

Edward dogged her heels. "Until what? Tell me."

Barely above a whisper, she murmured, "I met someone."

Edward shrugged. "You must have met many people." He matched his steps to hers. A simple gesture, yet reassuring. Some things remained the same. Joan's insides fluttered. "I mean someone special."

"Special?" Edward raised his brows "What do you mean?"

In some ways, Edward was still a boy. "A man, Edward. I met a man." Joan stretched out her arms, threw her head back, and twirled in a circle. She wanted to revel in her joy, even if only for a moment. "I fell in love!"

"What?" Edward's voice cracked.

Joan looked about the garden to make certain they were alone. No one must hear what she was about to confide to Edward. She breathed deeply to steady herself and clasped her hands together. "I am married, Edward."

"Married?" Edward shook his head. "You cannot be."

"Shhh…keep your voice down." Joan raised a trembling finger to her lips. "It is a secret. You must promise not to tell."

"I do not understand. You are married and no one knows? How is it possible? Whom did you marry?" Edward paused, his brow furrowed as the questions tumbled out of him.

"I do not think you know him, though you may know of him." Faeries danced in Joan's belly. "I first met him when Lionel was born."

Edward screwed up his eyes. "Go on. You married in secret?"

She nodded. "Much later, though, when John was born."

"And you dared wed without my lord father's permission?"

Joan looked away. The leafless rose vines would require pruning soon. When Edward started to walk away, she tugged his hand to stop him. "Do not go." She needed Edward's understanding. The king would be furious with her.

"Who is this man, Jeanette? Whom did you marry?"

The faeries swooned and Joan's legs trembled, but she raised her chin and bravely met Edward's scowl. "A respected knight in your father's service. Sir Thomas Holland." She read the shock on her cousin's face and understood what he must be thinking. Of royal lineage, a granddaughter of the first King Edward, she married beneath her station. Maidens like her wed for position, unions forged for political advantage and wealth. This king, the third Edward, might well believe she married to thwart his intentions for her. She did not.

"Joan—"

"There is more, Edward, though p-please, do not scold me." She took a few breaths and gripped his hand. "Please, I beg you."

Edward questioned her with his eyes.

Joan's throat was so tight, she groaned. "I am scared and may be in the gravest trouble."

"More? How can this possibly be worse?"

She cringed at his tone. "Y-yesterday," she rasped, "M-my mother came to my chamber before the banquet...."

"Yes?"

"She told me I am to wed."

"Wed?"

"W-Will...Will Montagu." Tears slipped down her cheeks.

"Your mother has pledged you to Will?"

Joan winced at Edward's tone. "The contracts were signed, but I cannot possibly marry him. I cannot." A shiver skimmed down her spine. "Lord, help me. What am I to do?" She covered her face, and turned away, sobbing.

Edward touched her back.

She spun and flung herself at him like when they were young, when her mother left her behind or scolded her for some trivial misstep.

Edward held her and patted her shoulders. "Jeanette, you must tell your mother." He spoke calmly, with deep concern.

She sobbed harder, clinging to him. "Oh, if only it were so simple!" She fought for breath. Edward must be wondering what he said to cause her to weep all the more. After a time, she raised her head, and swiped a hand at her tears and dripping nose. Staring into her cousin's soulful eyes, with ragged breath, she moaned, "The problem is, I have told her."

February 1341- Westminster

Joan tilted her embroidery frame to catch the light streaming into Queen Philippa's solar. The queen, more than five months into another pregnancy, dismissed her demoiselles, and retired to her inner bedchamber to rest as she often did in the afternoons.

Joan was alone in the anteroom with her mother and studied

her from beneath lowered lashes. How could her mother persist in her dogged pursuit of the union with Will Montagu knowing Joan was already married?

Not quite a year had passed since Thomas secreted her from the royal household in Ghent to the nearby inn. Despite the crackling fire in the chamber's hearth, Joan shivered, her stomach in knots. Thomas held her icy hands in his oh-so-warm-ones and smiled reassuringly while they spoke their vows. When he kissed her, heat flared within her and butterflies replaced the knots. She barely remembered the prick of pain at their joining, recalling only the surge of joy which followed.

The memory of it warmed her even now. However, in too little time, with the risk of discovery, Thomas returned her to Queen Philippa's care within an unsuspecting household.

Shortly after they spoke their vows, Thomas sailed with King Edward to battle the French at Sluys. She hid her fear for him beneath concern for the king, and rejoiced with Queen Philippa, and all England, at the news of the king's victory. However, six months passed since Thomas left her, and throughout the last months she received not one word from him.

After the sea battle, and the terms of the Truce of Espléchin were agreed, King Edward released his troops from service. Upon Joan's return to England, she asked Edward if he might discover Thomas' whereabouts. Envisioning her husband's return and their reunion, set butterflies winging within her, but her dream soon faded.

"I know how anxious you have been about Thomas," Edward said, "but what I have learned will not please you." A line appeared between his brows. "Holland joined the crusading forces headed to Prussia."

Joan wept against Edward's shoulder. How could Thomas sail off without a word to her?

"I am so sorry," Edward said.

Alarmed by her mother's determination, Joan begged Edward to help get word to Thomas about her predicament. Though her

cousin tried, nothing came from his efforts. At her husband's continued silence, fear gnawed at Joan. Not only for her current plight,
but for Thomas. Was he lying injured in Prussia? Was he killed?
As the days passed, calamity loomed ever closer. Joan prayed for
rescue.

For weeks, she suffered her mother's petty snipes and scowls
of disapproval. Joan mulled in the silence, tugging her stitches, her
feelings as tangled as her threads.

"I must say, my dear," Lady Margaret said, "Your appearance
is quite unbecoming. Your gowns are beginning to hang on you.
Looking as you do, you will never gain a man's favour."

The reproach added to Joan's apprehension, the coil tighten-
ing around her like a coney caught in a poacher's snare, with as
little hope of escape. She must speak and put an end to this deceit.
Her chest taut, Joan secured her needle and took a breath. "Mother,
please listen to me."

Lady Margaret's eyes barely left her cloth.

"Please, I beg you. End this betrothal." White-fingered, Joan
gripped the embroidery frame. "You know full well we cannot go
through with it. I am already married."

"You mistake the situation, my dear." Lady Margaret tied and
clipped a dark thread.

"Mother, why must you persist? If you refuse to put an end to
this, you force my hand. If I must, I shall seek out the Earl of Salisbury myself. Will's father will put a stop to this."

Lady Margaret did not deign to look up. "The Earl is well
aware of your, er…shall we say, indiscretion?" She pressed her lips
together.

"What?" Joan's eyes widened. "You told him?" She glared at
her mother. "How can you do this to me?"

"How can I?" Lady Margaret's voice rose sharply. "You are
the one who created this muddle."

"You cannot mean for me to go through with it!" Joan tossed
her stitching onto the floor.

"Calm yourself. Do behave like a lady." Her mother spoke as

if to an ill-mannered child. "In truth, would you imagine your Uncle Wake and I would not consult the Earl?" She poked her needle into the fabric. "Fret not, my dear. The Earl is of our opinion; your professed nuptials with Thomas are not binding. You and William will marry as intended."

Blessed Virgin help me! Joan sprang to her feet. "You bully me into wedlock with Will knowing full well I spoke sacred vows to another?" She paced to the hearth and back, hands fisted, blood rushing in her ears. "You want me to commit a mortal sin?"

"Enough." Lady Margaret's lips curled, and her eyes blazed. "Thomas Holland is a nobody, the son of a traitorous churl. He has nary a friend at court and scant prospects."

"But—"

"You little fool!" Her mother spat. "He tricked you, then tupped you!" She sniffed as if scenting a rotting carcass.

"Mother!" Joan's hand flew to her heart. She never heard such venom spewed from her mother's lips.

"Someone has to have a care for your future, dear." Lady Margaret sneered. "Even if you do not." She stabbed her needlework.

Joan fumed as she paced the room. Her mother was wrong. Thomas did not trick her; he loved her. Retrieving her embroidery, she sat down again, though her hands shook too much to continue. Her thoughts churned. Why-oh-why was Thomas silent?

Though Joan hated to admit it, her mother was right in one respect. As a younger son, Thomas' prospects were limited. He must earn his way through military service. She understood how her mother's mind worked. The Earl of Salisbury possessed marked influence. Against such a man, Thomas held no power, natheless, the vows she pledged were sacred. No matter the struggle, she would not commit a mortal sin.

Joan broke the silence. "Well, heed me, *Maman.* You and the Earl may bludgeon me to marry Will. God knows I can do little against you, but I refuse to consummate the union." She shuddered at the thought of bedding Salisbury's arrogant son, then pinned her mother with a glare. "Do you hear me?"

Lady Margaret smiled wryly. "Well, I dare say, dearest, refraining is only prudent."

Joan started. Did she hear right? Her mother yielded? "You agree?"

Lady Margaret pursed her lips and laid down her needlework. "Under canon law, William may renounce the union until he comes of age at fourteen. Were the two of you to consummate your vows and a child resulted, and should Will renounce the union, the Salisbury inheritance could be called into question. So, it is only sensible to delay until William is old enough to consent."

Joan pressed her temples. Such guile! Her mother considered every aspect of this odious matter.

"My dear, it is not uncommon with unions at your tender years to delay consummation. It would not seem at all amiss to wait before bringing a child into this world. After all, you are only thirteen."

Joan clenched her hands. She wanted nothing more than to smack the smug look off her mother's face. "How good of you to consider to my welfare, Mother."

Lady Margaret pulled a face. "Quite so. You will carry on in Queen Philippa's household, and William will remain with young Lord Edward. A satisfactory arrangement for the present."

Although enraged by her mother's duplicity, Joan breathed easier at her reprieve. She sighed. If only Thomas would return.

Every day's dawning brought Joan renewed hope. As was her custom, she attended mass, and prayed for her husband's safe return, and her deliverance from sin.

The next Sunday, Joan slipped quietly from the royal bench in the crowded chapel. By the time she pushed open the stout oak door, tears streamed down her cheeks. The priest had announced the first of her marriage banns.

Three weeks passed. Though she prayed for rescue, no saviour arrived.

In the presence of King Edward, Queen Philippa, her stalwart friend, Edward, and the entire court, Joan stood at the altar on trembling legs. From this day forward to all in her world, she became the future countess of Salisbury. As she spoke false vows to William Montagu, once a childhood playmate, her mind, heart, and stomach rebelled at the sin she was being forced to commit.

Would Thomas forgive her?

Would God?

June 1341 - Kings Langley

Joan gazed through the back of the travelling wagon's arched canopy. The dust was so thick at times it obscured the caravan of carts and wains lumbering behind. She sighed, grateful the journey for the queen's confinement at King's Langley neared its end. The wagon jolted in a rut and tipped precariously. Joan threw out her arm to catch the dozing queen before she tumbled from her cushioned berth.

Queen Philippa blinked awake. She laid a hand upon her rounded middle. "My babe took exception to that."

"Travelling is burdensome, my lady." Joan leaned closer. "Is there anything I might do to ease your discomfort?"

"Thank you, *ma petite*." The queen dabbed at the perspiration beading her flushed face. "The ills are of my own making. I should have removed to Kings Langley weeks ago but put it off. I did not wish to be separated from my husband again so soon after our return from the Low Countries."

Joan understood. Every day of her separation from Thomas weighed heavily upon her. Still, no word from him nor did Edward's inquiries prove fruitful.

High-pitched squeals issued from the wagon behind them. The queen pressed her temples. "Why did I not think to separate the girls?"

"Something to consider in future, my lady." Joan waved a fan to cool the queen and savored the relative peace of traveling separately from the princesses.

Queen Philippa shifted. "Dearest, are you certain you prefer to remain in my household rather than make a home with your husband? Do not stay with me from a sense of obligation."

"Have no concern, my lady. I am more than content with this arrangement. Joan shuddered at the alternative, trapped at one of the Salisbury estates under the hawk-like watch of Will's grandmother.

Dense stands of ancient beech and oak stood as sentinels along the track. "I so admire the beauty of this wood," Philippa said. "Langley means long wood, you know."

Above the trees, the sky was brushed with wispy, ladder-like clouds, as if some ethereal being painted them there. Patches of sunlight filtered through the leaves onto the clusters of bluebells, yellow cowslips and red clover.

The wagon slowed as the team climbed a hill. At its crest a church steeple appeared in the distance "My lady, I believe we have arrived."

Queen Philippa peered forword through the opening in the canopy. "We have topped Langley Hill. See there? All Saint's Church and the River Gade. Welcome sights, indeed."

Horns pealed as the escort of outriders and first royal wagon rumbled over the bridge.

Queen Philippa said, "One last right turn through Corte Gate and our journey comes to its end."

Alerted to the arrival of the royal entourage, the palace steward posed in front of a tidy row of liveried servants waiting to welcome their queen. Stable boys rushed forward to catch bridles while groomsmen readied the steps to aid the ladies' descent.

Queen Philippa sighed. "We have not stayed here for quite some time and you were so young, I doubt you remember." Philippa smiled. "Kings Langley offers many comforts thanks to the first King Edward's consort and I do not mind admitting a desire to spoil myself after enduring my last two confinements abroad."

An ear-piercing shriek burst from a wagon drawing up behind

them. Before it stopped, Johanna leapt out, skirts flying, and raced toward the walled garden.

A glowering, Isabella sprinted after her. "Give me that, it is mine!"

Queen Philippa pressed a hand to her heart. "Blessed Saint Marie, give me strength."

"Shall we get you settled inside where you may take your ease?"

Once out of the wagon, Joan brushed the worst of the wrinkles from Queen Philippa's gown and adjusted its folds. Then the queen greeted the palace steward and acknowledged the staff, all the while the aroma of roasting beef wafted in the air.

"That smells delicious," Philippa said. "I do believe this child of mine is ravenous."

Joan helped the queen hobble toward the Great Court. She grimaced. "My ankles are so swollen."

"Wait my lady. Let me call for a litter."

"*Non*. It is best I walk and work out the stiffness."

Queen Philippa rested in her scarletto-covered bed propped up with feathered bolsters. A sweet floral scent drifted from the vase of roses on the bedside chest, and light streamed through the window latticework onto the queen's Book of Hours. From a stool beside the queen's bed, Joan read, "Behold the inheritance of our Lord, children the reward, the fruit—"

Queen Philippa gasped.

Joan looked from the Book into the queen's eyes, wide with pain and wonderment—the singular expression would be forever sealed in Joan's memory. When the queen clutched her rounded midriff and moaned, Joan set the book aside and knelt beside the bed. "My lady?"

The queen's favoured lady, Mathilde, rushed from the antechamber where she and several other ladies were stitching garments for the royal babe. "Lady Queen?"

Philippa winced. "My time has come, *ma chére*. Let it not distress you. Thank you for reading to me, though it is best you leave now." The queen squeezed her eyes shut and clenched the coverlet, struck by another wave of pain.

Lady Mathilde called to a serving maid. "Fetch several soft linen cloths and a basin of cool water."

The queen's breathing returned to normal. "Though you are married, Joan, you have not yet consummated your vows. As a maiden, it would be unseemly for you to remain." The queen clasped Joan's trembling hand. "Do not fret. All will be well."

Joan spoke through a tight throat. "Yes, my lady." Should any harm befall the queen, Joan knew not what she would do. She kissed the queen's ringless fingers, too swollen now to wear them.

The queen winced and stifled a groan. "Jeanette, might I call upon you to find my steward and have him fetch the midwife and send word to the king?"

"At once, my lady." Joan marvelled at the queen's calm. *Holy Mary, Mother of God, watch over our Lady Queen in this time of travail.*

After speaking with the steward, and unable to return to the queen's chamber, Joan wandered the palace passages, the vineyard, all three of the castle courts, the Great and Little Parks, and the kitchen gardens. She retired early; no word on the babe.

The next morning, she awoke after a fitful night's sleep. Her maid reported the queen's safe delivery of another boy, a healthy one. Joan agreed, judging by his lusty wails coming from the queen's chamber, as she passed on the way to the Little Park. King Edward would be overjoyed, and Edward, too. She saw her cousin less often now and missed his compassionate understanding, so like his mother.

Joan rambled the walkway amidst the sweet fragrance of the pink-budded vines webbing the walls. The garden reminded her of the lonely times spent in Antwerp and Ghent, before the births of

Lionel and John—when she met Thomas. Memories of him taunted her. Did he miss her? Did he think of her at all? Not for the first time, she wondered if his continued silence was due to injury. Or worse? She prayed God did not, would not, claim him in the Holy War and he would return to her.

Bees hovered over the roses, their hum and the sweet bouquet a balm to Joan's troubled thoughts. Rapid footsteps tapped behind her.

"I have been searching everywhere for you," Lady Eleanor said, out of breath. "The queen is asking for you."

"How fares our queen?"

Lady Eleanor retraced her steps, calling over her shoulder, "She and the lad do well."

Joan hastened down the corridors, passing the chapel where she paused and offered a prayer of gratitude for the queen's safe delivery. When Joan entered the queen's outer chamber, Lady Mathilde put a finger to her lips and motioned Joan to the damask-covered bench near the window.

The door to the inner bedchamber stood open. Inside, Queen Philippa napped with her newborn in her arms, half-hidden by an ivory knitted blanket. Eyes closed, the queen napped, propped up with pillows. Her dark lashes rested against the shadows below her eyes. The ruffled neck of her linen shift framed her face, and her long brown hair lay across her shoulders.

Sitting near Joan, a wet nurse rocked one-year-old John in her arms while two-year-old Lionel played with wooden blocks on a blanket, his nursemaid watching over him. When his tower tumbled, he giggled.

Mathilde spoke in a hushed tone, "Our lady requested her boys be brought to her chamber."

Joan noted the querulous princesses were nowhere in sight. A few peaceful minutes passed before the babe burped, and the queen blinked awake. She nuzzled her son's downy head, then smoothed her fingers over his cheeks.

Joan rose and crossed to the entry. "May God keep you and

your infant son, my lady." She curtsied. "He answered our prayers for your safe delivery."

Queen Philippa crooked a finger. "Is my Edmund not a handsome boy?" She nudged the blanket aside. Edmund yawned and stretched his arms. "Is he not perfect?" Philippa placed a kiss upon Edmund's cheek.

Joan leaned closer. "He is, indeed." She marvelled at the baby's flawlessly formed miniature hands and fingers.

"Would you like to hold him?"

"Oh, may I?" Joan's heart beat a little faster. "You would trust me with him?"

"*Certainement.*" Philippa set Edmund into Joan's arms. "Fear not. Edmund will not break." Her eyes twinkled. "His father will bounce and wrestle him about soon enough."

Joan cradled Edmund, taking care to support his head. "I do not doubt it." She stroked her fingers through Edmund's chestnut-coloured fuzz, charmed by his miniature nose, ears, and eyelashes. She rocked him, swaying her hips. Hope sprang in her heart she would be blessed with children one day, though the bliss of motherhood would be denied her until her wedded state was put right. How did she end up in such a muddle?

"Have faith, *ma petite*. Your time will come." The queen's words sounded so faintly Joan thought she imagined them. Did the queen sense Joan's thoughts or was she aware of Joan's secret union with Thomas? If the queen knew…Joan's breath caught. King Edward knew.

July 1341 - Kings Langley

Dozens of squires and pages bustled beneath the tournament pavilion's striped canopy assisting the knights to prepare for the competition. The games were in honour of Edmund's birth, and today Chandos represented Edward's princely household. Edward perched on a table, resting his foot on the bench alongside it, smiling.

Chandos ran his fingers over his surcoat's red and gold embroidered threads. "Lord Edward, I am humbled by your generosity." Although knighted two years earlier at Cambrai, Chandos possessed no garment displaying his newly-created coat of arms. Until now.

"*De rien*. Think nothing of it," Edward said, recalling the tenet of knighthood Chandos taught him. *Judge not a goodly knight by his earthly possessions but by his heart's largesse.* The surcoat was little enough in recognition of the knight's encouragement and patience in tutoring Edward. "I owe you a debt, Sir John," Edward said. "Yesterday, my father watched me spar and praised my sword skills."

Chandos rested a hand on Edward's shoulder. "You are pleased?"

"Indeed, I am."

Since the knight joined Edward's household, he and Chandos were close, like brothers. Edward could count on Chandos to keep his confidences. The knight held himself to high chivalric standards and other knights held him in great esteem, not only for his prowess in arms, but for his honour and humility. Edward hoped to warrant a similar regard one day.

Chandos bent over at the waist and extended his arms. Edward, acting as squire, lowered a padded gambeson over his knight's head.

"I wish I were old enough to compete," Edward said, yanking the ties.

Chandos stayed Edward's hand. "Patience, Lord." Then he added, "You are but eleven. A wise warrior learns to bide his time."

Edward grumbled under his breath as he fitted the mail hauberk overtop his knight's gambeson.

"Mayhap, if you are accomplished enough, you may compete next year. You display great promise." John circled his arms, testing for restrictions in his movements.

"You mean it?" Edward's voice cracked.

"Indeed," Chandos said, solemn-faced. "In fact, when next we spar…I shall let you win!"

Edward grinned and smacked his friend's shoulder. The knight cuffed him back. Edward bent over and butted Chandos in the gut. "Ow!" Edward stood up, grimacing, and rubbing his head.

Chandos grinned. "I doubt you will do such again." He rocked back on his heels and chuckled.

Edward narrowed his eyes. "It is not funny!"

"Oh, ho!" The knight laughed harder.

Heat scorched up Edward's neck. "Stop laughing at me!" When the knight failed to hide a smirk, blood roared in Edward's ears and he charged, fists swinging.

Chandos planted a hand on Edward's forehead and stiffened his arm.

Edward flailed, red-faced and panting. Though he hit nothing, he kept swinging. Suddenly, his body lifted, the room spun, and his back hit the ground.

Pphhttt! The sound broke from Edward's backside. He froze. Chandos loomed over him and at the shocked look on his face, Edward burst out laughing, his belly rolling in waves.

Chandos began laughing, too, the commotion causing heads to turn in their direction.

Edward put a stifling hand over his mouth and snorted…like a pig. He laughed harder, clutching his gut. He could not stop himself, laughing so hard his stomach ached, but oh, it felt so good—an unguarded moment to be himself. Gradually, they quieted.

Chandos, standing over him, smiling wide, grasped Edward's hand and hauled him to his feet.

"*Je regrette mon*—" Edward began.

Chandos clapped his shoulder. "Say nothing of it, my lord."

King Edward lingered in the pavilion amidst a group of competitors lobbing challenges at one another. A commotion at the far side of the pavilion, where his heir played squire to Chandos, drew his attention.

"Sending Chandos to your son's household appears a wise decision," Salisbury said.

"Indeed, I believe it was. My heir shows great promise, as does your return from Paris, *mon ami*."

"You pay me and Suffolk great honour as these games are in celebration of Edmund's birth."

"I am relieved my two most stalwart commanders are back on English soil." More than relieved. King Edward called to Suffolk. "Fifteen months without you both was far too long. God answered my prayers with your safe return."

"And mine, Lord King." Suffolk bowed

"Though how you and Salisbury managed to get yourselves captured remains a mystery to me. Perhaps you desired a respite in Paris?" His commanders' capture before Sluys was more disturbing than he let on, and no one was more relieved than he to have them back on English soil.

"Imprisonment is not how I would wish to spend my time," Salisbury said. "Please, accept my thanks again for paying our ransoms."

King Edward laid a hand on the Earl's shoulder. "It is little enough. I do not forget what I owe you for your aid against Mortimer. It is a debt I can never fully repay, though I would rather you not put me to the test." He glanced from one man to the other. "Try not to get captured again."

"I take no credit for it and blame Suffolk," Salisbury's squire lowered the Earl's surcoat over his head and struggled to fit it over the Earl's middle.

"While your captivity did prey upon my mind, it appears I need not have worried. From all appearances, you fared quite well in the French usurper's custody."

Salisbury raised a bushy brow. "Sire?"

King Edward patted the Earl's bulging paunch. "Methinks, your steed may be hard-pressed to gallop the tilt today."

Suffolk chucked.

Salisbury said, "We shall see, Lord King, we shall see."

Spurs jangled as the earls and knights spilled out of the pavilion. A dozen well-muscled sorrel, black, bay, and chestnut chargers stood hitched at the rail, spaced well apart to prevent injury from a well-aimed kick or gnash of teeth.

King Edward walked among the competing knights, offering greetings and encouragement. "*Bonne chance, mes amis,*" he called to the earls as he withdrew to join Philippa in the viewing stand

Edward exited the pavilion behind Chandos toting his knight's helm and gauntlets. The earthy aromas of horseflesh and leather, the sounds of competitors mounting up, and calls from the crowd to their favourite knights heralded the start of the competition.

Jack waited near the horses and tipped his head toward the sorrel. "Your stallion is by far the finest, Sir John."

Edward took pleasure in Jack's praise as the charger was another of Edward's gifts.

Chandos ran his hands down the stallion's legs and inspected each hoof. "Never ride without checking your mount's feet," he reminded them. He slid his hand under the girth and waited for the horse to exhale before cinching it one last time.

Edward put down his bundle, and helped Jack drape a red silk caparison over the stallion and fasten the buckles. Jack handed him the polished steel chanfron and Edward secured it over the stallion's white-blazed muzzle.

Jack gave Chandos a leg up. "Who is your first draw?"

Collecting his reins, Chandos said, "Pembroke."

Horns sounded the call for competitors. Edward handed Chandos his helm and gauntlets and Jack adjusted the caparison one last time. "I carried your lance to the lists earlier."

"I wish you good fortune, though you will not need it," Edward said.

"I appreciate it all the same." A flourish of trumpets and drums heralded the start of the tournament procession.

"Time to find Joan," Edward said. "She promised to save places for us in the stand."

As Chandos walked off, Jack called, "May you triumph, Sir John."

Edward and Jack wove their way through the villagers vying for the best places to view the competition. Catching sight of Edward, they made way for him and he tipped his head in acknowledgement as he saw his father do many times.

Minstrels played outside the perimeter rail, while inside jugglers tossed flaming torches and tumblers bounded across the field. Laughter and cheers burst from the spectators. Standing at the bottom of the *berfrois*, they searched faces for Joan.

The queen and honoured countesses of Salisbury and Suffolk sat in the Ladies' Court beneath an awning of red striped cloth of gold. Joan, sitting a good distance from Lady Catherine, Salisbury's countess, waved to them with a small pennon bearing Chandos's coat of arms. Isabella and Johanna sat on Joan's left, with their governess wisely between them. He and Jack climbed up and squashed onto the padded bench on Joan's right.

She nudged him with her elbow, tilted her head toward the countesses, and leaned closer. "*Maman* is sitting over there." She covered her mouth and added, "Mind what you say, she has sharp—"

"What is Will doing down there?" Jack's gaze fixed on the entry gate where Will mingled with the knights assembling for the *pas d'armes*.

"He is only thirteen and cannot compete," Edward said, "so why is he there and who gave him permission?"

"He is wearing the Salisbury colours," Joan said, "Perhaps the king gave permission at the Earl's request?

"You may be right," Edward said. Joan could only guess because she avoided Will as much as possible to discourage his attentions. If Will were aware of her other marriage, he never mentioned it in Edward's hearing.

Trumpets and drums announced the entry of the riders. The two honoured earls rode at the fore of each of the two sides of twelve. The countesses waved ribbons sporting their husbands' colours and cheered along with the crowd. The competitors paraded past the base of the ladies' court where the helms of the previous day's champions were displayed, then exited to await their calls for the tilt.

"Which side are you for, Edward?" Joan asked.

"Sir John rides for Suffolk's side."

Heralds announced the first pair. The knights reentered individually and cantered the customary prefatory lap while the herald proclaimed each man's honours and feats at arms. The knights took their positions and readied, as jesters rhymed and spouted clever quips prompting guffaws from the crowd.

After the first four matches, the scores were even. A trumpet sounded for the next pair, and Laurence Hastings, Earl of Pembroke, loped in and circled his sleek black destrier.

"Oh, aren't they splendid?" Isabella clapped with enthusiasm.

Pembroke cued his stallion into a high-stepping piaffe in front of Queen Philippa, displaying his destrier's four white stockings and fetlock feathers to advantage. Halting his mount four-square, Pembroke dipped his lance to the king and queen and after the queen's nod to acknowledge his salute, Pembroke spun his mount and cantered to his end of the tilt.

Joan tugged Edward's sleeve and when he leaned closer, she asked, "Have you any word of Thomas?"

A trumpet blared. Chandos entered the lists, his stallion's glistening copper coat peeking from under the silk caparison, and light sparked off the polished steel chanfron. He reined in before the queen and dipped his lance. At her nod, he signalled his stallion, performed a one-handed pirouette, and then whirled away to take up his position.

A trumpet sounded, and the crowd hushed.

Edward grabbed Joan's hand and held his breath.

The flag dropped.

Equine haunches thrust, and the earth rumbled. Thundering hooves dug deep, catapulting clods of turf into the air while the knights lowered and seated their lances. The rods struck with a thunderclap. Shards flew. Pembroke teetered but did not fall. The crowd roared its approval.

Edward grabbed Jack's arm. "Did you see Sir John's hit?"

Joan poked Edward in his ribs. "Did you hear me?"

"Forgive me, Jeanette. I was distracted."

"H-have you heard anything? About Thomas?"

Edward shook his head. "I am afraid not, *mon amie.*"

August 1341 - Kings Langley

King Edward lounged against the feathered bolster with his consort enfolded against his chest. Philippa's gaze rested on their newborn, tucked into the crook of her arm. In profile, the small, barely noticeable bump on Philippa's nose, which so displeased her, charmed him. She turned her face and caught him grinning.

"We have so few moments like this." She nestled deeper against his heart and he brushed a kiss atop her head.

"Which makes those we share more cherished."

The sun met the horizon, saturating the chamber and bathing mother and son in an aureate light. His union with Philippa, against his father's wishes, was a diplomatic arrangement to suit his mother's ambitions. He never imagined, at the time, how unbelievably blessed his life would be with a wife who was, in many ways, foisted upon him.

Gazing up at him, Philippa sighed. "Must you return to London today? I hoped you might remain a few more days." Philippa's eyes reminded him of a woodland fawn.

"Already, I have lingered longer than intended. Thanks to you, *mon coeur*." He nudged her playfully. "I cannot ignore Philippe's attacks on my Gascon lands. The usurper agreed to the treaty's terms after his defeat at Sluys, yet he ignores them." His voice rose.

"Shh…you will wake Edmund."

King Edward lowered his eyes to his sleeping son and rested his head against the pillows. How much should he tell her? Fretting for him might delay her recovery. Damn, Philippe! Would there be no end to his interference? He lowered his voice. "There is another matter demanding my attention."

Philippa tipped her head, a crinkle between her brows.

"The Scots are raiding deep into the Northern shires and the Lords Percy and Neville call for aid."

Philippa narrowed her eyes. "What more are you not telling me?

He conceded. "As you know, Scotland's child-king sheltered in Philippe's court in Paris for the last eight years."

"Yes, and?"

"David has returned to Scotland."

Philippa sighed deeply. "With King Philippe's blessing and troops, no doubt. So, David leads this latest uprising? He is what takes you from us again?"

"Yes, I must go north."

During Queen Philippa's recovery at Langley, Joan spent the mornings walking in the garden, often with Edward before his lessons or arms practice. She thanked God for her friend. Edward's unceasing praise of Chandos distracted her and kept her disquiet at bay. She envied her cousin his companion, though she was happy for him, too. The knight's company banished Edward's ache for his too often absent father. In the afternoons, Joan resumed reading to Queen Philippa.

"I love my lord husband," the queen said, "and cherish my children, yet three births in three years…well, it is God's will."

"Your marriage is blessed, my lady," Joan said, unlike her muddled union.

As the queen's health improved, Joan's concern for the queen eased, though concern for her own marriage remained. She received no word from Thomas—still—and Lady Margaret's appearance at Langley only added to her disquiet. To avoid her mother, Joan spent long hours in the nursery. One afternoon, her brother stuck his head in the doorway.

"Care for a walk in the garden?" A grin lit Jack's face and his blue eyes twinkled.

"What a splendid idea!" She rose and called her leave-taking to the children's *maistresce*, then held out a wooden block to Lionel. "Be a good boy."

She and Jack ambled in the garden amidst the fragrant scent of roses. Joan plucked a yellow bud and tucked it in her hair.

"Mother and I depart for Surrey in a few weeks," Jack said. "For the harvest."

"Not surprising. Mother toils endlessly on your behalf and it is wise for you to oversee your Kent lands, though why our father was granted lands spread so far and wide is beyond me."

"Would you care to join us?" Jack brushed a hand through his hair, its color similar to hers, and in the sunlight it shone almost white.

"It is sweet of you to ask. How many times as a child did I beg mother to go with you only to be denied? Thank you, brother, but I prefer to remain with the queen."

"Now you are married, would not you prefer a household of your own?"

She patted Jack's arm. "Trust me, I am content."

A week later, she heard from Edward the fighting in Prussia ended. When Thomas returned to England, he would look for her where he left her—with the queen. Joan prayed daily for his safety and God's forgiveness for her sin.

As time passed, Joan slept little and ate less. Her clothes began to hang on her in a noticeable way. One evening, she dismissed her maid and sat in her chamber brushing her hair before braiding it for bed. By now, Thomas should have returned. She lowered the brush. A thought struck her.

The next morning Joan met her mother at Langley Chapel. The grey sandstone walls and somber interior suited her mood. When the bells pealed at the end of the mass, she followed Lady Margaret out the arched doorway. Several ladies of the court gathered with the queen beneath the field maples displaying tinges of early autumn color.

Joan veered away toward a small, well-tended garden, a distance from eager ears. The unease in her belly grew. She stopped near an arbour entwined with a vine, its pink blooms beginning to wither. She took a deep breath. "Mother, what have you done?"

Lady Margaret raised a brow. "Whatever do you mean, child?"

Joan crossed her arms. "Do not play the innocent with me. I doubt you are at a loss as to my meaning." Challenging her mother was more difficult than Joan imagined it would be. "The fighting in Prussia ended, and the crusaders have returned. Thomas would have come to claim me. H-have you prevented it?"

"Do calm yourself, my dear," Lady Margaret said, about to step away.

"Do not try to placate me, Mother. Thomas is my husband."

"Keep your voice down." Lady Margaret glanced over Joan's shoulder. "You may consider yourself married to Thomas Holland, but those of us charged with protecting you do not." Her mother scowled. "The ceremony was a sham and I shall not allow a knave such as him to tarnish our good family."

"Such as him?"

"A traitor's spawn," her mother hissed. "My brother understands how to deal with the likes of him."

"My uncle, Lord Wake?" Suspicion crawled in Joan's belly.

Lady Margaret raised her chin and pressed her lips together.

"Why did I not see it?" Joan said. "The two of you have conspired to keep Thomas from me. How could you, Mother? H-how could you?" Joan's voice broke on a sob.

"Quite easily, my dear." Lady Margaret spoke with the coldness of death.

Joan's legs trembled. Thomas came for her and was turned away. A tempest of emotions struck—shock, anger, betrayal, despair, grief—so fast, one after the other, as if she were battered in a small fishing boat threatening to break apart on the rocky shore.

"Listen to me!"

Joan blinked, numbed by Lady Margaret's betrayal.

Joan?" Her mother shook her. "Listen, I tell you. Thomas Holland is a nobody, a nothing, has nothing. No lands. No means to support you save the pittance he earns in service to the king." Lady Margaret's face twisted. "You deserve better. You are royal-born. Leave off your childish fantasies and accept the truth. You are married to William Montagu, the future Earl of Salisbury, and you are his future countess."

Joan yanked her arm free. "No, I am not!"

Lady Margaret narrowed her eyes. "We shall see, my dear. We shall see."

October 1341 - Westminster

Westminster's great hall swelled with bonhomie on the last evening of the four-day tournament. Light from the wall torches danced upon the Arras tapestries draping the chamber, seeming to bring the hunt scenes to life. Edward sat with Jack on the dais, recounting favourite moments of the competition. Melodic notes from the pipes and lutes floated beneath the conversations of the richly garbed noblemen and ladies seated according to rank.

Trumpets blared, Heads turned as the heavy oak doors swung wide. A procession of varlets strode in flourishing platters of roasted swan, stag, boar, and fowl. Enticing aromas drifted through the hall and a rumble emerged from Jack's stomach. He glanced down with a sheepish expression. "Dare I admit I am starving?"

"So I hear." Edward grinned. "Of late, cousin, you have stuffed yourself like a bear after a winter sleep."

Serving maids scurried between the tables refilling cups with mead, ale, and Gascon wine. Edward placed small portions on his trencher from the courses presented to him.

As the evening wore on, wine and ale flowed as freely as the minstrels' melodies. The assembly grew more lively with each passing hour, their waves of laughter and conversation winning out over the music.

When the candles sputtered and smoke curled up, the king and queen rose signalling the end of the meal. The assembly stood, moved off, and mingled in small groups while servants hastened to clear away the tables and benches. Edward and Jack wandered to the side of the hall when Edward noticed his father beckoning him.

"Your pardon, Jack. I shall meet you later."

At the foot of the dais Edward bowed. "Lord Father…Lady Mother." His mother's red velvet gown complimented her dark colouring, yet despite its brilliance, she appeared ghostly. With another babe on the way, mayhap she felt ill. Or perhaps his sisters' behaviour, as they stood giggling nearby, was causing her distress. She must have yielded to their wheedling, allowing them to remain for the entertainments. Though their chaperone hovered close, chiding their ill manners, they paid her little heed.

The king laid a hand on Edward's shoulder. "Have you enjoyed the games? It will not be much longer until you possess sufficient mastery to compete, *n'est ce pas*?" He smiled. "Ah, I see our cousin Derby and his countess approach."

Edward straightened, standing taller, slightly awed in the presence of the vaunted Earl of Derby, only recently returned from a year's captivity in Flanders, serving as surety against the king's debts. Not many men would be so loyally inclined as his cousin.

"Lord King, Queen Philippa, Lord Edward." Derby bowed and his countess curtsied.

The king clapped the Earl on the shoulder. "Good to have you back in our company."

Edward dipped his head in respect. "My lord…countess, God give you good day. May I offer a warm welcome home, cousin?"

"Lord Edward, I barely recognized you." Derby grinned. "There appears a new look of a man about you."

The king patted Edward's back. "Indeed, my heir has grown. Eleven years on his last birthday."

An embarrassed warmth crept into Edward's cheeks, spreading through Edward's chest, pleased at his father's notice.

Queen Philippa laid her hand on Lady Isabel's arm. "Countess, you must be relieved your lord has returned."

"Indeed. In good health and spirits, I might add. And of course, he is grateful the king arranged his release. As am I."

Derby laughed at something but Edward missed his father's comment, only catching a word about the Earl's appointment as Lieutenant of the North. The king mentioned Derby's forthcoming departure for Roxburgh.

"Sire, what word have you of the succession in Brittany?" Derby asked.

"The French Parlement decided against de Montfort's claim, siding with Charles of Blois."

"Not surprising," Derby said and sipped.

"Charles is King Philippe's nephew, is he not?" Edward asked.

"Yes, yet another Valois who makes claim for what is not his."

"What of de Montfort?" Derby lowered his voice making it difficult for Edward to hear above the din in the hall.

"As soon as de Montfort heard word of the decision, he fled Paris."

The Earl raised a brow. "And?"

King Edward leaned closer and spoke in a confidential tone. "As you might surmise, he seeks my aid."

"The man is no fool." Derby said. "He knows full well he cannot prevail against Blois without help. Should he succeed, with your aid, through him Brittany will be yours."

"Indeed." A grin teased the corners of the king's lips. "Once Brittany swears allegiance to me, Philippe will feel another bite from his realm."

His father and Derby changed subjects, argued about which knight was the most skilled, while his mother and Lady Isabel chatted of family matters. Edward's mind drifted. What did his father mean providing aid in Brittany? England could not offer aid to de Montfort unless his father broke the truce. Was his father not honour bound to uphold it?

A subtle tug on Edward's sleeve brought him back. His mother inclined her head toward the scene his sisters were making despite the efforts of their beleaguered chaperone. By the queen's gesture, she wanted him to intervene without drawing further attention. He pardoned himself and wove through the guests, crossing paths with Joan and her mother.

Edward offered a bow. "Good eve to you, Lady Margaret and to you, Jeanette."

"Blessings upon you Lord Edward," Lady Margaret said.

Joan curtsied. "Lord Edward."

Edward reached for Joan's hand and held it out to her side. "Is this the new gown you described to me? The yellow color becomes you."

"Thank you." She twirled, displaying the gown's hem of embroidered flowers, her smile dimpling her cheeks and her eyes twinkling the same shade of blue as the silk threads in her skirt. Suddenly, Joan fixed her gaze over Edward's shoulder and her smiled faded.

He glanced behind him. Will was threading through the guests who were enjoying the jongleur, making his way toward them.

"Stay with me," Joan whispered, a plea in her eyes.

Will bowed. "Good eve, Lord Edward, Lady Margaret, Lady wife." He took Joan's hand, but before he raised it to his lips, Joan withdrew it. Will stiffened almost imperceptibly, though his expression remained pleasant.

My lord." Joan offered a weak smile and busied herself

smoothing the folds of her skirt.

Lady Margaret pressed her lips in disapproval at Joan's rebuff while Joan's eyes flitted from one member of the court to another, looking anywhere but at Will.

"I beg your indulgence," Edward said, "I promised my lady mother I would look upon my sisters, and I owe a personal welcome to Baron Neville." He paused, then added, "Might you care to join me, Jeanette?"

"Of course." Joan took Edward's arm. "If you will excuse me, Mother? Will?"

As they moved away, Joan's hand on his arm relaxed and she moaned softly.

"Thank you. My mother unsettles me enough, and while Will is not to blame for this muddle we are in, his attentions are nettling. No matter how cool my manner, he takes no notice."

"It pains me to see you so disquieted."

After pausing to express his mother's strong suggestion for his sisters to retire, Edward guided Joan through the milling guests, searching for Baron Neville. Not finding him, he abandoned his hunt and steered Joan to the side of the hall where their conversation would be less likely overheard.

"Dear cousin," he began, trying to find the right words. "We both know Will can be off-putting, yet he is not an entirely bad fellow. He seems genuinely pleased with your match."

Joan stared at the floor.

He continued, "Have you heard anything at all from Thomas?

Joan's lips trembled. "No."

Her distress tore at Edward's heart. Though he made discreet inquiries, careful not to raise suspicion, his efforts failed. God rot that man!! Why did he not send word to Joan?

Edward waited for a couple to pass. "I regret I have been unable to learn of Holland's whereabouts for you."

Joan raised doleful eyes. "When I heard the fighting in Prussia ended, I expected Thomas to return, yet with summer's passing and no word...." A welcome breeze wafted from the entry and Joan slipped through the door.

He followed her down the steps to the torchlit courtyard. Guards stood silhouetted on the parapets above them and moonbeams lit Joan's face.

"I believe Thomas to be honourable, not the sort of man to go back on his word." Before Edward could respond, she held up her hand. "No, hear me out." Her voice firmed. "Before Mother and Jack departed Langley at summer's end, I approached her about Thomas. Though she did not admit it outright, I believe she and my Uncle Wake have kept Thomas from me."

"You are certain?" If what she said were true, it did not bode well.

"No, but given my mother's manner, it is likely."

"I do not mean this question to distress you. Are you certain of Holland? Perhaps your family is right—your vows may not be binding." The breeze shifted, and with it smoke from the flambeaux. They stepped away. "Ought you reconsider Will's suit? To all the court, you are joined with him."

"Oh, plea—" Joan's voice broke. "My vows with Thomas were sacred. In the eyes of God, I am married to Thomas, not Will." She clutched Edward's fingers. "Promise you will support me in this. Promise. I have no one else. Not even my brother. I believe he knows none of this." Her grip tightened. "*Please*, Edward."

Tears rimmed Joan's eyes. How could he refuse? Chivalry called upon men to care for and protect women. Joan was family. "All right, for the time being, but understand me. I do not own your same trust in Thomas. An honourable knight does not treat a lady, especially his wife, in such an offhanded manner. However, there may be more to his silence than we know."

Joan squeezed his fingers. "Thank you. What should I do without you?"

"Let us go inside before we are missed." He took hold of Joan's hand and climbed the stairs. Joan's situation nettled him. If serving as Guardian taught him anything, he learned to question below the surface. His father once counselled him not to ignore his gut, to trust his instinct. Thomas Holland's behaviour was off; it set the hairs on back of Edward's neck to prickle.

Eyes On Brittany

February 1342 - Dunstable

King Edward rose before the sun and was in the saddle with his escort by dawn, like every day since riding south out of Roxburgh ten days earlier. The jingling of harness and his palfrey's rocking gait lulled him, his thoughts drifting over the past three months of battling the Scots and his recent victory at Stirling.

The ongoing conflict compelled him to remain in the north through the season of Christ's birth, although he would have preferred to spend it with his family rather than his cousin, Derby. He grinned when he thought of Edmund, at six months of age, sitting up, giggling, and displaying a tooth or two.

"A thought pleases you, sire?" Sir Nigel Loring rode beside him.

"*Oui*. The reunion with my family in Dunstable." King Edward adjusted his seat; he spent too many hours in the saddle. "If I recall, your family estate is at Chalgrave, is it not?"

"Indeed, sire. The Chiltern Downs were my boyhood playground; I hope my knowledge of the area is helpful in organizing the tournament."

"Your knowledge and assistance are very much welcomed."

Far ahead, shadows veiled the white chalk cliff face as the winter sun lowered behind the escarpment marking Dunstable's southwestern reaches.

"If I may ask, Lord, what word of Brittany? Rumors say de Montfort was forced to surrender Nantes."

"Sadly, he did."

"Is it true King Philippe holds de Montfort in Paris?"

"Yes, though de Montfort's countess fights on for her husband's cause and has claimed the Breton title in right of her son."

"Sweet heaven! Well played, is it not?"

"Indeed." Jeanne of Flanders, de Montfort's countess, lost no time in claiming the duchy in her young son's name. Securing the duchy's treasury was her next priority. Her courage, and her cunning, impressed him.

Loring's smile faded. "What of Charles of Blois?"

"Ahh…Philippe's favoured nephew. The false king sent his heir, Duke Jean, to command Blois' army. The pair have made inroads, reclaiming towns loyal to de Montfort."

Their success compelled Countess Jeanne to seek aid—his aid. In return, de Montfort and his supporters would renounce Philippe and pledge allegiance to King Edward as France's rightful sovereign. But until the truce expired, he could not engage. At least not overtly.

The French defeat at Sluys sent Philippe's rule into turmoil, yet the underlying conflict between them remained unresolved. To his mind, the truce provided time to prepare. His first step was to send Derby to attend to a private matter already in motion. Then, at Dunstable, he would gather his senior commanders and Derby would join them after attending to the matter on the king's behalf. When the truce lapsed in June, England would be ready, its course set.

He chuckled. "Ignore me, Loring. My mind turns to the surprise for my heir."

"A most gratifying thought, sire."

They rode on in silence. Tournaments, like Dunstable, were viewed as merely amusement by some and since the Church opposed them, many rulers banned them. The fools! Why outlaw the use of sword and lance, and practice of command, when it kept men fit for battle? While England readied for the fray in Brittany, Philippe would be none the wiser.

De Montfort sought to secure his claim to the Breton Duchy, once ruled by the first King Henry, but lost to France by his inept son, John. Once de Montfort succeeded, with King Edward's help, the count's pledge of fealty to King Edward ensured the territory would again be a part of England. King Edward would take another bite out of Philippe's realm.

From the Great North Road, the entourage approached the outskirts of Dunstable. At Church Street, the three Norman towers of the Augustinian Priory of St. Peter appeared through the trees. King Edward gazed with satisfaction at the progress made on the Lady Chapel, the cathedral's rounded arches slowly ceding place to the favoured pointed ones.

"Loring, in the morning, you will ride with me to inspect the field at the Downs."

"My pleasure, sire."

"I rely upon you, also, to attend to the other matter concerning my son."

"As you wish."

While Loring rode on to the priory stable, King Edward reined his palfrey toward the cathedral grounds. Squeals from the Priory garden pierced the mauve-hued dusk. Several children, and no less than four nursemaids, were presided over by a well-rounded woman draped in a gold and red brocade gown.

She spotted him, raised her hand, and smiled.

His heart, and loins, throbbed at the sight of his wife, no matter the advanced state of another pregnancy. He returned her smile and wave. He missed her.

King Edward opened his eyes to the bright rays of the fully risen sun seeping through Philippa's bed curtains. The gold-embroidered dragons decorating the green panels seemed to breathe displeasure for his failure to rise early.

Fatigue from his travels did not keep him from Philippa's bed, though mindful of her condition, he only held her close until her breathing signalled she slept. Her peaceful rest waned within a short space, replaced by a restlessness which disrupted his slumber. Exhaustion won out in the end, and he slept through the Priory bells tolling for Matins.

Bereft of his wife's warmth, he rose, donned his robe, and padded barefoot to his chamber to dress, eager to witness his son's reaction to his surprise. Not halfway to the stable block, hurrying footsteps sounded on the path behind him.

"My Lord! Father!" Edward called.

The smile on his heir's face shone brighter than light sparking upon gold. King Edward spread his arms, and Edward raced to him, surely a reflection the father did not show affection often enough to the son. "*Bonjour mon fils*." He embraced his son, then held him at arm's length—another inch taller, at least.

"Good morning, *mon père*…Lord King." Edward bowed.

King Edward tousled his soon-to-be-twelve son's shaggy dark locks. The days of hugging were numbered. Too much of the boy's childhood was lost; he vowed not to miss his son's journey to manhood. They continued to the stable, his son chattering in the way of young boys, relating his hunting adventures with his new rock falcon.

Loring waited in the stable yard, one shoulder resting against a post and holding braided leather reins. He straightened and bowed at their approach. "God's blessings, my liege."

King Edward laid a hand on Edward's shoulder. "Sir Nigel, have you met my son? Edward this is Sir Nigel Loring."

Loring bowed again. "It is an honour, Lord Edward."

"Good morning, sir." Edward dipped his head, then raised adoring eyes to the king.

"Would you like to ride out with us, Edward?"

"May I? Oh, I should like that." Edward beamed, his front teeth too large for his face.

King Edward turned aside and winked at the head groomsman. A few minutes later, a stable lad led out the king's bay courser, tightened the girth, and held the horse's bridle for the king to mount. A slightly smaller, well-muscled sorrel with a white blaze followed a second groom. King Edward settled in his saddle with an eye to his son. "Edward, what are you waiting for?" His strident tone echoed off the eaves.

Edward spun around twice, searching the yard for his pony. "Where is Jaiet?" He demanded of the stable lads.

The king kept a straight face until he could hold out no longer, then gestured to the groomsman. The man leading the sorrel offered the reins to Edward.

The boy's forehead crinkled. "Whose horse is this?"

"Yours," King Edward said. His heir's bewildered scowl vanished, replaced by a grin spreading ear to ear. "Now, mount up! We have wasted enough time." The king heeled his courser and cantered out of the stable yard.

Edward vaulted into his saddle. "Wait, *mon père!*"

The king glanced over his shoulder, laughed and urged his horse to lengthen stride. Loring kept pace beside him as they cantered down the lane with Edward galloping in pursuit. When they neared the Eleanor Cross at Watling Street, the king slowed and made the sign of the cross at the monument honouring his great-grandfather's queen. May she rest in peace.

He waved Loring into the lead, and when they veered south, the king reined down to a jog so he might savour his son's joy. It did not take Edward long to catch up. Both his son's and his new mount's chests heaved. The king eased his horse to a limber walk. "Tinto is from Spain, bred at a stud alongside a red-colored river. He takes his name from it."

Eyes bright and between panted breaths, Edward said, "*Merci.* Thank you. Thank you."

King Edward lengthened his reins. "Might Jaiet be jealous?"

Edward patted his new sorrel's satiny neck. "I do not believe so, Lord Father. Jaiet has carried his burden long enough; his muzzle is rather white now, you see. I think he will be glad of a rest."

"You may have the right of it, Edward."

They caught up with Loring at the fork leading to the downs and continued three abreast, with Edward moving in easy rhythm with his mount's loose walk. The king dangled a little bait. "Sir Nigel knows John Chandos."

Edward swivelled to the knight, his face alight. "You are a friend of Sir John?"

"We served together at Sluys."

No doubt, Edward admired the knight. Sir John's name peppered his son's tales. Sending the Derbyshire knight to his son's household was a stroke of genius. Under the knight's tutelage, Edward showed remarkable improvement in arms.

The king trotted his courser up the track to where the terrain levelled and reined in.

Edward's eyes widened at the sight sprawling before him. "Oh, Father, look! There must be hundreds of knights here." Horses whinnied, and banter drifted from the men. Smoke billowed from forges and hammers clanged across the field.

Edward nearly bounced in his saddle. "Surely, this is the grandest of all tournaments!"

Loring swept out a hand. "The arrangements meet with your approval, sire?"

King Edward eyed the expanse. "Indeed, Loring."

"If I may direct your attention, Lord?" Loring pointed to a wooden viewing stand at the far end of the grounds, beyond which the undulating downs stretched toward the western horizon. "For the mêlée, sire."

King Edward followed the knight's direction. "*Bon*. We will not lack for space."

Edward twisted in his saddle, trying to take in everything. "The grounds seem unusually free of mud for February."

"A keen observation, Lord Edward." Loring flashed a grin. "The soil contains chalk, so the rain tends to run off, and the dense grasses growing here are cropped short by the sheep. The combination makes for firm footing."

"It is why we chose Dunstable," King Edward added.

"What about those, Father?" Edward pointed to a dozen red banners displaying golden clouds entwined with green vines. "I have never seen the like before." His son craned around to view them, then read the embroidered words aloud. "*It is as it is.*" What does that mean?"

King Edward winked at Loring. The idea came to the king months before, when he first conceived of the tournament. "Perhaps, Edward, you might ponder on it." He urged his horse forward, pleased with his son, and Loring's arrangements. "With so much to distract England's commanders, he must convene them before the hastilude exhausted their bodies and dulled their wits."

Edward spent the morning touring the grounds with the king, happier than in a long time. But, as usual, weightier concerns soon drew his father's attention. Edward excused himself and, escorted by Sir Nigel, raced back to the priory in time to meet Joan as he promised. Drawing Tinto to a halt in the stable yard, he jumped down and called, "My thanks for your escort, sir." The knight reined around to return to the downs while Edward handed his reins to a stable lad. "See to my horse; cool and brush him down." He would do it himself, but he would be late.

Edward missed Joan's company, though he would never admit it to his companions. Once in his chamber, he donned a fresh tunic, then hurried down the passageways to the hall. He paused on the threshold of the wood-paneled room humming with conversation. Servants bustled between the trestles with platters of cold meats, cheese, and pitchers of ale and cider. His stomach rumbled at the aroma of bread warm from the ovens, reminding him he missed breaking his fast.

The chamber stilled as those gathered noticed his presence.

Everyone stood. He searched for Joan, finding her among the queen's ladies seated at a table near the hearth. She motioned to the bench beside her.

Northampton's countess curtsied. "God's blessings, Lord Edward."

"Lady Elizabeth…ladies." Edward bowed.

Joan clutched his arm. "Oh, I am so pleased you are here," she said. "I heard you rode out with the king and thought you would be unable to meet me."

Edward sat, and the assembly resumed its mellow hum.

Joan added, "You did not tell me you were to spend the morning with your father."

Edward washed his hands in the basin presented by a servant and wiped his hands on a linen. "I did not know." He tore a piece of bread from his trencher and slathered it with butter. "I am starving." He bit into it and licked butter from the corner of his mouth. "Father surprised me."

"You must have been pleased." Joan ate a piece of cheese.

"Yes, and riding out with him was not the only surprise. He gifted me a new horse, Jeanette, a courser!"

Joan clapped her hands. "How splendid!"

"We shall go riding." He stabbed a slice of ham. "My father tells me Tinto is from Spain. He has the smoothest gaits."

Joan picked up her cup and peeked over its rim, saying sweetly, "Hmm…I shall have to forego my embroidery to ride with you. You ask a great sacrifice, Edward."

Edward bumped Joan's shoulder. "You tease." Hunger taking over, he piled his trencher with roast fowl and added a scoop of pears baked in syrup. "You and I will ride out, just the two of us, I promise."

Joan leaned closer and whispered, "Have you learned anything of Thomas? Your letter said he retur—"

"You have not heard from him, *still*?"

Joan shook her head while maintaining a pleasant expression. She knew not to draw undue attention.

Edward spoke low. "This does not bode well. If Holland's intentions were honourable, he would do everything in his power to resolve this matter."

"What power, Edward? Surely you understand he has little, not compared to the Earl. Salisbury has wealth and your father's ear."

"True."

"You know I believe my mother and Uncle Wake prevented Thomas from contacting me. Perhaps I could seek out Thomas without their knowledge…if you were to discover his whereabouts."

"Tell me you are not suggesting to meet him in secret again?"

Joan glanced around. "Please, Edward. If Thomas is in England, I must see him before the king calls him into service again."

"Meeting him in secret is what caused this tangle in the first place." He shook his head. "It is not a good idea."

She raised her chin. "Yet, I must try."

"Why must you?"

"Because…well… Will's birthday is in June."

"What does that have to do with anything?"

"The marriage vows we spoke were a sin. If Will wanted to, he could disavow our union, but only before he reaches fourteen years."

"I don't understand."

"Do you not see? Thomas could prevail upon Will to renounce our union. Such would remedy everything."

"Heaven help me. No! It is not a good idea to meet again in secret." Edward could not support Joan in this, but understood her desire to end Will's attachment. Holland might be able to persuade Will, but Holland was likely to be called to serve in Brittany very soon.

Joan squeezed Edward's arm. "Please? You must help me."

The Lady Chapel bells tolling for vespers greeted King Edward upon his return from the tournament grounds.He made his way to his apartment along the Priory House walkway passing servants lighting torches. He dismissed his escort, entered the anteroom of his chamber, and halted. "Who let you in?"

Derby lounged before the fire, a smug grin on his face and a cup in his hand.

"*Jesu*," the king cursed. "You certainly took your sweet time getting here."

Derby crossed his legs.

King Edward accepted a steaming cup of spiced wine from the serving lad, waved him away, and waited for the oak door to shut behind him.

"Well?" King Edward raised his brows.

Derby uncrossed his long, well-formed legs. Rising without haste, he offered the semblance of a bow. The corners of his lips twitched. "Sire, I live to serve."

King Edward broke his aggrieved façade and thumped Derby's shoulder.

His cousin chuckled. "My late arrival is through no fault of my own. A storm delayed the Breton emissary's crossing."

King Edward settled on a bench, eager to hear of Derby's clandestine encounter. "How did you find de Montfort's emissary?" His cousin had met with Amaury de Clisson in the king's stead to avoid tipping his hand should word about the meeting leak out.

Derby resumed his seat and leaned forward, resting his forearms on his thighs. "You were right. De Clisson confirmed the terms for aid to which de Montfort agreed last autumn still hold." Derby raised his cup in salute. "England supports de Montfort's claim to the Breton duchy, and he, and all his supporters, swear homage to you as the rightful king of France."

King Edward gazed into the glowing embers in the hearth and sipped the mulled wine. To assemble an army was one thing—to supply and pay the troops quite another. A lesson hard-learned in the Low Countries; some debts haunted him still.

Derby cocked his head as if hearing the king's thoughts. "De Clisson opened Brittany's war chest and paid the first installment."

The king raised his cup. "Well done, *mon ami*! Now, we take back Brittany!"

King Edward studied the faces of his most trusted commanders —Derby, Northampton, Pembroke, and Suffolk—dining with him in his chamber while Queen Philippa hosted their wives and other court nobles in the Priory's great hall. Both entertainments celebrated the betrothal of Lionel to the Irish heiress, Elizabeth de Burgh, but this private gathering concealed a second purpose.

Amidst the conversations, a serving lad circled the table refilling goblets. Suffolk pushed away from his trencher and wiped a hand across his grey-flecked beard. "Before we take to the tournament field, sire, let us drink to your son's brilliant match and future."

"To Lionel!" Cups raised, they saluted.

King Edward sipped and over the rim of his cup, slid a pointed glance at Derby.

The Earl took his cue, rose, and shifted to stand at his shoulder. "Gentlemen, while we celebrate let us consider the purpose for our gathering, the weightier one."

"Ho! Now there is a surprise!" Pembroke smacked a hand to the table setting the candlesticks to wobble. Everyone chuckled.

"Brittany." The king's sober tone pierced the good humour. "Charles of Blois battles John de Montfort for rule of Brittany. His success, should he defeat de Montfort, threatens our wine trade."

All humour gone, his solemn-faced commanders fixed their attention on him.

"However, a friendly power in Brittany would not only secure our trade but offer us entrée into France's heartland and, perhaps, an opportunity to forge new alliances."

"Lord King, are we not barred from interference by the truce?"

Suffolk asked in his customary gruff tone. The earl's surly manner and grizzled appearance belied the calculating mind beneath. "The truce extends until June, does it not?"

King Edward fingered the tails of his moustache. "Indeed, it expires then."

Suffolk's eyes flashed, his mind leaping ahead. "Yes, June. Indeed, sire, Time enough to prepare. We will catch Blois and the French king's son unaware."

As the other men fit the pieces, fiery comments fanned between them.

"*Ecoutez!*" King Edward waited for the heated murmurs to fade. "Before joining us here, Derby met with Brittany's emissary. Our esteemed Earl is eager to share Amaury de Clisson's proposal" For the next two hours, they plotted England's next moves.

When the tournament ended, the king made for London while Queen Philippa's household lingered in Dunstable. True to his word, Edward arranged for Joan to ride out with him. Though the day's sullen clouds threatened rain, Joan mounted the docile dun palfrey Edward chose for her.

"I thought we might wander the ridge beyond the *mêlée* site," Edward said, running his hand along Tinto's sleek neck.

"I am happy to ride wherever you want as long as we are away from the court's sharp eyes and wagging tongues." With no word from Thomas, hiding her disquiet was becoming more difficult by the day.

"I agree. The ridge it is."

They rode side by side down the road in companionable si-lence. Edward was right when he said Thomas should have found a way to get around her mother and uncle. After all, Thomas was clever enough to conceal their trysts and spirit her away to wed. She thanked the Lord for Edward as he remained her only support.

When they reached the track leading up to the tournament grounds, Edward took the lead and Joan followed, urging her less-than-enthusiastic gelding up to the hilltop. Gone were the glorious pavilions and billowing banners. Now, across the trampled expanse, dozens of workmen laboured to dismantle the paddocks, stack and bind the planks, and load them into the wagons.

Edward reined in and Joan pulled up beside him. "Men are to haul all this to Northampton for the tournament in April. I am to meet father there." Edward pressed Tinto to walk on in a long, easy stride.

Joan tapped her crop, encouraging her palfrey to keep up. "Tinto suits you. Your father chose well."

Edward's smile reached ear to ear. "Come! Race me!" He heeled Tinto into a canter and gave him his head.

Joan laughed and galloped after them, tapping her crop for encouragement. The wind brushed Joan's cheeks as they chased across the rolling grey-green down, past the grazing sheep, herders, and dogs keeping watch. Muted bleats and a distinctive musky odor scented the air. They enjoyed a lengthy gallop, hardly a race, and then Edward slowed to a walk. Joan reined up beside him. Though she hesitated to interrupt their genial interlude, she yearned to ask if Edward knew anything more of Thomas.

"Are you to attend the games in Northampton?" Edward asked, lengthening his reins and encouraging Tinto to stretch his neck.

Joan shook her head. "It is not likely. Your lady mother's time approaches and so much travel is not good for her. From here, we are to make slowly for London for her lying-in."

Edward made the sign of the cross. "May the Holy Trinity safeguard my mother…and the babe."

"Amen," Joan said. The breeze freshened, and silence grew between them. Her stomach skipped as she prepared to ask her question.

"Edward."

"Jeanette."

They spoke at once.

Edward halted, turned Tinto to face her, and waited.

The changes in her childhood playmate hit her. His cheeks were more angular, and his dark brown eyes rested beneath a heavier brow. He sat his horse differently, too, more erect and with his chin slightly raised. The broadening of his shoulders showed beneath the rich fabric of his tunic and mantle, bringing Edward's tales of swordplay and lance practice to mind. Though not tall, Edward was nimble and strongly built for his age. He would be twelve in June; her best friend showed signs of becoming a man.

When she did not speak, a glimpse of a smile crossed Edwards lips. "Jeanette," he repeated as Tinto stomped a hoof. "I have made inquiries about Thomas Holland as you requested. Chandos often hears of such matters." He paused, wearing a pinched look.

Joan's heart thrummed a faster beat. "Go on. Any word is better than none."

"You are aware my Lord Father went to London?"

She nodded.

"Before he left, I overheard a conversation. Do you know of the competing claims between de Montfort and Blois over the Breton duchy?"

"A little."

"You must promise not to say anything, for I share the next in confidence." He waited for her nod. "I believe my father gathers an army for Brittany. While I am not certain, it is likely Thomas is among those contracted to serve."

Joan gripped her horse's mane. "Oh." Thomas supported himself by military service. If the king mustered forces intending to fight in Brittany, Thomas would be gone again, perhaps lost to her should he die. She stared unseeing at Edward.

It was all she could do to breathe.

October 1342 - Port of Sandwich

The *George* slipped out of Sandwich harbour encircled by yellow-billed kittiwakes crying and plunging into its wake. King Edward balanced at the stern rail staring at his twelve-year-old, blue-mantled son, waving from the dock and slowly disappearing from view.

In April, at the Northampton tournament, Edward displayed a growing interest in governance, peppering him with questions about the Scots, the clash over the Breton succession, and affairs in Gascony. Thinking to shield his son from kingship's harsher realities, he responded vaguely at first, but given Edward's burgeoning maturity, he changed his mind. His son needed to learn. While breaking their fast privately one morning, he put down his cup of cider and said, "Admiral Mauny is assembling ships in Portsmouth. Once the troops are assembled, he is to sail to Brittany to secure the ports and towns loyal to de Montfort."

"But Father, the truce does not expire until June."

Bon. His son paid attention, but would he comprehend the significance of the next statement? "Admiral Mauny is to sail under de Montfort's colours."

Edward's brow knitted. "Under de Montfort's colours?" After a moment, he said, "Oh, I see. Flying de Montfort's colors will make it appear England has not broken the truce."

The king's lips curved up. Bright boy; he is catching on fast. "Just so." He explained, by the end of April an additional two hundred ships and troops were ready to sail under Northampton. Regrettably, the sailing was delayed by a political issue.

King Edward loosened his grip on the rail and faced fore. Was it a trick of the fading light, or were the clouds to the south thicker and lowered? The wind freshened, and the ship's timbers shuddered beneath him.

"Best find shelter, Lord King," the captain called.

He staggered across the rolling deck to his cabin, lay on his bunk, and laced his hands behind his head.

Throughout the summer, one delay after another prevented their sailing for Brittany, the most critical concerned the Flemings. Having heard reports of an English fleet assembling, they believed he intended to attack France, which would have violated the truce and prompted Philippe to retaliate with a counter-attack on Flanders. To prevent such an attack. the king sent English emissaries to meet with Philippe's ministers and the Pope's envoy.

The misunderstanding caused months of delay, time in which he could have campaigned in Brittany. Only now, six months later, could he sail. Yet, his resolve to reclaim the Breton duchy was as strong as ever. His determination surged like the ship beneath him, forcing him to seize a handhold. He groaned through clenched teeth as his gut rebelled.

Though Pope Clement urged peace in Brittany, why should King Edward heed his pleas when this Pontiff was as wedded as his predecessor to safeguarding Philippe's interests? Both Popes denied his requests for dispensations for a union between Edward and Margaret of Brabant. Both Pontiffs justified their refusals by citing consanguinity, as Margaret and Edward were both descended from the first King Edward, but the real reason was to prevent England from forging an alliance which might tip the scales against France.

The *George* crested a swell and lurched down a trough, the king's thoughts thrashing about the Holy See's enmity. Word reached him Pope Clement had lifted the interdict imposed on Flanders by his predecessor. Pope Benedict's sanction had resulted in Flanders recognizing King Edward as the true monarch of France. King Edward could not allow Philippe, the dog, to win Flanders back to his affinity. Nor would he abandon his campaign to bring Brittany under his rule. Damn, the French! Damn, the Popes! Brittany would be his.

Incense permeated Canterbury Cathedral's vaulted nave while candlelight flickered upon its blackened stones and sainted niches. Hands clasped, Edward bowed his head as the priest intoned the Psalm's blessed words.

"Like Mount Zion which endures forever, those who trust in the Lord cannot be shaken."

Gooseflesh raised on Edward's arms. He had paused his return to London to offer devotion at the tomb of the revered Saint Thomas á Beckett. From the quay in Sandwich, he had stared out over the bay at the billowing white peaks of his father's flagship until it vanished from sight. Once again, his father—his king—sailed to war, trusting Edward to resume his duty as Guardian of the Realm. Proudly would he serve.

Thomas Beckett was once trusted by his king, too, until Beckett accepted his appointment as Archbishop of Canterbury, the highest position of the Catholic Church in England. How did a man like Beckett, known for his grasping nature, transform from serving the king for personal gain to self-sacrificing service to God and the Church?

"As the mountains surround Jerusalem, so the Lord surrounds his people." The priest's intonation of the Psalm's holy words washed over Edward.

Beckett was humbled by the Grace of God.

Edward squeezed his eyes shut and called upon the Holy Trinity for guidance. First, he prayed death would not claim his father, then he asked for strength to fulfill his duty, and lastly, to not disappoint the king.

After the service, Edward made his way to the stable. Dust filtered up in the sun's slanting rays while the horses nickered and banged buckets to hurry the lads tossing their afternoon feed. While brushing Tinto, Edward breathed in the earthy scents of horseflesh and hay. On the other side of the wall, a hoof thumped.

"Enuff now, laddie," a stablehand scolded.

Edward paused to stroke Tinto's velvety muzzle, finding the silky feel quite soothing.

"I thought I might find you here." Roger poked his head around the stall door. "Care to stretch your legs along the river?"

Edward put down the brush. "All right." A walk with a friend might do him good.

Willows lined the Stour's bank, obliging Roger to duck under the low hanging branches. On the river's opposite bank, grey-robed monks distributed bread to the poor gathered at the Franciscan friary gate. Though Edward tried to put aside his disquiet, his concern for his father in Brittany consumed him.

In May, Admiral Mauny landed in Brittany to secure Brest and other towns in the duchy's western territory still loyal to de Montfort. French forces held most of eastern Brittany and they recaptured Rennes. When the fighting stalemated, Admiral Mauny returned to England with Bretons captured during the fighting. Edward happened to witness a disturbing exchange between his father and Mauny. He could not shake it from his mind.

"With all due respect," Mauny said, "we do not have enough troops to hold Brittany. Not against the combined forces of Duke Jean and Blois. The wisest course would be to agree to a truce."

"No. No truce. I will not have it." His father slammed his fist on the table. The scowl on his father's face and guttural tone reminded Edward of a cornered wolf. His father's reaction, no, his overreaction, was so extreme it shook Edward then and troubled him still. Like the time John flipped Edward onto his back at the tournament and he lost his temper. John's words came to mind. *"Never hand your opponent an advantage by losing your temper. It could cost you your life."*

The king was widely known for his temper. What if it got the better of him while in Brittany? His father might act rashly which could put him in unnecessary danger or get him killed. Edward kicked at a rock in his path.

Roger laid a hand on Edward's shoulder. "If it might help, I can listen."

The East Bridge lay ahead with the hospital's arched portal opened wide to welcome weary pilgrims. Edward stepped through and climbed the steps to the chapel, glowing bright white, so unlike Canterbury's grand cathedral. Behind him, fabric rustled as Roger closed the privacy panels separating the chapel from the stairs.

Edward lowered himself onto a bench, admiring the workmanship of the beams vaulted above him. A simple wooden cross, with the hovering dove of the Holy Ghost, was suspended over the linen-draped altar. "What distresses me is what awaits my father in Brittany."

Roger made the sign of the cross then seated himself. "The king does not battle alone."

"True, yet Northampton's early success was due to surprising Blois at Brest. The Frenchman fled rather than fight."

"Does his flight not prove Blois' lacking?"

"No." Edward twisted the ruby ring on his index finger. "Blois retreated because King Philippe recalled the reinforcements marching to aid Blois. Philippe recalled them because he believed my father was readying to attack Calais."

"Your father told you this?"

Edward nodded. "If not for Philippe's decision, Northampton's rout of Blois would have failed. "Since then, Northampton and Artois have achieved little. Morlaix was a standoff."

Roger toyed with the cuff of his tunic. "All may be true, but perhaps you fret overmuch. You know King Philippe shies from battle. If our king can outwit the Scots, Philippe offers no challenge whatsoever."

Edward shrugged. "I pray you are right, Roger." He looked up at the cross, then bowed his head. *O Holy Father, guide my father, allay his hunger for victory so it does not blind him, that he does not take one chance too many.*

Edward had never doubted his father before. The realization shook him.

December 1342 - Kennington Palace

Birdsong carried through the horned window panes in Edward's chamber, all lit a uniform grey. A fire burned low in the hearth easing the chill while he broke his fast. The wooded grounds at his Kennington estate, across the Thames from Westminster, offered respite from his duties. He did not regret his decision to set up residence there upon his return from Canterbury for he did not miss London's clamour and foul odors.

He sipped spiced wine and reflected on events since the king's departure in October. The first dispatch from Brittany reported the king, upon landing, made directly for Brest to confer with his commanders. Buried among other details in the report was one of interest to Joan.

From Dunstable, Joan had departed with Queen Philippa for her confinement in London. In July, he received a letter from Joan expressing sorrow at the passing of baby Blanche, only weeks following her birth. She also confided her personal disappointment; Will failed to renounce their union as she hoped.

When the king's letter from Brittany reached him, Edward wasted no time responding to Joan and lightening her spirits. Finally, the mystery of her delinquent husband's whereabouts was solved; Holland served under Northampton in Brittany.

Following a light rap on the door, Edward's chamberlain entered and bowed. "Your horse is being saddled and brought around, Lord Edward."

While he waited, he reread part of his father's November letter.

> *My commanders all agreed our main objective was the recapture of Vannes, the finest city of Brittany after Nantes, and the best position from which to reduce the lands beyond it to our obedience."*

Other than the king's one letter, no dispatches arrived from Brittany. Edward's concern grew. He finished the spiced wine and wiped his mouth. A ride would lessen his disquiet. He pulled on his boots, grabbed a cloak, and headed outside.

A week later, after resolving a few matters with his steward, Edward strode into the hall. Will and Jack sat at a table near the hearth, rattling cups with dice. Nearby, Roger set out a chessboard.

"Care for a game, Edward?"

Edward pulled out a stool and sat. "White or black? You choose."

Roger opened with a white knight. "Have you any word from Brittany?"

Edward fingered a pawn. "No report since the one in November relating my father's progress. His forces captured Rédon, Malestroit and Ploermel. He stated the French garrison at Roche-Periou surrendered, the cowards."

"Without a fight?"

Edward nodded. "According to my father's letter, Northampton led an attack on Viscount Rohan's lands."

Jack rolled his dice. "I overheard Arundel say Rohan is one of Blois's staunchest supporters."

"Neither Blois nor Rohan must have been happy to learn the Earl's troops razed Rohan's estate and then captured Pontivy."

Roger advanced a pawn. "Northampton's a cunning commander."

"He and Warwick joined forces after Pontivy and raided Nantes."

Will scowled. "You boast of Northampton and Warwick, yet never credit my father."

Roger rolled his eyes. "Allow Edward to finish. Do not be so quick to take offense."

Will's face twisted. "Do not chasten me, you fawner."

Roger's jaw clenched, and he stood, tipping the chessboard.

"Come on," Will taunted, rising and wiggling his fingers.

Jack jumped between them.

"Enough!" Edward glared at Will. "You best leave."

Will did not move, his hardened face inches from Roger's.

"I said… take your leave."

Will glared at Roger.

"Now!" Edward's voice cut like a blade.

For a few more heartbeats, Will stood his ground.

Edward leaned toward Will and sniffed. "Something smells foul."

Will's face flamed. Hatred flashed in his eyes and he stalked away, knocking over a stool.

"One of these days," Roger said, "he is going to push me too far."

"Something is gnawing at him," Jack said.

"His troubles do not give him cause." Roger righted the stool and sat down. "I do not relish being the target of his venom."

"Nor should you." Edward reset several chess pieces. Jack was right about something eating at Will. If Edward were to hazard a guess, Joan's continued rebuffs rankled the Earl's overweening son.

The following Tuesday, Edward boarded the barge ferrying him across the Thames to a Council meeting at Westminster. Battered by the wind, he pulled up his hood, and as soon as the barge bumped the landing, he hurried down the walkway to the palace.

At the door to the Painted Chamber, a servant took Edward's mantle and he exchanged greetings with his advisors. Then Edward seated himself upon the dais in the king's high-backed chair.

Chancellor Stratford began by holding up a parchment. "According this latest dispatch, several more Breton nobles have sworn allegiance to our king."

"Thank you, Lord Chancellor. That is good news." Edward cleared his throat. "If I am not mistaken, the contracts of service for soldiers in Northampton's service have expired. What is being done to find replacements?"

"Foot soldiers are being mustered in Brittany," Pembroke said, "and our bailiffs are recruiting archers in Wales."

"Good. What about spare bow staves and arrows?"

"Requisitions were sent, Lord," Pembroke said. "May I add that Gloucester and I conferred, and between us, we believe we can muster three or four hundred bowmen from those already in our service." He rubbed his jaw. "However, that number is not nearly enough to meet the king's needs."

Gloucester added, "If we are to sail before winter deepens, we must speed the muster."

"The good archbishop will send out urgent writs," Edward said.

Stratford shifted in his seat.

Edward aimed a stern look at the archbishop. "Today," he said, his voice a command.

"To assemble where, Lords?"

Gloucester said, "Plymouth?"

Pembroke nodded. "I agree. A western port offers a shorter crossing and reduces the chance of being caught in a winter storm."

A week before the feast celebrating Christ's birth, Edward trotted Tinto into Kennington's courtyard. Roger, Jack, and Will reined in behind him. Large white flakes billowed in the rising wind and snow crunched under the horses' hooves.

Will dismounted, steam rising from his horse's flanks. He clutched his hood. "Damn, it is freezing. A mug of mulled wine before the fire would suit about now."

Edward leapt down, and a groom hastened to take his horse.

The manor door banged open and William St. Omer trudged from the residence. Bundled in a woollen cloak, its hood was tucked up about his ears.

"Lord Edward." White puffs rose with St. Omer's breath. "You have guests."

Only then did Edward notice the two pairs of footprints marking the snow to the door.

"The Earls of Arundel and Huntingdon await inside," St. Omer said.

Edward arched his brows. "On such a day?" It had snowed quite heavily the previous evening, and flurries began again that morning as the four of them set off on their ride.

"Your good fortune, Edward," Jack chided from astride his grey. "Their arrival saves you from the loss of your coin."

Edward grinned. "My besting you at dice only suffers a temporary delay." He followed St. Omer into the residence, brushing snow from his shoulders. Inside, he handed his cloak and gloves to a servant.

The scent of freshly laid rushes and the warmth of the fire greeted him as he entered the hall. The two broad-shouldered Earls rose and offered sober-faced greetings. Edward settled himself on a stool and held his hands toward the fire. A serving maid brought him a cup of steaming cider, and after offering refills to the two noblemen, she scuttled away.

"My lords, I doubt a desire for a sojourn in the country roused you out of London today."

The Earls shared a glance and resettled themselves. Huntingdon gripped his cup with both hands and sipped. His tone grave, he said, "A dispatch arrived."

Arundel leaned forward. "A courier from Cornwall."

"Cornwall?" Edward's brow furrowed.

"Yes, Lord." Huntingdon cleared his throat. "A gale struck our fleet and a large number of our ships floundered into port at Falmouth."

"What? Those ships carried the archers and provisions to resupply the king."

Arundel paused, his cup halfway to his mouth. "Only the ships of Gloucester and Pembroke made it through."

"Not carrying nearly enough men and provisions to aid my father!"

The scar on Huntingdon's left temple stood out in the fire-light. "Lord Edward, we are no less concerned than you."

Edward twisted the ruby ring on his index finger. "Are you? Despite this foul weather, King Philippe will march his forces against my father and without the archers and supplies, we chance losing all the Breton territory my father has won." Edward rose, paced a few steps and turned back. "Assemble the Council."

The next afternoon in Westminster, Chancellor Stratford presided over the summoned advisors. While Arundel and Huntingdon related the situation in Falmouth, Edward studied the faces of the men.

"To chance a sailing in this weather would be foolish," the archbishop said. "We cannot afford the loss of more ships."

Edward bristled. "What about the loss of our king? Do you suggest we leave him stranded in Brittany?" Edward searched for an ally. Only Huntingdon met his gaze.

"While your concern is justified," the Earl said, "to sail right now is unwise."

Edward opened his mouth to speak.

Huntingdon held up his hand. "Hear me out. The foul weather does not prevent us from sailing. The captains, crews, and all the men mustered will stand by, ready to sail." He paused. "Arundel and I will sail with troops at the first break in the weather."

Edward scowled. "Tell me, Lord, when might that be?" He feared he knew the answer.

"Understand, Lord Edward, to lose ships means the loss of provisions, but more importantly, the loss of skilled archers."

"We vow to sail as soon as possible, perhaps by March," Arundel said.

Edward closed his eyes and breathed deeply. March. More than two months away.

"You have our word," Huntingdon added.

"I see." If only he possessed his father's skill for persuasion. Edward looked Arundel in the eye. "I do not doubt your word, Lord, but March is too late."

January 1343 - Tower of London

Two weeks later, having been summoned to London, Edward sat before the fire in the Tower's great hall. Somehow, a ship from Brittany, carrying a letter from his father, managed the crossing despite the winter storms. As he reread the letter, a rock lodged in the pit of his stomach.

> *"Philippe, the man who calls himself king, mustered a great army but chose not to command the forces himself. His heir, at the troops' head, arrived in the duchy not long before the day of Christ's birth. To my great vexation, Duke Jean retook Rédon, Malestroit, and Ploermel and forced Warwick to abandon Vannes.*

As Edward feared, much of the Breton territory his father fought so hard to win was lost. While the letter went on to describe other actions, its message was clear.

Edward failed.

He crumpled the parchment, about to toss it into the fire, but stopped, smoothed the wrinkles and refolded the letter. He would keep it as a reminder of a failure he hoped never to repeat.

During a break in the tempestuous weather, Edward removed his household to Berkhamstead Castle, near enough to London should he be needed, but far enough to provide distraction. Not a week later, a courier arrived bearing a letter in the king's hand directed to Edward. Yet another ship managed the sea crossing? Edward took the packet to his chamber to read; fearing it bore word of disaster, his fingers trembled as he broke the seal.

He skimmed a few lines, then collapsed onto the bed. His father absolved him of all blame for the lack of reinforcements and supplies. His father's absolution only added to Edward's guilt.

Toward the end of January, Archbishop Stratford sent for

Edward, reassembling the Council at Westminster. Unease, Edward's constant companion, travelled with him to the meeting. While he sat in Westminster's Painted Chamber waiting to begin, the colourful murals depicting scenes from the Bible reminded him to have faith. Sober-faced advisors gathered around the table, including the newly appointed Earl of Surrey.

Chancellor Stratford stood and cleared his throat. "Let me begin by saying why we assemble here today may come as a surprise to you, as it did to me." The archbishop paused. "We are here to review the proposed terms of a Breton truce."

"What? My father has agreed to a truce?" Edward recalled the king's heated outburst at Admiral Mauny's mere suggestion of a Breton truce. Now, he agreed to one?

"Indeed." Stratford read from the parchment.

"First, Flanders remains an independent territory and Count Louis is prohibited from returning from his refuge in Paris without leave of his Flemish subjects."

"Unbelievable," Arundel burst out. "For three years Philippe has tried everything to entice the Flemings to accept him as overlord of Count Louis and reestablish Flanders' allegiance to France. That will never happen if the Count is unable to return to Flanders."

"French brains must be addled to agree to such a stipulation," Huntingdon said.

Several men echoed the Earl's view.

Stratford held up his hand. "My lords, your sentiments may be well grounded, yet permit me to continue."

Gradually, the room quieted and Stratford continued.

"All territories remain in the hands of their current possessors and remain thus for the duration of the truce, set to last three years, until September 1346."

For several moments, the men sat in stunned silence until Huntingdon sputtered, "By all that is holy, the Valois must be mad. Under these terms, he cedes dominion over half of Brittany."

"Not to mention the loyalty of all the nobles who declared for our king." The Earl of Surrey shook his head. "It seems inconceivable Philippe should surrender so much."

Huntingdon asked," Archbishop, do these terms apply to disputed lands in Gascony and Scotland, too?"

Stratford nodded. "As I understand it."

Murmurs filtered around the table as the men questioned why the French would agree to such terms.

"My lords," the archbishop said, "there is more." He waited for quiet, fingering the gemstones on his cincture. "The king has appointed Northampton as Lieutenant in Brittany, along with a select group of Breton noblemen to advise him and oversee the duchy's administration in de Montfort's name."

Edward sat forward. "The Count is being held in Paris. What of his fate?"

"He is to be released," Stratford said.

"Countess Jeanne will be relieved," Arundel said. "What possessed Philippe to agree to such generous terms, I cannot imagine. However..." The Earl chuckled. "It appears nothing is beyond our king's wiles."

Edward eased back. His father did not lose his temper as Edward had feared, and, despite being outnumbered, his father won.

February 1343 - Byfleet Manor

After months of worry, Edward escaped to his favourite estate at Byfleet. He had his grandmère to thank for gifting him the property he enjoyed so much. One morning, he and Jack were returning from a morning ride.

"Race you back!" Jack said, and touched his spurs to his courser's flanks.

Edward crouched low over Tinto's withers. "Yah," he called. Tinto's hooves dug deep and his pounding strides cut Jack's lead to only a half-length despite his head start.

Jack glanced over his shoulder and mimed a wicked, blue-eyed challenge.

"Run boy, run." Tinto responded to Edward's urging. As Tinto's forelegs clawed ground-eating strides, branches whipped past. The horses thundered neck and neck toward the gateposts.

Edward pressed his heels. "Come on, Tinto, you can do it!" Ribs heaving and nostrils flaring, Tinto streaked through Byfleet's stone pillars a neck ahead.

Edward circled and reined in. "Ho, Jack, a fine race!"

"You would not have caught us if the footing were dry," Jack panted. "Though I grant you, Tinto has heart." Steam rose from the horses and both would require hand-walking before being put up.

Edward rounded the corner of the newly renovated half-timbered stable, admiring the skill of his carpenters and stonemason. Two unfamiliar horses stood hitched to a rail and muffled voices drifted from inside. Two figures emerged from the shadows.

"Father!" Edward leapt down, sprinted the distance, and then stopped short. "My liege, Lord King." He bent to one knee.

Solemn-faced, the king offered his hand. Edward pressed his lips to his father's ring, then gazed up, his heart beating as fast as Tinto's.

"Edward." With a smile, the king nodded permission to rise and clouted Edward's shoulder. "Are you not going to greet our guest?"

In his joy, Edward failed to notice the man with his father. "Sir John!"

The knight tipped a bow. "A pleasure to see you again, Lord Edward." The creases at the corners of John's eyes deepened.

"When did you dock? Where? How was the crossing? How do you come to be at Byfleet?" Edward glanced around. "Are others with you?" He said a silent prayer of thanks his father and loyal friend were safe.

Chandos reached for Tinto's reins. "Lord King, you and your son have a great deal to discuss. Jack and I shall see to the horses."

"Thank you, Sir John." John's gait seemed off, as he and Jack led the horses away. He also appeared thinner. Could he have been wounded? The thought of losing his friend made his stomach sink.

In the king's chamber that evening, tapers flickered upon the remnants of the meal he and Edward shared. The king sipped wine and marked the changes in his son during the past four months. Edward would be thirteen in the coming June and a young man's urges would soon send him seeking release, if not already done. Better he spill his seed with a wife.

Margaret of Brabant was the ideal choice although his original petition to the Pope was denied. A second appeal to the new Pope was also denied and he cited consanguinity as the reason. This was nothing more than a ruse to mask the true motive; neither pontiff dared offend the French monarch who provided the Holy See a sanctum in Avignon.

"Father?"

"Pardon my scowl; it was not directed at you. Quite the opposite, in fact. I am pleased by the accounts of you I received while away."

"I should not want to disappoint you."

The pitch of his son's voice vacillated between the boy and the soon-to-be man. He envisioned his son fully grown and savoured the image even more than the robust wine on his tongue.

"You cannot know my torment when I learned the French repulsed your assault on Vannes." Edward's voice wavered. "Please, forgive me, sire, for I failed in my duty to send aid."

His son blamed himself? "*Non*, Edward. The weather foundered, not you. The cursed narrow sea and its infernal squalls." Edward, twisted his Uncle John's ruby signet ring still too big for his ring finger.

"But, you were depending upon me."

"What could you have done to change the weather? *Rien*. Nothing." The king tapped his fingers against his cup. "A prudent man learns not to fret about what he cannot change. A clever one reasons about what he can achieve. A much better occupation, *n'est ce pas?*"

Though his son nodded, Edward's lips remained downturned. The king sat back. How might he help his son grasp this matter? "A wise leader gauges his enemy's strengths and weaknesses. What say you, we sort through this together?"

Edward's face brightened.

"Think upon my situation, then tell me what my enemy's advantage over me might have been."

"King Philippe's army was larger?"

"*Très bien.* Now, what might have been my advantage?"

Edward's brow knitted. "Although I do not see what it was, there must have been one for you gained more from the truce than King Philippe."

The king chuckled. "*Bon.* Let us say, I was aware my of enemy's greater force. Must it follow my enemy knew mine was smaller?" King Edward allowed time for Edward to consider, then said, "If my enemy does not, is his lack of knowledge not to my advantage?"

Edward edged forward on his seat. "Oh, I see."

"Now, what did we know of our enemy from previous encounters."

His son squeezed his eyes shut, then opened them. "In the past, King Philippe chose not to take the field."

"*Exactement.* So, given matters in Brittany, what does that knowledge imply?" The king waited. It was important for his heir to work this out, for he must learn to think like a king.

Edward stared at the fire, tapping a finger to his lips. Thinking out loud, he said, "Your enemy might have more soldiers, but he would rather not fight."

A warm pride welled in King Edward. He poured more wine and raised his cup. "You are a clever boy and will make a fine commander one day."

"You think so?" A red hue brushed Edward's cheeks.

"Indeed. Now, shall I share the details? *Oui.* Our Pope sent his emissaries—"

"The same cardinals you refused to meet last summer?"

"The very ones. Although this time, it was to my advantage to negotiate and, if the terms were favourable, to agree to a truce." He winked.

"So you met with them?"

"No, no, no, not me. My representatives traveled to Malestroit for the negotiations." He paused. "Nineteen miles from our camp."

Edward's eyes lit up. "They could not see your army to judge its strength."

"Just so." King Edward sipped. "You see, I know my enemy. Philippe would not chance his heir's life on a battlefield with me in command. *Non*, he knows better."

"I would not want to go against you either."

King Edward leaned back. "The terms were generous; we gained much more than what is written on the parchment."

"What do you mean?"

"It is true, a great deal of Breton land and many nobles now come under my rule, however, their influence extends beyond the duchy, to others who owe allegiance to Philippe. Perhaps they will discern an opportunity?"

"Opportunity?"

"To forge an alliance with England. Consider for a moment. Brittany borders Poitou to the south, and Poitou borders what to its south?

"Gascony. Aquitaine."

"What if all came under my rule?"

Bad Blood

January 1344 - Windsor

For the next four days, the king and nineteen hand-picked comrades would take on all comers. The tournament lists were impressive: one hundred and fifty yards enclosed by a stout barrier rail. A good length for a solid run-up to the tilt and, despite the previous day's drizzle, the footing remained firm.

On his way to meet Chandos, Edward passed the banners along the perimeter rail displaying the coats of arms of the nine earls being honoured. He pictured the combatants galloping toward each other and judged the point at which they would lower and seat their lances. He imagined he could hear the deafening clash and splintering of wood, and the roar from the crowd.

A sturdy wooden *berfrois* occupied the south side of the lists. A canopy bearing England's royal arms billowed overtop the loge to provide shade for the privileged guests. His mother, grandmère Isabella, and the earls' countesses would enjoy the hastilude in comfort, judge the winners, and award the prizes.

Two large pavilions, and several smaller ones, were erected outside the lists. Horses milled in paddocks or rested tied to hitching rails scattered throughout the grounds. Shrill whinnies dueled with blacksmiths' hammers while smoke drifted from blue-burning forges as last-minute repairs were made to mail and plate.

Edward entered the royal pavilion filled to overflowing with competitors readying for the competition. Men shouted and harness jingled, while servants scurried through the jumble offering food and drink. Squires helped their knights don hauberks and mail, then overlaid luxurious surcoats displaying their coats-of-arms.

Edward spotted Chandos and threaded his way through the labyrinth to join him.

"Lord Edward, quite a stir, is it not?"

Edward sat on a bench alongside a trestle spread with John's kit. "I recognize some of the knights, but I see many unfamiliar.faces."

"Your father's invitation drew an impressive number of knights, many from across the sea. Knights from Brabant and Flanders, and even a few from Austria."

"Is it true King Philippe banned French knights from attending?"

Chandos checked the ties on his hose. "He did. I do believe our king's lauded reputation rankles the French king." He winked.

"I sought my father's permission to compete, but he said no… again." Edward picked up a gauntlet. "Did you tell him of my progress?"

"I did." Chandos glanced behind him. The king chatted with Salisbury a few tables away."My advice is to accept your Lord Father's decision with good grace. And by the saints, keep your voice down."

Edward launched the gauntlet onto a bench. "My father should have made the exception…for his heir. After all, I will be fourteen in June.

Chandos ignored him.

Edward sounded like a bad-tempered child and regretted his words. If he wanted to be considered a man, he must act like one.

Snatches of a heated conversation between his father and the Earl of Salisbury drifted to him. Without drawing attention, Edward maneuvered closer.

"That the Scots retook Roxburgh and Stirling is not terribly concerning just now, not compared to Philippe's continual transgressions in Gascony. He has no right. Those lands are mine!"

"The French dog cares naught for the terms of the truce."

The two lowered their voices and, unable to hear more,

Edward made his way back to Chandos and retrieved the gauntlet he discarded so callously. "Each piece of equipment symbolizes a knightly virtue," Chandos taught him. "Gauntlets represent largesse and protect a knight from avarice."

Edward fingered the platelets, admiring the expertly crafted union of leather and steel. The glove also represented qualities essential to a knight: steel for physical and mental strength and leather for the resiliency so vital against adversity.

The king's voice cut through the din. "Salisbury, you know as well as I, few Gascon lords possess the resources to withstand the Valois imposter."

"Nor the fortitude to resist Philippe's bribes and remain loyal to you."

"Malestroit's truce means nothing to that French cur. But hear me, these latest incursions will not stand."

Joan threaded her way through the townsfolk milling along the rail, swilling ale and munching hot pasties. She paused at the base of the viewing stand, lifted the hems of her silk-edged *côtehardie* and fur-lined mantle, and climbed up the tiers.

"Jeanette, come, sit here." Queen Philippa beckoned with be-jeweled fingers. A diamond coronet rested upon her upswept hair and a netted veil shimmered past her shoulders. Luckily there was little wind.

"God's blessings upon you, my lady." Joan settled on the queen's left, beneath the gold and red striped silk canopy. She adjusted her skirts and folded her hands in her lap. The queen's invitation solved at least one of Joan's concerns. Seated beside Queen Philippa, Joan was able to avoid Lady Catherine and the pressure she exerted on her son's behalf.

Will's annoying possessiveness and the pretence of their marriage unsettled Joan. She was tempted to expose the fraud, though she dared not. The scandal would ruin her, and its consequences might be far worse for Thomas. She prayed and clung to the belief Thomas would return for her, yet time's passing tested her resolve.

Joan smiled and nodded politely to the honoured countesses as they found their places. Lady Catherine was among them and Joan could not ignore her altogether. When their eyes met, Joan dipped her head. "Good day, Lady Catherine."

"Joan." The woman's tepid smile did not reach her eyes.

Disquieted, Joan fixed a smile on her face and she chatted with two of the queen's favoured ladies-in-waiting sitting in the row below her. When a strand of Joan's hair loosened from a pair of pearl-studded combs, she tucked it back into place. Below them, a minstrel and his troupe of performing dogs entered the lists, yapping, running in what looked like chaotic circles, and jumping through hoops. The dogs' rollicking antics delighted the crowd, drawing laughter and applause from the ladies.

Joan's mind drifted. After serving in Brittany, Edward told her Thomas signed on with the Earl of Derby to fight the Moors in Granada. Thomas had asked her to be patient while he built a reputation so he could approach the king. Three years had passed; how long was she supposed to wait? The only letter she received recently was from her mother. It kept her tossing most of the night.

"It will not be long until your situation is resolved."

Joan felt dread perching on her shoulder. What did her mother mean?

The next morning Joan freshened her face and donned a gown, preparing to meet her mother. When Joan's maid finished pinning up her hair, she gathered her cloak, dashed down the passageway, and across the leaf-strewn courtyard to the chapel. She struggled to open the door against the morning's bluster. It seemed a fitting meeting place given her mother's attitude toward Joan's sin, for the chapel was named in honour of Edward the Confessor.

Joan's footsteps scuffled, yet if Lady Margaret heard her, she did not move. Her mother posed halfway down the aisle with her back to the door, contemplating a tapestry of Christ and the Blessed Virgin.

"Mother." Joan's voice muted in the chapel's expanse.

Lady Margaret glanced over her shoulder. "Daughter."

Joan made no move.

Her mother slowly turned. "Such a warm greeting." Lady Margaret's face held no welcome and her lips were pressed into a thin line.

Joan advanced a few paces to perch on a bench not far from the door, like a wary bird about to take flight. "Your letter…you wanted to see me?"

"Yes, here, so we might speak in private."

Joan clasped her hands to hide their shaking. "What is it you wish to discuss? Your letter was vague."

"Simply this. The Earl of Salisbury and Thomas Holland have reached a settlement."

The rush in Joan's ears nearly drowned out her mother's chilling next words.

"For a sum, Thomas Holland has agreed to release you."

Joan's heart pounded.

"The Earl wrote to your Uncle Wake. It seems the arrangement was struck when Salisbury and Holland were serving in Granada together."

Joan lifted her chin. "I do not believe you." Joan heard herself as if from a long distance."Why are you doing this, Mother?"

"For your own good."

"You are lying."

"It is done." Her mother's voice reeked of victory.

Joan fled the chapel. She held her skirts in bunches and blinded by tears she bounded through the palace courtyard, out the gate and into the park. Yes, Thomas served in Granada, but he would not have agreed to this. He would not. What her mother claimed could not be true.

Joan's stomach lurched. She clung to a tree trunk and retched. Sobbing, she stumbled on, tripping several times and almost falling.

She paused, wiped her mouth and found herself on the path leading to the pond.

She was not consulted; every decision made for her. She was nothing more than a chattel and her desires were of no consequence. The tree downed in her youth still rested near the edge of the pond, rotting and insect-ridden. How could her mother and uncle, those presumed to love her, do this? Worse, how could Thomas? The Church would dissolve her marriage, its decay just a matter of time, like the tree.

King Edward bowed his head. Candles in the many sconces lit the chapel, yet did nothing to lighten his spirit. This mass, on the last evening of the tournament, was intended to serve as a celebration; instead, he prayed for God's intercession on behalf of William Montagu. The Earl of Salisbury, his esteemed friend, lay injured, perhaps dying, from a wound suffered during the tournament.

The king squeezed his eyes shut, remembering the day Montagu helped free him from Mortimer's crippling regency, and recalled his boyhood friend's staunch loyalty since. Silently, he prayed. *O Heavenly Father, humbly do I beseech thee to look upon Thy injured servant with eyes of mercy; comfort him with Thy goodness, and restore him to health.*

The mass ended and the king, with Queen Philippa, exited the chapel at the head of a sombre procession. Behind them came his mother, dowager Queen Isabella, and his three eldest children. Philippa stroked his forearm, leaned close, and whispered, "Our Lord God holds William in His all-powerful and loving hands. Try not to fret overmuch."

He murmured, *"C'est impossible."*

When they entered Windsor's great hall, horns sounded and conversation faded. Heralds announced them to the foreign nobles and knights, as well as to the local barons and ladies who could not be accommodated in the chapel. The assembly bowed as one as King Edward, holding his sceptre, proceeded to the dais. After he and Philippa sat, the company found their places according to rank. The honoured earls with their countesses were situated in the row just below them.

Despite the Earl's grave condition, Salisbury's countess was in attendance with her son and Joan, surprisingly seated beside him. Salisbury's heir pressed his shoulder to Joan's and whispered. King Edward did not miss her slight stiffening.

Horns sounded again creating a lull in the resonant conversation. The king nodded to the castle steward, and servants entered, trays aloft, bearing roasted peacocks, fully dressed in regal plumage. A smattering of applause and delighted exclamations burst forth.The aromas of roasted fowl, stewed eel, and spiced oysters wafted from the platters.

The minstrels played gentle melodies throughout the meal while serving lads circled the tables, refilling cups with spiced cider, wine, and ale. When the main courses were removed, serving maids offered baked quince, damsons in wine, apples, and cheese. The king ate little, only toying with his food.

A flurry of activity at the entrance drew his attention. A sober-faced page in royal livery scurried toward the dais clutching a note. He kneeled and King Edward accepted the parchment, broke his physician's seal and read. He met Philippa's eyes. "Salisbury worsens."

What little food he consumed sat like a rock in his gut. He could do nothing, nor could anyone, save pray. After a few minutes. Philippa nudged him and covered his hand with hers. "Do not be dissuaded, my lord. William would want you to proceed."

The course the king decided upon before this tragic event, swelled with importance now. King Edward aimed a pointed look at his chamberlain and the man rushed forward with a gold-embossed bible.

Trumpets blared and King Edward stood, with Philippa beside him. The assembly clambered to its feet. He and his queen stepped onto a rostrum, draped with England's royal arms, and he placed his right hand upon the Lord's holy book.

The assembly hushed.

"On this day, in honour of the many who fought so bravely in years past, and for all those who will do so in future, I swear to the foundation of a new brotherhood of knights, one based upon the legend, and in tribute, to the courageous and acclaimed King Arthur. Today, I hereby pledge the founding of a new Round Table."

Gasps and excited murmurs spilt from the crowd.

The king's eyes welled with tears. Beside him, Philippa shimmered in a purple satin gown, her coronation crown sparkling atop her head. Though it took years, he finally rescued it from his creditors. He kissed her fingers and raised their hands into the air.

The assembly cheered.

As the lauding faded, he and Philippa resumed their places. Whispers began circling the room; heads paired as word of the gravity of the Earl's condition slithered from person to person, table to table, like the tentacles of a monstrous creature in tales of the deep.

These last few years, glad tidings were scarce. His realm suffered losses in Scotland, his ties with Flanders weakened, Gascon loyalties eroded, and trade disrupted. And now, Salisbury suffered grievous injuries. A creeping darkness threatened; the realm teemed with ominous premonitions. Might Salisbury's wounding be an omen?

Storms raged for an entire week after the tournament, but today, though it was grey, the wind ceased. Edward huddled in his mantle on the downed log near the pond with Joan beside him. He could not remember how many times they played here as children, stirring up minnows or skipping stones.

Joan's shoulders slumped and her puffy eyes held no joy.

Looking lost, she tossed a rock into the pond and watched weak rings ripple outward.

Edward sensed what might be troubling his friend. At the banquet, he chanced to overhear Will.

"My father's injury reminds me of my duty as future earl," Will said. "It has been three years since we wed and I believe I have given you sufficient time to accept our union." Will brushed a finger across Joan's hand. "It would please me should you welcome our joining." Joan murmured something and Will's eyes blazed.

Edward broke the silence. "I hate to see you like this. Tell me what troubles you so."

Joan shuddered a sigh. "The dispatch from Bisham…of Salisbury's passing."

"It is hard to believe, my father's loyal friend and trusted commander is gone from us. Let us pray he has passed directly into Our Lord's Heavenly peace."

Joan wrapped her arms around her middle and rocked back and forth. "Do you know the king's intentions regarding the Salisbury title? At fifteen, I believe Will is too young to inherit."

Edward shook his head. "I do not know. My Father has not spoken of this, though you are correct. Will's majority is still six years away and he cannot inherit the title before then, unless my father grants it early."

"Is he likely to do so? Or might he hold the wardship himself?" She picked up a stick and peeled the bark.

Edward raised his brows. "Why all these questions about Will's inheritance? What are you not telling me?"

Joan answered with quivering lips. "M-my mother informed me the Earl offered Thomas a sum t-to disavow our union."

"What? Thomas agreed to a settlement?"

Joan's jaw tightened. She pushed away her tears. "My mother lies, damn her. She thinks to trick me into consummating my union with Will."

Edward took a moment; never before had he heard Joan speak with such cold fury. He hesitated. With what he was about to say, she might turn her rage on him. He cleared his throat.

"Forgive me if this sounds harsh, but I think you do not want to believe your mother. Indeed, Thomas may well have agreed to Salisbury's proposal. Consider. You have heard nothing from him in over three years."

"You need not remind me." Joan crossed her arms. "If my mother has spoken true and the two did reach such an agreement, with the Earl's passing nothing may come of it."

Edward let out an exasperated humph. "I do not understand you. After Holland's long silence, and knowledge of this arrangement, you cling to him still?"

A tear slid down Joan's cheek.

Edward's heart ached for her. He wrapped an arm around her shoulders as she cried. Joan's instincts were right. If the king did not grant Will the title and thereby its wealth, he would not have the means to fulfill his father's agreement with Holland.

Joan's fate rested with the king.

December 1344 – Clare Castle

Barren tree branches rattled above them as Edward and Elizabeth hurried to the stable. Beneath a sun haloed a hoary white, their breath misted, and their footsteps crunched through the ice-crusted snow. Edward had broken his journey at Clare Castle while on his way to Norwich to celebrate the Christmas season with his family, and welcome his baby sister, Mary, into the world.

Two stable lads, caps snugged down over their ears, led out the horses. Edward checked his stallion's girth, then mounted. Lady Elizabeth smoothed her riding gloves over aging fingers before accepting assistance from a groom to climb the mounting block and settle atop her gelding.

His cousin tugged up her hood, reined around and led the entourage out of the courtyard. "Although I made no mention yesterday, Edward, I was struck by how much you have grown. Taller, certes, and I discern the air of a man about your face, not so much in evidence when you visited last spring."

Heat flushed Edward's face as he bent to adjust a stirrup, pleased she noticed the changes, especially his moustache. When he glanced up, laugh lines surrounded Elizabeth's twinkling blue eyes. The lady missed little.

He could not remember a time when cousin Elizabeth was not a part of his life. He recalled a visit when he was about five. She gave him a chest of toy soldiers which belonged to her beloved son, killed in his twenties. With each visit, they grew closer and in truth, she was more of a nurturing *grandmère* than his own. Over the years, he learned his secrets were safe with Elizabeth.

Edward's stallion pranced along the snow-covered lane lined with red-berried holly. A winter wren flitted from branch to branch, flicking its tail and twittering sharp warning notes. The scent of damp loam mingled with wood smoke drifting from the manor.

Lady Elizabeth patted her chestnut's sleek neck and said, "You have assumed formal duties now, have you not?"

"Indeed. My father honoured me with a seat on his council in April, after conferring my title as Prince of Wales." Edward squeezed his reins to check Tinto's enthusiastic prancing. "Stop showing off," he scolded.

"Your father is an astute ruler and is wise to engage you in the realm's affairs." Elizabeth halted her gelding at the verge of a fallow field. "You are young; watch and learn. He needs men around him he can trust and a son, moreso."

"Speaking of the realm's affairs, I suspect you know the conflict in Brittany worsens."

"Yes, I have heard the rumblings."

"Are you aware King Philippe beheaded several Breton lords who were loyal to my father? A nobleman from Poitou, I believe, Oliver de Clisson, regrettably lost his head, too."

"Yes, a bad business."

"The French raids on our Gascon lands grow ever more

frequent."

Raucous barking announced the arrival of the huntsmen with the dogs. Elizabeth spoke over the tumult, "I wonder if the Breton succession issue and enmity over the duchy of Aquitaine will ever be resolved between your father and King Philippe."

"My lord father says the only message Philippe understands is defeat in battle."

The falconer transferred a merlin to Elizabeth's gloved hand. When he removed the bird's leather hood it blinked several times and rotated its head.

"War, Edward?" At Elizabeth's nod, the huntsman released the dogs. Noses to the ground, they crisscrossed the field flushing skylarks into flight. The merlin took to the air flapping its wings with deadly intent, yet it missed its quarry. At the falconer's raised fist, the bird circled back to his hand.

"King Philippe has no right to sanction companies of routiers to make private war on my father's lands, nor to confiscate them. And he incites the Scots to rebel. My father is hard-pressed to protect his Gascon lands in the South with the Scots threatening in the North."

Elizabeth arched her brows. "Indeed?"

"Our Valois cousin is not even France's rightful monarch. He must be stopped!"

At Edward's outburst, Elizabeth's mount skittered sideways. "Easy, easy," she crooned. "While you may be right about Philippe's interference—"

"My father is the true king of France, not some imposter cousin from the House of Valois. Peace is unlikely as long as the pretender sits on the throne."

"Though your father's claim as King Philippe's grandson has merit, the current Philippe, is not about to give over his crown."

"Until the false King Philippe is forced to concede, the hostilities will continue. Parliament agrees or it would not have granted my father a two-year subsidy." He paused for a breath. "If it comes to war, my duty is clear."

"If King Philippe were defeated, would England be any safer? Truly?"

"Of course. How should you think otherwise?" Edward collected his reins into one hand while the falconer removed the rufter from the second bird's head. Edward rolled his shoulders, took several deep breaths, then extended his hand. As the goshawk hopped to his glove, it surveyed the area with its dark-rimmed, golden eyes. A moment later, Edward lifted his arm, sending the bird into flight. With powerful strokes of its wings, the falcon circled the meadow, caught an updraft, and soared ever higher with a familiar scree.

"Lord Edward, your paternal grandfather, God rest his soul, also believed force was the answer to resolving disputes with those who challenged him. It cost him his crown. And despite his efforts, to this day, the Scots still rebel."

The dogs sniffed and crashed through the brambles and meadow grasses, while the goshawk circled high above. A covey of pheasants took flight and the hawk tucked its wings and dove as swift as a longbow's arrow. Talons outstretched the bird struck, and both pheasant and hawk tumbled into the field grass.

"A perfect strike, my lord," the falconer said.

"Thanks to expert training." Turning to Elizabeth, he said, "*Grandpère* dispatched troops against his own nobles. My father does not use such tactics. He works with Parliament to find a peaceful solution to internal conflict."

"So, it may be, but—"

"Philippe spurs the Scots to act against their sovereign. What manner of monarch encourages another king's subjects to rise against him? A man with no honour, no integrity. *Un faux*. Make no mistake, my father is the veritable king, not the Valois dog."

Elizabeth glanced from the fallen birds to Edward, a crease between her eyes and her lips pressed together.

"England's safety depends on defeating Philippe."

Elizabeth shifted her gaze to the falconer's lad striding through the field to the goshawk and its fallen prey. The lad extended his arm and the bird hopped onto his glove, taking the offered reward. With his other hand, he grabbed the dead pheasant and raised it aloft.

January 1345 – Westminster

King Edward summoned his advisors to his privy chamber. A lad laid another log on the fire, sending sparks flying, then scurried out. Sir Hugh Neville, waiting for Derby, Northampton, and King Edward to settle, ran a shaky hand through his thinning hair. The king's diplomatic emissary displayed signs of unease.

King Edward sent Neville and Offord to Avignon in the autumn as his delegates to Pope Clement's peace convocation, the pontiff's attempt to resolve issues regarding the terms of the Truce of Malestroit. Neville returned recently while Offord remained in France. Two years had passed since the Breton hostilities ended, yet the French continued to stall, hesitating to sign the official treaty confirming the terms of the truce.

King Edward said, "Let us begin."

"My lords, let me speak plainly," Neville said. "Most regrettably, the negotiations have come to a standstill. The French are no closer to signing the treaty than when the most recent negotiations began."

Though Neville's report annoyed him, the king tempered his words. "In May, Derby, was received cordially by Pope Clement and met privately with him on several occasions. Perhaps my cousin's elevated stature might prove more persuasive, given the circumstances.

The terms of the truce ceded close to half the Breton duchy to King Edward, but more importantly, it freed him from owing homage to Philippe for the Duchy of Aquitaine. Those French dogs were still stringing him along. His patience was near its end.

"The French are entrenched in their position," Neville said. "With all due respect, I do not believe further diplomacy is likely to accomplish anything."

"It is true Pope Clement afforded me cordial audiences in the past," Derby said, "but too many churchmen in Avignon are biased in France's favour."

The Earl of Northampton muttered one word. "True."

"The longer this truce lasts, Lord King," Derby said, "the more time Philippe has to pressure your Gascon nobles and offer lucrative inducements to sever their loyalty to you."

"Derby is right," Northampton said. "Each passing day weakens our positions in Brittany, Gascony, *and* Flanders."

Parliament made the king promise to exhaust all peaceful means. The king laid his palms on the table. "*Messieurs*, I am grateful to you for speaking your minds. Do I understand rightly you oppose sending another delegation?"

Heads nodded.

"Then it is time to consider other options."

Inwardly, the king rejoiced. He met Parliament's dictate. Now, with the subsidy they granted, he was free to settle the conflict on the battlefield.

A few weeks into February, King Edward sipped ale in his chamber while Derby and Northampton faced off over a game of chess. A rap sounded on the door.

"Come." His chamberlain entered and bowed.

"Your pardon, Lord King. Bishop John Offord requests an audience."

"Offord? Here?"

Derby looked up from the chessboard. "I thought he was in Avignon."

The king set his cup aside. "Send him in."

The bishop entered, walking with difficulty, and with a face wreathed with concern. The cleric dabbed at his perspiring brow, despite London suffering a bitter cold. He kneeled stiffly. "Pardon my intrusion, sire."

The king waved him to his feet. "We thought you in Avignon."

"Yes, yes…well, I beg your forgiveness most humbly, Lord, for I fled Avignon, er…without Pope Clement's leave."

"You did what?" King Edward stood.

"The French are outraged at the extent of the Breton lands ceded to you at Malestroit. Their manner was so hostile, I feared for my life." The bishop wrung his hands. "It is with regret I tell you the French refuse to ratify the treaty."

"Those knaves! For two years they have dragged their feet and for the last nine months they led me to believe they would sign. Now this." King Edward slammed his hand on the table, turned and stalked to the window. "You may leave us."

In truth, he understood the French position; the truce favoured King Edward, granting him great swaths of Brittany. He was not about to give them up, nor was he backing down from his claim to the French throne.

One morning not long after Offord's return, the king broke his fast in his chamber with Derby. He handed his cousin a dispatch received the previous day and sat back, waiting for Derby's reaction.

His cousin skimmed the parchment, then raised disbelieving eyes. "Philippe dared confiscate Aquitaine? Your duchy?"

"Indeed, invading in force—a direct violation of the truce."

"Philippe ventures this at the same time as Pope Clement sent delegates here to appeal for peace?" Derby threw up his hands. "These churchmen are naught but spies!"

Throughout the Spring, hostilities worsened. King Philippe's raids penetrated deeper into Gascon lands, claiming ever more territory. In England, citizens' fervour grew, resentment rumbled like a brewing storm. A war with France was now viewed as inevitable, prompting nobles of military age to volunteer for service.

One afternoon, while King Edward reviewed petitions in his privy chamber and dictated judgements to Offord, a knock sounded on the outer door. With the king's nod, Offord went to determine the cause of the interruption but returned in quick moments. Surprise showed on his secretary's face.

"Sire, Brittany's Count seeks an audience and awaits in the outer chamber."

King Edward paused from scratching his signature on a parchment. "John de Montfort? Here?"

Offord nodded.

King Edward laid down his quill. "Send him in, then leave us, but have someone fetch refreshments."

Muted voices sounded from the outer chamber and boot heels rapped closer. The inner chamber door opened. Offord bowed."Lord de Montfort, sire."

"My liege," de Montfort said, lowering to one knee. The Breton's face told the story: hollow-cheeked and pale, with worry lines webbing his brow.

The king stood. "God's blood! What are you doing here?"

De Montfort rose unsteadily. "It is with utmost regret I seek your shore." The man's exhaustion spoke volumes. "My meager forces could hold out against Blois no longer. I come to beg your aid yet again."

"You look done in. Sit before you fall."

De Montfort wobbled to a bench and dropped onto it. He closed his eyes and let out a deep breath. "Thank you."

A soft rap and the door opened. His steward ushered in a lad with refreshments. King Edward rested across the table from de Montfort. He motioned the lad to set out the platter and pour wine.

De Montfort accepted a cup. "Lord, I am a proud man. I must regain my lands."

The king was not unmoved by the Count's plight. "Eat, drink and tell me all."

Not long after de Montfort's arrival, another exile landed in London seeking refuge. Though quite unexpected, King Edward welcomed Godfrey de Harcourt. The Norman Vicomte pledged him liege homage. Word of the Norman's defection would reach his French contemporaries, further undermining Philippe's authority.

De Montfort and the Norman Vicomte held influence and possessed military experience. King Edward would not hesitate to use both men to his advantage.

Late one evening, King Edward entered his wife's apartment and dismissed her maid. A lone candle fluttered on a bedside chest in Philippa's inner bedchamber. Behind the half-drawn bed curtains, Philippa rested against the bolsters. Her unbraided hair flowed over her shoulders, dark against her ivory nightdress. A coy smile played on his wife's lips, and her eyes danced.

"Husband." She patted the bed beside her.

"*Ma belle femme*," he whispered, slipping into her enticing and addictive warmth.

Philippa stroked teasing fingers along his forearm, raising his flesh. "Sleep eludes you?"

"You noticed." He rested against the bolster beside her, laid an arm across her shoulders, and settled her head into the crook of his neck.

His wife stilled her hand. "Ahh, you wish to speak with me?" She smoothed the quilt over her thighs.

"*Oui*." The king's heart paired a steady rhythm with hers, and they breathed as one. What he was about to say would likely disquiet his wife. "It is about Edward."

Philippa twisted to look at him, her brows arching over smokey eyes. "What about Edward?"

"Do not be alarmed." He tucked her back against his heart. "Our son is fine."

"What then?"

He waited until she eased. "You and I have discussed my intention to renounce the truce, yes?" He waited for her nod. "While Derby sails to Gascony, Northampton and I depart for France with troops, under my personal command as Parliament decreed." He rested his chin atop her head. "Edward is to accompany me."

Philippa stiffened.

"Lionel will act as Guardian, with you and the Earl of Lancaster as Council."

Philippa sat up. Alarm scribed her face. "My lord, Edward is but fifteen. You would not chance your heir in battle at such a tender age?"

"*Non.*" He shook his head. "Our son is young for the battlefield, though what Edward believes…." He tugged Philippa against him again. "My heir considers himself a man. He serves as one of my advisors and has proven his skill at arms at any number of tournaments this past year.

Conflicting emotions flickered like candlelight across Philippa's face.

"I believe our son begins to chafe. One day he will rule. Should we not prepare him in every way and who better to learn from than his sire?"

His wife yielded into his enfolding arms but not wholly. Would she understand his reasoning, or would her motherly instincts to protect her son prevail? He waited.

She sighed. "Tell me your mind."

The harbour brimmed with ships, men shouting and hauling cargo. Aboard his flagship, King Edward signed the last document in the stack and handed them to his scribe. "The Chancellor is to review those straight away."

"Very well, sire." The young man dipped a bow.

As he was leaving the cabin, a courier arrived with a worn leather pouch.

"Here, give it to me." King Edward strode to the other end of the long table where his son studied an unfurled map weighted at the corners.

"Edward, if you are to aid me, a working knowledge of the territory is essential." King Edward retrieved the letter from the pouch and read it. He stared straight ahead, letting the parchment drop onto the table.

Edward looked up.

"A change of plans.""We must postpone our sailing. The situation in Flanders has changed." Though his heir was learning, would he grasp the political significance? "Count Louis of Nevers returned to Flanders from his exile in Paris." He paced a few steps. "The Count is attempting to lure his people back to his affinity. It appears his efforts are bearing some success." King Edward rubbed the back of his neck. "This, I cannot allow. Flanders must remain loyal to me."

Edward fingered the edges of the map. "Why? Does the Count's return pose a threat to our wool trade?"

"That is true, but not the main issue. With Flanders loyal to me, Philippe's eastern border provinces are subject to attack."

"Ah, I think I understand." Edward re-rolled the map. "The threat on Philippe's eastern territories forces him to divide his troops, some to guard his eastern provinces and others to guard his lands bordering Gascony and Brittany."

King Edward smiled. "*Exactement.*"

Edward sipped wine in the Painted Chamber, enjoying his father's reception of Pope Clement's emissary, Archbishop Canali. The king sat upon a small dais and he kept Canali standing in front of him.

"Most gracious King, it is my duty to remind you Malestroit's truce does not expire for another nine months."

"Remind me?" King Edward shouted, tapping his chest. "Philippe, the pretender, needs reminding, not me!"

Canali flinched. "But—"

"In June, I sent formal notification renouncing the agreement and if His Eminence mistook its meaning, let me make myself perfectly clear here and now."

Canali squirmed at the king's sharp rebuke.

Edward hid a grin.

"I am the rightful king of France, not that Valois pretender." He heaved a breath. "Brittany belongs to me, as does Gascony. By all that is holy, I will defend my rights, my lands, and I will not hesitate to do so by force of arms!"

King Edward stood, turned his back on Canali, and walked away.

"Lord King," Canali called in his most deferential tone. "His Holy Eminence seeks peace and I am here on his behalf. May I ask you to state a date and place at which negotiations might resume?"

The king spun like an enraged bear. "Resume? Resume? Of all the—" Red-faced, the king threw up his hands. "You can tell him this from me…after I defeat France's faux King Philippe, should the Pope send a delegation to me then, I might be gracious enough to receive them."

The archbishop looked about to burst, choking off whatever he might have said. His face flushed a light purple as he stood wringing his hands.

The king jabbed his arm toward the door. "Get out, Canali. Get out of my sight right now before I have you thrown out!"

The archbishop scurried from the room, tapping a hasty retreat.

Edward continued to sip while the tension in the chamber eased. Whether sent by the Pope or not, Canali should have known England's king was in no mood to hear the archbishop prattle on about peace. Not when France temporized and delayed approving the formal treaty for years while continually violating the truce and the French Parlement reneged on signing the treaty altogether.

As the envoy's footsteps faded to silence, King Edward returned to the dais and picked up his cup. He rolled a sip of wine over his tongue, and waggled his brows.

"You are amused, sire?"

"*Oui*. The look on that oily cleric's face." His father raised his cup in salute and chuckled.

"With all due respect, *mon père*, I ask you, what happens now? You called off our summer campaign to repair relations with Flanders. Our cousin Derby remains in Gascony, Northampton in Brittany, and Parliament refuses the ships necessary to replenish either force. "So, what now?"

He was keen to know the answer, for he had missed the opportunity to campaign with his father in Brittany. While he waited for an answer, he toyed with the ruby signet ring on his little finger.

"Now?" The king lowered his cup. "We proceed, of course. The French believe they can dishonour the Malestroit truce without repercussions. I have no intention of allowing them to do so. Though I postponed last summer's campaign, nothing has changed, save for its timing."

Edward straightened. "Do you mean it? Truly?" He did not intend to be left behind this time. He was proficient at arms and almost sixteen. "Are you to go to France?"

King Edward put down his cup. "Derby's campaign recovered most of the territory Philippe confiscated and I have extended his command. With the sad death of his esteemed father, the Lancaster title and wealth pass to Derby. He now has the means to fund the campaign."

Edward nodded. "Yes, I was sorry to learn of his father's death and Derby's success in Gascony is well known." Edward admitted he envied Derby, and his success

"Over the winter, our cousin is to continue his raids on Philippe's southern lands. Northampton is to secure our holdings in Brittany and seek a port closer to our southern harbours than Brest or Vannes."

Edward's question remained unanswered, so he probed again. "Even should you wish to invade, sire, *our* fleet has been disbanded."

The king shook his head, a wry smirk on his face. "*Non*, the ships were not released, only licensed to trade until February. I will recall them and come March, *mon fils*, we sail."

Edward's grin spread ear to ear. His father said '*we*'.

Once And For All

12 July 1346 ~ Sainte Vaast La Hougue, Normandy

Edward balanced in the ship's forecastle, his back against the rail with his arms outstretched staring north into the inky darkness. The *Thomas'* wake snaked a glowing white under the waning moon.

Throughout the long months of the fleet's preparation and assembly, Edward's anticipation grew. When raging storms forced the ships to shelter in port for two weeks before finally putting to sea, he cursed in frustration.

Grey seamed the eastern horizon, distinguishing the charcoal-colored sky from the black depths of the sea. Ships of all shapes and sizes stretched behind the *Thomas*. Hundreds of billowing white sails dotted the swells as far north as he could see.

Before long, seabirds dipped and squawked above them, signalling land ahead. Edward faced fore; his future beckoned.

A lemon hue lit the shoreline of the small, horseshoe-shaped bay of Saint Vaast La Hougue. Several jagged rock formations jutted above the waterline and a squadron of French ships, with their hulls aground, lined the western shore.

Sails lowered and the *Thomas* slowed.

Boots scuffed the ladder behind him. Chandos stepped alongside and nodded toward the western shoreline. "Perhaps the French anticipated our landing."

"I count fourteen," Edward said, "and half are fitted with fighting castles. Do you see any defenders?"

Chandos searched the shore. "None that I can see."

Edward frowned. "What fool leaves his ships unguarded?"

Three flat-bottom cogs, flying the Earl of Warwick's colours, slid into the cove while the king's flagship, *George*, with England's royal arms fluttering atop its mast, hove to in the safety of the deeper waters outside the bay.

Warwick's three cogs drew closer to shore, slipping into the shallows. Welsh archers manned the shore-facing rails as ten score men-at-arms slithered over the sides of the ships into the waist-deep water. They waded toward shore covered by the archers with bows at the ready. If the French were near, they would attack now when the soldiers were most vulnerable.

Edward gripped the rail.

Warwick led in his surcoat of gold crosses on a field of red. He signalled Godfrey de Harcourt, his second in command, and the Norman led his men left while Warwick motioned his to the right. Half of the bowman remained alert on deck while others streamed to shore, bows aloft, to help secure the beach.

Without taking his eyes off the shore, Edward said, "If the French were warned of our intended landing, they would not have left their ships undefended."

"Agreed," Chandos said. "I wonder what brought them here and what took them inland."

Edward scanned the tangled thicket beyond the beach. "Whatever it was, I doubt they have gone far."

The Earl's men ferried pitch and hot coals to shore and within minutes, smoke curled up from the French ships. Thick plumes spiralled skyward and flames crackled up the riggings.

"For England!" Warwick's men shouted.

A shriek pierced the cheers.

Edward's pulse notched up. The French had not gone far.

Warwick's archers fired a flurry of arrows into the thicket

beyond the beach while his men scrambled for cover. The wounded man was dragged to safety by two others, leaving a trail of blood in the sand.

Edward winced at the crossbow bolt jutting from the man's thigh. Silently, he urged the men to hasten.

Warwick raised his sword, and more arrows flew into the thicket. "Forward!" His force charged and disappeared into the tangled brush. The odour of burning pitch wafted over the bay as oiled canvas went up in flames. The distant sounds of weapons clashing and men screaming carried across the water. Edward's stomach churned.

Chandos laid a hand on his shoulder. "It is not uncommon to feel a small sickness, Lord Edward. This is no tournament."

King Edward paced the deck of his flagship, listening and scanning the shoreline for movement. Save for Warwick's cogs, the fleet remained in deep water.

In the time since the Earl and his men vanished, the sun crested the horizon fully. How did the French come to be in this harbour? Did Philippe's spies somehow unearth the English fleet's destination and landing location? Where were Warwick and his men? What was happening?

The rattle of weapons and English voices drifted across the bay before the men emerged from the brush. King Edward's eyes flew to Warwick's red-stained surcoat.

The Earl waved the all-clear.

Relieved, the king took a deep breath. "Captain, take us in."

Once the anchor was set, King Edward climbed from the *George* into a lowered longboat and oarsmen rowed him to shore. Meanwhile, several more English ships anchored in the shallows and dispatched forces to shore to secure a larger beachhead.

When the longboat scraped bottom, the king's guard hopped

out and dragged the craft from the shallows onto the sand. Warwick and de Harcourt hastened toward him.

"A skirmish, sire, nothing more," the Earl said. "The French saw they were outnumbered and fled."

"Perhaps four or five score, no more," de Harcourt added. "Too few to repulse us."

King Edward stepped from the boat and gestured to Warwick's bloodied garment. "What of our men…and you?"

The Earl grinned. "Not mine."

King Edward nodded. "*Bon.* Any losses?"

Warwick shook his head. "None. Only a few injured who need tending."

"*D'accord.*" The king said to de Harcourt, "Did you get a good look at them? Recognize anyone?"

"Indeed, sire, Robert Bertrand leads them. His family holds high favour with the Valois pretender. Bertrand's brother is Bishop of Bayeux."

When de Harcourt first sought refuge in England, he named Bertrand as the cause for his exile. "Robert Bertrand is an old adversary of yours, is he not?"

"Your memory serves you well, sire."

Warwick raised a brow to the Norman. "A score to settle?"

A bitter expression etched de Harcourt's face, as if swilling wine gone to seed. "It is no secret I am eager to meet Bertrand again, this time with a force at my back."

"Not without my leave," King Edward warned.

De Harcourt blanched. "As you command, sire, I meant no disrespect."

"Normandy is rightfully mine and I would have these Norman lords swear homage to me. Despoiling these lands is forbidden. Warwick, what say you? Was Bertrand warned of our landing?"

The Earl shook his head. "No. We surprised him. Although once he gathers his wits, he will send word to Philippe and seek local reinforcements."

"He is cunning, that one," de Harcourt said. "As former Marshal of France, Bertrand does not lack military experience.”

Warwick spat. “I sent men to intercept his couriers.”

“*Bon.*” King Edward studied the small bay. “De Harcourt, send orders for the ships to use the entire length of the shoreline to speed the offloading, then find my undermarshal and have him summon Northampton and my son.”

“Warwick, with me.” King Edward headed toward the north end of the cove and trudged to the top of the dunes. The king shielded his eyes and scanned the coastline. English ships bobbed its entire length northward, their masts like a floating forest. Transporting an army of fifteen thousand was no small feat.

The Norman Vicomte caught up with them. Breathless, he pointed west. “See, there, La Pernelle and Quettehou.” Then, he pointed north.“You see those distant masts? That is Barfleur.”

King Edward smiled. “Only a handful of warships. *C'est jolie.*” He had taken great pains to ensure the secrecy of this landing place. Not until the ships were at sea did his captains break the seals on their orders to reveal their destination. So few French warships meant his ruses succeeded.

“Lord King!” His son called as he scrambled up the dune. “Is it not wondrous no enemy force harries our landing?”

The king narrowed his eyes. “I take it, Edward, you are no longer angry with me for keeping our landing a secret from all, including you?”

His son blanched but did not look away. “I admit my ire was misplaced, sire.”

“Do not question me again. I am no novice at war.”

Warwick broke the tension. “Indeed not, lord king. Leaking rumours to King Philippe’s spies paid off.” Warwick grinned. “I wonder what King Philippe made of your intention to unite with Lancaster in Gascony? Or what he thought when he learned of Hugh Hastings’ forces landing in Flanders. His head must have spun.”

“Whatever his reaction, let us wield our advantage. On the morrow, you march to Barfleur and make certain the port is no longer a friend to French ships.”

"As you wish, sire."

King Edward pointed west, toward the town on a rise. "There. Quettehou is it? That will serve as our base." He started back down the dune.

"*Mon père*." Edward caught up. "Begging your pardon, sire. I-I was wrong to act the way I did when you refused to reveal our destination. If King Philippe had learned of it, well, your prudence saved the lives of many."

"Indeed." His son's admission demonstrated a growing maturity. "By the time we are done here, we will have need of every one of them."

Later in the morning, from atop a marram-riddled dune, Edward observed the crews unloading cargo. Wooden panels, axles, and wheels were hauled to shore where workmen assisted wheelwrights and carters to reassemble the wagons.

Pigs, sheep and calves lowed and bleated as the herders drove them into make-shift pens, while fowl squawked from dozens of crates. "Soldiers require more than swords, shields, staves and arrows," his father had explained. "They must be fed, and food-stuffs will be hidden when word spreads of our army's approach."

Ear-piercing whinnies burst from the beach. The first horses unloaded from the ships splashed out of the shingle, folded onto the sun-baked sand, rolled, and grunted. Then, abruptly, shifted onto their haunches, extended forelegs, and heaved upright.

The stockmen had erected barriers along the beach and set grooms as guards. More horses trotted from the shallows, joining the others. The herd pounded through the sand, slid, wheeled as one, and raced back again. Shrill whinnies resonated across the water. It would take days for the horses to recover after two weeks of confinement. Many would sicken and die; Edward hoped his destrier would not be one of them.

Late in the afternoon, he made his way to Quettehou. A temporary lodging had been established for him and his squire and page
laid out his best garments, including his gleaming kit. They helped
him prepare for the evening's ceremony and when he was ready, he
joined the king's entourage outside the Church of St. Vigor.

"Lord Edward, it is with great pleasure I witness your knighting
today," Chandos said.

"Any mastery I possess is due to your training, John." Through
a throat tight with emotion, he continued, "Not to mention your
goading when I was wont to ease off." He grinned. "I owe you a
great debt."

A smile played on the knight's lips. "You owe me nothing,
lord. It has been my honour."

A steady flow of knights, surcoats ablaze with their colors, hastened toward the church. Glistening metal plate, mail, and weapons
rattled. Roger and Will paused briefly to voice greetings before the
ceremony. Both would be knighted with him.

Chandos tapped Edward's arm. "Begging your pardon, my
lord, the king bade me to speak with him prior to the ceremony. I
shall see you inside."

Edward strolled over to de Harcourt and Warwick, conversing at the arched portal with the Earl of Arundel. Warwick had
exchanged his bloodstained garment for a clean one. Quite un-
commonly, the Earl's unruly mass of dark hair was dampened and
combed neatly into place. Edward hid a grin.

"Lord Edward." The veteran campaigner's face bore a perma-
nent crease between his brows, and lines webbed the corners of his
eyes.

De Harcourt turned and bowed. "Lord." The red and gold
stripes of the Vicomte's surcoat stretched tight across his broad
shoulders. The Vicomte served in the vanguard, second in command
to Warwick.

"*Messieurs*," Edward greeted.

"I was just explaining," de Harcourt said, "about my brother
and me roaming this area as boys. This church, did you know, was

named for a hermit who preached here centuries ago?"

"The lands of your seigneury are where, lord?" Edward asked.

"Sainte Sauveur lies ten miles southwest."

Curious, Edward probed. "You must long to see your home again. My father mentioned a falling out with Bertrand drove you to Brabant, and from there to England."

De Harcourt stiffened. "I make no secret of my hostility toward Bertrand. His estate of Bricquebec lies not far from here."

Arundel broke in, "The ceremony looks to begin."

Edward caught a glance from Warwick, perhaps a warning to leave off pricking the Norman's festering wound?

The dark wood interior of the church flickered with candlelight. All eyes focused on the tall, tawny-haired king posed before the altar in a surcoat proclaiming his right to France's throne—England's golden leopards on a crimson field quartered with France's fleur-de-lis on azure.

Edward's tunic displayed the same device with the addition of a horizontal white stripe with three vertical bars across his chest, marking him as eldest son. His fellow initiates—Montagu, Ros, de la Warre, de la Bere, and Mortimer — stood shoulder to shoulder in the transept. As Edward joined them, Roger winked.

The Bishop of Durham stepped forward; the assembly fell silent.

"*In nomine patris, et filii, et spiritus sancti,*" the bishop began. Thomas Hatfield was not only the Bishop of Durham, he was in joint command of the rear guard with Arundel. As the bishop continued the prayer, he passed his hand over Edward's scabbard, sword, and spurs laid out on the altar.

Edward stepped forward. His chest tightened and his legs trembled. He hoped no one noticed. The king picked up Edward's sword and gem-encrusted scabbard and secured them around Edward's hips. The Earl of Warwick took up Edward's golden spurs and knelt to buckle them in place, then rose and backed away.

Edward drew his sword, held it before him, and knelt. When the king placed his hand on Edward's head, a tingling raised the hairs on his arms. All his life, Edward dreamed of this moment.

O Merciful Lord, bestow your blessing upon me, a warrior of your creed, that I may deign to serve you and protect your servants against all evil according to your holy will. In the name of Father, the Son and the Holy Ghost. Amen.

The king tapped Edward's shoulder. "Rise, Sir Knight."

"Sir Edward!" The cheer reverberated in the modest space.

Edward rose, and the king embraced him. "Sir Edward," his father whispered into Edward's ear, raising gooseflesh.

Beaming, and numb, Edward backed away. Silently, he prayed for courage and the strength of character to uphold his vow, not only to God but to his king and his duty to safeguard England and its people.

Montagu stepped into place, and one-by-one by the ritual was repeated.

The knighting finished, the king beckoned Edward to stand beside him for the remainder of the formalities.

De Harcourt hobbled from the ranks, his slight limp more noticeable after the day's labour. He knelt before the king and in a voice loud and clear, the once highly-placed Norman formally pledged fealty to England's king, France's rightful monarch. He rose and stepped back as men brought England's furled standard forward to stand beside the king.

A hush descended.

King Edward raised his hand, and with a flourish pulled the cord. The banner unfurled.

"For England!

"For King Edward!"

The invasion officially began.

The next morning, as they prepared to march, Edward's gut twisted relentlessly while he wound through the ranks of soldiers breaking camp. His father honoured him with command of the vanguard, but he lacked any actual battle experience, let alone leadership. Thankfully, he shared the command with the Earl of Warwick, one of the army's most tested battle veterans.

Horses stamped and snorted while being saddled and packs were loaded. Edward's squire handed him his helm and gloves as he waited for his horse to be brought around. Edward adjusted his scabbard, stuck his foot in the stirrup, and swung his leg over. "Mount up!" Edward called. All down the line, saddle leather creaked.

Thomas Ughtred trotted up and reined in beside Edward. "All is ready, lord." From this day forward, Edward would rely on this seasoned campaigner assigned as the vanguard's undermarshal.

The Earl of Northampton, the army's Marshal, headed the vanguard column this morning and Edward urged his horse forward to ride beside him. Northampton held authority over all three of the army's divisions, and personally commanded the main body, the middle division responsible for safeguarding the king.

Edward remembered as a boy huddling with others, listening to the knights' stories of Northampton's victories. During this campaign, Edward would learn the ways of war, and he could have no better tutors than Northampton and Warwick.

At the Constable's nod, Edward motioned and shouted, "Move out!"

The horses jostled each other for position in the column, then settled into a steady pace. Edward said, "I understand Warwick and his retinues ride the coast today."

Northampton nodded. "They do, while Huntingdon's fleet shadows them just off-shore."

"Is the Admiral's purpose to protect Warwick's flank should

the French attempt to land a defensive force?”

Northampton nodded again. “Exactly.”

In the distance, dust rose from the track where the vanguard’s outriders scouted the English army’s advance. Fifteen thousand strong, the army marched southwest in seemingly endless ranks of mounted men-at-arms, foot soldiers, and archers. The supply wagons and herds of spare horses and livestock followed, the rear guard commanded by the Earl of Arundel. The dust stirred up by the troops could be seen for miles.

Normandy’s unfamiliar terrain unfolded before Edward. To the East, tangled scrub and marram yielded to the peninsula’s sandy shore and the bay beyond shimmered orange with the rising sun. To the West, verdant fields gave way to granite outcroppings rising up to merge with the grey-shadowed skyline. The army marched a diagonal route southwest from the coast into the heart of the Cotentin peninsula.

“Lord Edward,” Northampton broke into his thoughts. “What do you make of the way ahead?”

Edward studied the narrow track. Lined on both sides with ferns and shrubs, it cut through a dense wood.

Northampton inclined his head. “Prime for an ambush, perhaps?”

Edward took the earl’s meaning, halted the column, and called for his under-marshal.“Choose eight men with good eyesight and even better instincts,” Edward said. “Send them to scout the wood. Have them report back in relays.”

Northampton, his hands resting on his pommel, nodded approval while a slight smile played upon his lips.

Ughtred called out names and issued the orders. The riders split up, four to the right and four to the left and jogged off through the trees.

Fueled by inexperience, Edward’s doubts marched in time with the infantry’s boots. France’s bounty beckoned, as did the prize his father sought—France’s crown. Yet, an arduous journey lay ahead of them before victory was won. Edward’s first task, no small one, was to earn his men's respect.

They encountered no resistance throughout the day, easing Edward's apprehension.

The sun slid behind the western ridge as the vanguard crossed a small river and rode into Valognes. The unwalled town appeared prosperous with several mills lining the stream and, from the odor, a tannery. The steeple of a modest church rose at the town's center with an enclosed priory.

"Ughtred," Edward called, "send men ahead to secure the town before my father and the main body arrive."

By the time Edward reached the village square, the most prominent townspeople, judging by their attire, were lined up in front of the church portal. He reined his horse aside to await his father's entourage. Pennons flying, the king and his guard advanced toward the churchyard. The people sank to their knees and lowered their heads.

A heavyset, grey-haired man with sagging jowls raised his eyes. "Lord King, we surrender ourselves to you. Most humbly, we plead for mercy."

"Good Norman citizens, you do me honour." The king spoke with a voice that could be heard across the square and carry to anyone who might be hiding. "By swearing allegiance to me, your rightful sovereign, I spare your lives and property."

Edward appreciated his father's prudence; he rewarded his Norman subjects' acquiescence rather than force acceptance through bloodshed.

That evening, Edward supped with his father at his temporary headquarters, a commandeered manor house owned by Duke Jean, King Philippe's heir. He would be little pleased that King Philippe's rival made use of it. While Edward and his father dined, the scent of smoke filtered into the residence. The king sniffed with a puzzled expression, then rose and strode out to the courtyard. Edward followed.

Several smoke plumes, dark against the sky, swirled in the distance. His father stiffened; a vein in his jaw pulsed. "Find my deputy constable, Edward." His father spun back toward the manor. "And have my commanders summoned, now!"

Edward conveyed his father's order, then waited outside until Northampton and the others arrived. When all were assembled, the king stalked into the hall.

"What is this nonsense?" He gestured toward the door. "I gave orders…no looting, nor properties fired. God's blood! There is little reason in destroying what is mine." He glared at them. "Do I make myself clear?"

In a calming voice, Arundel replied, "Sire, there is only so much we can do. Our knights heed our command but the foot-soldiers—"

"Soldiers are motivated by plunder," de Harcourt broke in. "With all due respect, sire, the lure of riches is why men go to war."

"Enough!" King Edward glared at the Norman. "This must stop and I rely on all of you to see that it does." He turned and marched from the room.

Edward exchanged sympathetic glances with the chastised commanders. In truth, there was little any of them, including his father, could do to halt soldiers who viewed the spoils of war as their right.

At dawn the following morning, Edward mingled among his men as they readied to march. All appeared rested and well-fed from the town's stores. In the distance, despite the king's order and threats of punishment, men seeking plunder swarmed like ants over the farmsteads. Retribution was sure to follow.

De Harcourt's banner fluttered above a nearby column. As Edward strode over, the Norman vaulted into his saddle

"Lord Edward." The Vicomte tipped his head.

"Do you ride with the vanguard today?" Edward asked.

"No, lord. I am ordered southwest to guard the western approach to the river crossing near Carentan."

Edward nodded and waved a hand. "Go with God."

Like de Harcourt, Edward's force would leave the main column today. While Northampton led the main body, supply train, and rear guard along the old Roman way, Edward's retinues would gallop across-country, searching for any French force intending to thwart the English advance. Carentan, at a strategic crossing, must be seized and secured before the French mounted a strong defense. From there, the army would advance east to take Caen.

Edward's horse was brought around and Chandos reined in beside him. Edward stepped up into his saddle and called, "Mount up!"

The vanguard advanced across a dawn-rippled plain of fields of golden wheat and barley. The land was dotted with occasional clusters of cottages, vegetable plots, and pastures with long-legged, red-brindled calves lazing under the trees. All afternoon, the vanguard paralleled a meagre stream flowing southeast from the higher land to their west.

Chandos tilted his head toward the runnel. "De Harcourt mentioned a river called La Douve. Do you suppose that is it?"

"Not much of a river," Edward said. "Flat-bottomed and as languid as a moat." He slipped his feet from his stirrups and rotated his stiff ankles. "We have met little resistance since landing."

"We will not march unopposed for long. Bertrand is mustering troops somewhere.

By late afternoon, the riders Edward sent to scout the army's rendezvous point at Sainte-Côme-du-Mont returned, reporting the town deserted, and no signs of the French. Then they rode out again.

When Edward and his retinues reached the outskirts of town, he called, "Ughtred, post sentries and hold the division here until I return. The men may dismount, but stand ready."

Edward proceeded into town with Chandos and his guard, riding to the southern end and halting on a small rise. From there, the land sloped down steeply to a vast marsh where three ribbons of water joined.

"There. Our scouts." Chandos pointed to movement in the distance below them.

For several minutes they watched, then rejoined Ughtred and the vanguard. The sun dipped below the western plateau when

Northampton rode in at the head of the main body. He ordered all three divisions, supply wagons and herds, to set up camp on the outskirts of town. The Earl and the king, surrounded by his guard, proceeded to the central square where they commandeered the largest home to serve as the king's command. At twilight, Warwick and his retinues marched in from the coast.

Edward settled into a deserted house in the village and when his scouts returned their report set his gut to roiling. In responding to the king's summons, he arrived early and was admitted by his father's steward.

"Sire." Edward bowed and waited for the steward to leave.

"You are early," his father said, sipping from a mug of ale.

"I thought it prudent to share my scouts' discovery before the others arrive."

"Sit then, and tell me."

As Edward did, a dark expression clouded his father's face. Not long after, Warwick tramped into the chamber.

"God's blessings, my lords." Covered with dust, he offered a bow, then joined Edward and the king at the table.

"Help yourself," the king said. "It has been a long day."

The Earl poured himself a cup of ale, gulped it down, then poured another.

One by one, the other commanders filed in, found seats and handed ale around. The chamber overflowed with banter and the rising stench of sweat, leather, and horses.

The king caught Warwick's eye. "Begin, *mon ami*."

The Earl wiped his mouth with his sleeve and leaned forward, elbows on the table. "We saw no signs of the French along the coast. The townspeople of Ravenoville and Montebourg surrendered willingly enough, after which we loaded Huntingdon's ships with the bounty we collected." Warwick picked up his cup and sipped. "The holds are packed so full with plunder; it is hard to imagine the vessels staying afloat."

"*D'accord*." King Edward nodded. "Let me add, de Harcourt sent a dispatch and reports no sightings of the French." The king's face hardened and Edward steeled himself for what was coming.

"My son reports much the same, however, he advises me the bridge between here and Carentan was destroyed."

"Bertrand would have reckoned our route," Northampton said, "and breaking the bridge is one way to delay us. No surprise there."

"True, and he has several days lead on us." The king rubbed his nose. "Edward, tell them the rest."

Edward's heart ticked faster. "About three miles south of us, two rivers join with *La Douve*. The channel is wide with steep banks and beyond the channel, the land flattens into a large marsh. Though my scouts searched, they found no way around it. The bridge connects to a raised levée winding through the wetlands to Carentan about a mile beyond that point."

"And the town?" The Earl of Oxford, Northampton's second in command, asked.

"Walled," Warwick said, "according to what de Harcourt told me. A market town with strong defenses and a fortified keep."

"Did the Vicomte offer a guess at the number of defenders?" Oxford asked.

Warwick shook his head. "None I recall."

"The number is of little consequence," King Edward said. "Set the carpenters to work through the night to rebuild the bridge. Those defending Carentan will not expect that, nor our attack at dawn."

July 1346 - Carentan

The next morning, in the home of a local merchant, Edward lay working the sleep from his brain as his eyes adjusted to the shades of dark painting the chamber. A scuff sounded and wavering candlelight flickered through the door left ajar. He threw off the linen covering, swung his legs over and rose as his page entered the room.

"Good morning, my lord." Simon placed the candle and a tankard of ale on the chest.

"Fetch Hal with my mail."

Edward's hands trembled as he tightened the ties on his hose after relieving himself and waved away Simon's offer of bread and cheese. Facing his first real assault, he had no stomach for food.

Hal entered and helped him don his gambeson and after snugging its ties, lowered Edward's mail into place, and layered a clean surcoat overtop. Edward ran his still-shaking fingers over the embroidered silk threads marking him as heir. Hal handed him his scabbard and after buckling it on, Edward grabbed his helm, and headed to the door.

In the near blackness, the eerie forms of his mounted guard emerged from the shadows. He mounted and they rode from town to the camp, greeted by the rattle of mail and weapons as the vanguard's men prepared for battle. Edward called to Ughtred, "When the men are assembled, meet me at the bridge."

"Yes, lord."

Edward wheeled his horse, signalled his guard, and they trotted off to inspect the carpenters' progress. A dawn attack would catch Carentan's defenders by surprise, but for the assault to succeed, the bridge must be completed before first light. The French were fools to believe a broken bridge would stop England's advance.

Edward trusted his stallion's night vision as he cantered down the track. In the distance, fires flickered and before long, the pounding of hammers sounded above the pounding of hooves. Sentries alerted their arrival.

Edward circled his horse and halted.

"Lord Edward!" Roger broke off a conversation with Ned Despenser and Bartholomew Burghersh, both assigned with Roger to oversee the men guarding the workmen.

"Any trouble, Sir Roger?" Edward said over the noise of the hammers.

Roger smirked. "Nothing, lord.

Several lads retrieved deadfall from the surrounding wood and kept the fires burning bright for the carpenters. Within the firelight, workmen planed hastily cut timber into planks. Apprentices hauled the boards to the carpenters nailing them onto the new bridge supports.

Distant hoofbeats and the jingle of harness signalled the vanguard's approach. When the column halted, firelight flickered upon the faces of Warwick and Ughtred. At the undermarshal's signal, a retinue of men-at-arms and equal number of archers broke off and relieved those who had guarded the area during the night.

"The men have their orders, lord," Ughtred said. "An advance party is ready to ride.

"Good. What word of de Harcourt?"

"A messenger arrived," Ughtred said. "His force will ford the Sèves at Baupte, to the southwest of Carentan, and hold position there."

"He knows the country," Warwick said. "By the time we launch our assault, he will be in position."

The hammering gradually stopped. A master carpenter grabbed a torch and closely inspected the joists underneath the planks and made certain the nail heads were pounded in properly. After the final inspection was complete and a brief conversation, lads led several horses across the span to test it. "All clear, my lords."

"Time to ride," Warwick said.

Edward reined his horse alongside the Earl and adjusted a stirrup. His hands trembled. In the next hours, he would face a real enemy, a true test of his battle skills.

"Forward!" Warwick called.

Hooves pounded across the newly-laid planks. Edward's heart drummed with the hoofbeats. Once across and on softer ground, Warwick motioned Edward closer. "In this first encounter, Lord Edward, you are to stay with your guard and follow my lead." Warwick's sober tone brooked no objection.

Edward nodded. "For now, *mon ami*." Edward would comply *this time*. Duty demanded *he lead*, not follow.

Warwick halted the column a fair distance from Carentan to prevent alerting the guard. He signalled his men to dismount and lads came forward to take the horses.

"Tread wisely, lord," the Earl murmured. "Allow my men do their jobs."

Edward accepted the caution with a nod.

At Warwick's signal, the archers crept forward until they were within longbow range. The Earl moved up and took cover within a thicket. His men-at-arms fanned out, interspersed with the archers.

Edward crouched at Warwick's side, a tight grip on his hilt. Atop Carentan's crenelated walls, torches flickered upon only a handful of helmeted heads.

Warwick raised his arm.

"Nock!" A ventenar hissed.

More enemy heads appeared above the walls, and a warning shouted.

The Earl dropped his arm.

"Loose!"

Bowstrings hummed.

Arrows soared overhead providing cover, while a dozen soldiers sprinted to the base of the walls. Grappling hooks flew upward, caught, and men began scrambling up the ropes.

Carentan's defenders hurled rocks and wielded axes cutting some of the ropes. Despite their efforts, the men-at-arms kept climbing and though the Frenchmen attacked, they were soon overwhelmed by the English assault. When Warwick's men clambered over the top, his archers cheered.

Weapons clanged, and men shrieked. Dozens more men-at-arms poured over the walls. Within minutes the sounds of battle faded, and soon after the massive oak gates swung open.

Edward turned to Warwick. "Too easy."

The corner of the Earl's lip twitched. "Did you count the number of helms atop the walls?" Then, glancing over his shoulder, he signalled.

A trumpet blared.

"For England!" The vanguard roared.

His heart in his throat, Edward lurched to his feet and surged forward alongside Warwick, past the barbicans, and through the gate. A handful of French sprinted through the central square toward the safety of the castle keep. Other than these, the town appeared deserted. Where was Bertrand? And his forces?

"With me!" Warwick and his retinue sprinted toward the castle keep. The gates were flung wide and England's colours waved from the castle walls. Hundreds of soldiers dashed through the town, shouting, and eager for plunder.

"Halt! By order of the king! No looting!" Edward shouted. "God's teeth, stop!" No one listened. Carentan had fallen but at what cost?

July 1346 – Carentan to St. Lo

That evening, King Edward gathered his commanders in the fortress hall. Though still vexed at the town's sacking, he set his ire aside and focused on the discussion. Given what occurred, what was their best course of action?

"The French captives confirmed Bertrand is in command," Northampton said. "And after some persuasion, confessed his force is not large, no more than two hundred." He brushed his tangled hair from his brow. "They claim he has withdrawn south to Saint Lo."

"As I see it," Arundel said, "we have two options. We can march south and attempt to catch Bertrand and take Saint Lo, or we advance directly east to Caen."

King Edward turned to the Norman Vicomte. "What have you to say?"

"Saint Lo sits at a crossroads between Mont Saint Michel and Coutances. Seizing it would give us control of all western Normandy."

"No small advantage," Warwick said.

"But why change our course?" Edward asked.

King Edward was pleased by the question. Despite his son's inexperience, Edward was not afraid to challenge his more seasoned mentors.

"Lord Edward makes a good point," Northampton said. "Chasing after Bertrand only delays our advance on Caen, which is likely Bertrand's aim."

Arundel rested an arm on the table. "If taking Saint Lo gains us control of the roads, why not do it?"

"Because," Northampton said, "the delay allows Caen time to mount a stronger defense."

"Trapping Bertrand would demonstrate your strength, sire," de Harcourt said, "and influence other Normans to support you."

"Indeed." King Edward stroked his beard. The capture of the man who contrived de Harcourt's downfall would undoubtedly please the Vicomte, yet, in the Norman's desire for revenge did he overstate the importance of taking Saint Lo?

"Bertrand's ransom would certainly add to our coffers," Arundel said.

Several others murmured agreement.

King Edward weighed the two courses of action. While Northampton might be correct regarding Bertrand's intention to delay their advance, if capturing Bertrand and taking Saint Lo swayed more nobles to pledge him fealty, the delay would be worth it. He rose. "We make for Saint Lo."

In the morning, Edward's retinues cantered out of Carentan on the heels of Warwick's advance force. Within minutes, they clattered over a bridge spanning the River Taute. The bridge was not broken. Was Bertrand so hard-pressed by the speed of the English advance that there was no time to destroy it? Or did Bertrand leave it standing for a reason? The hairs on the back of Edward's neck prickled. Was Northampton right? Was the Frenchman leading them a merry chase?

The track began to climb and dip, traversing a series of ridges. About two miles farther on it forked; one track leading east to Bayeux and Caen, the other south to St. Lo. Edward took the southern route. The terrain became marshy again, forcing them to ride single file. Along the way, they crossed several more undamaged bridges. If Bertrand withdrew along this track, why did he not destroy them?

As his troops rounded the next bend, two men of Warwick's advance party galloped back toward them. "Lord," one called, breathing as hard as his lathered horse, "the bridge ahead is broken."

Northampton's suspicion about Bertrand appeared correct. "How far?" Edward asked.

"About five miles, lord."

"You have ridden hard. Find my squire for a drink." Edward called to Ughtred. "Alert the carpenters. They are needed to repair another bridge. Send men to aid them to gather whatever tools they require and hasten forward as fast as they can."

Five miles on, Edward heard the river's rush before he saw it. The track descended about a hundred feet through a dense wood lining the river's steep banks to where the water cascaded over large granite boulders. They walked slowly forward. God rot, Bertrand!

Warwick waited near the broken bridge. He removed his bascinet and sweat trickled down his temples and forehead. "No signs of an ambush, only this." Jagged sections of timber beams and planks rested upon rocks jutting out of the fast-flowing current below. "Though my men have searched, they found no way around."

Edward called to the master carpenter. "Walk with us."

They dismounted and approached the gap. Bertrand's force destroyed all save the stone footings.

"Lord Edward, whoever did this performed his task well." Lines fanned from the corners of the carpenter's eyes. "Not one of the salvageable beams below is long enough to straddle the gap."

"Bertrand will pay for this." Edward glanced skyward, gauging the position of the sun. "There is time before nightfall to accomplish much and afterward, you work by firelight."

The carpenters laboured through the afternoon, into the evening, and through the night. At first light, Edward and the vanguard retinues crossed the rebuilt span and arrayed on the hillside overlooking it. They stood guard while the king and main body traversed the bridge and ascended to the top of the hill.

Several hours passed. While there were no signs of the French, the previous day's sensation of being watched persisted. When the last of the heavily-laden supply wagons lumbered up the rutted slope, Edward stretched his back and called to Chandos, "Time is wasting."

Chandos nodded. "I think the wagons are safe enough with Arundel and rear guard shepherding them."

Edward waved to round up his men. "If we ride cross-country, we should catch up with Warwick's troops before they reach Saint Lo."

He urged his mount into a gallop, his desire to capture Bertrand so strong, he could almost taste it. Accomplishing such a feat would earn respect, from his men and, more importantly, from his father.

They rode all out, the dust swirling above and behind them and soon reached the outskirts of St. Lo where Warwick paused his advance force. In the distance, twin church steeples jutted above the trees.

Edward reined in, but his stallion's blood was up and he resisted, tossing his head, pulling on the reins, and pawing. When Edward curbed him, his stallion threw his head and reared. When his horse returned to earth, still snorting and too full of himself, Edward bent his stallion and displaced his haunches until his mount settled.

"Still no sight of Bertrand," Warwick said.

They pushed on into town at a cautious walk. A shop sign creaked. Not a soul in sight. Not even a dog to growl a warning.

St. Lo was deserted.

Later in the day, Edward strode across St. Lo's abandoned marketplace to confer with his under-marshal and Chandos.

"Sentries are posted, lord," Ughtred said. "Two crews search the town: one gathering valuables and the other collecting grain, smoked meats, and anything edible.

Chandos said, "Quite a haul so far." He pointed toward the growing pile of stores.

Edward shielded his eyes from the glare.

"Thomas!" Chandos called to a man on a well-built dappled grey stallion. "Thomas Holland!"

The rider spun his horse."Chandos," he called, urging his horse into a trot. The man wore an eye patch over one eye.

Edward stood motionless as the rider approached. Here was the man Joan wed in secret. Although Edward knew Holland served under Warwick, their paths had not crossed— until then.

Holland noticed him, dismounted, and sank to one knee.

Chandos said, "Lord Edward, may I present Sir Thomas Holland? Sir Thomas, this is Lord Edward of Woodstock, Earl of Chester, Duke of Cornwall and Prince of Wales." Chandos grinned.

Edward did not smile nor signal permission for Holland to rise. Outrage on Joan's behalf surged through him.

Chandos continued, "Holland and I served together in Brabant several years ago, under the old Earl of Salisbury."

Edward studied Holland. Had he flinched at mention of Salisbury? "I have heard your name and believed we might meet." Edward deliberately addressed the knight without using his courtesy title. Would Holland discern the slight?

How might the king handle such a situation? Edward motioned the knight to rise. "Your reputation precedes you."

Holland rose, avoided Edward's gaze, and shifted uneasily. "My affairs are insignificant to one as esteemed as you, my lord." He offered a weak smile.

"On the contrary. Though we have not met before, we share intimates do we not?" Edward looked pointedly at Holland. "Indulge me with your company and we will reminisce about our mutual acquaintances."

Chandos made no comment but his brow furrowed.

Holland's eye twitched. "You do me great honour, Lord Edward."

"We march again at dawn," Edward said. "Find me when we make camp tomorrow evening." Edward turned his back, dismissing Holland.

"Something afoot between you, Thomas?" Chandos asked.

Saddle leather creaked and hoofbeats faded as Holland rode away.

Edward exited his lodging the next morning, intending to seek out his father. By the looks of the men, many suffered the ill effects of the previous evening, cradling their heads and scurrying green-faced into back alleys.

He found the king in the square conversing with the Earls of Northampton, Suffolk, and Oxford near a wagon piled high and covered with canvas. His father's scowl evidenced a foul humour.

"Bertrand seems to have vanished into thin air, sire," Warwick said.

Edward broke in. "We ordered riders east at dawn to search for signs of him."

"The Vicomte suggested Bertrand might have ridden south," Northampton offered, "in an attempt to draw us farther from Caen."

"Quite likely," King Edward said.

"I ordered a retinue, under Thomas Holland's command, to scout the road to Torigni," Northampton added.

"With men riding all three roads," Edward said, "we will soon find Bertrand." That Northampton granted Holland command of a unit meant the Earl possessed confidence in him. Holland bore watching.

Throughout the morning, St. Lo buzzed with activity. Men

loaded crates, sacks, and barrels into a least a dozen wagons. Edward recorded everything and at midday, he took a break, wiping sweat from his face.

Hoofbeats sounded and a rider atop a lathered mount loped into the square. The scout spotted the king and reined his horse toward him.

As Edward reached his father's side, the messenger halted and jumped to the ground. Doffing his cap, he knelt. "My lord king," he said between breaths, "we picked up the Frenchie's trail on the road to Cormolain."

"Well done." The king turned to Edward. "Get with Warwick. If you move fast, you might catch Bertrand out." The king bellowed, "Oxford, send word to Holland to break off his pursuit. Tell him Bertrand is headed east and to meet us on the road to Cormolain."

While Ughtred assembled a mounted retinue, Edward's horse was saddled and brought forward. Within minutes, Edward galloped out of St. Lo with Warwick, leaving Ughtred to organize the foot soldiers and archers to follow at speed.

The day's sullen grey was fading to charcoal when Edward halted the vanguard on a ridge above a loop in the same river they forded earlier in the day. "God's teeth," he cursed under his breath. The wily Bertrand had evaded them yet again.

Ughtred reined in beside him. "We pushed the horses hard today, lord, and many are not yet fully recovered from the voyage."

"The men are exhausted, too." Edward swivelled in his saddle, scanning the terrain. "This looks a likely spot to camp with good fodder for the horses at the river's edge below." On another ridge not far in the distance, fires flickered from the main body's camp. Should an enemy approach, his vanguard was close enough to provide protection.

The vanguard settled in near the river. Shadows deepened and a moisture-laden breeze rattled through the wooded couloir. Edward consulted briefly with Warwick, then returned to his tent. He ducked under the canopy and rolled his shoulders before sitting at the table his page laid with refreshments. A small fire smoked at his feet.

Rain began a soft tattoo upon the canvas and a crisp scent drifted reminding him of home. With it came thoughts of his family and Joan. Beneath a moon riddled by clouds, the rain drummed harder, trickling brown rivulets down the sides of the tent. Edward downed a cup of wine and snapped at his page, "Add another log to the fire." He frowned into his cup. Simon did not deserve to suffer Edward's irritation at being kept waiting.

Hollow thumps drifted from restive horses on the picket line. Minutes drew on. He poured another cup of wine. Where was Holland? If his father were to confront Holland, how might he handle the matter? Edward twisted his ruby signet ring.

Muted hoofbeats announced the knight's arrival. Holland dismounted his muddy, rain-streaked mount and handed his reins to Edward's squire.

"Did you mean to keep me waiting?"

"Your pardon, Lord Edward." Holland ducked under the dripping awning and kneeled. "I hope I have not kept you waiting overlong."

"Long enough." Edward waved at the stool opposite. Simon poured wine for Holland, and stepped away.

Holland had combed his hair and changed into clean garments. In the light from the fire, his one good eye appeared bloodshot.

Raindrops plopped into the puddles forming below the sides of the tent. Edward sat quietly, as the king did at times, allowing the silence to stretch.

Holland shifted, crossed and recrossed his legs.

"You have some thought regarding my request for you to attend me?" Edward sipped.

"Indeed, though I know not why, I am honoured."

The knight's false-hearted manner annoyed Edward. He savoured his wine and settled in as if for a genial tête-à-tête and

200

studied Joan's erstwhile husband through half-lowered lids. On many occasions, the king enticed an unwary victim to lower his guard by employing a similar manner.

Holland shifted restlessly while maintaining a cordial smile.

"You are aware my cousin and I are close?" Edward spoke in dulcet tones.

Holland raised a brow.

"My cousin, Joan."

The knight's smile faded. "My lord, begging your pardon, my knowledge of your affinity is limited." The knight's good eye twitched.

Above the fire's hiss, men in the distance argued while redistributing loads among the wagons.

Holland leaned forward. "What is it you want of me, lord?"

"Answers." Edward spoke sharply. "And you best be truthful." Only a fool would mistake the threat in his voice. "God's blood, Holland, it has been five years!"

Holland winced. "My lord, you perceive I have abandoned your cousin?"

"*Perceive*?" Edward rubbed his temple. "*Mon Dieu*! You deny it?"

The knight blanched and his eye twitched again. "It-it is not what you think, lord. If I might explain?"

"I am listening." Edward's lips pressed in a firm line.

"After Sluys, my contract for service with your lord father expired. I have no other means of support. I signed on for the holy war against the Moors in Prussia, leaving Joan in the queen's household believing she would be safe there. Upon my return, I discovered my *wife* married to Salisbury's heir. *Jesu*! Might you imagine my shock?"

Edward clenched his jaw. Did the knave expect sympathy?

"I attempted to see Joan, but Lady Margaret and her brother, Lord Wake, refused me. They denied the validity of our marriage and barred any contact."

"Go on." Edward said.

"What power did I have to enforce my claim and challenge Salisbury? Until my circumstances improved, mayhap by gaining the king's regard, my only recourse was to entrust Joan to the safety of your lady mother's household." Holland spread his hands. "I beseech you to believe me."

Edward weighed the knight's words.

Holland pressed on. "Did not the king sanction the Montagu marriage? The old Earl was the king's intimate and greatly esteemed." Holland soughed a shaky breath. "I intended to appeal to the Earl, lay my case before him. Though, if you recall, after being captured, he was held in Paris. Seeking resolution at the time was not possible."

Edward crossed his arms.

"Certes, I was in no position to approach the king and challenge the marriage. In truth, I knew not what to do. I am here now, to prove my value to our king."

"Mayhap, you would have been wise to consider your lack of means and influence *before* secretly wedding my cousin." Edward hardened his tone. "Tell me, did you think to elevate your station by marrying my cousin for her royal blood? God's wounds! Your first concern should have been her welfare."

Holland retreated. "I admit my actions were rash and poorly judged."

"How do you explain the years since then? Salisbury's power died with him, yet you have done nothing. Your behavior sickens me." Edward sneered. "How dare you call yourself a knight? You have no honour!"

Holland flinched. "Lord, might you consider I left Joan with the queen for good reason? Perhaps, she preferred marriage to the future Earl."

Edward stared into the distance, twisting his signet ring around and around.

Raindrops puddled.

Edward pinned Holland with his eyes. "Do not take me for a fool. My cousin bears no blame in this deceit. For now, I shall reserve judgment and safeguard Joan's secret. For now." Edward steeled his voice. "Tread carefully. This is not the last you will hear from me." Edward stood. "Now, get out of my sight!"

July 1346 - Cormolain

Two days later in Cormolain, Edward awoke to shouts outside his lodging. Half-asleep, he grabbed his sword and rushed to the door, colliding with Simon. Ash covered the lad from head to toe, and tears streaked his face.

Edward backed up a step. "What has happened?"

Simon swiped his sleeve across his face, smearing the ash. "The-the archers, m-my lord."

"Archers?" Edward gripped Simon's narrow shoulders. "What about them?"

"My c-cousin…Tom. D-dead, m-my lord."

"Dead? How?" Edward jiggled Simon's shoulders.

Jesu! He could make nothing of the lad's babble. After hastily donning his hauberk and mail, Edward hurried out into the lane and sprinted in the direction of the king's command, dodging men racing in the other direction. What could have happened to cause such a stir? The evening before, he posted guards, ordered the watch rotated, and took every precaution to secure the town against an enemy attack.

Simon mentioned the archers. The army depended upon the bowmen, each worth his weight in gold. It took years to develop the strength to draw and wield a longbow with accuracy. His father, already vexed by Bertrand's game of cat and mouse, would rage if any of his bowman were harmed.

Edward paused to catch his breath outside the half-timbered building serving as his father's command. Hoofbeats clattered behind him. Oxford reined in and dismounted.

"Lord Edward." The scowl on the Earl's face did not bode well.

Edward followed him inside.

Oxford bent to one knee. "Your pardon, Lord King."

King Edward was breaking his fast. He glanced up, his brows drawn close.

Edward bowed. "Sire."

The king laid down his knife. "What is all this clamour?"

Oxford rose. "Northampton sent me to report…personally." Odd for the Constable to send Oxford rather than a messenger.

The king wiped his lips. "Well?"

The earl hesitated.

"Out with it!"

Edward braced himself for Oxford's report.

The earl cleared his throat. "A company of archers bedded down at a farmstead outside of town. During the night, the barn they slept in was set on fire."

"What? They are unharmed?"

Oxford shook his head. "No, sire, the timbers smolder still."

"God's wounds!" The king stood abruptly nearly capsizing the table. "How? Did no one smell the smoke? See the flames?"

"Regrettably, no. The farmstead was situated between two hills. When our guards took note of the lightened sky, they rushed to the site and found the barn fully ablaze. They could do nothing."

"No one heard cries for help?"

"No sire. The smoke likely took the Welshmen in their sleep."

Edward imagined the horror and the stench. He cringed.

"While the archers should have posted a watch, they did not," the Earl said. "However, their neglect does not absolve me of responsibility. At our advance, the townsfolk fled. It was imprudent of me not to anticipate they might return to seek revenge. I was a fool not to post more guards." Oxford kneeled again. "Most humbly, do I beg your pardon, Lord King."

A vein pulsed in the king's temple. "How dare these Normans defy me!" The king began to pace, all the while cursing under his breath.

Oxford rose and caught Edward's eyes; the Earl's spoke volumes.

Edward twisted his signet ring. What torment his father must feel. Not only for the fate of the archers, but he believed the Normans would forsake their false Valois king and rally to him. Such brutality demonstrated they did not view England's king as their liberator.

His father halted, his face mottled red and his body as rigid as Dover's white cliffs. "Burn it," the king spat. "Burn this town and everything in it. Burn it to the ground."

July 1346 - Torteval

Leaving Cormolain in ashes, the army moved on to Torteval. Overnighting there provided time for the king to reconsider his course of action. He spread a parchment on the hastily assembled plank table in his temporary lodging and studied it while he awaited his commanders. What a fool he was to have trusted de Harcourt's assurances the Normans were so aggrieved with Philippe they would renounce him and pledge fealty to King Edward. He fell for the exiled Vicomte's wishful thinking. The king shook his head. The archers paid a grisly price for his vanity.

Studying the map, he estimated distances, and considered a way to salvage an advantage from the bowmen's ashes. Caen lay only thirty miles east.

Boots thumped, announcing his commanders' arrival. They lumbered in, muttered greetings, and settled around the table.

"*D'accord*," he began, met by glum faces. "I have decided the main body should rest here for another night, perhaps two."

Jaws dropped. His bewildered commanders stared at him.

Northampton rubbed his jaw. "Are you suggesting we delay our advance on Caen, lord?"

"Indeed, that is exactly what I am proposing."

To a man, confusion played across their faces. The army's sharp-minded Constable would likely be the first to discern the reason for the delay and the wisdom in it.

"The main division only, sire, or all us? Edward asked.

"Yes, we will all rest and then march on Caen." His son's question showed his growing confidence. "But we will progress quite slowly."

Warwick laid burly arms across his chest. "Sire, our halt gives Caen time to prepare its defenses."

"Just so. A gathering is what I have in mind." He searched their faces for signs of comprehension.

Northampton nodded his head. "Yes. A slow march." He grinned. "Fear will grow and people will panic."

"Indeed, *mes amis*. We will fuel their fear. Stoke it, in fact. With fire." He turned to his son. "The vanguard is to set flame to our surroundings and then, as we march, fire everything in our path. Your job is to fill the sky with mountains of black smoke, a swath so wide, the horizon so full—"

Northampton chuckled outright. "The locals will flock to Caen for safety and create chaos."

The chamber came alive, everyone talking at once.

Warwick shook his head, grinning. "You are a wily one, lord."

The assault on Caen would be the first real challenge to England's army. King Edward laid a hand on his son's shoulder, and the first real test of his heir.

The next day, Edward's vanguard ranged east atop a steep ridge—their orders to fire everything in their path. Every farm. Every village. Every town. Normandy's simple country folk would run screaming to Caen for safety while French couriers bore urgent messages to Philippe—he must march to repel the invaders. In a pitched battle, the English would destroy Philippe and his army.

At the base of the hill, the neat rows of a thriving homestead furrowed the land. Though Edward understood what needed to be done, he hesitated, considering the destruction he was about to set in motion. Burying his remorse, he shouted, "For England!" and led the charge down the slope. Like rampaging bulls they galloped, hooves churning, through the pastures and fields, shredding the summer crops.

Edward slowed while his troops whooped past him. At the far end of the field, a family of five—a mother with a babe in arms—ran in terror through the vegetable patch and into a wood.

Chandos reined in beside him, both bearing witness to the havoc below. "We will catch the locals by surprise at first," Chandos said, "but our slow advance provides time for them to strip produce and livestock from the farms, leaving little to feed our men."

"I was thinking the same." Edward urged his horse into the farmyard where a dog barked a frantic warning. He shouted and his men gathered around. "Half of you search the barn, the others, the outbuildings. Gather all the food stores and livestock small enough to carry."

Edward dismounted. "John, see what lies around the back of the cote while I look inside."

"I doubt there is much of value in the family's belongings."

"Mayhap not. Their wealth lies in the livestock and fertile land."

A growl halted Edward's approach to the farmhouse. Six honey-coloured pups cowered beneath a bush guarded by a shaggy bitch, hackles raised and teeth bared. She was determined to protect her pups. What courage!

He side-stepped the dog, opened the weather-beaten door and ducked under the lintel. He paused for his eyes to adjust—cob walls, an overturned chair, and a kettle resting in crimson coals. A subtle movement in the corner. The lid of a chest inched closed.

He strode forward and flipped it open. A pair of terrified, wide-set blue eyes, under an unruly mop of flaxen hair, gaped up at him. The waif shrank back, her mouth in a snarl much like the dog, and as menacing.

"*N'ai pas peur*," he said. "I will not hurt you." He reached in, and though she stiffened at his touch, she did not fight him. He lifted her from her hideaway and settled her tautly-strung body on the floor. He motioned for her to stay. "*Restez.*"

Frozen in fear, wide eyes stared at him.

He gathered floor rushes and jammed the bunch into the embers until they caught. Then he grabbed the girl's hand and towed her outside. He held the flaming rushes to the thatch, watched it spark, and tossed the burning bundle back inside.

Shouts sounded from the barn where the men worked with determined fury. Smoke billowed from the hayloft, and flames fingered their way across the roof. Edward felt a tug on his fingers. The girl stared up at him with strangely familiar eyes, clear blue, forsaken and welling with tears.

"*Tu vas!* Run!" He released her hand and pointed to the wood.

She bolted like a panicked hare. Long golden locks streamed out behind her as she raced past the herb garden and through the ravaged field. At the edge of the wood, she looked back.

Jeanette. He felt for the tiny bump beneath his surcoat. Joan's hart pin.

Spurs chinked behind him and a hand rested on his shoulder. Chandos gazed at the girl vanishing into the trees.

Edward closed his eyes. The sun seared his face, and rivulets of sweat trickled down his back. He could use an ale. Opening his eyes, he strode to his stallion and hauled himself into the saddle. He swiped his forehead, his sleeve coming away smeared with dust and ashes. "Move out!" he shouted.

Sacks and saddlebags bulging, the men mounted. Rounds of soft Norman cheese, spring lambs and red calves were draped over their pommels. They would eat well tonight.

Edward loped his horse partway up the slope, halted and scoured the landscape. About a half-mile distant, bright banners whipped in the swirling smoke. Warwick and Northampton gathered their retinues. Edward cantered to join them.

July 1346 - Windsor Castle

Joan hastened to the queen's solar as quickly as she could without calling attention to herself. A messenger in royal livery had arrived, her maid learning of it through a serving lad, such tidings winging from servant to servant swifter than a hawk after a rabbit.

Although official dispatches had arrived in the month since the army's sailing, perhaps this courier brought a personal missive for the queen from the king, or from Edward. He promised to write.

Joan's thoughts flew to the young men serving alongside Edward, of Roger and even Will. Most concerning of all, what of Thomas? Would the war put a sad end to her marital muddle? Was she wife not to two but one? Or none? Her stomach listed.

Sunlight streamed from the queen's solar into the dim passageway. At Joan's entry, Queen Philippa raised her eyes from a parchment.

"Ah, Jeanette, *ici*, come in." She held up the letter. "From *mon fils*. I was about to send someone to fetch you."

"How kind, my lady." The queen's ladies were nowhere in sight. Joan sighed, relieved to have a few private moments. She lowered herself onto the tiny stool near Queen Philippa's feet. The queen cleared her throat and read aloud.

> *"Most revered queen and beloved mother, you will want to know of our good health and safe landing in Normandy on 12 July. The day witnessed the occasion of my long-awaited knighting. Our most esteemed King bestowed a second honour upon me, entrusting me with command of the vanguard."*

Joan clapped her hands. "Oh, for Edward to be knighted! He laboured so hard."

"Indeed, he did."

> *"We have greeted each dawn eager to confront our French foe. Along our line of march, several towns surrendered and the citizens pledged fealty to our king."*

Pausing, the queen looked up. "My husband must have been pleased."

"Though we have met little resistance, a small enemy force hampers our advance. Several bridges were broken forcing halts to repair them. Northampton deployed a retinue to hunt them down, led by a Lancashire knight, Sir Thomas Holland."

Joan's skin tingled and though she was careful to school her expression, Queen Philippa seemed to be studying her. Did she know of Joan's secret? Bless Edward for slipping in this mention. "What else does your son write, my lady?"

While we have advanced our landed army, Huntingdon's fleet has laid waste to Normandy's ports from our landing on the Cotentin east to the mouth of the Orne, much to our king's great pleasure. Huntingdon's destruction of French ships and Normandy's harbors deprives our enemy of the means to ever again attack our homeland. It is long past time we taught Philippe a lesson."

"In the next days, Huntingdon's fleet will join us for our assault on Caen, so for now, I must end. With God's blessings and your prayers, victory will be ours."

Lively voices sounded from the passage.

"Thank you for sharing Edward's letter, my lady."

Upon the ladies' return Joan removed to a bench near the window where she might tuck herself away from their prattle. Before sailing, Edward spoke of courageous deeds and glory. How might the war change him? What about Will? Over the years, he had been patient with her, and loyal, signs of maturing. Could she trust his behaviour, or was he attempting to trick her into submission?

A branch rattled sharply against the window. Joan was trapped in a battle between opposing powers, not just now but had been for years. Will's patience would not last. She must find a way out, but how?

The Best Laid Plans

26 July, 1346 – Caen

Edward jerked awake before dawn, his every nerve on high alert. He held his breath and listened, straining to hear over the thrumming of his heart. Noises drifted to him—muffled voices, coughing, horses stomping, the clatter and chink of harness—the sounds of camp coming to life.

He slipped his legs over the side of his traveling bed, sat up. and rubbed the grit from his eyes. Sleep had eluded him for much of the night. His father's emissary, the cleric Geoffrey de Maldon, had ridden to Caen to present the king's terms for surrender but he never returned. It appeared Caen intended to resist, unlike previous towns in their path.

Today would see him tested in his first major battle. A hollow formed in the pit of his stomach. Scuffled footsteps neared the tent's entrance.

"Lord Edward?"

"I do not slumber, Simon. Come." His page entered carrying a flickering candle and a mug of ale. In between sips, Edward's fingers trembled. The tent flap opened again. His squire, Hal, entered carrying Edward's battle harness.

Edward donned his padded gambeson, then struggled to pin Joan's petite gold brooch over his heart. *You are not alone.* He tugged on his boots, then motioned for his hauberk and raised his arms. Hal lowered Edward's hauberk, then mail over his head and shoulders, its weight a heavy reminder of his knighthood pledge. Hal smoothed Edward's surcoat overtop, its quartered arms and white horizontal label marking him as heir. Edward belted his scabbard into place and Simon fastened leather and metal greaves around Edward's calves and buckled on his spurs.

Hal secured protective vambraces to Edward's forearms and handed Edward's gauntlets to Simon before grabbing Edward's bascinet and helm with mail aventail. Edward made a final tug to his surcoat and left the tent with the two lads following on his heels.

Spurs jangled as human forms stirred in the shadows, the only light cast by a silver crescent hanging low in the west. No fires betrayed the army's location. Edward crouched so Hal could place Edward's bascinet on his head, and adjust its linked aventail into position to protect Edward's neck and shoulders.

"Enough Hal. Hook my helm to my back."

Edward pulled on his gauntlets and flexed his fingers, pausing a moment to reflect: steel for strength and leather for resiliency, as well as a knight's obligation for largesse. A groom held his horse and Edward grabbed his reins, stepped into his stirrup, and threw his leg over.

"Both of you, stay safe. Shelter behind with the wagons."

"Yes, lord."

In the twilight, Edward discerned Warwick's silhouette among the mounted men gathered beneath the vanguard's banners. He urged his stallion forward.

"God's blessing, lord," the Earl greeted. "The men are ready."

Distant trumpets sounded from across the valley. Edward swallowed hard. The king's division prepared to march.

With trembling hands, Edward collected his reins. "May God in his wisdom and grace favour us this day."

Warwick crossed himself. "Amen."

Leather creaked and the men's voices pitched higher as the vanguard formed up.

Ughtred called from the column, "All is ready, lord."

"Forward," Edward ordered.

As the column headed out, Edward concentrated on remembering Caen's layout, picturing it in his mind as de Harcourt described it at the meeting the evening before.

The city was situated at the joining of the Orne and Odon rivers. A massive fortress stood guard on the north bank of the Orne, and the land behind it rose steeply, while to the east, the slope was more gradual. The oldest part of the city, *Bourg-le-Roi*, was situated to the citadel's west.

According to the Norman, dwellings and shops swelled Caen's walls to the west and south, while a bend in the Orne encircled a small island, the *Île St-Jean*. A bridge at its north end connected it to the old town and a bridge to the island's south led to the surrounding faubourgs.

The king and army's main body would advance from the west at a deliberately slow pace, to allow troops time to take position. It would enter the city through its western unwalled faubourg.

The vanguard would assemble on the city's north, above the old town, market, and storehouses. Arundel's rearguard would approach from the south. Edward recalled his father's strict orders; no assault would launch until his scouts reported back on the exact dispositions of the French and until Huntingdon's ships were spotted. In coordinating forces bearing down on Caen from three directions—and from the river—timing was crucial.

At this, Edward's first major battle, he could not afford to make a mistake.

Partway down the slope from camp, Edward reined to the side and halted while his force of two thousand continued to march past him. Behind them, vibrant yellow and red flames scorched the still-dark sky as the village of Cheux burned.

Chandos rode up beside him, accompanied by Sir James Audley, a recent addition to Edward's guard. Chandos gazed east. "Caen will pay a high price for refusing our king's offer of surrender."

"Imagine the French panic," Audley said with a wry grin. "Each tower of smoke a sign the marauding English are closing in."

"When the city falls," Edward said, "Philippe will feel the

English lion's bite." He gathered his reins. "Let us to work!" He set heels to his stallion's flanks and cantered off. All three ranged ahead of the main body's advance, to fire the fields and farmsteads in the vanguard's path. Gradually, the sun's golden light feathered the eastern horizon and smoke funnelled upward across the plain as the army closed the distance to Caen.

Edward called a halt as he and his men rejoined Warwick's retinue on a small rise at Caen's northern boundary. He nodded downslope. "Though de Harcourt described Caen as prosperous, I never imagined its size would rival London."

"France's dog Bertrand may have proven himself shrewd, yet I doubt he has a force large enough to defend a city of this size," Warwick said.

"Indeed." Edward searched below for landmarks, noting the confluence of the two rivers, the smaller channel of the Odon running through the old town and the Noe channel beyond it. Defensive walls encircled the *Île St-Jean*. A few places showed cracks and missing rocks, though it was difficult to determine any weakness at this distance. Water levels in both rivers were low, exposing a marsh to the island's west.

French banners hung limp from the crenellated ramparts of Duke William of Normandy's ancient fortress. South of the stronghold but on the river's north bank, golden spires soared from the Church of St-Pierre. Beyond it, to the east, the Abbey aux Dames rested within a hillside orchard, exactly as drawn on de Harcourt's map.

Hoofbeats sounded from behind. Ughtred and Chandos trotted toward him, both covered in ash and smiling.

"Look, the king and main body." Chandos pointed to a dust cloud nearing the western outskirts of Caen.

"We dismount and hold here," Edward said. "Ughtred, remind the men to remain alert. When we go in, we advance on foot."

"As you say, my lord." Ughtred trotted off.

Warwick turned in his saddle and scanned the river to the north. "We should see the masts of the fleet by now. Where is Huntingdon?"

Edward studied the northern reaches of the river. "Huntingdon will be here."

"Your father will have his arse if he is not." The Earl twisted back toward the old town. "Nothing moves. The place is deserted." He threw his leg over and slid to the ground.

Chandos dismounted. "Bertrand must make a stand somewhere."

"He would not dare surrender this city without a fight," Warwick said. "Not and face King Philippe's wrath."

"It appears the old town's walls offer slight protection," Audley said.

Edward tossed his reins onto his horse's neck and jumped down. "What say you we find out?"

Warwick grinned. "You read my mind."

After conferring with Ughtred, Edward and Warwick headed down the slope accompanied by Chandos, Audley, Edward's guard, and several retinues of men. Weapons rattled as they scrambled downhill, and upon nearing the old town, a dozen men spread out to skirt its walls.

"Here!" The shout came from the right.

Edward's gut tightened.

They hastened along the crumbling bulwark to a wooden gate, hidden beneath a blanket of twisted vines. The guard drew their weapons while a half dozen men put their shoulders to the gate and shoved. The old boards creaked.

"Again!" Warwick called.

They heaved once more and with a loud crack, the hinges gave. No enemy guarded the other side. Two wiry men squeezed through the narrow opening while others tore away the vines, clearing a larger opening.

"Looks clear, lord," came a voice from the other side.

At Warwick's signal, his men opened the gate fully, and a dozen men-at-arms darted forward and hared down the lane in fits and starts while archers held bows with arrows nocked.

The wind gusted, swirling dust and scattering feathers.

Edward's pulse beat in his ears. He drew his sword.

"Keep sharp," Warwick called.

Edward crept forward into the marketplace, empty save for stacks of crates and dozens of barrels. Several good-sized storehouses lined one side, with merchant stalls along the other. A collection of fishponds occupied the middle. The men-at-arms spread out, searching building by building, the only sounds those of spurs and weapons rattling.

Edward scanned the abandoned square and the lanes running from it. "Lord Earl, if you were Bertrand, where would you position your forces?"

Warwick's eyes narrowed. The stronghold's ramparts, lit by the morning sun, loomed in the distance. "Mayhap the fortress will provide answers." He paused, an intensity aimed at Edward. "I lead. You follow with your men."

Edward nodded, accepting with good grace.

Warwick signalled and he and his men advanced toward the fortress. Edward, his guard, and retinue fell in behind. They proceeded with caution, the streets eerily quiet. When they neared the stronghold, Warwick halted his force out of crossbow range. Edward counted the pikes bristling atop the ramparts.

Chandos came alongside. "I would wager some number of Bertrand's men are guarding Caen's women and children within those walls."

"No doubt," Edward said, "but where might he have stationed the bulk of his men?"

Shouts and a scream from the right broke the quiet. The sounds came from the direction of the river. Edward's pulse quickened.

Warwick and his men ran toward the voices, toward the Church of St-Pierre. One of the Earl's men broke off and raced back.

"The Earl bid me to say," he panted, "for you to wait here while he judges the situation."

Edward bristled. "You dare—"

Chandos caught his sleeve. "Listen to him."

"I am no coward, John."

"No, you are a commander." The knight held his gaze.

Neither a coward nor a fool. His father's words sounded in Edward's head. *A king leads.* And a wise commander does not lead his men into a trap. Edward concentrated, trying to place an alley they passed on their way to the stronghold. It led directly to the river. He needed a better vantage.

"On me!" He sprinted, reversing direction, found the alley, and headed toward the river. As they neared the street running alongside the Odon, the screams grew louder. Then more shouting and wails.

Edward slowed and signalled his archers to advance with caution, and for his men to spread out. He crouched behind a stack of crates alongside a shed, and beckoned to Chandos and Audley. They crept up beside him.

Straight ahead, the river flowed between his position and the *Île St-Jean.* To his left, a bridge, lined with shops and houses, spanned over the waterway. French forces massed at the guard towers at each end, and at the far end, at the entrance to the island, wagons were tipped on their sides, piled with a mountain of crates, barrels, and chests. French men-at-arms guarded the barricade and were augmented by Caen's residents brandishing make-shift weapons.

Genoese crossbowmen crammed several boats moored beneath the bridge. Several dozen English foot soldiers were pinned down near the church. As the Genoese fired and the crossbow bolts struck, the English soldiers howled and the Genoese laughed.

Edward ground his teeth as Warwick's forces approached from the fortress. The archers nocked their bows and arrows flew.

Screams erupted from the Genoese in the boats as English arrows hit their marks. Bodies spun upon impact and toppled into the river.

The English soldiers trapped near the church cheered.

"At such a small distance, our archers cannot miss," Chandos said.

Edward cursed. "*Jesu!* Those idiots at the church ignored my father's orders and jeopardized our assault."

"The lure of riches makes fools of men," Audley said.

Warwick's archers began firing flaming arrows into the shops' thatched roofs on the bridge. Black smoke swirled skyward. With a roar, the French guards rushed at Warwick's men-at-arms.

"For England!" Warwick's retinues met the French head-on, matching them stroke for stroke. Smoke drifted to Edward. His men were awaiting orders.

"For St. George!" Warwick's men shouted.

Their battle cry stirred Edward to action. Orders from the king or not, honour demanded he not leave the Earl to battle alone. He stood and called to his standard-bearer, "Sir Thomas Daniel, raise my banner higher." Edward said to his men. "We cross the river and find a way onto the island. Now, on me. For England!"

Edward sprinted toward the river, launched down the bank and into the water. He sank calf-deep in the mud, the river to his knees.

"God's bones!" Audley cursed as he hit the water.

Edward looked over his shoulder. Chandos slogged alongside Edward's standard-bearer, who struggled to keep his balance while holding Edward's Welsh dragon aloft. Though the waterway was merely ten yards, it felt like a mile as the muddy bottom sucked at Edward's feet. He stumbled up the opposite bank, his boots and lower legs weighted with muck. He waved to his men. "Spread out!"

The clash of weapons and battle cries on the bridge spurred Edward forward and down a narrow alley to his left. Boots pounded behind him, Chandos and Audley, James cursing all the way.

At the end of the alley, Edward heaved for breath, then gagged. The stench of rotting carcasses and entrails came from the back of a butcher's shed. *Jesu!* He covered his mouth and nose.

Audley grimaced. "Keep going, do not stop here!"

Edward hurtled through a maze of shanties and then plunged into another narrow channel of murky water. On the opposite side, an overgrown footpath ran along the island's stone wall. He ploughed ahead, his heart pumping as hard as his legs as he raced toward the sounds of battle, louder now. He searched the wall for signs of a breach, weakness, crack, or a gate. Thickening smoke burned his throat.

"With me. Heave!" Voices came from ahead.

 Edward bolted around a curve where two men shoved against a rotting wooden gate.

"Wait!" Edward shouted.

Chandos and Audley caught up, with Thomas Daniel close behind, clutching Edward's banner.

"There may be French men-at-arms on the other side," Edward said.

Chandos scowled. "This gate looks as rotten as the one in the old town.

Several more men pounded up. "You!" Audley motioned to the smallest. "Hop on my shoulders." The man climbed up and peeked overtop. "No soldiers, lord," he panted, "nothin' but a lot o' fancy houses." He jumped down.

Five men lined up with their shoulders pressed against the gate. Edward counted, "One…two…three…heave!" The gate squawked in protest, but held.

"God's rot!" Audley shouted.

"Again," Edward said. "Ready? Heave!" With a loud crack, the gate gave. The men stumbled, regained their feet, and piled through the gap. Edward paused on the other side. "Thomas Daniel!"

Edward's banner man raised Edward's banner and waved it, rallying the men.

Edward faced them, smoke clouding the sky behind his left shoulder. He raised his sword. "With me!" He spun, charging toward the fighting on the bridge.

The island's residents swarmed the streets. A stout man, brandishing a sword, rushed at Edward. He dodged and stuck out his foot. The man tripped and collided with an ample woman wielding a red shutter.

"Forward!" Edward urged.

Smoke engulfed the bridge. Warwick's banner fluttered in and out of sight. Another shop roof burst into flames, and sparks showered on the Earl's men. They were gaining ground, forcing the

French back, more than halfway toward the island.

The men defending the island stood behind the barricade with their backs to Edward's men. The French were riveted by the fighting on the bridge. Edward raised his sword to signal his archers.

"For England!"

The men at the barricade spun directly into the barrage of arrows. They screamed, their. bloodied bodies hurtled backwards onto the barricade. Arrows punched through leather and mail.

Edward charged. "Saint George!" Weapons clashed, steel rang, men grappled and cursed. The French lacked room to maneuver and fought with a ferocity born of desperation. Edward refused to hang back, despite the coat-of-arms he wore marking him heir.

When a French knight spotted him, Edward's focus narrowed. He parried the Frenchman's first strike and the second, retreating several steps to evade his taller foe's longer reach, then pretended to falter. The Frenchman took the lure and lunged. Edward spun away, swiping his blade across the back of his foe's unprotected calf. The knight stumbled forward, and as he fell, Audley rammed his blade into the back of the man's neck. An odor like forged metal wafted up.

"Lord!" Chandos shouted.

Edward caught a blur to his left, he dodged right just enough for the blow to glance off his helm. He punched the haft of his sword into his attacker's eye while hooking a foot around the man's ankle. As the Frenchman toppled, Edward slid his blade up beneath the man's helm. Blood gurgled from his throat as he sank to the ground.

The vanguard's men had made quick work of the French at the barricade. Only a few skirmishes remained. Edward dashed forward to join the others tossing chests and crates, creating a gap to slip through to trap the French on the bridge between his forces and Warwick's.

A trumpet sounded from the far end of the bridge. Edward caught a glimpse of Northampton's banner as hundreds of his men surged into the mêlée. Pressed front and rear, the battle grew fiercest at Edward's end of the bridge, near the guard tower. The French were forced back and many retreated inside. Despite the strong French defence, it was only a matter of time before the smoke choked them into surrender.

The battle tide turned.

Edward backed away, his attention focused now on securing the island. "To me!" he called to his men. As they rallied around, a high-pitched scream issued from a commotion down the street. Two young girls, not likely more than ten or eleven years, struggled to break away from soldiers eager for sport.

"Chandos!" Edward pointed. "Do what you can to help."

Everywhere soldiers ran rampant, looting and ransacking houses. Shouts and furious howls burst from the upper story of one of the grander homes. Basins, chairs, and storage chests rained down onto the heads of the soldiers ramming the door below.

At the southern end of the island, the masts of Huntingdon's ships jutted up. Edward sprinted toward them. In the field beyond the river, men wearing Huntingdon's and Arundel's colours chased a score of French soldiers through the marshland. None could be allowed to escape to threaten an ambush later.

Butchered, fly-riddled bodies, too numerous to count, bestrewed the streets, riverbanks and marshes. Most were French, yet death claimed many English, too. Flies swarmed everywhere.

Edward said a silent prayer for the men who fell in the battle and prayed their victory might allay the king's temper at his disobeyed orders. Their three-prong assault succeeded despite its muddled start. As an afterthought, Edward added a prayer for himself, fearing his father's wrath when word reached him of Edward's role in what ensued.

In the evening, Edward patrolled among the wounded English, lit by the flames of burning houses. Though choking at the stench, he paused often to offer kind words to the injured, many likely dying, while he searched among them for one particular face. Edward could not recall when he and his standard bearer were separated.

"My lord." The voice came from the shadows.

Thomas Daniel swayed as he lowered himself to a knee, his surcoat dangling from one shoulder, the bloodstains black in the dim light. Through the soot and crusted blood streaking his face, Thomas smiled his familiar lopsided grin.

"*Dieu Merci*! God be praised!" Edward rushed to help his man stand. "I cannot tell you how relieved I am to see you!"

"And I you, my lord." Thomas coughed. "Forgive me, for I failed in my duty to stand with you."

"Never think it. Battle is chaos." Edward placed a careful hand to his banner man's back, uncertain of the extent of his injuries.

Thomas Daniel frowned. "Yet, I do and the chaos is no excuse, lord." A grin replaced the frown. Mayhap what I have to report makes up for my failing."

"Finding you alive is more than enough."

"You heard of the surrender, lord?"

"What of it?"

"You have not heard fully, then. It happened in the press of men; France's Marshal, the Comte de Tancarville, recognized the banner I held. Your banner. He surrendered to me. To me, in your name." Daniel's proud smile could have lit the sky.

A warm tingling sensation flowed through Edward. "Come, let us get you to my physician."

The moon rose blood red in the smoke over the smouldering city. The men of the vanguard were billeted on Caen's eastern slope to keep a close watch on the fortress and Bertrand's garrison. Edward sat with the men sharing tales of their exploits in the frenzied battle. He learned his father established his command at the Abbey aux Hommes, paying respect at Duke William's tomb.

An archer began his tale. 'I heard from one o' Northampton's archers about the king getting wind of the battle already startin' n' sent Northampton ter put a stop ter it. When the Earl got ter the bridge, he sized up the French n' saw Warwick's men had the better of it. Instead o' callin' a halt ter the attack, he joined it. Against the king's orders…quick as—" He snapped his fingers.

Edward sipped his ale. So, the king did not send Northampton to aid Warwick.

The archer wiped a sleeve across his mouth. "The smoke were comin' thick but some o' us were able ter move forward n' pick off any Genoese daring to show a face." He belched.

"What then?" someone asked.

"Our men-at-arms hacked through ter one o' th towers where a couple dozen Frenchies were holding firm. But the Prince of Wales here," he waved a hand at Edward, "showed up on t'other side o' the bridge. Caught 'em from behind, he did." The archer grinned, revealing several missing teeth.

"Go on," another man said.

"They was caught like rats, France's Constable n' Marshal. Forced ter surrender, 'cept theys too high n' mighty ter hand over their noble arses, yer pardon lord, ter a villein. No. The Constable recognized one o' our knights...fought with 'im in the Holy Wars." He paused for a gulp.

Edward rubbed his jaw. He knew of Comte d'Eu's surrender, though not the details.

"More n' likely you 'ave seen 'im. Lost 'is eye n' wears a patch."

Jesu! The Constable surrendered to Holland? The nobleman's ransom was worth a fortune and when paid, Holland would be a wealthy man.

Five days later, Edward watched from the bridge over the Orne as knights escorted the two high-ranking French nobles onto his father's flagship. The king offered to spare Caen's residents further hardship if the pair persuaded Bertrand to surrender the fortress.

Edward was there when his father heard of their refusal.

The king's eyes shot daggers. "Those two, pig-headed French sods can sit and rot until every groat of their ransom is paid, no matter how many years it takes!"

The English stripped Caen of its wealth, searched every building in every quarter, gathered anything of value and loaded it all onto Huntingdon's ships. Those who took part in the battle would share the bounty. Tidy sums to fill the soldiers' pockets. They earned it.

A shadow fell onto the planks at Edward's feet.

"My lord."

He turned. "Holland." The knight must have heard the chill in Edward's tone, for he bowed his head and took to one knee.

"When first we met, you reserved judgement on my knightly honour, for your cousin's sake, you said."

"Yes." Edward needed no reminder of Joan's plight at this miscreant's hands.

Holland raised his gaze. "You must know what Comte d'Eu's ransom represents for me."

Edward arched his brows. "Must I?" He hardened his eyes.

Holland did not flinch and held Edward's gaze. "Perhaps now, my lord, I might redeem myself."

Edward could have signaled Holland to rise. "You might try. Indeed, you might try." He turned and walked away. While Holland may have charmed his way into Joan's affections, he would learn Edward's regard would not be easily won.

Crossing the Seine

30 July 1346 - Caen to Liseux

Edward rode with Warwick and Chandos as the army advanced out of Caen, leaving behind a small guarding force to prevent Bertrand's troops from attempting to retake the city. Chandos was sharing his opinion of the Genoese bowmen, when Warwick interrupted.

"Lord Edward, do not fool yourself into thinking a battle proceeds as imagined. A commander must think on his feet and make quick decisions in response to an enemy's actions."

"Like Northampton did when he joined your assault on the bridge instead of signalling a withdrawal?"

"Just so." Warwick nodded. "And like you did when you searched for another way onto the island."

Chandos added, "Without a doubt, your quick action helped win the day."

Edward warmed at the veterans' praise. "I admit I am in awe of my father's foresight in keeping our landing location secret. Because he did, we were unopposed and now we have handed the French a major defeat." He paused, grinning. "Can you imagine the Valois' face when he learns most of Normandy's ports, and ships docked in them, were destroyed?"

A smile played on Warwick's lips. "Your father would be pleased to hear you grasp the importance of preparation. Think on this. What advantage have we gained in taking Caen aside from the obvious?”

“I do not take your meaning.”

“Caen’s riches have fallen into our hands as have many high-ranking prisoners. Might there be value in their capture aside from their ransoms?”

Edward considered, then shook his head.

Chandos said, “Many of the men we captured possess military experience.”

“Of course!” Edward grinned. “While we hold them, their expertise is lost to Philippe.”

“Exactly.” Warwick said.

“If I correctly view the campaign thus far,” Edward said, “its only failing is Normandy’s nobles have not embraced my father as their rightful overlord.”

“A good point,” Warwick said. “Our king judged wide of the mark there, though it matters naught now, not when our men discovered documents revealing Philippe’s intention to invade England and seize your father’s crown.”

“When Philippe learns of it, his reaction would be a sight to behold,” Chandos said.

Following the battle, Edward had supped with his father and he explained their next course of action. While the army advanced east, the fleet would sail home with the plunder and hostages. Huntingdon would offload, then return with provisions and troop reinforcements. They would rendezvous at Le Crotoy near the mouth of the Somme.

“Philippe must have heard of Caen’s fall by now,” Warwick said. “We must advance quickly, before he musters his forces.”

For the next two days, Edward’s vanguard ranged ahead of the army’s main body and at each town, after the men scavenged valuables and gathered foodstuffs, they set fire to everything. A mile after torching one particular holding, Edward took a deep breath and coughed. His chest rattled. Despite riding at the front of the column, breathing was difficult. “Ughtred!” he called, his voice more rasp than a bellow.

The under-marshal trotted forward. "Lord?"

"Make certain to rotate the order of the march. The combination of smoke and this dust must be near to choking the men in the rear. They need relief."

Three days later, after descending into a valley and fording a river, the vanguard rode up another hill into the village of Liseux. Modest houses lined the lane to the market square and the stately bishop's precinct. Just beyond the square, England's arms swayed from the eaves of a two-story, half-timbered house. The king's division usually traveled a more direct route and often arrived before the vanguard.

Edward dismounted at his father's temporary command post. Not a dozen yards away, three dust-laden, scarlet-robed clerics broke off their conversation. Edward ducked inside the home and found his father at a table with a map spread before him, his moustache and beard damp.

"Sire." Edward bowed. "The churchmen outside wait to attend you?"

His father scowled. "Sent by the Pope to broker peace."

Edward strode back to the door and glanced out. The cardinals abruptly ended their conversation—again—and then moved farther away. One man, pasty-faced and beady-eyed, offered the semblance of a bow.

Edward returned inside. "Something is amiss." He rubbed the nape of his neck. "I feel it. Do not trust them."

"Your concern may be warranted, yet I cannot refuse to speak with the Pope's red birds. Let us hope their chirping is more melodious than their customary song."

For the sake of courtesy, King Edward halted his march and granted the Pope's emissaries an audience, but he intended no more than a brief respite. He was willing to listen; if the Pope wanted peace, what might he offer in exchange for it?

Hoping the clerics' homilies for peace would be brief if they were made to stand, he did not give permission for the delegation to sit. Natheless, they droned on. The king listened half-heartedly while he assessed the campaign. Caen's defeat proved profitable and his son, to his credit, showed some cleverness of command. Looking ahead, Hugh Hastings should have landed in Ypres and united with Henry of Flanders by now and their troops begun their advance to rendezvous in Picardy. Before then, his main army must cover many miles and cross several rivers. First, the Seine at Rouen, before Philippe assembled a force to stop them. He pressed his temples. The sooner these damnable clerics ended their discourse, the better.

A day and a half later, the king's belly buzzing like a nest of hornets, he sought out the Norman Vicomte at his tent. De Harcourt bowed and gestured to a stool.

"No need, this is not likely to take long." King Edward fingered his beard. "My audience with the Pope's envoy lasted longer than I intended. Now, we must make up the lost time."

"Indeed, Lord King."

"I rely on you and your knowledge of the region."

"Yes, sire. The bridge at Rouen is our best way forward. If we push, we can arrive there in two days, but...."

King Edward raised his brows. "But what?"

"It requires a march of forty miles...and a night without water."

Jesu! The lengthy delay in discussions with the Pope's delegation better be worth the cost. "If that is our best route, then we march." How would the Pope respond to his proposal?

2 August 1346 – Liseux to Le Neubourg

Two evenings later, as the sun lowered behind a ridge, the army's main body trudged into the deserted village of Le Neubourg. King Edward dismounted with a groan. He had pushed the march at a taxing pace and prayed Philippe lacked sufficient time to muster forces at Rouen.

He needed to do more than pray.

That evening he invited de Harcourt to share a cold supper with him. Over the meal, they discussed the Vicomte's relationships with other Norman nobles and their inclination to switch allegiance. Toward the end of the meal, the king laid down his knife and wiped his mouth.

"In the morning, I want you to scout Rouen and determine the size of the garrison and assess the security at the bridge. Take two retinues with you, entirely your choice of men."

The next morning, not long after sunrise, King Edward ambled through camp chatting with his tired men. Should Philippe's forces hold the Rouen bridge, he would be obliged to find another crossing. A less direct march would drain his men's stamina further and stretch the army's supplies. He risked a great deal to meet with the Pope's delegates as long as he did. Were they only sent to delay him?

At mid-morning, while he conferred with Northampton, scouts shouted a warning of dust billowing above the road to the north. He and the Earl hastened outside. A few minutes later, de Harcourt's column clattered into the square. Rivulets of sweat scored the dust caking the horses' heaving flanks.

The Vicomte hauled himself from his saddle, his face bleak and his brow beaded with sweat. "Lord," he said, "Philippe occupies Rouen."

King Edward stiffened. "You are certain?"

De Harcourt wiped his face. "His banner and the Oriflamme fly from the city's walls."

"*Jesu!*" Northampton said.

The king pretended calm. "Come, let us talk."

The Vicomte handed off his horse and went inside. He sank onto a stool and downed a cup of ale in one gulp. He gestured to the page for more.

"Father?" Edward hovered in the doorway, Warwick behind him. "Might we join you?"

The king gestured them in.

De Harcourt began his report, sipping between breaths. "The French have barricaded the entire width of the bridge and dozens of pikes jut up from behind it. Several retinues of men-at-arms patrol it." He paused, frowning. "I sent two men ahead, on foot, but they were spotted."

"Killed?" Warwick asked, concern in his voice.

"Wounded and bleeding badly." The Vicomte set down his ale. "You should have seen them, Holland and de la Marsh."

"What?" Northampton leaned forward.

"The hotheads galloped full tilt at the bridge, whooping and howling at the top of their lungs." The Vicomte closed his eyes and shook his head. "They drew attention, and the crossbow fire, while four other men hauled the two injured men to safety."

"The damn fools could have been killed," the king said. "But I give them credit; they have courage."

The Norman nodded. "And quick thinking, sire."

"Holland and…de la Marsh, did you say?" Northampton rubbed his jaw. "Holland served with me at Sluys and in Brittany but I do not recognize de la Marsh."

The king tugged his beard. "So Vicomte, the skirmish aside, what did you learn?"

De Harcourt's face grew grim. "At least ten score men-at-arms and as many bowman are stationed at the south end of the bridge, plus there are four more heavily-manned blockades along its length. We counted at least twenty standards flying on the northern bank."

"Four thousand men." Edward shook his head. "Far too many to force a crossing."

At dawn's first light, as the vanguard prepared to march, Edward checked and tightened his girth one last time, then mounted his stallion. All around, horses snorted and stomped, metal clanked, and orders were shouted.

"God's blessings upon you, Lord Edward," de Harcourt said as he trotted up.

"Vicomte" Edward nodded. "I understand we ride together today. My father informs me you know our direction well."

"Indeed, we traverse my fool of a brother's lands. With all our family has endured at Philippe's hands, why my brother remains loyal to him I cannot understand."

Why any man remained loyal to a coward like Philippe, Edward could not understand. The men assembled, he signalled the column forward. De Harcourt rode beside him, keeping a silent vigil. The silence suited Edward. Why had his father delayed to march for so long? While his father could hardly brush aside the Pope's intimate, Cardinal-Bishop of Ostia, what reason or matter discussed justified spending a day and a half with the Pope's emissaries? It cost them the ability to cross the Seine at Rouen. Edward prayed the alternate route they found would not take them too far afield.

They had descended into to a small verdant valley, then climbed to a heavily-wooded ridge they traversed for several hours. At a break in the trees, the vista cleared. Edward halted. "*Jesu!*" The ridge sheered straight down three hundred feet to the Seine flowing through a U-shaped gorge.

De Harcourt said, "Now, you see why Rouen offered the better crossing." He pointed. "That town is Elbeuf."

From their scouts' report, Edward was aware the bridge at Elbeuf was broken, but he was curious and urged his horse down the cleft in the white stone bluff to the river's edge. He halted and studied the shattered bridge timbers half-submerged in the river.

Could the carpenters repair the it?

A whirring brushed past Edward's left ear followed by a thud. He reined back. "God's bones!" The crossbow bolt barely missed him. French taunts burst from the opposite bank. Edward raised his fist, flipping a fig sign, then spun his horse and returned to the column. "How far to the next crossing?

The Vicomte nodded. "Following the river, Pont de l'Arche. is about five miles from here."

They rode the ridge for another mile then Edward called an early halt. He had pushed the pace most of the day and the men needed rest.

The next morning, Edward saluted farewell to Elbeuf's smouldering embers. The vanguard headed southwest and not long into the march, de Harcourt rode up beside him. "That village is Criquebeuf; Pont de l'Arche lies a few miles beyond it."

Edward squinted and could just make out the outline of the village. While the sun crested over the treetops, his men ransacked Criquebeuf. At the loud swoosh behind him, Edward swiveled in his saddle. Sparks flew from a collapsing roof.

Edward spotted Warwick, touched spurs to his horse, and loped off to join the Earl at the head of the column. Mile after mile, the vanguard marched beneath an azure sky with not a single cloud to ease the blistering heat. Though they had traveled for several hours, Edward saw no signs of enemy troops tracking them from the opposite bank of the Seine.

Pont de l'Arche appeared in the distance when a sentry shouted. Several scouts were galloping toward them. Warwick signalled a halt. The leading scout slid his winded horse to a stop.

"Lord," he blurted, "the bridge is broken but the town is deserted and we saw no defenders this side of the river."

"None?" Warwick glanced at Edward.

"No," the scout said, "though a small force guards the northern bank."

Edward's insides buzzed. "We have a chance." He called over his shoulder, "Ughtred, hold here while we judge the damage."

Edward, Warwick, and the carpenters, with a guarding force, trotted into the deserted town, the clatter of hooves sounding off the buildings. Nothing stirred save whirlwinds of dust.

The river's roar drew Edward forward, though he advanced with caution after the near miss at Elbeuf. They halted at the river's edge. A gap yawned between them and the remnants of the bridge jutting from the northern bank, while below, the river rushed over broken beams.

Edward caught movement from across the river. While he studied the dense stand of trees, he said, "Lord, what do you think?" He tipped his head toward the opposite bank.

The Earl stared across the river. "No more than a handful of French."

Chandos drew up alongside. "Dust rises above the trees. Looks to be a good-sized force."

Edward scowled. "Damn them!"

9 August 1346 – Pont de l'Arche to Vernon

Thwarted at Pont de l'Arche, the vanguard advanced another ten miles, skirting a forest stretching south as far as Edward could see. A church steeple rose from among the trees.

"The Priory and Church of Notre Dame," de Harcourt explained. "Where the Eure joins the Seine."

Edward rolled his stiff shoulders. "Fresh water, ample stores, and comfortable lodging for the night." He grinned.

Near dusk, the king's division and rear guard rode in and set up command in the Priory Hall. Later, Edward responded to a summons from his father. Upon entering the hall, he discovered it empty save the king. Edward strode forward and bowed. "My liege."

His father had washed, cleaned the grit from his moustache and beard, and donned a clean tunic. "Sit." His father said, grim-faced. Several quiet minutes passed.

Edward waited, twisting his signet ring.

His father tapped his fingers on the table, then stopped. "Philippe plays a game, delaying us and depleting our supplies."

Edward nodded. "As long as he prevents us from crossing the Seine, he holds the upper hand. The Valois may lack courage but he is proving himself wily as a fox." Though Edward might be a novice at war, he understood Philippe had checked them, just like in a game chess.

"Two things we must accomplish, Edward. Cross the Seine and stir Philippe from his lair." The king pinned Edward with a dark look. "Find a way."

Edward swallowed hard. *Jesu*! He had no idea what might force Philippe out of hiding, yet his father laid the task upon him. Here was an opportunity to prove himself. He stood, bowed, and bade his father *bon nuit*.

Beneath a sliver of a citrine moon, Edward wandered circles through the priory grounds, his gut and mind churning. He brooded on the problem, twisting his ruby signet ring round and round and round. He halted; the kernel of an idea sprouted.

At daybreak, the king and main body lumbered away, to follow the course of the Seine, while Edward's vanguard set to flame all save the priory church. Then he and his men galloped five miles south to a property Edward recalled de Harcourt mentioning a few days earlier.

The Chateau Louviers and surrounding property were owned, and held in great affection, by Jeanne de Bourgogne, Philippe's queen. If she were to suffer the full brunt of the English king's ire, see her cherished Louviers destroyed, her royal husband might be spurred into action.

The vanguard galloped through the stone pillars into the courtyard sending chickens squawking and servants shrieking. The few French guards present drew their swords and weapons clashed. Outnumbered, the guards soon fled.

"Ughtred!" Edward called from atop his stallion. "Have the men scour every chamber for valuables, including the chapel, then take axes to anything too heavy to carry. I want kindling made of the furniture and the tapestries shredded."

He dismounted, handed off his horse to his squire, and strode to the far end of the yard to the kitchen where he ducked inside. Loaves of bread were cooling on a shelf and at the yeasty aroma, his mouth watered. He grabbed a baguette, a wedge of cheese, and a half-bottle of wine, then wandered into the herb garden. There, surrounded by sweet herbal scents, he sat cross-legged on the ground and ate, serenaded by the staccato sounds of axes. No bread, nor cheese, nor wine ever tasted so satisfying.

The hacking waned, replaced by dark fingers of smoke curling up from the château. Edward retraced his steps to the gate to where his squire held his horse, seized his reins, and mounted. "Hand me one of those," he called to the men lighting torches. He heeled his stallion toward the chateau and heaved the flambeau through the shattered portal. Perhaps this pyre would smoke Philippe out of hiding.

Hours later, the vanguard caught up with the main body at another great bend in the river curving around a promontory. Château Gaillard, the Lionheart's legendary fortress, rested at its top. Below, at Andelys, sunlight glinted off the helmets and weapons of a large French force guarding the bridge.

Edward halted beside Warwick. The Earl massaged the vertical crease between his eyes and spat. "Too well guarded to force a crossing."

They rode on, travelling along a high, flat plateau above the river. When de Harcourt loped up beside the Earl, Edward dropped back to ride with Chandos and Mortimer. The pair were arguing Lionheart's merits. De Harcourt's voice, although muted, drifted back.

"But you share the king's confidence."

"Even so," Warwick said, "he has shared nothing of why he spoke at such length with the Pope's emissaries."

"Courtesy be damned," de Harcourt said. "The king was fully aware of the importance of reaching Rouen before Philippe rallied his forces. What was he thinking to dally a day and a half?"

"Like I said, I am not privy to the king's reasons and although it is unlike him to blunder, I fear he has handed Philippe the advantage."

Edward pretended not to hear them for such grumblings spoke ill of the king's authority. However, to himself, he could admit he shared their concerns.

Later in the afternoon, de Harcourt drew up alongside Edward. "Vernon lies ahead, lord, another of Queen Jeanne's holdings. The town lies on the southern bank and, if fortune is with us, boasts few defenders." The Vicomte rubbed his jaw. "The bridge at Vernon is the last for another sixty miles."

"Then, let us pray our Lord God is with us."

Desperate to reach Vernon ahead of the French, Edward pushed an arduous pace through the forested bluff above the river. At each town in their path, a retinue broke off to ransack and fire it while the column rode on. The track gradually descended and Vernon appeared in the distance. The steeples of two abbeys towered above the cotes and shops which spilt into Vernon's faubourg beyond the town's walls.

Edward halted the column about a half mile away and sent a half-dozen of the vanguard's most trusted men to scout the town. He dismounted and paced, stopping now and again to search for signs of his men. Mortimer and Chandos were the first to return.

Edward, Warwick, and de Harcourt crowded around Mortimer when he crouched and began scratching a hasty map in the dirt. "The town is situated on the river, here, with the bridge here." Mortimer marked each with an x. "The bridge is sturdily built on stone pilings and shops line its length." He paused. "The only way to reach the bridge is through the town."

Chandos took the stick. "A modest force of men-at-arms and crossbowmen patrol the walls, with most positioned here, near the gate." He marked an x.

Warwick tugged his ear. "A modest force, you say?"

"Even with only a handful of defenders, with a direct assault we chance the loss of many men." Edward said. "Perhaps we should stage a ruse to lure the garrison out?"

"There is more, lord," Mortimer said. "A French force guards the northern bank."

Edward glanced toward the town and the bridge. "How large?"

A rustling sound came from within the tangled scrub. Thomas Holland emerged and hunched down beside them. "By my reckoning," he said, "perhaps a thousand or more with a Genoese crossbowman behind every tree."

Edward gagged and covered his nose.

Mortimer and Chandos scooted backwards. The Vicomte waved a hand to dispel the foul odour.

Warwick studied the map. "We might manage to overwhelm the guards and take the town—" He sniffed, grimaced, and slowly turned in the direction of the odour. "God's blood, Holland, you are covered in shite!"

"Your pardon, lords." Holland gestured at the muck caking him from shoulders to toes. "I probed the fosse a tad too deep."

Warwick snorted. "*Jesu*! You stink."

"Truth be told," Holland grinned, "it is quite possible I smell no worse now than I did before."

Warwick raised a hand as if to clap Holland's shoulder, then caught himself and chuckled. The filth-covered knight stood, and with a self-mocking grin, lifted one muck-covered boot and shook it, rousing a round of laughter.

The Earl cut the mirth short. "With such a large force, we can do nought here save teach these mongrels a lesson."

Warwick rallied his men, and within minutes, archers entered the faubourg. Once in position, they loosed a flurry of flaming arrows over the town's walls into Vernon proper. The vanguard's men-at-arms cheered as smoke rose above the palisade. Roofs sparked and smouldered. Warwick signalled and his men fanned out and pillaged every abandoned shop, cottage, shed, and warehouse before setting them afire.

August 1346 - Windsor

Joan entered Queen Philippa's outer chamber where her ladies gathered around the nurse holding infant Margaret, the fifth princess and newest addition to the royal family.

"Bring her to me," Queen Philippa said from her bed. Only a few weeks since delivering her tenth child, the queen returned to her customary robust health.

Joan stood in the doorway. Queen Philippa gazed at her infant daughter with a mother's doting affection, her lashes fluttering down, dark against her glowing complexion.

"Come, Joan, sit with me."

Joan lowered herself onto a stool beside the bed and the queen leaned close. She whispered, "Admiral Huntingdon came to inquire after me."

"The Earl came here, my lady?" Joan kept her voice low. Perhaps she misunderstood?

The queen smoothed the blanket from baby Margaret's face. "I yielded to temptation and agreed to speak with him despite my lack of the church's cleansing. I pray our Lord, in his mercy, forgives my transgression."

"The Earl recently returned from Normandy, did he not?"

"Indeed, and I could not rest until I heard of my loved ones and Caen's surrender from one who bore witness to the battle."

Joan folded her hands in her lap. "Quite understandable." Though highly irregular. What would the gossips say if they heard of the queen's indiscretion?

"I feared my son, in his eagerness, might act foolishly, but the Earl eased my disquiet, offering nothing but praise for Edward. It seems my son's quick actions turned the battle tide."

"Edward has never been one to lose sight of his purpose."

"Still, it is good to know he keeps his head about him even during the heat of an engagement."

"Did the admiral share anything of my brother?" Joan did not ask after Will. Would the queen notice, think it odd? Joan lowered her gaze and fingered the folds of her gown.

"Regrettably, nothing of Jack…nor of your husband. During the voyage the Earl spoke often with one of the captives, Count d'Eu. The Count related his surrender at the battle at Caen. As he explained it to Huntingdon, while in the final stages of battle the Count recognized a knight who fought with him in the crusades, and who sadly, had lost an eye. The Count stated he much preferred to surrender to a man of honour, so when he spotted Thomas Holland, the Count surrendered to him.

Joan's breath hitched. *Blessed Virgin*!

The queen soothed her daughter's whimper. "A remarkable story, is it not?"

"Indeed, it is." Joan was unaware of the surrender, nor did she know Thomas had lost an eye.

"I believe a knight by that name served the king in the Low Countries. A handsome young man from a Lancashire family, as I recall. Too bad about his eye, though the Constable's ransom will be the making of Sir Thomas."

Joan busied herself pouring cool drinks from the pitcher on the small table in the corner. Queen Philippa seemed to know quite a bit about Thomas, more than was warranted by someone of his low rank. Why? And, why did the queen confide her interlude with Huntingdon to Joan?

Philippa motioned to Margaret's nurse. "Take her. I should like to rest now."

Several days later, while the queen's ladies strolled in the garden, Joan chatted with Lady Elizabeth a few paces behind the others. Beneath a morning sky blanketed in clouds, the fragrances of rosemary and mint mingled with the scent of coming rain.

Elizabeth paused to admire a shrub cleverly trimmed in the

shape of a rabbit. "Baby Margaret bears a good likeness to the king," Elizabeth said. "More fair in coloring than her mother or Johanna."

"Yes, like Lady Isabella, Margaret seems to favour the king."

"Over time Margaret's hair may darken."

"It may, indeed." Time. Days spent waiting, becoming weeks, months and before long, a year, then another. Joan's thoughts hovered on the queen's revelation. Thomas said Joan must be patient, his military service his only source of income. Now, with the Constable's ransom, Thomas might have the means to support her when he came to claim her. Yet, after being abandoned for so long, did she still want him to claim her?

The ladies slowed their pace and talk of the war drifted back. "Did I tell you," Lady Mary said, "I overheard two guards discussing a recent skirmish for a river crossing in France? It sounded frightful. Several of our knights were wounded."

"I hope no one was killed," Maud said. "Did you recognize anyone?"

"One, if I remember correctly…from our time in Flanders. Sir Thomas Holland?"

Joan's stomach sank. Thomas was wounded?

"I remember him," Maud said. "Handsome and quite gallant, as I recall."

Though Joan's pulse thrummed, she schooled her face and voice. "Eleanor, I beg your pardon. Where did this skirmish occur?"

"At a town called Gaillon, I believe."

Joan kept her tone light. "Were the men seriously injured?"

Eleanor shook her head. "I do not know. The men I overheard did not mention any details."

Joan calmed herself. Thomas had lost an eye, and now this. The strength of her reaction provided an answer to her question. Despite the years apart, she wanted Thomas still, and hoped their separation ended with his return. *If he returned.*

10 August 1346 – Vernon to Mousseaux

After Vernon, the next possible crossing was the bridge at Mantes. To reach it, de Harcourt mentioned a large bend in the Seine which lay not far ahead. The French would be forced to march the long way around while the vanguard could cut cross-country, reach the bridge and take it, before the French defenders arrived.

Edward wasted no time in assembling the troops and as they moved off, he and de Harcourt loped their horses up and down the ranks of marching foot soldiers calling encouragement. Dripping sweat, the soldiers passed skins of watered ale from man to man. They could not afford to stop, not if they were to secure the bridge ahead of the French.

Several hours into the march, Ughtred waved from the column's head. "Lord!"

Edward cantered to the front and not two hundred yards distant, white flags fluttered. Edward halted the column. Ahead of them, an armed guard escorted three men in red robes.

"God's bones, Ughtred! Another papal envoy? At this exact place and time?"

Edward called for a fresh mount and galloped with four guards to intercept his father and the army's main body coming behind. When he reached them, he reported the arrival of the papal delegation.

The king's eyes blazed. "Churchmen, now?"

Edward checked his fractious mount. "No doubt they are sent to delay us. Sire, you must refuse them. We cannot afford a delay. It is urgent we secure the bridge at Mantes."

King Edward shook his head. "*Non*, Edward, I cannot decline to see them." He rubbed his brow. "You and the vanguard must hasten to Mantes. As you say, we must secure the bridge."

Though Edward had plenty to say, he kept his thoughts to himself. As he galloped back to his troops, he could not help but question the king's decision. Why could his father not refuse? What was so important?

He reined in beside Warwick and de Harcourt. "My father says he intends to meet with the delegation and orders us to Mantes."

"What? He has agreed to pause our march again?" Warwick's face grew red.

Edward curbed his stallion "Even should we secure the bridge, how long can we manage to hold it? We do not know the king's mind nor the length of this delay."

"And consider this," the Vicomte said, "Rolleboise is about three miles from here, with a standing French garrison."

"Yet the king orders us to Mantes?" Warwick shook his head.

"Lord Earl, you disregarded my father's orders at Caen. Mayhap it is time to do so again. Despite his command, leaving him is out of the question." Edward circled his restless stallion. "I do not trust the cardinals, nor the garrison at Rolleboise."

"Then Mantes ceases to be a possibility," Warwick said.

The Earl and de Harcourt must be asking the same question as Edward asked himself. What was so important the king would pause again to meet with the emissaries?

De Harcourt frowned. "After Mantes, only two crossings remain. One at Meulan and the last at Poissy—only seventeen miles from Paris."

11 August 1346 – Mousseaux to Meulan

Having lost the chance of crossing at Mantes, Edward pushed the vanguard's pace to Meulan even harder. The horses' hooves pounded a three-beat rhythm, labouring under another cloudless sky, offering no respite from the searing heat. The track they traveled hugged the river, and by mid-day, they crossed the Maudre, a small tributary of the Seine.

Late in the afternoon, Edward halted the column with a view of the river near Meulan. The sun glared upon the water rushing under the arches of an unbroken bridge from the western shore of the river to a large island in its middle. Stone walls encircled the island with a barbican guarding the gate.

Edward took a deep breath; relief washed through him. They

had found a crossing. Northampton and Warwick eased their horses alongside him. Warwick made the sign of the cross. "God and Saint George are with us."

"Walls or not, we take the bridge," Northampton said, his voice steeped in determination.

12 August 1346 – Meulan to Ecquivilly

King Edward sat beneath the awning of his camp tent, clenching and unclenching his fist while his commanders made their reports. The light morning breeze rustled the leaves on the trees, yet did nothing to cool his ire.

His son brushed his hair from his eyes. "We launched our assault on Meulan before dusk, sire, and while the archers laid down a barrage of arrows, our men attempted to scale the walls, but we failed to breach their defences."

"Regrettably, it matters not, lord," Northampton said.

King Edward rounded on the Earl. "Tell me, Constable, how does failure not matter?"

"Lord King, we did all we could," Edward said. "Many men chanced their lives in the current trying to skirt the island's walls. Then Warwick's men discovered the span of the bridge from the island to the northern bank was broken."

Warwick picked at a scab on his face. "We withdrew believing it the wiser course. No sense in suffering further injury or loss of men if the northern span was broken."

"Assuredly," Northampton said, "we are no less vexed than you at yet another setback."

King Edward girded his temper. If his two most experienced commanders saw fit to withdraw, then he must accept their verdict. The hoped-for crossing was lost. He stood. "You may go," he said to the earls. "Ready the men to march."

The king gestured his son outside. "Look around, what do you see?"

"Smoke plumes."

"Indeed. While your vanguard attacked the island, my troops laid waste to Philippe's cherished *Île de France*. Each day Philippe thwarts our crossing our army is that much closer to Paris."

"Yes, I see."

"Do you?" The king's lips twitched. "Tell me. What do you see, Edward?"

"Destruction."

King Edward grinned wryly. "*Non, mon fils*. That," he waved a hand, "is an invitation. The French imposter believes us stymied, *n'est ce pas*? Perhaps, we need not cross the Seine after all."

Edward's brow wrinkled. "Not cross? I do not understand."

King Edward tucked his hands behind his back. "Only forty miles separate us from Paris." He paused. Would Edward discern his intention?

"Word in camp says Philippe's heir, Duke Jean, has withdrawn his troops from Gascony and marches here. Is this true?"

The king nodded.

"If we cannot cross to unite with Hastings, mayhap we best devise a new course before we are trapped between King Philippe's and Duke Jean's forces."

"Indeed." The king smothered a smile. He wanted his heir to ponder the chessboard a while longer. One bridge remained. Poissy. Seventeen miles from the gates of Paris.

The city held the key.

The army overnighted not far from Meulan and King Edward rose before dawn to catch Edward before the vanguard left camp. The king approached his son as he was about to mount his stallion. "Torch everything in your path," the king said. "The smoke must be visible as far as Paris."

"You may rely on me, sire." Edward settled in his saddle,

adjusted his reins in one hand, and raised his other. "Forward!" He set his heels to his stallion and cantered away, leaving Ughtred to follow with the rest of the column..

When the sun crested the horizon, smoke plumes spiralled in the distance. The king judged his son's forces were already several miles ahead. The king mounted his horse and the army's middle division, supply wagons, and rear guard left the Seine behind, climbing to the forested ridge above it.

He breathed in the woodland's cooler air finding the myriad shades of green soothing after the weeks of dust-riddled tans and browns. Easing into his horse's rolling gait, King Edward flexed his shoulders and stretched his neck from side to side, smiling to himself. Philippe believed him cornered, and in the faux king's arrogance, he failed to recognize his peril, one of his own making.

When the army reached the village of Ecquevilly, King Edward called an early halt. His men needed to rest to rebuild their strength in preparation for battle come sunrise. And his son needed time…as did Philippe.

As twilight descended, the king spread a map on the table in his 'borrowed' chamber while a serving lad lit candles and another refilled his cup with wine. The king sat studying the map and reconsidered his course of action.

Hoofbeats sounded outside, followed by voices. At the knock, one of the lads opened the door. A messenger stepped inside and doffed his cap.

"Lord King." The hobelar bent to one knee. "Lord Edward bade me tell you he is camped atop a ridge near Bures. It lies not five miles from Poissy."

The king nodded. "*Bon.*" Less than a day's ride from Paris.

13 August 1346 – Bures

In the morning, camp pulsed with a raw energy that matched Edward's. *Lord, grant me strength this day.* The barest sliver of amber lit the eastern skyline as he climbed into his saddle.

"Form up," Ughtred called. Weapons rattled, and leather creaked as several hundred men mounted. Horses snorted and pawed; Edward's vanguard retinues formed into line. Chandos and Audley halted beside him while they waited for de Harcourt's retinues to join their column.

Today, they would carry out a mission separate from that of Northampton, Warwick and the bulk of the vanguard. The earls' success this day depended upon him, and he vowed to do all in his power to ensure the earls succeeded.

He urged his horse forward. "*Bonne chance!*" he called to the two veteran commanders. The rumble of hooves, jingling harness, and chink of weapons echoed through the trees as his force descended the ridge. Halfway down, the sun peeked in the east, casting a fiery light upon the Seine, snaking in the distance. To the north, Poissy beckoned from a bend in the river, but Edward's targets lay east and south, nearer to Paris—much nearer.

Not long into their journey, Chandos sniffed. "Do you smell something?"

Edward swivelled in his saddle. Dark plumes blackened the sky to the north, confirming Warwick and Northampton's rampage toward Poissy. Villagers would panic and flee to Paris, causing great havoc like that at Caen. The citizens of Paris would wail for protection, pleading with King Philippe to defend them and Paris at all cost.

The vanguard rode fast, covering the miles to the first targeted village east of Poissy before the sun cleared the trees. The rapid clatter of hooves echoed off the empty shops and homes bereft of life, a result of his previous day's work. He halted the column and turned to de Harcourt. "You and your men begin at the other end."

"My pleasure, lord." The Vicomte's eyes glinted. He called his men and spurred away, an unholy smile on his face.

Chandos and Audley remained while Edward studied the deserted structures. "Yesterday's labours were not wasted. It appears our French friends have all fled to Paris."

Audley grinned. "They think it safe. Do we ride there next, lord?"

"By the manner in which Philippe persists in denying us our chosen course, one might perceive his actions as an invitation to join him there." Edward inclined his head toward the center of town and winked. "However, let us first celebrate, perhaps with a dance around a blazing pyre?"

Audley chuckled.

Edward ordered Ughtred and Mortimer to lead retinues to the villages in the surrounding areas. "Your orders are to induce as much panic as possible."

De Harcourt's knowledge of the region proved invaluable; throughout the day the communities within easy reach of Paris went up in flames. As dusk descended, the sky blazed crimson between thick layers of a charcoal haze. To the northeast, smoke billowed skyward above Nanterre and dark pillars marched southward to St. Cloud, only four miles from the gates of Paris.

Edward swiped at the beads of sweat dripping from his brow and spit ash from his lips. Drifting smoke and ash must be engulfing Paris. Embers, caught on the wind, likely threatened homes. What were the Parisians thinking? Feeling?

The retinues of the middle division, the supply wagons, and the rear guard had encamped overnight atop a ridge in Ecquevilly. The sun breached the eastern horizon while King Edward strolled through camp greeting his men and extolling the virtues of victory. The vanguard troops, under Warwick, Northampton, and Edward, had encamped overnight at Bures and by first light would have embarked on their assignments.

The countryside surrounding Ecquevilly sheltered the chateaux of France's highest-ranking nobles. Earlier that morning, he ordered dozens of the middle division's retinues to ride out and set fire to every dwelling within twenty miles. Flames devoured Philippe's prized heartlands—he would feel the bite of England's lion.

Not until mid-morning did the middle division rumble from camp, King Edward at its head. While thousands of feet marched in rhythm to the beat of the drums, England's quartered arms and the cross of St. George fluttered in the breeze above them. Bright crimson pennons danced alongside, signalling King Edward's challenge to France's false sovereign to meet on the battlefield. Would the coward-who-called-himself-France's-king take up the gauntlet?

From atop the ridge, the formidable Seine appeared through the trees, stretching northwest toward the sea and southeast toward Paris. The river presented no barrier to English troops nor protection for Philippe's cherished city as Paris, the jewel of Philippe's crown, lay directly in the English army's current path.

As smoke billowed ever closer toward Paris, King Edward smiled. Did Philippe recognize his city's peril?

With the sun at its zenith, dust shimmered in the distance, above the track they were travelling. A rider in Northampton's livery came into view as he galloped toward them. Did he carry the message the king most desired?

The courier slid his horse to a halt. "Lord King." He doffed his cap and used it to mop the sweat from his brow. "The Earl bade me report these words: 'The gates of Poissy swing open.' The town is abandoned, sire. The French have withdrawn."

King Edward allowed himself a brief inward sigh of triumph, then braced himself. "What of the bridge?"

"Broken, sire."

"Can it be repaired?"

"My lord says, 'With God's blessing.'"

Throughout the day, outriders relayed messages between the king and his commanders in Poissy. As much as he desired to push his army's pace, he dared not exhaust his men. They may yet be needed to engage in battle.

By late-afternoon, the main body entered the southern reaches of Poissy. The king and his guard trotted their horses past the shops and down the main street, passing the priory and royal palace. The French had spared no expense in their construction. Rather than the common rough-hewn beams and rubble, the priory and palace were constucted of planed wood and ashlar blocks.

King Edward smelled the river, the odours of fish and marshy vegetation, long before it came into view. He cocked his head. Faint sounds…shouts…coming from the river. Alarm raced through him. "Cobham, alert the troops."

The king set spurs to his horse and galloped headlong down the street with his escort thundering around him. To the north, beyond the rooftops, dust billowed.

Riders! Hundreds of them.

The shouting grew louder. A trumpet blared.

As he closed the distance to the river, the vista opened. Stone foundation piers, supporting the northern and southern ends of the bridge, jutted from the Seine's racing current. Both ends appeared intact with a large gap yawning between them.

One single beam spanned the breach which, according to dispatches, had been retrieved from the river and hauled into place.

The dust cloud in the north loomed closer. French soldiers galloped full-tilt beneath blue and gold banners. They were closing the distance to the northern end of the bridge where a handful of English carpenters were working.

"For England!"

The king's eyes flew to the man who cried out.

Northampton! Sword in hand, and in full armour, the Earl balanced his way across the beam, little more than a foot wide.

King Edward's breath seized. One misstep would see his steadfast friend plunged to certain death in the swirling river below. He slowed his mount.

"For Saint George!" The Earl's men chorused his cheer, following him across the narrow timber. Despite being encumbered with armour and weapons, dozens dared the beam. Northampton's force was small, not above two hundred, all bound to defend the north bank.

A knot formed in the king's gut. He urged his mount forward again and called, "Archers! Ready the archers!"

His heart raced; the bravest of his bowmen, staves in hand, sprinted onto the beam and traversed to the northern bank. Other archers positioned themselves along the river's southern bank, within longbow range of the French soldiers, swarming the northern bank and wheeling ballista-armed carts into position. French crossbowmen cranked and loaded their weapons.

Someone grabbed King Edward's bridle. "Get back, sire! Out of crossbow range."

With his guard forming around him, the battle unfolded before King Edward's eyes. The French men-at-arms launched out of their saddles and formed into line. They were as desperate to retake the crossing as Northampton's men were to hold it.

The Earl raised his sword. "For England!" The two forces collided with a roar. Weapons clanged. Men grunted and cursed. Screams ripped as crossbow bolts pierced English bodies.

The king winced with each wail from a bloodied Englishman. As each man fell, he choked down bile.

"Loose!" Longbows sang.

King Edward's chest thrummed as hundreds of arrows clouded the sky. The first flight felled the French loading the ballistas. The second toppled most of the crossbowmen. Shaft after shaft, the archers aimed into the line of French men-at-arms attempting to form a wall at the top of the riverbank.

The howls of wounded and dying men echoed across the divide.

Northampton's surcoat flashed crimson and gold amid the mêleé. His men battled uphill, their backs to the river. The French were fighting with admirable courage. *Damn, them!* The king's heart ran rampant.

Northampton and his men fought like cornered boars. Foot by

foot, they drove the French back while arrows winged from English longbows, picking off defenders.

Suddenly, the French broke and ran.

Late in the evening Edward returned to Poissy. The sound of hammers resounded off the buildings. Edward dismounted in front of Philippe's palace, draped with England's arms, and went inside.

He threaded his way through the throng of men swigging ale in the Great Hall, reeking of sour sweat, and smoke; Edward smelled no better. He approached the head table and bowed. "Lord King."

"Ahh, *mon fils*, you join us." His father grinned and clapped Edward's shoulder. Dust and ash floated up.

Edward pulled up a seat. "By the sounds outside, I take it the carpenters continue repairs on the bridge." A serving lad was passing and Edward motioned for ale.

Cobham lowered his cup. "Laying more support beams and heavy planks to accommodate the wagons. All now loaded with Philippe's treasures." He winked.

Edward slumped, and downed a cup of ale. "Lord Father, did I hear right, you received a message from Philippe? Delivered by yet another churchman waving a flag of truce?" Edward belched.

"That whoreson, Philippe, calls our king a false vassal." Warwick's lip curled. "The Valois orders our king to cease his attacks, and to refrain from burning any more of his liege lord's territory." He bit off the roughened skin around his thumbnail and spat.

Northampton wiped ale from his beard. "Philippe responded to our king's offer of battle with a challenge of his own to meet southwest of Paris."

"Oh ho!" Edward said, grinning. He motioned for a refill.

While the men ate, Philippe's challenge dominated the conversation. They dined on plundered goods: beef, goose, doves, partridge and widgeon, accompanied by sauces, four cheeses, and pickles. The hall overflowed with men lauding Northampton's balancing act and the king's cunning, for their success at Poissy was owing to it.

Edward ate and drank his fill and when the candles burned low, he leaned toward his father. "What was your reply to Philippe?"

"As we speak, the Pope's cleric of peace hastens to Philippe with an expression of my great pleasure at his invitation." The king glanced at the men surrounding him. "Should Philippe want to find me, he will know where I am by the smoke in the air. Tomorrow, we march to meet him." The king chuckled. "At least that is what I intend Philippe to believe."

He laid an arm across Edward's shoulders. "Your efforts today convinced Philippe of an imminent attack on Paris. So believing, he withdrew the troops here in Poissy, stationed to secure the bridge. On the morrow, Edward, you are to execute an encore, one equally if not more persuasive. Tomorrow, you burn Philippe's precious Saint Germain-en-Laye."

The next morning, Edward, de Harcourt, and their men rode out of Poissy while still dark. Over several cups of wine the previous evening, de Harcourt regaled him about the birthplace of France's sainted King Louis. By the time they rode into Sainte Germain-en-Laye, the sun crested the eastern horizon. Its rays glinted upon the tall, narrow windows lining the length of an ornate building's massive walls, supported by pale stone buttresses soaring skyward.

"Unless I am mistaken," Edward said to Chandos, "here stand Philippe's royal château and Sainte Chapelle." He could not deny their magnificence. "According to de Harcourt, when the chapel was first built, it housed a holy relic from Christ's crown of thorns."

"Certainly its grandeur befits such a treasure," Chandos said.

Edward rested his hands on his pommel. After admiring the

elaborate buildings for a few moments, he reined around and called back over his shoulder to his men, "Burn them."

He trotted away. Behind him, glass shattered. He halted partway down the street and twisted in his saddle, witnessing a man-at-arms lob the first torch through the broken glass. After several moments, tendrils of smoke eddied.

Edward rode on, but not without a twinge of regret. He trusted Chandos and his men to make short work of destroying the buildings so dear to French hearts. He caught up with de Harcourt on the way to Marly and as they galloped side by side, the exiled Norman wore a satisfied expression. He had exacted revenge on Philippe by singling out the king's most cherished royal properties and causing their destruction.

At Marly, they reduced the palace of Montjoie to ashes. From there, they thundered on to Chastel le Roy. When they halted before the palace, the Vicomte turned to Edward. "This is one of Philippe's favourites, completed just two years ago."

At the sound of axes splintering wood, a wide grin spread across de Harcourt's face. He called to one of his men. "Hand me a torch." He pressed spurs to his horse's flanks, urging his mount up the polished stone steps, his steed's hooves slipping and clattering as it scrambled. De Harcourt paused a moment, then tossed the flambeau through the door onto the shattered remains of a tufted velvet bench in the entry hall. "Such splendour," he murmured. Hungry flames fingered up the satin window panels and devoured the ornate *setle*.

De Harcourt's face, as he pivoted his mount, was painted black from smoke and ash and his teeth gleamed white from a humourless grin. His horse clambered back down the steps.

Meeting Edward's eyes, the Vicomte said,"May it please God to vanquish all our foes in like manner."

Race For The Somme

18 August 1346 — Poissy to Milly

The previous day's feint on Paris might have fooled Philippe into believing the English were marching to meet him south of Paris, but he would learn soon enough his quarry escaped. Before Philippe learned of his folly, the English army must march with all speed.

Edward donned his kit with help from his page, and went in search of his undermarshal. His footsteps drummed upon the tiled passageways of Poissy's old palace and echoed off its vaulted arches. Philippe's precious palace would not stand much longer.

He emerged into damp river air and fog misting over the river. He nodded a greeting to Ughtred. "The men are to burn everything save the buildings guarded by the king's retainers."

"As you wish, Lord."

Edward grabbed his reins from his squire and swung into his saddle as the fog began to burn off. Groups of men remained behind to fullfil orders in town while most of the vanguard were already advancing with Warwick and Northampton. Edward trotted toward the head of his column, pausing at the southern end of the bridge to inspect the recent repairs. When he trotted onto the planks, his stallion's hooves beat hollowly across the span. Beyond the Seine's north bank, the land rose steeply and the dray teams strained in their traces, hauling the heavy wagons up the slope.

The English travelled the plain of Pontoise and by mid-morning, the heat-scorched air whipped dust and grit into unprotected faces, the cool river mist only a memory. Edward swiped at the sweat beading his brow. Hoofbeats approached from the rear, and within moments, the riders slowed their mounts to match pace alongside him.

"Lord, as soon as the wagons and rearguard passed over the bridge safely, Arundel ordered the bridge broken again," Chandos said.

With a wry grin, Mortimer said, "I would have loved to see the faces of the French dogs pursuing us when they found the bridge broken and heard their curses when they were forced to go around."

Edward spat the windblown grains clinging to his lips. "The feint buys us a little time, but Philippe will appear the fool when he learns we marched north. His rage and fury will spur France's pursuit."

They rode on, Edward pressing the vanguard to great effort beneath a cloudless sky offering not a shadow of relief from the blazing sun. The men's shoulders sagged, and their steps grew sluggish. The faux king's stranglehold on the river crossings had taken a heavy toll. The men were weakening, and the supplies pillaged in Poissy would not last.

"Heed me, Edward," his father said before leaving Poissy. "You and your men are to scavenge for provisions but only at farmsteads and villages that are unprotected. You will not attack any fortified towns."

"But—"

"I forbid it. We cannot afford to squander even one minute nor chance the loss of men. Do I make myself clear?"

Edward simmered at his father's lecture, treating Edward as if he were a willful child. At least his father took the trouble to speak with him in private.

The air hung thick with dust and smoke. Perhaps they would breathe easier when they reached the summit of the rise ahead. At the top, Edward called to Ughtred, "We halt here. A brief respite only."

The weary men slumped where they stood, and slaked their

thirst with skins passed from hand to hand.

Edward trotted a little way beyond and stopped, then tugged off his gloves and flexed his fingers. After a few moments, he dangled his legs from his stirrups and rotated his ankles. From the rise, the land fell away, offering clear views to the south and east. Dust billowed from the king's division, wagons and rearguard, but he saw no sign of French pursuit. Not yet. He brushed a finger across his cracked lips and came away with blood.

The days unfolded much the same with each town they passed sacked and burned. The countryside rolled before them in ever-increasing swells. The columns began to string out. Men straggled and stopped to plug the soles of their boots with bits of leather, fabric torn from their clothes, or whatever came to hand, even leaves.

"My lord!"

Edward twisted toward the rider galloping to meet him.

The sun-scorched hobelar reined to a stop. "The king bids you attend him this evening."

They encamped beneath a stand of poplars near a small, clear-running stream. Edward washed the grime from is face and headed to find his father, following Northampton into the king's tent. He and Edward were the last to enter and they found places while the others passed mugs of ale. A serving lad placed two full jugs on the table and left.

The king rose, a grim look on his face. "*Mes amis*, I shall speak plainly. The provisions gathered at Poissy already run low. I need not tell you our men cannot march, nor fight, without sustenance. Yet, fear not for our Lord God provides for us as He did the people at Galilee. The town of Beauvais, lies in our path only a half-day ahead."

De Harcourt nodded. "A good-sized, prosperous town." Pale squint lines webbed the Vicomte's sunburned face. "Beauvais is situated on steep buttes which rise above the joining of two rivers."

Northampton lifted a hand. "Our scouts report the town's walls appear recently fortified and count more than four score helms and pikes top the parapets."

Edward leaned forward. "Not a great many, not against a force such as ours. These French dodypolls need a lesson in England's might."

"Perhaps," the Earl replied, "yet there is no need to take the city. Merchant shops, storehouses, and shambles crowd the lanes of the faubourg outside the walls."

"Wisdom must prevail," the king said. "We take what we require and march on to rendezvous with Hastings."

"Might I suggest we divide our forces, sire?" Northampton said. "Retinues to guard each of the city's three gates to stave off any who may think to sally forth, while other retinues gather provisions."

Warwick flicked a bug from his jupon. "Agreed. Quick, simple in and out, with no loss of men."

"*D'accord*," the king said. "On my orders, the churches and priories are not to be harmed nor looted."

The next morning on the approach to Beauvais, all three divisions advanced together and Edward rode beside his father. He studied the town's defences while they traversed a nearby ridge.

"Lord Father, the town is not as well defended as our scouts reported. Look there, the old walls show cracks, and missing stones. The repairs were not well done."

"*Non*, Edward."

"Capturing another city enhances your reputation with the region's nobles, and encourages them to abandon the feeble Valois."

"I said no. Why do you not listen? We can ill afford the time." The king spoke with a steely tone. "Perhaps it is your pride which prompts this fervour. *Non*, I shall not chance the lives of men who will be sorely needed later."

Edward jerked his stallion's head around and, cursing under his breath, trotted away. The king's division remained on the ridge, while Edward's forces advanced. At his signal, two dozen men-at-arms dismounted and crept forward to probe the faubourg, their approach covered by the vanguard's archers. A short time later, a soldier shouted and waved the all clear. The faubourg residents had abandoned their dwellings to seek shelter within the ramparts.

His men tramped from deserted building to deserted building, scattering squawking chickens while Ughtred shouted orders. A one-eared cur tucked its tail and slinked down an alley. The men loaded their scavenged haul onto sure-footed pack horses and small carts. These relayed the loot to the bulkier wains too wide to navigate the faubourg's narrow lanes and alleys.

When the search ended, fire licked the wooden shops and sheds. Smoke clogged the air and embers leapt from roof to roof, sparking dry thatch to flames. Horses snorted and baulked in fear until carters draped cloth over their eyes and led them past the flames.

Edward's thwarted desire to capture the town festered.

Soldiers darted in and out of structures not yet torched and stowed smaller valuables, jewelry, and silver candleholders into pouches and saddlebags. At the abbeys of St. Quentin and St. Lucien men swarmed the grounds and buildings, stripping the abbeys of their most precious items, then set the buildings ablaze. Despite the king's edict, Edward did not curb them; he would not begrudge his men their plunder.

A small contingent of Edward's men remained behind to secure the provisions in the wagons while Edward and others departed. Soot-covered and in high spirits, they bantered good-naturedly as they advanced out of town. For several hours, the column traveled through a wooded draw and followed a track hugging a small stream up the gully it carved. A faint scent of smoke drifted in the air.

Edward's outrage at his father's rebuke still smouldered, like Beauvais. His successful feint on Paris allowed Warwick and Northampton to secure the bridge at Poissy. Yet despite this, his father did not trust him enough to grant him leave to attack Beauvais. Edward worked his jaw, realizing he was clenching it. He crested the ridge and the terrain opened to a wide plain. As they gradually descended the rocky track, his horse stumbled. Edward collected himself, surprised to find Chandos riding beside him. For how long had he been there?

"You should know our Lord King hanged twenty of our soldiers today."

The statement hovered between them while their horses plodded the path. At dusk, the army camped outside the village of Milly, near a fast-running brook edged with tempting fodder. Thirsty horses nickered in eagerness, while upstream, his men discovered a deeper pool with pike and carp. In his lodging later, the aroma of roasting fish floated to him.

He sat down to eat in no humour for company. Though he picked up his knife, appetite eluded him. Images of men with coarse ropes around their necks, eyes bulging, and urine staining their breeches swam before him. He pushed away from the table. Candlelight glinted upon the ruby in his signet ring.

Stirring memories of Westminster's vaulted nave supplanted the grisly pictures in his mind. Incense and choir music surrounded him as he knelt before the altar. Sunrays filtering through the stained glass windows cast coloured patterns across the stone floor. A pale linen vesper cloth glowed in the light of dozens of glimmering candles while the archbishop intoned solemn prayers.

"In nomine patris et filli et spiritus sancti."

"Amen," he murmured.

Edward had lifted his eyes and held out his hand. The archbishop slid a ruby-studded gold ring onto Edward's thumb. The ring once belonged to his uncle John. Upon his death, at only twenty years, the king granted his beloved brother's title, lands, and ring, to Edward — Duke of Cornwall. With the investiture came duty—the ring a symbol.

Over time, Edward grew into the ring and believed he grew into the duty. Had he? Today, his disobedient lapse caused the needless deaths of twenty men. He choked on the guilt of his failure. The lone tallow candle in his chamber flared and guttered out, but its acrid, animal scent lingered. Removing only his boots, Edward lay down on the cot, crossed his arms under his head, and closed his eyes.

O Heavenly Father, cradle in the palm of your loving hand the souls of those who died today. Let them not languish in hell's fire for their earthly sins but bestow mercy upon them. O Lord, fill me with your wisdom and strength so that ever I shall do right in your name. Amen.

The moonlight faded long hours before Edward fell into a penitent sleep.

19 August 1346 — Milly to Airaines

King Edward awoke before the blare of trumpets rallied his army. He broke his fast with bread and cheese while carters hitched the horses, men refilled water barrels, and loaded wagons. He drove his footsore troops at a demanding pace. For the past days, they trudged through endless fields of wheat stubble, the remains of an abrupt harvest. His commanders encouraged the men to step lively with reminders of fresh supplies and reinforcements awaiting them at Le Crotoy. And they spoke of the glory from the victory to come.

Thomas Hatfield, Bishop of Durham, rode beside him. "Philippe's arrogance gained us a few days march."

"*Oui, mon ami,* but the French cur is not stupid. *Non,* he is cunning, as all kings must be." King Edward shifted, his body stiff after a another long morning in the saddle. Since they left Beauvais, his headstrong son had done his job without argument, leaving a trail of smoke, a lure, Philippe could not fail to follow.

King Edward glanced around, wary of unwelcome ears. "My son's imprudence was unfortunate."

"I cannot say his disobedience was not noted, yet most young men learn from their *faux pas,* do they not?"

"Perhaps I have been too lenient, too quick to excuse my heir's missteps."

The bishop rode in silence while King Edward pushed aside his qualms and imagined the defeat of his enemy once England's army united with Hastings and the Flemish troops. Yet, before then, his army must cross the Somme and they must do so before Philippe and his troops could cut them off.

"Sire!" The bishop gazed southeast. In the far distance, dust billowed.

God's blood! Philippe!

The race was on.

The English reached Airaines and promptly seized the priory sitting atop a promontory to use as the king's command post. King Edward summoned his son and waited on the terrace. He gazed out at the plain of Ponthieu. Footfalls sounded behind him.

"Lord King."

King Edward did not turn, instead waving a hand toward the land below rolling to the east. "All the lands from here to the river. belonged to your grandmère. Given to her as part of her dowry." The king continued, "As a boy, I toured these lands with the seneschal who managed my mother's holdings here in Ponthieu. Bartholomew Burghersh was his name."

Edward raised his brows.

"Indeed, the same Bartholomew Burghersh who serves with me now."

"That is quite remarkable."

King Edward counted upon Burghersh's past labours to prove useful.

Rocks skittered behind them. King Edward turned.

"Your pardon, sire." Northampton bowed. "Our scouts report the French reached Amiens."

Unfortunately, his nemesis had made good time. Too good. "Amiens is there, Edward." He pointed southeast.

Northampton cleared his throat. "Among the standards is that of King Jang of Bohemia."

"Ahh, so, Philippe has rallied allies. Well then, *mon ami*, with no more than a day's ride between us, we best be about our business."

Although no blaring trumpets disrupted the English army's slumber the next morning, King Edward was already awake and pacing outside the priory in the pre-dawn grey. The wily Valois had advanced much quicker than expected.

Hoofbeats signalled the arrival of Warwick and de Harcourt. As they trotted their mounts into the courtyard, the king sidled alongside them and he grabbed hold of Warwick's bridle. "Should you find a crossing lightly guarded, *mon ami*, do not hesitate to take it. Then send your fleetest horse and rider with word."

Warwick made the sign of the cross. "God be with us, sire."

"You have enough men?" That he asked, signalled his apprehension.

"Our fate rests in God's hands," de Harcourt said.

The two men reined around. "*Bonne chance!*" the king called as Warwick and de Harcourt spurred away. He prayed they would meet with success; his army must slip through Philippe's fingers once again.

Hour after hour, the king waited, hoping to hear the sentry shout of incoming riders. The sun passed its apex and still he waited, apprehension mounting. Grinding hours later, a shout, hoofbeats and the rattle of weapons alerted King Edward to his commanders' return. He hastened to the courtyard, its ancient stone walls glowing blood-red in the setting sun.

Warwick dismounted, leaning heavily against his horse. Sweat streaked the dust caked on his face and blood crusted his surcoat. Behind him, riders gripped the tethers of horses draped with bloodied bodies. The king closed his eyes, offering a brief prayer for their souls.

De Harcourt slid from his saddle, easing his bulk onto stiffened legs. He hobbled forward, visibly favouring his lame leg to a greater degree than usual. "Sire."

King Edward searched both weary men's faces for any hint of success. Dreading what he would hear, he said, "Come inside."

The other commanders waited, too; the priory hall smelled of rank bodies. Edward poured two cups of ale, passing one to Warwick and one to the Vicomte. The earl downed his in one draught and set the cup on the table, the tap audible in the strained silence.

"When we reached Pont Remy," Warwick began, "we believed only local levies guarded the bridge. Our archers waded through marshy ground and once they were in position, we launched our assault." Warwick paused and raised his mug for a refill.

"That is when we spotted King Jang of Bohemia's colors," de Harcourt said, "and his crossbowmen let loose. Though we made several attempts, we were losing too many men to their bolts. We withdrew." The Vicomte gulped his ale. "From there, we rode to Fontaine-sur-Somme and were shadowed the entire way by a French column flying Duke Jean's colors."

"At that point, we thought it best to split up," Warwick said. "The Vicomte and I rode to Hangest while one of my retinues scouted Longpré, and another Picquigny." Warwick shook his head. "At every crossing, the bridges were destroyed, or barricaded and heavily manned. Damn Philippe." The Earl rested his head in his hand. "Sire, I am sorry to have failed."

King Edward stood and paced; the hall's heavily worn planks creaked into an unnatural silence. God's teeth! The Earl and Vicomte had ridden thirty miles, probed six towns, and lost men in a hard-fought skirmish. He halted.

"*Mes amis*, we have not come this far to be defeated now. There must be an unsecured crossing somewhere."

"We might consider a coups de main in Abbeville," Northampton said. "Though to succeed, we would need to draw away a significant number of troops."

King Edward rubbed his temples. "*Oui*, that might work, though at great loss of men should the French flank us."

Amid dispirited grumbles, heads nodded.

The king studied the disheveled and weary men. He asked much of them. "Burghersh, from your time as seneschal here, what do you know of Blanchetaque?"

The bishop's shoulders slumped. "It was so long ago, lord."

Edward pricked to attention. "The ford exists? It is not just a rumor?"

22 August 1346 — Airaines to Acheux

For several hours into the night, Edward's father and commanders debated the army's best course. After the discussion concluded, Edward bade his father *bon nuit*, and retreated to his chamber. He fell onto his bed fully clothed. His mind would not rest.

The foodstuffs gathered at Beauvais would not sustain them much longer. Huntingdon's fleet, stocked with provisions and reinforcements, was anchored at Le Crotoy, but to reach the port they must cross the Somme. The difficulty facing them now was the same as with the Seine—Philippe's army barred their way.

Edward bolted awake at the thunder of hooves and sprinted to the courtyard. Warwick and de Harcourt galloped away. Edward's heart faltered.

The king galloped with them.

Despite fears for his safety expressed by all, the king insisted on judging Abbeville's defences for himself. Edward prayed they would locate a crossing and return safely.

Returning to his chamber, Edward collected his kit and then went in search of his under-marshal. After the meeting ended the night before, his father pulled him aside. "In the morning, save the departing retinues, you will command the remainder of the army."

"Me? Above Northampton?" The king was offering Edward an opportunity to redeem himself after his foolish blunder at Beauvais.

"Do not deviate from my orders. I am counting on you. Should Philippe's army march out of Amiens toward our encampment, here is what I want you to do."

While the sun struggled through a sky layered with grey,

Edward walked the camp with Ughtred, taking stock. Soldiers sat in clusters, sharing portions of stale bread, cheese, and the little remaining ale. Others lounged against trees mending leathers, serenaded by blades whirring against whetstones. The responsibility weighed on Edward, his actions crucial. He must not fail.

"As you see, they rest now, Lord Edward, though all else has been made ready according to your orders." Ughtred gestured toward the wagons lined up and loaded. Horses picketed nearby carried packs stuffed full.

"Eyes up, incoming rider!" A sentry shouted. Men cursed, and scrabbled out of the way of flailing hooves.

"Here!" Ughtred raised a hand.

The hobelar swerved toward them and leapt from his saddle, his feet hitting the ground before his horse slid to a stop. He swept his cap from his head, dropped to one knee, and panted, "My lord."

Edward smiled at the familiar wisened face beneath the matted mop of ginger hair. "What word, Nick?" Extending his hand, Edward hauled the man to his feet. He wobbled slightly as he caught his balance, his chest heaving like his mount's.

"The French left Amiens at daybreak and march in our direction."

Edward's heartbeat ticked up. He paused, gauging the distance and possible speed of their march. "Good man." He thumped Nick's shoulder. "Ughtred, call the order and send word to Northampton and the rear guard. We move out. Now!"

Trumpets sounded. Men clambered to their feet, grabbed belongings, and hastened into formation. Edward's horse was saddled and brought forward. He checked the girth, then he stuck his foot into the stirrup and mounted.

Chandos and Audley trotted up. "My lord."

"Take your retinues south. Ride fast. Set fire to the farmsteads and villages, but skirt any fortified ones. By the time the sun reaches the treetops, I want to see smoke. Mountains of it!"

Chandos grinned. "We draw the French?"

Edward nodded. "When done, circle back."

"Until tonight!" Audley called as they cantered away.

Edward checked his stallion. "Ughtred, let the fires burn. Make sure several packs and at least two half-loaded drays are left behind."

Ughtred knitted his brows. "My lord?"

"Should the French track us here, they must believe we abandoned camp in a rush. They must pursue us without question." Edward was charged with convincing the French the English were in full retreat, that they had abandoned all hope of crossing the Somme. Philippe must swallow the bait just as he did at Poissy.

Edward paused a moment to view the columns, then gathered his reins in one hand, and signalled. "Forward!" They left with campfires smouldering behind them.

Edward settled into his horse's stride, recalling the map de Harcourt scratched the night before. The town of Oisemont lay due west. Chandos and Audley had disappeared over a small rise to the south. "Ughtred, you ordered scouts to ride our advance and rear?"

"Yes, lord."

"We take no chances."

The land ahead rolled like swells upon an endless sea. At the scent of smoke, Edward scanned the southern skyline pleased at the billowing black clouds. They rode west for several hours and by then the sun had broken through the grey and its rays scalded Edward's back. Beneath his surcoat and mail hauberk, sweat trickled between his shoulder blades. Scouts reported French forces to the south, though none approaching their rear.

Heat shimmered above the featureless plain. The silhouettes of five riders wavered in the distance. Edward squinted. One of Ughtred's scouting parties. The horsemen galloped toward him, closing the distance.

"Lord Edward!" Holland curbed his labouring mount. "Less than a quarter mile ahead, levies of armed men sally out from the walls of a town."

Edward rested his hands on his pommel. "The locals think to challenge us? "He rubbed his chin. "How many?"

"Not more than a hundred. A few carry swords though most wield farm tools."

Edward shook his head. "A local militia with rusted weapons, pitchforks and scythes?"

"They must be mad to venture from their walls," Ughtred said.

Edward reined around. "No matter. Order the battle lines."

Trumpets sounded. Several hundred men-at-arms dismounted, donned helms, grabbed weapons and shields, and hastened into battle formation. Archers stuffed arrow sacks and tested staves. Edward rallied his personal retinue, while Northampton mustered mounted knights.

Horns blared again. "Forward!" The English line advanced, chanting and banging weapons. Human figures emerged through the shimmering heat, steadily more distinct. A single horn sounded; the archers nocked arrows. Edward raised his hand. The villagers came into range.

"Loose!"

Bow cords hummed.

Arrows flew and townsmen shrieked and fell.

"For England!" The line surged forward.

The town's defenders froze. Courage vanished. Panicked, they turned and ran.

"For Saint George!" The vanguard gave chase.

"*Ouvrez les portes!*"

"*Laissez nous entrer!*"

Terrified, the villagers fled for the partially-open gate, cursing and shoving their way forward. Many stumbled, fell, and were trampled. The vanguard's men-at-arms hacked their way through the crush to force the gate before the French could shut it. Once inside, the battle was over.

Throughout the afternoon, Oisement was ransacked, and the provisions pillaged—sacks of grain, vegetables, tuns of ale, and crates of squawking fowl—created a mountain just outside the town's gate. Under Ughtred's competent eye, men streamed from the stockpile to the wagons and back again. The air shimmered in the heat, yet the hungry men did not complain. Their bellies would soon be full.

The lowering sun painted the town and terrain in yellow hues as Northampton and Suffolk were preparing the rear guard to set off to rendezvous with the king.

Edward joined them. "A feast awaits."

Suffolk shrugged. "For one night at least."

"Looks like you depart soon," Edward said. "When my men and I complete a few final tasks, we will catch up with you."

Warwick and Suffolk raised their hands in farewell and galloped to the head of the amassing column. Arundel and Oxford rounded up the men to guard the last of the teams and wagons in the rear.

Edward strode over to Ughtred, conversing near the gate with two burly men. "We have one more task before we go."

"Yes, lord?

"De Harcourt mentioned two villages, just there." Edward pointed southwest. "Assemble a raiding party to burn those towns and everything around them." Edward scanned the distance. "More scat for the French to follow."

Ughtred nodded. "Indeed. By the amount of smoke to the south of us all day, I would say Chandos and Audley were very effective."

A horse and rider trotted up. "Lord Edward!" Thomas Holland wore a smile so wide the lines around his eye deepened.

'Is something afoot?" Edward asked.

"Oisement's bounty overflows…with more than provisions. In the men's search, they unearthed several of the town's good nobles. The seigneurs de Louville, de Saines, Sempy, and Boubert were discovered hiding in a cellar." He chuckled. "I dare say, they are a most amiable group."

"Tell the men from me they did a good job and earned a share of the ransoms. If the captives are not already tied up, make sure to secure the knots and load them into a wagon. They may have something useful to tell us."

As Holland cantered off, the wind gusted for the first time in days. Dark clouds rolled in the west, blackening the skyline and promising rain. Given the smoke, it was almost impossible to distinguish where land ended and the sky began. He would welcome rain, for he was weary of the heat, the dust and the flies. He pictured England's green rolling countryside, longing for its cool breezes and misty rains.

Dusk had deepened to twilight by the time the vanguard crossed the trickle of a stream on the outskirts of Acheux. He left Oxford and Ughtred to organize the parcelling of the food seized in Oisement, though it would not last long. If the king's day of labour failed to find a river crossing, the dearth of provisions would matter little.

While trotting from camp into town, Edward's grumbling stomach dueled with the clopping of his stallion's hooves. A rising sliver of moon revealed England's quartered arms hanging from a dwelling. The horses tethered outside bore the livery of Warwick and Northampton, but curiously, not those of de Harcourt. Edward dismounted, tied off his reins, and entered.

"Lord King." He bowed, then studied the faces in the chamber. De Harcourt was definitely missing. Edward arched his brows at his father.

"The Vicomte rode north to Saint-Valery to investigate a rumored crossing."

"So, we await his return." Edward settled onto a stool surrounded by muted conversation and men drinking plundered ale. Not until full dark did hooves clatter in the lane. The chamber grew silent.

Outside, saddle leather creaked. "Take my horse and see to his water." De Harcourt's voice sounded grim. Dust drifted with every step as he entered the chamber. "Sire." He half-kneeled, then sank onto a stool. After tugging off his gloves, his arms dropped onto the table. Northampton handed him a cup of ale.

A muscle twitched in the king's jaw. "Well?"

All eyes rested upon the Norman.

"We managed to slip in quite close." He gulped half a cup. "Saint-Valery's walls are old but solid and show signs of recent repair. The banners of Jean de Huy, and Guy, Comte de Saint-Pol, fly from the battlements. The town teems with our enemies. I fear, sire, Saint-Valery holds no hope."

The king closed his eyes for a moment. When he opened them, his gaze rested on the army's marshal. "Warwick?"

"You saw for yourself, sire, Abbeville is a maze of lanes and alleys. A death trap."

"No argument there, *mon ami*," the king said. "Philippe's troops would attack our rear, trapping us between his forces."

A rap sounded on the door. "Come," the king called. His steward entered and bowed. "I beg your pardon, sire. Lord Edward's squire is here and seeks a word."

King Edward nodded permission and his steward stepped aside.

Hal entered and kneeled. "Lord King. B-begging your pardon."

King Edward waved the lad to his feet.

Hal stepped to Edward, whispered in his ear, then turned, and half-bowed to the king. As he hastened out, a restlessness rippled through the chamber.

Catching Northampton's eye, Edward nodded once.

The Earl cleared his throat. "My liege?"

King Edward turned questioning eyes to the Earl.

"You heard of the nobles captured at Oisement?"

The king's brows furrowed. "*Oui.* What about them?"

A warmth coursed through Edward. "Blanchetaque, sire."

All eyes wheeled to him.

"Seigneur Boubert was unable to control his tongue. We have our crossing."

Cornered

24 August 1346 – Crossing the Somme

Unable to sleep, Edward only rested in his cot. Following a light tap on the chamber door, it cracked open. "Lord," Hal said, "you are summoned. The scouts have returned from Blanchetaque."

Edward hastened to the king's quarters. He joined the other commanders crowding into the chamber, their faces expressed hope parrying with deep disquiet. Edward squeezed onto a stool. One face in the group surprised him—Sir Edward Despenser. Ned had served with the rearguard from the campaign's start and tended to linger in the background. The shame of his grandfather's treason haunted him, like it did Roger.

The king flicked his eyes at Cobham.

The veteran campaigner rose and gestured to the man hovering in the shadows behind him. "Step up, Tom. Tell them what you saw."

The gaunt-faced man shifted from foot to foot, his eyes flitting over the dour faces of the commanders. He dipped his head. "Lord King."

"Go on," Cobham said.

"Yes, lord." The scout swallowed hard, mashing his cap in his hands. "When me 'n the lads reached the edge o' the marsh, we tethered our horses. Wide it were, guessin' about a mile, mebbe more, a tangle o' reeds 'n grasses." He licked cracked lips.

"We waited fer the moon ta rise higher 'n the tide ta ebb. Ever so of'n we caught a whiff o' woodsmoke. Frenchies camped t'other side. When the wet were low, we dropt down the bank. 'Bout thirty feet. Freezin' the water was, n' the bottom soft as gruel. Mud like ta suck our boots off 'n the current swift enuff ta drag a man ta sea."

The king leaned forward. "What about the river channel and the ford itself?"

"A shelf o'rock glowing white in the moonlight. Mebbe three wagons wide. 'Twas t'only place could bear the weight, I reckon, the rest nothin' save bars o' drifted sand 'n stiff grass."

"How high was the water at its lowest?" Warwick asked.

"Mebbe calf deep, mebbe a bit more."

"Tell them the rest," Cobham urged.

"After the tide turned, we hurried back fearin' ta be cut off, though not afore countin' the fires atop the cliff on t'other side."

The commanders pelted the scout with questions. He answered as best he could, pausing often to wet his mouth. Then, with a final, gap-toothed grin, he bowed and left.

While conversation swirled, a chill seeped through Edward. The scout mentioned more than a hundred fires. Each accounted for how many men? Twenty? Forty? Yes, the ford existed, but it lay within a tidal marsh at least a mile wide with tidewaters rising twice a man's height.

To evade Philippe, they must force a crossing at low tide, battling the French on the northern bank and secure it. Edward's earlier joy at learning the ford existed, guttered with the candles.

God help them. They needed a miracle.

Under a waning moon, Northampton gave the order. "Mount up!"

Edward's heart pummeled as he seized his horse's reins from his squire and stepped up into his saddle. Orders passed down the ranks.

Chandos, gnawing on a heel of stale bread, rode up. "God's

272

blessings, my lord."

"And to you, my friend."

They jogged their horses to join Northampton and Warwick near the head of the column. After an exchange of solemn greetings, Warwick said, "Six miles between us and Blanchetaque."

Between life and death.

Edward's mouth was as dry as cotton lint.

The horses stomped and snorted, feeding off the men's unrest. Then, with the eastern horizon still dressed in darkness, trumpets sounded the advance.

The night before they agreed on the order of march. Edward was second in command of the vanguard to Northampton, the army's Constable. Despenser's men would march with the vanguard today. The king granted Despenser's request— the distinction of leading the charge across the Somme.

Chandos steered closer to Edward. "Despenser volunteered in order to redeem his family's honour, did he not?"

"A good man," Edward said.

"But a bad business all those years ago. Hugh Despenser's greed cost him his head."

"Yet, one must admire this Despenser's courage." Mention of Hugh Despenser reminded Edward of his grandsire's penchant for male favourites.

"No doubt Ned is apt to win your father's regard, given the dangers he faces."

"If he survives," Edward said.

When the horizon paled to charcoal, Northampton reined his charger alongside Edward.

"I would wager," the Earl said, "Philippe's army is marching out of Abbeville about now, intending to catch us out. We slipped through his grasp at Poissy and we will do so again today."

"God willing." Edward prayed his mentor was right.

All the foot soldiers, even those whose boots were worn through, marched with urgency, keeping pace with the horses. Gaunt-faced, with hunger gnawing at their bellies, the men bravely trudged the rutted track. No banter lightened their mood.

As the charcoal sky muted yellow, the trees and bushes took shape. A salt-scented breeze gusted, and in the distance gulls careened over the estuary. The terrain sloped gradually downward, and hooves began to squish in the sump.

Northampton twisted in his saddle. "Listen up," he said to his commanders. "We know little of this tide's ebb and flow, nor precisely how long low tide lasts. The ford's rock shelf is not wide enough for all these thousands of men and wagons to cross." The Earl rubbed the back of his neck. "After the vanguard, the wagons are to ford using the rock shelf, and the remainder of ours must spread out and wade through."

"The ranks are ten deep or more," Chandos said. "Our men must hasten; time is not on our side."

"The moment the tide weakens," Edward said, "we start across even if the water is still above our knees. We cannot wait."

Northampton stared toward the far northern bank. "With our numbers, the French cannot stop us, but they can delay us."

Despenser grimaced. "Long enough for the tidal surge to trap and drown us."

"Not if we do our jobs," Northampton said. "Time is against us, so there can be no holding back. The archers are key, but they will come into crossbow range before they can restring their bows and fire."

"Like sitting ducks," Warwick said.

The Earl's words sent a shiver through Edward.

Northampton spat. "Once the archers reach firm footing, they are to take out the crossbowmen." He turned to Edward. "I put this next to your lord father and he agreed, so do not argue." Then, with steel in his voice, he continued. "My retinues go first. You follow."

Edward stiffened. He was not some weakling to be mollycoddled.

Northampton continued, "Ned and his men, on our flank, are to advance slightly ahead drawing fire, buying time for our archers to reach firm ground and string their bows."

Despenser and his men would fall prey to the first volley of crossbow bolts. How many would perish? *Holy Spirit, protect these brave men.*

The Earl and Despenser trotted back down the column to Cobham. Chandos tipped his head to the far shore. "The height of that ridge gives the crossbowmen greater range."

"Maybe so," Edward said, "yet we take the north bank or we drown.

They plodded on, through shifting sand bars and brackish water. Hooves sank and squelched in an unsettling rhythm. Their lives depended upon Northampton's wisdom and battle array. The reason for Northampton seeking Edward's help the day before became clear. They hand-picked the most skilled fighters from each of the army's divisions and those men joined the vanguard this morning. The fighting would be fierce, and no matter the cost, they must not fail.

Edward must not fail.

They approached the small hamlet of Saigneville. Smoke drifted from no more than a handful of thatched cotes and a rat scuttled out of the reeds. A lone dog, hackles raised, barked in warning. A rock flew past Edward. The dog yelped, tucked its tail, and limped into the scrub, lame on its right front leg.

Edward looked over his shoulder.

Montagu grinned.

Upon reaching the marsh proper, Edward urged his horse to the edge of a sandy bank. Twenty feet below, tidewaters still too deep to enter, swirled in retreat to the sea. The vanguard's archers and men-at-arms crowded forward while foot soldiers bunched up behind them.

Word spread through the ranks; the French were already marching from Abbeville. Left with no other choice, the English were forced to brave the river's swell. They formed up; the rows stretched beyond Edward's line of sight. Across the marsh, on the river's northern bank, pinpricks of colour shivered amidst the trees.

"John, can you make out the banners on the clifftop?"

Chandos studied the ridge line. "Might be those of Godemar du Fay."

"Burgundian," Northampton said, spurring past them and down the bank, splashing into the marsh. "May God have mercy on them."

The vanguard's combined force, knights, men-at-arms, and archers, hunkered down to wait. Already bone-weary, the crossing and battle to come would test the limits of their endurance. Edward peered at the retreating water. "Not much longer," he muttered to no one. His bowels groaned a warning while he rode among his men. "Move as quickly as you can. Make yourself small. Do not bunch up," he called.

An archer cried out, "Lord, I cannot swim."

"No need. Stay on your feet and splash through."

While the water receded, men hauled forward extra sheaves of arrows. The archers stuffed their bags and hitched them high to keep them dry.

Northampton spurred his destrier back up the embankment, legs and leather trapper splattered with mud. "You know what to do, lads," he shouted. "Take out those God-cursed bowmen first. I want to see them bleed!"

Despenser joined the Earl and called to the men, "Aim true. Make each arrow count."

Northampton stood in his stirrups. "I want to hear them wail for their mothers!" He eyed the water level.

"For England!"

Northampton and Despenser launched down the embankment into the marsh, followed by two hundred men-at-arms and over fifty of the army's best archers. Bows held aloft, they splashed thigh-deep into the current, plowing into the muddy bottom. Their curses drifted to the ranks behind them until replaced by banter urging each other onward.

"Those Frenchies will shite themselves when they sees us coming."

"Run like rabbits, they will!"

Edward's arm shook as he raised it. "Forward!" He urged his destrier down the sandy cliff on the heels of Northampton's men. The frigid water struck Edward's groin; he sucked in a breath. The men around him swore as they sank into the soggy bottom.

Behind him on the embankment, riders careened through the ranks. "The French are closing from Abbeville!"

Edward's pulse jumped. "Forward!" Beneath him, his horse laboured, pastern-deep in mud. Edward focused on the coloured specks atop the far shore. Delay meant death. His destrier's hooves churned, sucking in and out of the soft bottom, creating a lulling rhythm.

Time slowed.

A splash and cry came from Edward's left. A fallen archer scrambled to his feet helped by a kinsman, both panting for air.

"Move! Keep going," Edward shouted. His destrier's nostrils flared and barrel heaved with each mud-weighted step. The mire was taking a toll.

The tide eddied, stilled, shifted, and with the barest ripple, began its inward journey

"Hold!" Northampton's order echoed across the wetlands. His men paused.

Upstream, Despenser and his retinue pushed harder toward shore. When the sun broke through the clouds, hundreds of human shapes appeared beneath the banners fluttering on the clifftop. The crossbowmen waited, silhouetted between the trees.

"For England!" Despenser bellowed.

"For England!" His men surged toward the far shore.

Iron bolts whirred. *Phfttt. Phfttt. Phfttt.*

A man shrieked.

Bolts peppered the water and ripped through Despenser's men. Many tumbled and sank, their blood turning the water pink.

Edward's heart pounded. *Holy Mary, Mother of God!*

Despite the carnage, Despenser's banner still flew.

The bolts stopped. The bowmen hurriedly cranked their bows to reload.

"Now, forward!" Northampton laid spurs to his stallion's flanks, leading the charge to gain solid ground.

Edward forced his mind to silence the shrieks of the vanguard's men. He waited only moments before lowering his visor.

"For England!" he shouted, spurring his horse forward. "For Saint George!"

Phfttt. Phfttt. Phfttt. Bolts whirred and pelted all around him.

Move. Faster. The words drummed in his head.

"Move!" Edward bellowed. "Faster!"

Bodies floated past—death dressed in pink.

Edward sucked in air scented with woodsmoke.

Thirty yards!

The water splashed lower.

Despenser's archers plunged onto the shoal, nocked arrows, and let loose. Beneath the white-fledged storm arching overhead, Despenser and his men-at-arms charged to shore.

Crossbow bolts flew. Men screamed.

Northampton bellowed, "Kill the bastards! Kill them!" His horse squealed; a bolt seared its rump. The Earl's archers, those still standing, surged onto firmer ground, whipped arrows from bags, and nocked their bows.

"Pick your targets!" the Earl shouted.

"Loose!"

Bowstrings hummed.

The second and third flights soared before the first enemy scream rent the air. Bowmen toppled.

A breeze rippled the tidewater. "Watch the wind!"

Flight after flight, feathered death thudded home.

On the clifftop, crossbowmen were pinned down, sheltering behind four-foot pavises. Unable to shoot, their aerial assault faltered.

"For England!" Despenser slogged through the body-riddled shallows toward shore.

"Montjoie St. Denys!" Burgundians charged down the slope.

"Form up!" Cobham yelled. The vanguard's knights locked

shield-to-shield.

The forces collided. Steel rang.

The English wall of men, shields, and weapons, hove forward like one giant being. Men pushed, shouldered, cursed. Swords and pikes hacked overtop. A break appeared in the enemy line and Northampton spurred into the mass. "Saint George!"

"Kill! Kill!" came the chant.

Trumpets sounded from the ridge top. More defenders poured down the embankment. English archers picked them off one by one. As they fell, the men behind tripped over their crumpled bodies.

Edward's destrier lurched onto firmer ground and leapt over a downed soldier. He ploughed from the shoal with his heart in his throat. He drew his axe.

A ventenar bawled, "Look to yours, boys. Over English heads."

Arrows whistled above Edward's head and punched through French padded jacks and mail. Edward spurred into the mêlée. "For England!"

A Burgundian couched his lance and charged. Edward pressed his right spur; his destrier whirled sideways. Momentum carried the Burgundian forward, his lance ripping Edward's surcoat.

Pressing his spur again, Edward spun his horse, body-slamming a foot soldier to the ground. Cobham jammed his bloodied pike into the man's throat.

Edward heeled into the press and swung his axe into an enemy shoulder, breaking mail. The man grunted, half-turned, and thrust up his spear. It glanced off Edward's visor. Bodies pressed him all around, hemming him in, and hands tried to pull him from his saddle. He spurred out of the tangle, jumped off, and with a slap to the rump, sent his destrier off, then rejoined the blur of blades and shields.

One of Northampton's knights grunted and crumpled to Edward's right, the man's helm split by an enemy axe. A French knight broke from the fray and charged. Edward raised his axe, catching his foe's stroke, and shoved hard. Edward spun away, striking the knight's thigh. He stumbled to one knee. Edward crashed his axe on the back of the man's helm. He slumped and fell.

Edward panted for air.

Beside him, Chandos, fighting like a demon, caught an enemy axe on the rim of his shield, then rammed his spear into the helmed man's eye slit. As he reeled backward exposing his neck, Chandos slashed the Burgundian's throat. Blood bubbled as he fell.

"For England!" Warwick bellowed on horseback behind them. He led his men's desperate scramble out of the rising water. Crossbow bolts whirred into Warwick's forces as they joined the mêlée. Men grunted, cursed. Metal sang. The Earl's archers fanned out, nocked arrows, and loosed.

Edward wielded his axe in constant motion. His throat burned. A lance struck his helm and his vision blurred. Dazed, he sheltered behind his shield, and willed his body upright.

Hooves pounded behind him. De Harcourt spurred out of the water leading another retinue. Stallions lunged, teeth bared at the disarrayed French. Riders swung weapons, splitting mail, flesh and skulls. Horses reared, hooves striking flesh and breaking bone. Blood splattered.

"Close up! Close up!" Cobham shouted. His men howled like mad dogs as they tightened ranks. Blades sliced leather hauberks and punched into flesh.

The sounds of weapons clashing, cursing, and wails were deafening.

Edward panted for air through his helm; his chest heaved. Inch by inch, they gained ground, backing Du Fay's men against the cliff bank. The archers picked off enemies on the flanks until only a handful remained fighting. Along the shore, pockets of defenders threw down their weapons and knelt. The men on the hilltop, turned, and sprinted into the woods. English knights pounded up the slope after them. "Cowards!"

Edward, soaked in sweat and bloodid, clambered up the bank, his breath seizing as he tugged off his helm. He swiped at the sweat stinging his eyes. Upstream and down, all across the marsh, thousands still trudged waist-deep against the onrushing tide. Camp followers, belongings bundled over their heads, plodded after the troops.

Wagons creeped axle-deep through the rising swell.

A whip cracked. "Get on, damn you!"

Herdsmen stampeded the army's spare mounts through the rushing water. Nostrils flaring, and tails swishing, the horses zigzagged through the flood, their hooves churning the water brown.

Edward's pulse galloped with the horses.

The relentless tidewater swept inward, engulfing the last of the wagons belly deep. Swamped teams whinnied in terror as the undertow dragged at their traces. A carter jumped from his wain and grappled his way to the team's heads. He grabbed their bridles and cajoled the panicked team forward onto firmer ground.

"Brave lad," Chandos said, climbing the slope to stand beside Edward.

A sudden roar burst from the atop the ridge. Startled, Edward looked back across the marsh. On the Somme's southern bank, France's gold and blue colours fluttered. The French amassed on the far embankment; their certain victory drowned in the floodwaters.

Edward searched the clifftop for the king's banner. It danced above his father, sitting astride his stallion, surrounded by Northampton, Warwick, de Harcourt, and Despenser. Though covered with mud and bloody gore, wide grins graced their faces.

Edward, his back against a tree, slid to the ground. Chandos collapsed beside him. They needed a miracle and God blessed them with one. Edward bowed his head. *Thanks be to you, O Lord.*

He jerked upright. What a fool! "The French only await the next tide!"

Edward leaned against the tree, trying to rest. Hours passed. Though the inland tidal flow prevented the French from attacking, they did not retreat, only bided their time until the water receded again.

As the sun marched across the sky past its zenith, the men's initial jubilation faded, replaced by a wary restlessness. Edward kept vigil along with his troops. The army dared not march, for their forces would be strung out and at risk of being caught from the rear.

When the tidewater eddied and began its seaward journey again, apprehension soared. Edward ordered the vanguard on alert, yet as dusk descended, their enemy did not advance. They all waited. Night fell. Why did the French not cross? At dawn, trumpets blared in the distance, startling birds from the trees. Edward's eyes flew to the Somme's southern bank, his heart beating as if it would burst from his chest.

The French were withdrawing.

25 August 1346 – The Somme to Noyelles

Edward joined his father and commanders on the clifftop. "Blessings upon you, sire."

"Ah, you join us. *Trés bien.*"

"It appears the Valois prefers to keep his feet dry."

The comment brought a chuckle and Warwick added, "Philippe has never been one to take risks. I suspect he heads for the bridge in Abbeville."

They shared opinions concerning their enemy's withdrawal. Edward was no less surprised than they and all too aware of how close they came to losing all. They must rendezvous as quickly as possible.

His father raised a hand for attention. "We must make the most of the time it takes our enemy to go around and cross the river at Abbeville. Hastings and the Flemings await us."

"We ask much of our men to march on empty bellies," Edward said. "What of provisions?"

"Despenser rode with a detachment to Le Crotoy before first light. Huntingdon's fleet should be at anchor, his ships sitting low in the water. Despenser is to assemble the reinforcements, load the supplies, and we will reunite on our the march."

"We best put some distance between us and the French," Edward said.

Northampton ran a hand through his sweat-matted hair. "Prudence dictates that our divisions march separately and forage as we go."

Their forces must march no matter their exhaustion. Until they united with Hastings and the Flemish forces, a face-to-face battle must be avoided.

At mid-day, Edward eased his legs from his stirrups. With each mile of the advance, the sky grew more sombre. They traveled northwest encountering Noyelles, but found little to scavenge. Alerted to the army's advance, the townsfolk hid their foodstuffs. The men's bellies rumbled.

Many hours later as dusk fell, shouts sounded ahead, and several riders galloped out of the trees.

"Ours," Ughtred said from beside him, "wearing the king's livery."

Edward swiped at the sweat beading his face. "Perhaps they bring word of camp."

Chandos glanced over his shoulder at the column behind them. "Our men are dead on their feet." An understatement if there ever was one.

The king's hobelar guided Edward's force into a dense wood. Clouds dulled the meagre moonlight, while deadfall crackled beneath them. The men cursed as they stumbled in the underbrush.

Edward dropped his reins, trusting his stallion to pick his way. Edward searched the darkness ahead for firelight. His horse pricked both ears forward. Muffled voices soon followed and then a sentry's shout. In another hundred yards, silhouettes appeared in the shadows. Small groups of men rested beneath the thick forest canopy.

"See to our men," Edward called to Ughtred. He rode on, seeking the king and passing men chewing on scraps and sharing ladles.

Others slept where they fell. He made the sign of the cross. What sort of commander allows his men to starve?

A guard directed him to the king's command tent. The Earl of Oxford came out as Edward dismounted. "No fires?"

"The king's orders," Oxford said.

Another man, dust-caked and disheveled and one Edward did not recognize, exited and disappeared into the darkness.

Oxford spoke low. "Despenser's detachment returned from Le Crotoy."

Edward's spirit lightened. "Provisions for the men?"

Oxford shook his head. "The harbour was empty. Not an English ship in sight."

"*Jesu!*" Without quizzing Oxford, Edward ducked beneath the tent's awning and threw back the canvas flap.

King Edward rose from his travelling altar.

"*Bon,* we have a few moments before the others arrive." His father's face was etched with foreboding.

"Sire?"

"Hastings and the Flemings disbanded."

"God's blood!" Edward choked on the words.

"Reports of bad faith and skirmishes between the troops."

"*Jesu,* Father!" Edward strode in a circle. "This would not have happened if not for the delay to meet with the Pope's envoy near Rouen." He caught himself. Though he may have said too much, he did not care.

The king pressed fingers to his temples. "You do not understand."

Edward's breath came short. "Oh, but I do." He did not hold back. "Your audience with the cardinals cost us, allowed Philippe time to assemble his forces. Ever since, he has held the upper hand, forcing us to march farther than what was necessary and wasting precious time. The delay drained our supplies and our men's energy." Edward rubbed his brow. Never before had he ever spoken to his father in such a manner.

"Tell me, sire, what could have been so important you would

chance our mens' lives in such a way? Tell me. I need to know."

The king paced a few steps, spun around, and met Edward's eyes. "*You.* I did it for you."

Edward's blood rushed; his temples throbbed. "Me?"

"Yes, for you. For years, the Pope refused to grant a dispensation for any unions proposed for you."

"Yes, but what—"

"A dispensation is vital!" His father's face mottled red. "Without it, you cannot marry, nor sire a legitimate son, so I put it to the Pontiff's envoy. If the pope agreed to a dispensation, I would concede a truce."

Edward sank on a stool, the wind taken from him. They would face Philippe's army alone. Their chance for victory slim. Victory? With God's mercy, they might survive.

26 August 1346 - Crécy en Ponthieu

Before sunrise, the army broke camp. Edward rode racked by guilt, his father's revelation landing upon him like the weight of an anvil. After marching a few miles, they reached the hamlet of Crécy. On a ridge east of town the king's planted banner waved in the wind. Here, they would make their stand. Beneath a blanket of grey, the army dug in.

Edward rested against the base of a blue-painted windmill situated atop the ridge, gazing downslope. The on-again, off-again misting drizzle did nothing to relieve the August heat and his clothes stuck to him as if he were covered with honey. He groaned and stretched his calf to relieve a cramp.

The hillside to the west, on his right, descended into a gully cut by the River Maye. The opposite, eastern end the slope was steeper and laddered with farming terraces. Another small village appeared in distance.

Edward coughed, hacked up *fleume*, and spat. Although hardened to the campaign's demands, he functioned on the last vestiges of his strength, exhausted from the roundabout march and the contest at the Somme. No army could survive without food, ale, and rest. Witnessing his men's plight was torment.

All due to him.

Raindrops mixed with sweat trickled down his brow. He swiped it away with his blood-stained sleeve and grimaced at the stench from his leather hauberk. Somewhere behind the lines, his squire scrubbed his mail in preparation for the coming fray.

Chandos folded onto the turf beside him. "Cobham's scouts reported the French marched north from Abbeville before first light."

"King Philippe is a fool if he believes we headed to the coast," Edward said. "As if my father would flee rather than face him."

"The Valois will realize his folly soon enough."

Whenever the French arrived, Edward would command the vanguard's front lines.

Duty.

He recalled his first taste when he learned his family was sailing to Flanders and he was to remain behind as Guardian. His mother comforted him, the color of her gown the same blue as the windmill's planks. A raindrop christened Edwards lashes; he brushed away the moisture but not the memory.

Duty tasted of terror.

"You owe your father, your king, your unwavering loyalty," his mother said.

Edward turned to John, his brother-in-arms, closer than his own blood and the one constant in Edward's ever-shifting life.

"Do you recall the day at Byfleet when we boys first rode our ponies at the quintain?"

"Odd to mention it now, but yes, I remember."

"It was then my father summoned me to join him on pilgrimage before he sailed to Sluys, to war." He paused. "I did not want to go. I did not want him to go."

Chandos chewed a stem of grass. "It was his duty."

"Yes…duty. Then, only a word to me. I had yet to learn what duty meant, what being king meant, means—to protect England

and its people, placing the interest of the realm before personal desires."

War then. War now.

If Edward survived today, in ten years, would he look back and realize even now, he did not understand the true meaning of duty? The enormity of a king's responsibilities struck him anew. He picked at the dried blood on his surcoat. Though he proved himself proficient at arms at many tournament mêlées, save for Caen and the Somme crossing, his battle experience consisted of raids and a few skirmishes. When the French appeared today, duty required him to command the vanguard. How? Edward scooped up a clod of earth. His hand shook.

"Lord Edward!" Holland beckoned from mid-slope. After the courage Thomas showed at Rouen and Gaillon, the king rewarded him with command of a retinue in the vanguard. Would Joan be pleased to learn of it? With the maiming of Holland's eye, would she still prefer him to Montagu? Would any of them survive?

Edward rose and joined Holland as he directed his men. "Dig about here." Holland motioned to a spot about three-quarters of the way up the slope. "Leave enough distance between the trenches for the archers to slip through." As the men began to dig, he turned to Edward. "Lord, where do you want the small pits? How many and how deep?"

Edward recalled Northampton's instruction. "Just there, about mid-way up the slope." He shouted to be heard above the shovels. "About three feet apart and a foot deep. Not in a straight line; stagger them so they are difficult to spot."

Chopping sounds came from the wood behind the windmill. Dozens of men felled small trees, chopped off the branches, and sharpened the ends. Others hauled the posts onto the battlefield and jammed them securely into the ground at an angle about a horse length upslope from the trenches.

"Place them along both flanks, too," Edward called.

The drizzle waned, and the earls of Northampton and Warwick joined Chandos at the base of the windmill. As the hammering eased, Edward climbed up and lowered himself beside them. Over the weeks, he benefitted from their experience. He owed them a great debt.

Work parties rolled wooden carts loaded with sheaves of arrows onto the battlefield's flanks while standard bearers crisscrossed the hillside planting banners to mark the divisions' positions.

Edward plucked tufts of grass. "John," he said, barely above a whisper. "Is this enough?"

"The cream of France's noble *chevaliers* will charge up this slope, four or five ranks deep, with overweening pride. Our men are tired, but determined, and when our archers pluck their bowstrings, English fury shall rain down." A bug crawled on his neck. He plucked it off and crushed it.

"I have served with the king many times. He chose this ground to defend and chose it well. We are fully entrenched, our defenses strong. My trust is absolute."

Yes, but the king would watch from atop the windmill while his barely bloodied son battled below. Edward breathed a shaky breath. "The king honours me with command of the vanguard. A duty I accept, but," Edward caught and held John's eyes, "am *I* enough?"

Cobham's scouts reported in. Philippe realized his mistake; his army reversed course and was marching back. Soon enough, Philippe's scouts would discover the English army's true whereabouts.

While they waited, Edward went behind the lines to prepare for battle. The morning's fitful drizzle made the August heat unbearable. He stripped off his overripe linen shirt, donned a fresh one and added his leather gambeson overtop. Hal slipped Edward's mail over his head and buckled it. Then he overlaid the cleanest and brightest of Edward's surcoats and secured Edward's belt. The coat of arms upon Edward's garment marked him as eldest son of the king. The chevaliers would scour the field for his banner. *For him.*

Edward strode along the top of the ridge and agreed with Chandos in his assessment; the king could not have chosen a better battlefield to defend. The vanguard arrayed at the top of a natural funnel formed by the gully to the west and the steeper incline to the east, and would bear the brunt of the French charge. Edward would command with seasoned men beside him: the earls of Oxford and Warwick, de Harcourt, Cobham, and Holland. The vanguard's archers were to muster on both flanks, slightly ahead of the men-at-arms.

Northampton positioned his division east of mid-ridge, with a view of the entire field. Not only would he direct the overall battle, he was charged with reinforcing Edward's forces when hard-pressed by the French. Archers flanked his men-at-arms, with those to the west positioned within bow range of Edward's lines. Farming terraces laddered the easternmost portion of the slope. The treacherous footing of the *radaillons* would foil any French cavalry attack from that direction.

Finally, the king's division mustered slightly back from the centre, near the windmill, with Arundel and the Bishop of Durham sharing command with the king. Suffolk commanded the veteran reserve force, made of up the most seasoned fighters.

On the field, when the French came, no English spurs would jangle. The English fought on foot.

Chandos, having donned his kit, strode up to Edward. "I have come from the king with his final orders."

Edward paused. "You stand beside me?"

"Always." They shared a look. Edward's throat tightened.

Steel blades whined against whetstones, and hammers rang as blacksmiths made last-minute repairs to weapons and mail. Whinnies carried from the horses corralled inside the ring of wagons behind the ridge top.

"Look." Chandos inclined his head toward men hauling three pipe-like iron devices, rounded stones and several barrels. Edward shook his head. "Bombards, I think they are called." The men positioned them on the vanguard's flank. "My father believes, if nothing else, the noise from those abominations are likely to terrify the chevaliers' horses."

"God help them," Chandos said.

With each passing hour, the gnawing inside Edward grew. Given the size of Philippe's army, England's was vastly outnumbered.

The Lord is my banner and my salvation, and though a host of men rise up against me, I shall not fear, for His hand lies upon my sword and shield.

King Edward mounted, trotted his horse to the edge of the slope, halted and scanned the divisions. After making the sign of the cross, he breathed deep, and signalled.

Trumpets sounded. The thousands on the battlefield turned to him.

The king, wearing no armour and carrying a white baton, jogged his pure white stallion along the ridgeline. Both were garbed in green silk embroidered with gold, his mount's caparison rippling out from his flanks, drawing all eyes.

The French were renowned for their battle prowess and with their outnumbering force, for any chance of an English victory he must inspire his men. He must lift fear from their minds by harnessing the power of his person and instilling the determination of their God-anointed king upon them. Today, they would prove wrong any who asked, "Who are these English to challenge the mighty French?"

King Edward reined to a walk and rode calmly through the ranks of grim faces and clenched jaws. He halted time and again to call out his battle orders so the men could hear them from his own lips.

"You fight this day not for your king but for your homes, your families, your country. Hold firm. Victory awaits us. Do not break rank, not for prisoners, not for any reason." They were sorely out-numbered; discipline must prevail. No soldiers could be spared to take or guard prisoners.

Not one.

The king pulled up near the centre of the field and searched the mass of men until he spotted his heir. Their gazes caught and locked. Sixteen. A frisson chased through him.

O Heavenly Father, watch over my son.

Silent and still, the king waited. All murmuring ceased. "Good men of England," he called, "we came to these shores to prove Philippe of Valois a false king, a usurper, a coward, and to end his unjust attacks on our lands."

Cheers burst over the hillside.

He waited for the lauding to fade. "Peace shall rule our lands once the crown of France rests upon my head, along with that of England, as is my hereditary right. You, the loyal men of England, have served me well since we landed upon these shores and for your support I humbly give you thanks.

Men hooted and banged shields.

The king signalled for quiet. "I beg you listen…*you* are the backbone of England. *You* are its power." He stood in his stirrups. "Today, it is up to us to prove to these French curs the English are not cowards. We *do not run.* England *will not* be beaten!"

Whistles and cheers swept the field, unsettling his horse.

"Hear me! Trust in my certainty…on *this* day, on *this* hill, God is with us and victory will be ours!"

The men roared, "For England!"

Banner men swept aloft England's quartered arms and the cross of St. George. The king smiled, stood in his stirrups, and saluted with his baton.

England's army cheered louder.

Let the French come.

Later, atop the ridge under the sky's mantle of leaden grey, Edward knelt at his father's feet. Both of them wore full battle harness and with the unrelenting heat pressing down, sweat beaded Edward's brow.

The king placed a hand upon Edward's head. "Go with God," he said.

Edward kissed his father's ring and rose. Just as when he was a boy, when his father went to war, Edward wondered whether he would see his father again.

Duty beckoned.

Fear remained.

Edward made his way back to his men, to his personal guard beneath his dragon banner, held once again by Sir Thomas Daniel. Edward folded onto the grass beside Chandos and other companions who would fight alongside him: James Audley, William Penniel, and Bartholomew Burghersh, the younger. They all seemed to scan the surrounding terrain for signs of the French.

Many men on the battlefield dozed while they waited, though how they could sleep, he did not know. Others guzzled courage from the remaining casks of ale looted from Le Crotoy. Several younger lads squatted in the verge, their bowels loosened by fear.

Dark-robed priests passed among the men, laying hands on bowed heads and murmuring prayers while soldiers confessed their sins. Edward had made his confession to the Bishop of Durham earlier, following the king's pre-dawn mass.

"Scouts!" Audley called.

Across the valley, a foursome of riders pulled up and remained still for several minutes.

"Likely counting our banners," Warwick called.

The horsemen circled around and galloped back the way they came.

Warwick chuckled. "Our king's message is clear."

"If the French doubted my father's intention," Edward said, "none remains."

Another hour passed before a low rumble drifted from the south.

Audley stood and squinted into the distance. "Still miles away," he muttered. He stretched his back and sat down again.

Warwick sprawled on the ground and chewed on a blade of grass. "Fighting is easy. The waiting is hard." He winked.

Edward would soon discover the truth of the Earl's words.

If he survived.

Minutes later, Warwick sprang to his feet. "About bloody time."

Edward stood, his heart drumming. Muffled shouts, the rumble of wagons, and chink of harness drifted from beyond the river, drawing every man's attention. Northampton jogged from across the slope to join them. "The French cannot mean to fight this late in the day," he said.

Warwick ran a hand through rain-damp hair. "I would not, not when my army marched all day."

"But Will Philippe?" Edward wiped the mist from his face.

"A *competent* commander would know to rest his men and sound horns in the morning," Warwick said.

The rattle of trappers sounded from the bottom of the slope. Several *conrois* of chevaliers cantered into view and milled about, their wild gestures and swirling caparisons blurred by the mist. Earlier, Edward walked that ground. The slope was deceptive, steeper than it appeared. The chevaliers' horses would struggle.

Just as the wind blew off the last of the rain leaving a flat light behind, the sounds of pipes and tapping drums drifted from beyond Edward's line of vision. Then, below him, scores of red and green-coated Genoese bowman, mercenaries, poured across the lower reaches of the hillside.

"*Jesu!* The idiots!" Northampton raced back to his division, shouting, "Form up!"

Warwick squinted downslope. "Look at the bowmen. No pavises?" The rectangular shields large enough to cover a man's body were heavy, but the Genoese were mad to take the field without them.

The tempo of the French drums increased, urging the chevaliers to form into lines and ready their lances.

Edward's chest vibrated with the rhythm, and despite the heat, he shivered. His squire helped him don his helm and gauntlets, and buckle on his scabbard. Before reaching for his shield, Edward made the sign of the cross. *Heavenly Father, defend us against our enemy.*

French horns sounded again.

"May God be with you lord!" Hal called, then sprinted for the shelter of the wagons.

"With us all," Edward said.

Chandos tugged on his gauntlets. "So it begins."

From atop the windmill, King Edward studied the battlefield. The sun had begun its descent, and if Philippe were prudent, he would rest his troops and muster at dawn. Philippe's decision to engage now gained England an advantage, and without the Flemish forces, he welcomed Philippe's folly.

He raised his baton. Trumpets sounded.

"Form up!" His heir's order, carried to the king, followed by the rattle of the men lining up shield to shield. Archers retrieved bow cords tucked away from the wet, restrung their staves, and tested their draw. The vanguard's four thousand men faced at least the same and half again, and would bear the brunt of the enemy assault.

"Do not worry overmuch, sire," the Bishop of Durham said. "Warwick, Oxford, Cobham, and the other veterans fight beside your heir to see him safe."

"Make no mistake, I have full confidence in my son." The knot in his belly sang a different song. Along the length of the slope's base, at least a thousand plumed chevaliers assembled into *conrois* no less than four ranks deep. Several knights gestured vigorously. A destrier reared, nearly unseating its rider.

Suffolk narrowed his eyes. "Are they arguing?"

The king shrugged. "A daft time for dissension." French drums beat a heady rhythm, and hundreds of crossbowmen advanced up the slope. "Like an army of ants," he murmured.

French horns blared and then a command, "*Pronto!*"

The Genoese levelled their crossbows.

"*Fuoco!*" Springs twanged and the air shivered with thousands of bolts.

"Listen," Suffolk said.

The king cocked his head.

Pfttt. Pfttt. Pftt-pftt. Midway up the hill, patches of dirt and grass burst.

"Their bolts are falling short," Warwick whooped. "Their strings are wet."

King Edward grinned. Not one bolt hit the English line.

The vanguard's archers nocked arrows. "Draw!" A ventenar called. "Loose!"

Arrows hummed.

The screams rent the field while the second and third flights still clouded the air. As arrows bit into bodies, blood sprayed.

"For England!" Bowstrings to ears, the archers' arrows winged.

"Make them bawl for their mothers!" Warwick bellowed below.

Hiss. Thump. *Hiss.* Thump.

The feathered shafts drove home. Without shields, the Genoese were vulnerable. Legs buckled and bowmen crumpled.

A dozen archers broke ranks, rushing forward. "For England!"

"*Non!*" King Edward shouted."*Non!*"

Flight after flight, arrows soared…thudded.

Enemy bowmen howled and toppled like pins in a game of skittles.

Draw… release. Draw… release.

The air whirred.

Edward winced as bodkin tips punched through Genoese leather jerkins, ripping flesh, as if piercing cloth. Men yowled, and fell. Their advance broke; the bowmen raced back down the arrow-studded slope leaping fallen comrades.

A single chevalier galloped from the *mélange*, shouting, *"Les traîtres! Les froussards!"*

"Non, Alençon! Attendez!" A second voice cried.

The Comte d'Alençon…King Philippe's younger brother, Charles.

"Les chiens! Traîtres!" Alençon charged. The feather plumes on his helm bobbed with his horse's strides. Alençon's guard galloped on his heels.

"Attendez! Arrêtez!" Someone attempted to halt Alençon's charge.

Clods flew from thundering hooves. The chevaliers seated their lances and rode straight at the retreating Genoese.

Edward froze.

"God's teeth," Audley muttered. "The whoresons are attacking their own bowmen."

The Genoese fired at the horsemen, but could not stop the charge. They tossed their crossbows and sprinted for the gully, crying for mercy. Their cries were cut off mid-scream as lances gored through Genoese backs.

Alençon and his knights dropped their bloodied lances, drew weapons, and spurred after the frantic bowmen. Blades hacked down. Dark stains spread across the bright green of the bowmen's coats.

Chandos shook his head. "If I did not seen it with my own eyes, I would not believe it."

"Nor I," Edward said. *God have mercy.*

Horns sounded below.

Edward bellowed to the archers, "Get back!"

A *conrois* of chevaliers galloped out of the crush, all sporting scarlet armbands and carrying brightly painted lances and shields.

Drums signalled the charge. *"Montjoie Sainte Denys!"*

Sod flew as the first rank of chevaliers charged up the slope. France's bright Oriflamme, signalling no mercy, streamed above them.

"Close up!" Edward bellowed. While the line tightened, flanking archers stuck arrows point-down into the ground, making them quicker to hand.

The chevaliers rode knee-to-knee as a tightly-packed, galloping wall of thundering horseflesh. Their pennons and caparisons rippled across the hillside, the slope a riot of color and motion.

"Préparez!" French lances lowered.

Edward closed his visor.

"Nock!"

The ground rumbled closer.

"Draw!"

Cobham shouted to the archers, "Take out the horses!"

"Loose!"

Thousands of arrows hissed. Shafts thumped as broad-headed barbs punched through leather trappers into equine chests. Destriers screamed and cartwheeled, pitching riders. Stunned, they staggered into the path of oncoming horses.

Whump! Whump!

Edward winced. The sound would haunt him.

Bones cracked. Bodies flew into the air and landed with legs and arms at odd angles.

English arrows feathered white against the leaden sky. Shafts thumped into riders, hurtling them out of their saddles to be trampled or trapped beneath fallen horses. Horrific wails echoed across the field.

"Still they come," Chandos murmured.

Hoofbeats drowned the moans of the injured as the fourth line galloped up the hill past their fallen brothers.

Edward sucked in a breath as the horses neared the pits.

Forelegs snapped. Horses tumbled. Riders and lances flew.

Chevaliers coming behind checked their mounts; the charge losing all momentum. The French skirted the pits and regrouped. They kneed their mounts forward again, up the hillside littered with fallen horses, shields, and bodies with arrows jutting from them.

"Here they come, lads." Cobham shouted. " Archers pick your targets!"

Arrows soared again.

"*Montjoie! Sainte*—" The French knight's words were ripped from him, his throat torn through by an archer's bodkin. He toppled, catching a foot in his stirrup and while his horse careened across the field, the knight's head banged the ground with every stride.

Those French still mounted, began to gain ground. "Archers, fall back!" At Edward's order, trumpets sounded. Gaps opened in the vanguard's line and the archers scrambled through.

The French cheered their retreat.

"Shields! Close up!" Edward wedged between Chandos and Audley, his Welsh dragon banner a few yards behind. Shoulder-to-shoulder, shield-to-shield, they braced for the assault. Beneath their feet, the ground rumbled as the French thundered toward them, the horses' chests heaving like bellows. With a deafening roar in his ears, Edward gauged the distance.

"Now!" The line scrambled back behind the sharpened stakes.

The chevaliers dropped their lances and hauled on their reins.

Too late!

Momentum carried them into the trenches, impaling their destriers on the sharpened stakes. Legs flailed. Whinnies erupted. Entrails spilled and the blood of courageous horses soaked the ground.

Edward closed his ears to the screams.

Wielding axes and spears, his men hacked at their enemies. "For England! Saint George!"

"Watch the hooves!" Edward dodged a pair, then plunged forward, his blade glancing off an enemy rib. He twisted it free. Blood gurgled from beneath the Frenchman's helm.

Edward dared a glance toward Northampton and then down-hill. His gut clenched. Dozens of chevaliers skirted the pits, weaving between the mounds of bodies. There were no arrows to stop them.

"Close up! Close up!" he roared.

The French dropped their lances, drew their swords, and bullied their horses around the stakes and into the crush. Blades rang.

Edward's shoulder jarred from a heavy blow. The chevalier who landed the blow spun his stallion, knocking Edward sideways. The knight slashed down again. Edward slipped and as he fell to his knee the knight's sword whooshed past, barely missing him.

The chevalier dug in a spur and as his horse wheeled again, Edward ripped his sword across the destrier's belly. The stallion screamed, took one step, and folded. The knight kicked free, landing with the horse between them.

Chandos charged the Frenchman. Steel met steel, stroke for stroke until Chandos stepped back and dropped his guard. The French knight took the bait, lunged and slipped. Chandos' blade broke through mail links, piercing the knight's neck. Blood spurted, and the Frenchman slumped onto the body of his dying horse.

In the press of horseflesh and riders, men grunted, cursed and hacked. Edward panted for air through his helm. "No prisoners!" he shouted. A destrier stumbled, slamming into Edward. Holland grabbed the rider from behind and tugged him backwards. As they toppled, Edward stabbed the Frenchman's exposed throat and he bubbled a last breath. Holland shoved off the dying man's body and stumbled to his feet.

Sweat streamed into Edward's eyes. He slipped in the gore; Holland thrust out a gauntlet and Edward latched on.

The Prince of Wales must not fall.

At a lull in the fighting, Edward raised his visor and gulped cooler air. On the vanguard's right flank, Northampton's archers loosed a flurry of arrows to stop the French *conrois* from breaking through a breach in the line.

Edward slammed down his visor. "On me!"

Holland and Cobham rushed to help plug the gap.

"Hold the line!" Edward bellowed, fighting for breath.

A knight with plumed helm, spurred at them. Cobham grabbed the knight's leg and tried to drag him from his saddle. The Frenchman crashed his shield on Cobham's head and spun his horse.

"*Sainte Denys!*" He slashed from side to side like a madman, then spun his horse again. The destrier reared and struck out, knocking a man to the ground. When the chevalier tried to spin a third time, Chandos grabbed him from behind and towed him back over his cantle. The French knight roared and, twisting in mid-air, he pinned Chandos beneath him when they hit the ground.

A bloody carcass blocked Edward's path. Cobham dove forward; the force of his blade pierced the Frenchman's mail and into his back. Blood gushed from his mouth, and as Chandos rolled him off, Cobham offered his shield. Chandos grabbed it and was hauled to his feet.

"*Là! Le fils du roi!*"

Edward whirled. The chevalier charged, intent on killing the English king's son. Edward parried the knight's downward stroke, the blade sliding down and catching on Edward's hilt. Off balance, he fell. As the horseman came again, Edward rolled and the horse's hoof caught his thigh. He slashed the stallion's pastern. It squealed and as it lurched sideways, the off-balance chevalier's arm flailed. Audley jabbed his sword into the knight's armpit. He toppled with his horse, his arm hanging useless.

From his perch atop the windmill, King Edward let go his breath when his son staggered to his feet. Though half-bent over and soughing for breath, his heir was holding his own. The king flicked his eyes across the field. Hundreds of chevaliers retreated downslope. Only a handful of skirmishes remained. *Bon.* Despite Philippe's numbers, the English lines held.

"This interlude will not last long," the bishop said.

King Edward shook his head. "The French...this." He waved a hand. "Alençon's assault of the Genoese...it makes no sense."

"The *Comte* is hotheaded."

"His arrogance has cost them."

"Go! Be quick!" Warwick ordered below. In the fading light, lads scampered across the hillside scavenging arrows.

"Check the fletches!" Edward hollered. "If undamaged, we can reuse the arrows.

The king asked, "How many sheaves do we have in reserve?"

"No more than a dozen, lord," the serjeant replied, "aside from your personal supply."

They would need every blessed one.

Boys crisscrossed the field, passing skins of watered ale.

French horns sounded over the hillside.

"Form up!" Warwick shouted.

"Archers!" Edward called.

The vanguard's men-at-arms reformed shield to shield with archers once again on their flanks. Discipline. No one ignored orders and broke rank to take prisoners.

The French chevaliers' line stretched the entire length of the ridge.

"At least a dozen new standards, sire," Suffolk said. "Shall I ready the reserve?"

Before the king could answer, three sharp French trumpet notes were followed by a fanfare of pipes and drums. The French line parted.

"Ahh, Philippe takes the field. France's imposter king has suffered enough shame."

Flying with the French colors was one of black bearing three white feathers.

"Is that the King of Bohemia's banner beside Philippe's?" Suffolk asked. "He is near blind! Does he mean to fight?"

"It appears so. The Holy Roman emperor's son is no coward."

"Look at them!" Burghersh snorted. "Their finery is better

suited for a Paris parade than a battlefield."

King Edward grinned. "Perfect targets."

As the sun's dying rays sliced through a bank of low-lying clouds, French drums beat a new cadence.

King Edward said a silent prayer. *O Heaven's King, bestow Your blessing and strength upon us this day.*

"*Preparez!*" The order sounded over the field.

Equine muscles bunched; hooves danced.

"*Avancez!*"

Curbs released, the horses thrust forward and scabbards rattled with each stride. Frustrated fury drove the chevaliers' charge.

The king raised and circled his baton, signalling the shawm player. Two notes sounded, setting the men below into action, lighting fuses. The king's heart raced.

Boom! Boom! Boom!

The ground shook. Thick, acrid smoke smothered the battlefield, making it difficult for the king to see, but he could hear. Panicked warhorses whinnied in terror. The smoke dissipated enough to see horses colliding and bolting in all directions. Riders fought desperately to stay seated and regain control.

English centenars called, "Nock!"

"Loose!"

Hundreds of bow cords hummed. Arrows hissed like thousands of roaches. The second flight soared, then the third. Iron barbs punctured leather trappers and impaled equine chests.

French destriers reared, hurtling chevaliers backwards. Horses scrambled, tripped by the pits. Legs splintered. Frenchmen tumbled making easy targets for English archers.

Runners hauled out the king's reserve of red-fletched arrows. "Make every arrow count, lads," Warwick bellowed.

A downed knight staggered to his feet with a feathered shaft in his calf. He grabbed the reins of a riderless horse and tried to mount. A red-fletched arrow took him in the back.

In minutes, fewer arrows flew, and then none.

"Fall back!" His son's order rang clearly. The archers dashed through the gaps in the English lines, tossed their bows, and pulled out their stabbing knives.

Again, the French cheered. "*Montjoie! Sainte Denys!*"

Shields up!" Came his son's command. "Hold firm!"

Resolute chevaliers found the gaps in the English line. Unyielding, the vanguard's men-at-arms pounded their shields into the horses' tender muzzles. The destriers shrieked, and tried to veer away, but others rammed them from behind. The horses bunched up with little room to manoeuver.

"For England!" The vanguard's men-at-arms hacked over their shields at the horsemen, while the archers stabbed at the French from between English legs.

On the battlefield below King Edward, the vanguard's line swayed and reeled. The French fought with skill. Outnumbered, many English fell—too many.

"Sire, my reserve," Suffolk cried. "Your son needs aid."

"Close up!" The Prince of Wales called from the field.

"*Non*, my son is holding his own." King Edward dismissed Suffolk, returning to observing the fighting below.

"Hold! Hold the—"

A half-ton destrier slammed into his son. The stallion writhed and screamed, trailing entrails and blood. King Edward searched. Where was Edward?

Edward lay in tall grass. White wings flapped all around him. *Honk! Honk*! Geese? Angry Geese? He rolled onto his knees and shook his head. *Honk! Honk*!

Someone grabbed his elbow. "Lord?'

Edward strained to hear above the honking.

"Get up, lord!" Hands tugged him.

He placed a foot beneath him.

"Lord Edward, get up!" Someone seized his shoulders, shook

him, and caught hold of his surcoat.

He clambered to his feet. The world reeled.

"For England!"

Edward's ears roared. He shook his head, blinked, and blinked again.

No geese. No honking.

His guard encircled him, battling a hoard of frenzied French knights. Arundel parried, feinted, parried again, then trapped his foe's sword with his hilt, put his foot behind the man's calf, and shoved. The knight fell. Arundel thrust his blade into the man's chest. He groaned a last breath.

Edward swayed, then steadied himself.

"This is no time for a nap," Arundel quipped.

Fitz Simon hauled Edward to his feet by his surcoat and helped him to stand. "By our God's blessed mercy!" He released Edward's bloodied garment and handed Edward his sword. Not five feet away, Thomas Daniel waved the Prince's Welsh banner, rallying the vanguard.

Edward grabbed his hilt, at the same time catching a blur of motion through his eye slit. He sprang sideways, avoiding the blow by a hair's breadth. He punched his hilt into his foe's visor, lunged, and jammed his sword into the man's unprotected groin. The French knight slid into the blood, pooling at this feet.

The Welsh dragon banner drew the French like the tide drew the Thames to the sea. Flanked by Arundel, Warwick, Audley, and Chandos, Edward's training took over—his only thought to stay alive. Time stilled.

Shadows grew deeper. Wraithlike figures scuttled past the mounds of lifeless humps littering the field and the few men still fighting, the hillside eerily lit now by only a sliver of a moon. Men slithered down the slope in retreat.

Edward's temples throbbed. He soughed for breath through

a throat scorched raw. The air reeked of blood and faeces. Voices drifted.

"*La bataille est perdue, mon roi.*

What? The battle is over?

Below him, a group of chevaliers surrounded a horse and rider. King Philippe?

"*Viens, il faut y aller.*"

Indeed…Philippe's guard was shepherding him from the field.

Edward's body was racked with tremors, his arms as if weighted with lead. Every muscle whined. He lowered the tip of his sword to the ground and leaned on it to hold himself upright.

Mournful cries keened over the hillside, the sound like an other-worldly being from hell.

Never had he witnessed such slaughter.

He shivered.

No one cheered. Not his guard. No one.

Contretemps in Calais

December 1346 ~ Calais, France

Joan rested a hand on her stomach and gripped the bench in the longboat with her other. The *mal de mer* she suffered aboard ship during the crossing was not yet settled. The ship had been caught in a sudden squall, transforming a one-day crossing into three days.

With each slap of the oars, the longboats ferrying the queen and her household drew closer to the windswept beach near Calais. Joan gave one last look to the king's flagship and then focused her attention toward shore and her future. After five years, it was long past time to end her life's uncertainty.

The December wind blew steadily as the boat scraped in the shallows, scattering the grey-and-white speckled birds skittering along the water's edge. The leather-faced oarsmen slipped the blades, and two others jumped into the surf and dragged the craft up the shoal. Accepting a crewman's hand, Joan stepped out, turned to the queen, and held out her hand.

"Allow me to assist you, my lady."

Queen Philippa tucked up her skirts, grasped Joan's hand, and stepped cautiously onto the wet sand. "At last," she sighed. The queen scanned the length of the shore, her gaze coming to rest on the fortress looming above the deserted harbour. England's army was entrenched below the stronghold's towering walls. Philippa's brow knitted. "So, this is the French bastion our lord king has vowed to capture."

Joan tightened her cloak against the bitter onshore wind. "Let us pray the siege ends soon." An icicle-sharp gust tangled Joan's skirts and whipped up grains of sand. She tucked her face into her mantle's plush hood to shield it from the pelting.

"Please take heed, my lady. The deeper sand beyond the wet verge and the wind make for treacherous going."

The queen drew the hood of her fur-lined mantle closer. "No matter, Jeanette. It feels good to stand on solid ground again."

"I could not agree more." Joan held the queen's elbow and helped her trudge through the sand.

"*Maman*!" Johanna stepped out of a boat and twirled along the shore, startling the shorebirds.

"Just look at my daughters! Neither appears to have suffered any ill effects from our voyage." While Johanna dashed along the shore, Isabella chatted gaily with the queen's ladies huddled near the chests unloaded from the longboats.

Queen Philippa smiled. "My ladies are as eager to reunite with their husbands, as am I to unite with mine."

"Do you not find it odd, my lady, that King Philippe has done so little in these three months to relieve the siege?"

"Philippe's defeat at Crécy caused great turmoil in his rule. Suffering another defeat could likely lead to its complete collapse. Unfortunately, while he wavers, the men holding the fortress for him go hungry."

Joan scraped her hair from her face. "My lady, look, Edward has arrived."

Her cousin dismounted nimbly and strode toward them; the set of his shoulders evinced a confidence not present when he left England. No one could doubt Edward's newfound authority. She smiled, proud of the man her friend had become.

Isabella pounced on her brother, grabbing Edward's arm. "Why were you not here to assist us?"

Edward grinned at his sister, but addressed his mother. "Forgive me, Lady Mother. Most regrettably, I was detained." He clasped the queen's outstretched hand, tipped at the waist and placed a kiss on her fingers. "You are well, *ma mere*?" As he straightened, he tugged his mother close, and brushed a kiss upon her sallow cheek.

"Ah, *mon fils*, I am as well as may be expected given the storms haunting the narrow sea, *n'est ce pas*? Let me look at you." She held Edward at arm's length. "You have grown taller, *non*?" The queen drank in the sight of her son, her love for him brimming in her eyes.

"Isabella, *ma belle sœur*, by the roses in your cheeks I see you suffered not." Edward chucked Johanna's chin. "And what of you, *ma petite*?"

Johanna wriggled into his embrace. "I missed you." He hugged her shoulders, then raised his eyes to Joan.

"Jeanette, *ma chère*, you are well?" Edward released Johanna and took both Joan's hands.

"I am well, Lord Edward." Joan curtsied. "You suffered no wounds in battle?" She studied him. All traces of the youth she held so dear were gone. A pang of melancholy tugged at Joan's heart as Edward squeezed her fingers before releasing them, their private signal.

"As you see." He waved a hand. "*Maman*, let us get you out of this wind." Edward called to his squire, "Hal, attend to the queen's ladies and the baggage." Edward rested a protective arm about his mother's shoulders. "It is but a short distance to the royal residence." He pointed to a second wagon.

Joan followed a few steps behind as Edward escorted his mother to the heavily-draped wagon and helped her up the portable steps. Edward lended a hand to his sisters, then Joan. He took his stallion's reins from the carter holding them, and instead of mounting as Joan expected, he tied his horse to the tailboard, and climbed in. "Drive on," he called, sitting beside his mother.

"*Maman*, you may be surprised by the size of the settlement."

"Indeed? What of this residence my lord husband has built for our stay? I am more than ready to rest upon a bed which does not sway."

"I share your sentiments, my lady," Joan said.

Isabella let out a deep sigh. "I agree."

"Your dwelling is solidly built. My lord father oversaw its design to ensure it provides suitable comforts for you, *Maman*."

The horses plodded up the shingle to the rutted track running through the army's vast camp. Thousands of tents and slatted huts sprawled a safe distance from the stronghold's stone ramparts. The rickety dwellings looked as if a strong wind might blow them down.

"A great many reinforcements sailed over to supplement our troops for the coming engagement," Edward said, "although rumors of Philippe mustering a force has come to nothing." He shrugged. "Our camp extends as far south as the marshlands, which, I might add, stretch for miles." The wagon passed by groups of men huddled around smoking fires.

"It must be hard on the soldiers," Joan said, shuddering at the thought of how cold they must be.

"Between the gales off the sea and the damp, the living conditions are poor at best. As you can see, the *Pas de Calais* is a less than hospitable place."

"From what I have experienced so far, I would not argue with that assessment," Queen Philippa said.

Joan gazed at the tumbledown cotes set in haphazard rows, casting occasional glances at Edward. She could hardly believe how much he matured, noting his fashionable moustache and beard.

Edward leaned against her shoulder and whispered, "It comes as no surprise you joined my mother on this sojourn."

Joan raised her brows. "As one of her ladies, it is only natural I would accompany her."

"I think it is not the only reason." Edward narrowed his eyes. "Thomas Holland is here."

Three days after Joan's arrival, she strolled with Isabella among the guests at Queen Philippa's welcome celebration. The king's forethought about the residence's design included the construction of a grand hall. It now blazed with color from dozens of banners hanging from the beams and lit by the wall torches. More candles than Joan could count flickered from pewter holders on the trestle tables. Gentle melodies drifted beneath the flow of conversation between the noble couples reuniting after so many months apart.

Isabella chatted with a group of knights who vied quite boldly for her notice. The green silk gown she wore set off her creamy complexion and auburn hair to perfection. Joan conceded to herself she enjoyed the knights' chivalrous attentions almost as much as her cousin.

"Lady Isabella, pray tell us your impressions of our king's settlement," Roger Mortimer suggested. Joan reminded herself to address her childhood friend, now knighted, as Sir Roger.

Isabella blushed. "Oh, I think you are all so brave for living here, let alone going into battle. I never envisioned you living in such harsh conditions." Isabella's eyes opened wide. "And the wind!"

Over Roger's shoulder, Joan spotted John Chandos and a companion at the far end of the hall. Pausing in the entry, the torchlight danced across their faces. Joan's breath caught; the man with Chandos wore an eye patch. She had expected Edward to be with Chandos, but his companion was none other than Thomas Holland, the errant husband she never set eyes on, nor heard from, in five years.

Joan folded her hands to stop them shaking. She stared, unable to help herself, but as the pair approached, she schooled warring emotions from her face, though she could do nothing about her spinning stomach and the heat spreading into her cheeks. To conceal her distress, she coughed and turned her back.

"Lady Isabella," Chandos greeted in warm fashion.

"Sir John." Isabella's gown rustled as she curtsied. "It gladdens my spirits to see you in such fine health after the rigors of battle."

Joan coughed again, her malaise no longer a pretence.

"Begging your pardon, Lady Joan," Chandos said, "are you unwell?"

Courtesy demanded she respond. Turning, she met John's eyes. Only his. "Thank you for your concern. I suffer merely from a tickle."

"What a pleasure to see you again." Chandos bowed. "Ladies, if I may, permit me to introduce my good fellow, Sir Thomas Holland." He paused. "Thomas, this charming young maid is Lady Isabella, Lord Edward's sister."

Isabella fluttered her lashes, offered a timorous smile, and curtsied. "Sir Thomas."

"Lady Isabella, it is indeed an honour to see you again." Thomas offered a bow.

Isabella tilted her head, a puzzled expression on her face.

"I served your lord father in Flanders years ago. You were a mere girl at the time and may not remember me."

Isabella dipped her head. "Indeed."

"Lady Joan," Chandos said, "allow me to present Sir Thomas, recently of Lord Edward's retinue at Crécy. Thomas, this is Lady Joan, Lord Edward's cousin and William Montagu's future countess, when the king grants him the Salisbury earldom."

Inwardly, Joan winced and searched for her husband's reaction. Utterly composed, he gave nothing away. How like him.

Joan bobbed a curtsy. "Sir Thomas."

"Lady Joan." Thomas bowed and as he straightened, his eye claimed Joan's. "John, I do believe this lady may have some small memory of me from the Low Countries." Holland's eye never left hers. "A young maid then, yet perhaps of an age to remember me. May I say the years have favoured you." Holland's eye twitched. "I am enchanted."

Joan gritted her teeth, keeping her face neutral. "You flatter me, sir." Did he think her still so naive as to be taken in by his charm and flowery words? Yes, she blossomed, or so the looks men bestowed upon her indicated. Yet, her mind, too, bloomed. No longer was she an innocent easily duped by a man's silver tongue.

"Sir Thomas, if I have any memory of you, it is hazy at best. I have met many knights in the king's service. It is impossible to bring them all to mind." Though tension rippled through Joan, she managed an insincere smile. For once, she did not lack for words, pleased with the set down the gave him, one he richly deserved. She broke off from Holland at James Audley's arrival, and caught the tic in her husband's jaw.

"Sir James." Joan offered a warm smile. "Such a pleasure to have your company."

Pleasantries swirled around Joan. Isabella carried most of the conversation. Distracted, Joan paid little heed to the teasing banter; her attention drifted around the assembly.

O Blessed Virgin!

Will and his mother strolled in her direction.

Joan's stomach listed. Could this be any worse? She should have prepared for this situation, well aware both of her husbands served the king. She must tread carefully.

"Good evening, lady wife." Will reached for Joan's hand and brought it to his lips.

Lady Catherine cleverly positioned herself in a way as to isolate Joan from the others—so much for safety in a crowd. Ignoring Will, Joan leaned toward Isabella's coterie, trying to maintain a connection. Though she heard the chatter, her mind struggled to make the words mean anything.

"Would not you agree, Lady Joan?" Lady Catherine asked.

Off-guard, Joan replied without thinking. "Yes, indeed."

"I am heartened to hear you agree," Will's mother said. "It is settled then."

Joan nodded meekly. What was settled? To what did she just agree?

After months of hardship, Edward feasted on the tastes, sights, and fragrances surrounding him while he half-listened to Warwick opining upon the siege. Floral scents supplanted the battlefield stench of death and decay, and the lush fabrics, sparkling with gemstones, made a pleasing divergence from the campaign's bleak livery.

"The king is right." Warwick stated with conviction. "Catapults and siege engines are useless in this boggy ground."

"Bombarding the walls would have little effect anyway," Cobham said.

"Our best strategy is to starve the garrison in order to force a surrender," Edward said. "Our ships blockade the harbour and our troops secure the overland supply routes. The garrison grows desperate without provisions and pressures Philippe to come to their aid."

"I think it unlikely Philippe is mustering forces," Cobham said.

Warwick nodded. "At least, not until spring."

Edward stopped listening. Across the room, Montague and Lady Catherine cornered Joan, separating her from Isabella and the company of knights, including Holland, who bowed to Isabella and strolled away.

"Your pardon, *messieurs*," Edward said, then cut across the room to intercept Holland. "You are departing so soon?"

Holland's forehead puckered. "Montagu abrades me like a whetstone."

Edward glanced toward the trio. "Sadly, as his wife, my cousin must suffer the future Earl's attentions."

Holland's gaze fixed on Joan. "When you spoke to me of Joan and our marriage, lord, you made no mention of Joan's beauty. I knew her as a budding maiden of twelve, yet now, she is nothing less than stunning."

"Yes, my cousin seems to turn many heads."

"Time has wrought changes in her beyond any I might have imagined," Holland murmured.

Edward glanced from Joan, in her azure gown and sapphires,

to Holland. "Montagu is besotted by her beauty. However, a husband who takes the time will discover Joan's genuine beauty lies within."

A week later, Joan climbed into the wagon with Isabella and Johanna for a tour of the countryside beyond camp. Edward had succumbed to his sisters' endless plaints of being cooped up indoors too long. He arranged for Sir James Audley to escort them into the countryside as far as the gatehouse on the road to Gravelines.

As the horses clopped along the rutted track, James rode beside the wagon, explaining the lands surrounding *Villeneuve le hardi*, the name given to the English settlement. Isabella's previous comments about the bravery needed to live in this new town proved true, based on what Joan experienced since her arrival. Bitter winds blasted off the narrow sea incessantly and the marshlands encircling the port reeked of damp and decay. Life here required fortitude.

Their outing began pleasantly enough, but too soon the sisters began to bicker. By the time they returned to the residence, Joan's patience was as withered as the bleak winter landscape. She could hardly wait to escape.

When the wagon halted in the courtyard, Isabella and Johanna scrambled out and disappeared inside. Joan stepped down from the wagon with a hand from Sir James.

"Thank you for your escort and your patience."

"It was my honour, Lady Joan." Audley remounted and waved as he trotted away, his expression one of relief.

Joan adjusted her cloak, then, seeking a few moments of solitude, she wandered into the small walled garden. Tiny brown birds chirped among the shrubs which grew in the lee of the walls, sheltering the birds from the gusts sweeping off the sea. Despite the warmth of her heavy mantle, Joan shivered, the day's chill deepening as the sun disappeared beyond the cliffs.

A boot scraped on the path behind her. She turned.

Heaven help her.

Thomas Holland halted not five paces away. "Pardon me for startling you, my sweet." The man was definitely too close for comfort. Joan crossed her arms. Her heart raced faster than a hare fleeing a hound.

"I do not believe startling me is all for which you need beg my pardon." Her voice, as sharp as the wind, gave no quarter. She would show no weakness.

Thomas dared another step.

Joan held up her hand. "Do not, sir."

He blinked a bloodshot eye. "I have been hoping to catch you for a private word."

Joan forced a thin smile. "Ho! Do not make me laugh. After five years of silence, you want a word?"

"You dare upbraid me, madam? I did not forsake my vows and wed another."

How dare he! "Pray tell, what say did I have in the matter?" Joan shook. "I had none! Not with my mother, Uncle Wake, and the old Earl of Salisbury gainsaying our marriage. My protests mattered not one whit. Without lawful proof or word from you, what could I do?"

Thomas opened his mouth.

"Do not say one word!" Pent up anger burst from her. "I am an insignificant female, considered nothing more than the property of parent, guardian, or husband. I am devoid of rights or say about my life." She raised her chin. "So, enlighten me, Thomas, why did you marry me if only to abandon me?"

"Oh no! Do not place the blame on me."

Joan gasped.

Thomas seized her by the arms. His nostrils flared and the heat from his battle-hardened hands seared through her cloak.

She glared at him. "Without a word, you deserted me to fend

as best I could."

"What? I abandoned you?" He eased his grip. "When I returned from Sluys, I sought you out first thing. Your mother barred me from seeing you."

"This is your tale?" Joan shook off his hold. "You forget, Thomas, I am no longer the naive young maiden you married in secret." She sat on a bench before her legs gave out on her.

He paced a step away and back again. "When your mother refused me, I wrote to you."

"You wrote to me? Do tell."

"Yes. I asked for your patience until I was in a better position to approach King Edward. I planned to seek him out. That, of course, was before I learned of your marriage."

Blood rushed to Joan's head. He had written to her?

"Joan," he paused, "you have a right to be angry at my lack of foresight. I confess, at the time of our union, I thought of naught save making you mine. I failed to consider our life after we married. When the king recalled me for service, I left you in Queen Philippa's care trusting you would be safe within her household until my return."

"No, you did not think." Joan's voice was as cold as the wind.

"I should have anticipated the strength of your family's resistance to a union with a mere knight. When you did not respond to my letters—"

"What letters? I never received any letters." Joan pressed her throbbing temples.

"No letters? Christ's blood!"

"Ah, I see my mother's hand in this. She must have intercepted them."

"How I should like to throttle your dam. We have paid a heavy price for my lack."

"We?" Joan jumped up, hands on hips. "*We*? Tell me, Thomas, what cost have *you* paid?"

"Yes, I say we." He roughed a hand through his hair. "Imagine my shock when I learned my *wife* married another? And I could not vent my spleen at anyone. So, yes, I dare claim we have both paid a price." He paced, his face screwed in frustration. "Dare I also admit to a wounding? I approached old Salisbury after I learned of your marriage, though, as King Edward's close friend, Salisbury held all the power. Despite that, I did not yield for I believed if I gained the king's notice, he might give credence to my claim to you. I have laboured ever since, striving to make it so." Thomas bowed his head as if sincere.

Was he? Joan crossed her arms. Did Thomas speak true?

"I worked even harder after your cousin Edward took me to task."

Joan started. Edward never mentioned any such encounter. She glanced away. Was Thomas more embarrassed by the reproach than shamed by his behaviour? Was her husband's act of contrition other than a false show? She steeled herself, unwilling to succumb to a slight show of remorse.

"What of your arrangement with the Earl before his passing? You agreed to a settlement. A lucrative sum for disavowing our union." Joan's throat ached from holding back tears. She sat again, dreading his answer.

"Ah, you heard about that." Thomas rubbed his jaw. "Forgive me." He sat beside her and brushed a windblown strand of hair from her face. "By then, several years passed and it occurred to me you might prefer Montagu and life as his countess. I persuaded myself releasing you was for the best and what you wanted. I lost hope." He reached for her hand and caressed her fingers. "Your happiness is important to me."

"My mother used your bargain with the Earl to convince me you married me for only one purpose—your own advancement. I did not want to give her words credence, but I heard nothing from you for so long, I feared her words were true." A tear slipped down Joan's cheek.

Thomas tugged her against him, stroking her back and shoulders. Gradually, she regained her composure and pulled away.

He dabbed the wet from her cheeks and, gentle as the touch of butterfly wings, he feathered his lips to hers.

Heat flooded Joan; she cradled Thomas's face and he deepened their kiss. After a few moments, he withdrew his lips and tenderly lifted her chin until their eyes met.

"Believe me when I say, I regret these lost years. If I were a man of means, I would have challenged Montagu and claimed you as mine long ago." He took a breath. "You heard of Comte d'Eu's surrender to me at Caen?"

She nodded.

"Once his ransom is paid, I will have the necessary funds to petition the church to recognize our marriage and enough wealth to provide for you. For us." He hesitated. "If you still wish for us to be together."

Joan withdrew to arm's length. "What I wish? For five years, I resisted the pressure from my mother, uncle, and Will to yield, yet I remained true to my vows. I am *your* wife. Of course, it is what *I* wish*." The temperature had dropped with the sun and Joan's teeth began to chatter.

Thomas bundled her cloak around her. "You must go inside. I cannot have my wife taking a chill." He rose and guided her toward the gate, but stepped to the side as they neared it. "It would not do should we be observed."

"Wait." Joan furrowed her brows. "I came to Calais to resolve what lies between us. Now, knowing what we do, when might we be together?"

Thomas urged her forward again. "Dearest, I shall not lie to you. I honestly do not know."

January 1347 - Calais

"Come away, sire, out of crossbow range." Edward steered the king to place more distance between them and the ramparts. Had not the great Lionheart walked beneath fortress walls when struck by a stray crossbow bolt? With the wind shearing across the mud-flats, anything might happen.

The siege engines sat idle and silent while seabirds sailed overhead, their mournful cries echoing off the bastion's walls. Trenches encircled the fortress, hindering any French relief attempts and providing shelter for the English soldiers guarding against any approach. Offshore, English ships patrolling the coast tossed in the white-peaked chop. So far, England's blockades succeeded, at sea and on land.

Edward pulled up his hood and placed himself between the king and the battlements. His father patrolled the trench lines daily. "If nothing else," the king said, "my presence relieves the sentries' boredom."

Edward suspected his father's real purpose. On the march through Normandy, Edward learned of a soldier's need to connect with the man for whom he risked his life. When a commander suffered the same deprivations as his men, the bond between them deepened.

Smoke swirled from the watchmen's fires burning at intervals along the line. As they trudged closer to one, the men warming themselves recognized the king and stood.

A banneret called, "God's blessings, sire."

King Edward raised his hand in greeting and then diverted his direction to stroll toward them. The soldiers, who began to kneel, stopped at the king's gesture. They shuffled to make room for Edward and the king at the fire. King Edward removed his gloves and held his hands over the flames.

"So, what goes here?"

The burliest among them said, "Not much, sire. 'Tis too cold fer these French buggers. We sometimes sees a few heads atop the walls and hears a few insults shouted now 'n agin."

The king nodded. "The waiting is hard, I know."

A few men mumbled agreement while they huddled closer to the fire and chafed cold hands above it. The smoke shifted and everyone adjusted positions. For several minutes, the men shared opinions of the French and memories from Crécy.

King Edward said, "You do well for your king." His praise left the men speechless but not without smiles. He pulled on his gloves, and they walked on.

Though the wind lashed at them, his father appeared not to notice. Deep inside his thoughts, a scowl crossed his face. "Damn Philippe! By now, he should have marched to relieve Calais."

"Is it so surprising? We humiliated him at Crécy and many of high birth were killed. Even should he rally a force, there is little here to sustain it, not with our raids from Guines to Sangatte."

"Lack of provisions is not what stops Philippe. He has the means to supply his army from Paris. He hesitates because he fears a second defeat."

A gust sheeted sand across the barren flats, forcing them to duck behind one of the wooden windbreaks stationed at intervals along the stretch from the watergate.

"Before we sailed, Parliament demanded I put an end to this war. To do so, I need another pitched battle and a second indisputable victory." His father's voice signalled a worsening mood.

Edward changed the subject. "How does my lady mother? Is she recovered fully from the voyage?"

"Your mother frets over leaving Margaret behind with her wet-nurse. I see no reason for her concern as the babe knows little difference whether Philippa is there or not." He shook his head. "While she left Margaret behind, she made the mistake of allowing Isabella and Johanna to accompany her. Their endless-bickering is distressing, though she seems to find solace in Joan's fellowship."

A point in Joan's favour. Good to know. The king's appreciative sentiment might aid Edward in his purpose. He glanced around, judging the distance to the nearest sentries making sure no one would overhear. How might he best approach the king? A bold offensive often won the day.

"About Joan, sire." Edward clapped his numb hands to warm them. "Might you consider her two marriages have carried on long enough?"

"Christ's blood!" King Edward halted, his legs planted wide. "You know about her cursed dealings?"

Edward nodded.

A glower on his face, the king resumed his steps. "How long have you known?"

"Does it matter?"

His father's black look deepened. "She dared to defy me."

"Did she?" Edward took a deep breath and plunged on. "Do you forget Joan was but ten years when she sailed with you to Flanders and barely a maiden of twelve when she joined with Holland?"

"Old enough to know better."

Edward ignored his father's crusty tone. "Joan was an innocent and easy prey for an ambitious man." Edward met his father's blazing eyes, steeling himself to continue. "You once said you admired Holland's daring, his initiative as you called it."

"*Jesu!* You venture to throw my words at me?" His father stormed ahead, then spun around. "You forget yourself, Edward." He tapped his chest. "I am king, not you."

Angry waves crashed along the water's edge. Edward stooped to pick up a rock as he bit back an angry retort. "If you recall, Father," he said with a level voice, "when my Lady Mother delivered John in Ghent was when Joan and Holland wed. Perhaps those charged with Joan's welfare were less than diligent about her care." Edward hurled the rock into the sea. "What better time for a clever man like Holland to press his advantage and secret Joan away?"

The king stiffened, working the muscles in his jaw. "Dare you blame me for this?" The king glared at Edward, and though Edward did not look away, he held his tongue. As Joan's guardian, duty required his father to protect her, to ensure nothing untoward happened to her. The fault did lie with his father, yet to enrage him further would be unwise. If provoked too far, the king's anger blinded him, and Joan needed the king's eyes opened. Until his father's temper cooled, *the king* would be unable to see what Edward hoped in time, *the father* in him would.

King Edward lay abed with Philippa, her head tucked beneath his chin while the tempos, of her heart and his, gentled. With each breath, her hair and floral scent tickled his nose. Candlelight flickered through the opening in the bed curtains while outside, the wind off the narrow sea howled.

Philippa sighed and raised her head to gaze at him. "What troubles you, Husband?"

Jesu! The woman's eerie ability to read him was unnerving. He sat up, leaned back against the bolster, and drew her to drape upon his chest.

"Edward."

"Edward? What about Edward?" Philippa popped up, lines creasing her brow. "He has not taken ill?"

"*Non,* nothing of the sort, *mon coeur.*" Robbed of her warmth, he chided himself for his heedless response. Edward and I had words today is all—heated ones."

"Ahh." She nuzzled against him again. "This sort of duel is natural between father and son, *non?* Do you forget boys grow into men?"

His silent agitation followed her question, underscored by the keening wind outside.

"Edward accused me of failing in my duty. My own son!"

"Hmm…are you certain Edward said as much?"

"He brought up our time in the Low Countries."

"My, my, so long ago?"

"He reminded me Joan was under my protection and suggested its lack allowed Holland to whisk her from under our noses to marry her."

Philippa's playful fingertips wandered over his chest.

"Our son suggested I am to blame for her wretched marriage."

"Hmm… well then, the fault lies with me," Philippa said. "Joan resided in my household. You were fully occupied with affairs of the realm at the time while I was too caught up in our Johnny's coming birth to notice anything amiss in Joan's behavior." Philippa lowered her eyelashes. "You must forgive me."

Philippa's softly spoken words acted like a pallative balm, soothing the sting of his eldest son's plaint. "Our son believes Joan has suffered long enough and it is time to end her muddle of a marriage."

"This has troubled you all evening?"

He sighed. "I cannot take sides in this, Philippa. The matter lies with her two…er…suitors to resolve."

"I see." Philippa reached for his hand. "As heir to the Salisbury title, Montagu wields more power and influence, placing Holland at a disadvantage."

Philippa astutely divined the heart of the matter and her words hinted at a clever solution. His lips twitched upwards. He need only level the playing field. "Tell me," he said, squeezing her shoulders, "however did the notion arise that females lack reason?"

"I shall take your question as a compliment, husband, though this female is not nearly as crafty as her lord." She kissed his cheek, a sultry invitation in her eyes. "Now, blow out the candle."

February 1347 – Calais, France

Amidst the tumult inside the tournament pavilion, while workmen assembled trestle tables and servants set benches and hung the competitors' banners, Edward inspected his kit for rust. The din of hammers from outside the pavilion, ebbed and flowed on the wind as carpenters finished constructing the lists.

What better way to offset winter doldrums, and sharpen the knights' swordplay, than through lively competition and prizes worth fighting for? Edward smiled at his father's cleverness.

His red-faced page appeared beside him and bowed. "Your pardon, lord. Sir Thomas Holland requests an audience."

"Bid him come, Simon, then fetch my dragon banners from the residence. Take Hal to help you." The lad hastened off and Holland entered.

"God's blessing upon you, lord." He lowered to one knee.

"Holland." Edward wagged a finger for the knight to rise and sit.

"I have come about Count d'Eu's ransom," Holland said.

"Good fortune smiled when the Constable surrendered to you at Caen, though it may be some while before he raises the funds to pay you."

"I thought so, too." Holland's eye twitched. "However, the king has offered to advance me one-third."

"My father did what?" Edward slapped his thigh. "Splendid!"

"Most generous and quite unexpected."

Edward raised his cup in salute. "God bless the king." And God bless *the father* who took his son's words to heart. What a clever ruse to aid Holland's cause and put an end to Joan's misery, without appearing to favour either Holland or Montagu.

Holland picked at a thumbnail. "I am at a loss to explain it."

Edward raised his brows. "How so? Our king often rewards those who serve him."

"Yes, er, the king may appreciate my sword, yet aside from my promotion at Crécy, he has shown me no particular favour. On the contrary, he keeps a cool distance."

"Perhaps he values you more than you think."

Holland eased back. "Well, he did mention initiative."

Edward smothered a grin.

Holland thumped his hand on the table. "It was you! You spoke to the king?"

"You might describe it as such, though a clash of wills might better describe our exchange." Yet, his father heard him. Edward chuckled to himself. He might do well to pay closer attention to his mother for she possessed a curious skill at handling the king.

Holland crossed his arms. "If I may inquire, why speak on my behalf?"

"Is it not obvious?"

"Not to me."

Edward leaned forward. "You did say without funds you were unable to petition the church to recognize your marriage to Joan."

"God's nails!" Outside, the hammering stopped.

Holland lowered his gaze. "I am at a loss for how to thank you, lord, for interceding on my behalf—"

"I did not do this for you." Edward's voice cut, galled by Holland's assumption. "Make no mistake, I did it for Joan. She deserves a better life, one not wasted due to your failing."

"No argument from me. Joan is a beauty. Little did I think she would mature into such."

"You believe her simply beautiful?" Edward's pitch rose. "She is worth ten of you!"

Holland raised his hands in surrender. "Your pardon, lord. I meant no offense. I have much to learn of my wife." He lowered his hands. "Please accept my apology as well as my heartfelt thanks. I owe you a debt I can never repay."

Edward tamped down his ire. "See you cause me no further concern. Make my cousin happy."

'

Easter 1347 – Calais, France

At the feast to celebrate Christ's resurrection, Joan sat at table between her brother and Will. Vibrant banners, and abundant light from the wall torches and table candles, lent a festive air to the otherwise dim hall. Enticing aromas drifted as servants presented platters of roasted meats, fowl, potatoes and root vegetables.

"I am so happy to share this time with you, Jack. As children, we were so rarely together." In many ways, she hardly knew her brother. How sad she shared less bond with Jack than with Edward.

"True," Jack said, "yet even now, my duties often separate us. Soon, I am to sail for London, on the king's behalf, to meet with Lionel's Guardian council."

Joan patted Jack's arm. "Then we must share what precious time we have." Her brother, like Edward, matured in the past year. He grew taller and broader, no longer the youth who sailed to Normandy eager for adventure and the glory of war. She suspected war's reality bore little resemblance to the tales men spun, for even when prompted, Jack spoke scarce words of his experience.

"This food is delicious, is it not?" Will said, drawing Joan's attention. "Everything tastes so good after the Lenten restrictions."

"I believe we will all eat more than our fill," Joan said. The savoury meats and fowl served in cream sauces were indeed a treat after nought but fish and fasting for six weeks.

Jack inhaled, his face alight with pleasure. "I am certainly glad to see an end to Lenten restrictions."

The strumming of lutes created a pleasing undertone to the building volume of heady conversation. Joan sipped her wine and gazed about.

Will leaned toward her. "When the siege ends and we return to England, it would please me, lady wife, should you consent to altering our living arrangements." He reached for Joan's hand.

Joan fought the urge to yank it away. Her stomach clenched and the hand holding her cup trembled. Carefully, she placed it on the table. While Will's request caught her off guard, it was not wholly unexpected. She smiled weakly, attempting to hide her distress.

Will's face remained inscrutable. While the minstrels played a familiar melody, he pressed her fingers. "You cannot fault me for hoping your feelings for me might have warmed? Mine remain unchanged."

At the slight waver in his voice, her heart went out to him. "You have been a constant friend to me, Will Montagu, and I shall treasure our friendship always, but I beg you to understand what you ask is impossible. My bond is to another."

Will swallowed hard, and for an instant, rage smouldered in his eyes.

The intensity startled her. Perhaps she imagined it. Were his feelings so engaged as to engender such savagery? Perhaps she underestimated his feelings for her, or was this simply wounded pride?

She fingered her cup. "I am sorry. Truly, I am."

His lips pulled back as if to smile, but his eyes frosted as bitter cold as an ice-encrusted pond. A shiver rippled through her. Though Will guarded their exchange from curious eyes, in an instant, he revealed his inner fury.

Will released her hand. "I beg your pardon." He stood, half-bowed and strode away.

Joan breathed a sigh of relief. "Do continue, Jack. You were speaking of your duties for the king."

Jack frowned. "What was that all about, pray tell?"

"Nothing." Joan plucked at her gown.

"Dissemble if you wish, sister, but whatever he said unsettled you."

"Pay it no mind." She shifted. "So, tell me of your future."

Jack shrugged and let it pass. "Our kingly cousin has entrusted me to represent him with Lionel's council. I am hopeful the king will grant me the Kent title and lands soon, though I am only seventeen and not of age for several years yet."

Joan squeezed Jack's hand. "I should be happy for you if it comes to pass."

King Edward and Queen Philippa promenaded through the hall with Edward and Isabella while servants cleared the trenchers and stowed the tables and benches to make ready for the jongleurs and entertainments. The royal party paused a few moments to converse with Joan and Jack.

Isabella's eyes gleamed as she leaned toward Joan. "There is to be dancing!" She pelted Jack with questions about the young nobles and knights in attendance while Joan half-listened and hunted the room for one particular face.

"He is not here." Edward's voice rumbled close to her ear.

She whirled around. "Oh, Edward. How good to see you, but how thin you are! Are you fully recovered from your illness?"

"As you see, I am on the mend. My father made the right decision to send me to Bergues. The nuns at St. Elizabeth provided great comfort and care." Edward angled his body away from Isabella and Jack and lowered his voice for Joan's ears alone. "It is Holland you search for, is it not?"

"Secreting anything from you is impossible."

The minstrels began to play a lively tune; Edward held out his hand. "Dance with me." They joined the other couples gathering for a round. As the dance began, Joan resumed their conversation in a tone only Edward could discern.

"I have not seen Thomas of late." She dropped Edward's hand and clasped the hands of the ladies to each side as the women circled in one direction inside the ring of men dancing in the other. When the couples reunited, Edward said, "It is for the best Holland is not here. Montagu watches."

Before she could respond, they parted again. While the two lines of men and women wove in and out, she glanced at Will. Edward twirled her, then they promenaded side by side.

"Will's eyes never leave me. It is disconcerting." She spun on Edward's arm again and asked softly, "What do you mean, Thomas is not here?" The couples parted, circled, and joined again.

"The siege drags on with little to do. The king released Thomas to return to England."

She could hardly believe her ears. The music ended, and she curtsied to Edward's bow.

"Am I to understand Thomas has sailed to England?"

Edward offered his arm and led them to a quiet corner. "Pressing affairs required his attention."

"In England? *Mon Dieu!* He has left me again without word!"

"Please, quiet yourself, *ma belle*. Holland is due to return. My father granted him leave is all. I assure you, the matters your Thomas attends at home are of great import."

Joan took several deep breaths. "Tell me, am I wasting my life? Married, yet wife to none?" She wrung her hands. "I long for a home and children. Am I asking too much?" Her throat closed with her anguish.

Edward squeezed her hand. "Have faith, Jeanette, Holland will explain upon his return."

"How can I have faith? I am in a tumult about Will. His patience is at a breaking point and I fear he may take me by force. I am at my wits end."

Edward leaned closer. "Heed me, you must be wary."

Joan's pulse raced. "What do you know?"

"Smile." He offered one himself, quite false, and aimed his gaze across the hall.

Joan smiled and followed Edward's attention. Isabella's flirtatious laughter drifted from where she conversed with Jack and Will. While Isabella nodded at a remark, Will regarded Joan as if he wanted to devour her. A thousand midges crawled up her spine.

Edward touched her arm. "Never forget. Montagu is caught as tight in this web as you. Until he comes of age, my father maintains a heavy influence, yet as the future Earl of Salisbury, he wields power. He is not likely to surrender you willingly. Do not underestimate him. Ever."

April 1347 ~ Villeneuve-le-hardi

Soon after Easter, a cold snap gripped the English encampment at Villeneuve-le-hardi, as tight as the English army's stranglehold on the Calais fortress. For six months, while King Philippe did little to relieve the siege, King Edward encouraged multitudes of English to cross the narrow sea to serve, and profit from, the burgeoning settlement.

Edward opened the Sea Bird's door and ducked inside, blasting the taproom with frigid air. Located in the heart of the ramshackle town, the inn offered a cheery warmth to many a bored soldier. As the chilled air punched into the room, the patrons' good-natured chatter suspended, all eyes fixed on the new arrivals. Chandos, the last of the five to enter, shouldered the door shut, and the crowd's mind-your-own-matters hum resumed.

The aroma of simmering fish stew dueled with that of sour ale and unwashed bodies. A plank bar lined one wall and the ginger-haired maid behind it paused in filling a tankard, eyeing Edward from top to bottom.

"Ooooh, ain't 'e a shiny penny," the redhead called to the barmaid working beside her.

Mortimer chuckled.

"Not the usual sort, neither," the second maid said. "Look at 'is cloak."

"Like ta warm m'self inside 'im," said the redhead,

"Lord Edward?" Chandos pointed to a table large enough to accommodate their party.

Edward noted its location in the back near the hearth and nodded for them to proceed.

The barmaid sent a flirtatious smile Edward's way as the group wove through the crowded trestle tables.

Chandos rested a hand on Edward's shoulder. "No doubt, those two are the secret to the pub's plentiful custom."

"Brimming with God's bounty," Mortimer quipped.

Though Edward shared their admiration, he turned a blind eye, mindful of the evening's business. The table Chandos selected was occupied by one fellow, slumped over, finding some spot on the floor of particular interest.

Montagu halted with his finely-tooled leather boots in the lone patron's line of vision. The man raised his bloodshot eyes and sprang to his feet. "Beggin' yer pardon, m'lords." He backed away, overturning a stool, and with a final, bleary-eyed glance at Montagu's scowling face, he scuttled off.

"Crook-nosed knave." Montagu drew his leg over a stool and sat.

Edward straddled an overturned barrel. Familiar with Montagu's high opinion of himself since boyhood, Will's belligerence was not hard to guess. Though three years passed since the old Earl of Salisbury's death, and despite Montagu's military service, the king withheld granting him the Salisbury title.

The emboldened redheaded barmaid ambled toward them, rolling her ample hips and wedging her abundant curves between Montagu and Mortimer. Her linen shift slipped to expose a tantalizing shoulder. A shapely form, long auburn waves, and wide-set blue eyes forged a heady appeal.

"What'l ye 'av, yer lordships?" Teasing eyes sparked above full, pouting lips.

Montagu slung an arm about her waist. "What are you offering?" He tugged, and the maid landed in his lap with a bawdy grin and seductive wriggle.

Edward tossed out several coins. "Ale all around."

After untangling herself, she waggled off with Montagu tracking her movements. She topped five tankards and returned. Plunking down the cups, she leaned forward, inviting closer inspection of her peachy orbs. Will licked his lips, grabbed his mug, and drank half in one swallow, still eyeing the maid as she sasshayed away.

Mortimer tumbled a pair of dice onto the table. "Care for a game, lord?"

Edward picked up the dice. "You do enjoy taking my silver, Roger." The game provided a guise for the night's true purpose. Edward rattled the dice. "Perhaps luck is with me tonight." If only he possessed his mother's gift.

The ale flowed freely and the crowded tavern grew more raucous as the night drew on. A crash and angry shouts sounded from near the door. A man jumped up, his face within inches of another patron. Seconds later, a ring of onlookers cheered the brawling pair.

"Od! You! Put down that stool!" The tavern keeper dashed from behind the bar, pushed through the crush, and dragged the two apart. "Not another drop fer the pair o' you. Out!" He crossed burly arms and waited. "Now!" The men shuffled out, ending the entertainment. The inn's custom settled.

Edward rolled the dice. "Ho!" He cheered his good fortune and noted his friends' piles of coins dwindling. Throughout the evening, he kept an eye on Montagu, who paid scant attention to the game or his shrinking stack.

Chandos handed Montagu the dice. "Your go."

Montagu's eyes followed the earthy maid as she worked the room. "It appears my appetite is honed for other than drink and dice this evening."

"She is a comely wench, I grant you," Mortimer said. "I wager she hungers for more lively sport than dice."

Edward did not doubt the maid noted Montagu's lustful gaze and judged her mark's ready coin by the rich fabric and cut of his clothes. As the other tables emptied and the tavern grew quieter, the bewitching maid winked at Montagu with a tilt of her head toward a curtain at the end of the bar. He did not hesitate.

Edward caught his sleeve. "A moment. Oblige me with a word."

"My lord." Will resumed his seat.

Edward twisted the ruby ring on his finger. "At the Easter celebration, you conversed with my cousin at some length."

"What of it?"

"Later, when I danced with Joan she seemed unusually disquieted."

"You need not concern yourself, Lord Edward." A facial tic betrayed Montagu's outward calm. "What passes between me and my wife, need not trouble you."

"You forget yourself."

The future earl's jaw tightened.

Edward tempered his tone. "Where would my knightly honour be should I not show concern for a lady of my royal line?"

"With respect, my…lord, this is none of your affair. Joan is my wife, not yours." A vein pulsed in Montagu's temple.

Mortimer and Chandos shifted away.

Edward pinned Montagu a steely glare and laid a sharp edge to his voice. "I offer you fair warning. Do not do anything you may come to regret. Make no mistake, *ma petite cousine* is cherished and I would not take it kindly should any harm befall her." Edward's eyes never left Montagu's as he picked up his ale, and took a long draught.

Montagu rose unsteadily, the cords in his neck bulging. With a glower at Edward, he stalked off, but halfway to the curtained doorway, he retraced his steps. His face mottled red and his nostrils flaring, he said, "Hail, the great Lord Edward, the soul of chivalry, hero of Crécy and king's lauded heir. Lest you forget, your father has other sons."

Montagu tilted his head. "Ask them," he scoffed, "for the truth of what happened at Crécy." He spun on his heel, strode to the curtain, and disappeared. None who heard Montagu's remark could mistake the snake's venom, but Edward knew not what he meant. What about Crécy? What did others know he did not?

Crécy.

Edward's vision blurred, and his limbs numbed. Montagu's toxin coursed through him. He rose, grabbed his gloves, and donned his cloak on the way to the door. Outside the tavern's entrance, he paused in the lamplight, the chill a compress to his fevered thoughts. He breathed deeply, expelling white clouds into the air. The Sea Bird's door behind him groaned open and creaked shut.

"Ignore him," Chandos said. "He knows naught of what he speaks."

Edward stared into the shadows. "Indeed? Of what does he speak, John?" Edward's chest was drawn as taught as a bowstring. "Tell me."

Chandos tugged on his gloves.

Edward untied his reins, jumped into his saddle, and, pressing spurs to his stallion's flanks, galloped down the track toward Gravelines. The wind whipped his hair across a wooden jaw. The moonlit miles flew by, yet no matter how fast his stallion raced, Edward could not outrun the demons. When his horse began to labour, Edward eased him to a trot and then a walk.

Hoofbeats approached from behind, and Chandos drew alongside.

Always beside him.

Edward smoothed a hand along his stallion's neck. "What do I not know?"

Chandos rubbed his jaw. "It is not what it may seem."

"*What* is not?" Edward halted. "*Tell* me."

"On the battlefield…when you went down and your guard surrounded you."

Edward nodded. "I have a vague memory."

"Men sped to the king to request aid."

"And?"

His friend glanced away.

"Enough! Tell me!"

Chandos let out a breath, his face pained in the moonlight. "He refused."

Edward froze, barely breathed, the air knocked from his lungs. *You forget, your father has other sons.* Montagu's venomous words echoed in his mind while the marsh's damp slithered down the back of his neck. He adjusted his cloak, shutting out the chill, but not the cold reality. His father thought to sacrifice Edward on the battlefield? To see him slaughtered? His own son?

Montagu always viewed himself as better than others, even better than a royal son. Perhaps jealously of Edward, and umbrage at Holland's rising favour, blackened Montagu's soul? So much so, he would impugn the king's honour? Edward shook himself, attempting to dislodge Montagu's odious allegation.

He kneed his horse around. "As you say, John, it could not possibly be as it seems."

May 1347 - Calais

While hurrying to the residence courtyard, Joan pulled on her leather riding gloves. Winter's grip was broken, finally, the sun shining bright in a sky more blue than grey. Bless Edward for inviting her to ride out with him after being shut inside for so long. Unfortunately, Will overheard Edward's suggestion.

"If you had made your desire known to me," he said, "I should have been pleased to arrange a ride for us." He pressed a kiss on her fingers. "It would be my honour to provide escort. With you beside me I am the envy of all men."

Joan shuddered at the memory. Deflecting Will's ardent attentions grew more challenging by the day. She crossed the threshold into the sunshine, where both men waited with the horses. Will stepped forward to assist her to mount. After adjusting her skirt, she collected her reins. "Where are we to ride, Edward?"

"I thought you might enjoy a gallop on the beach."

"Dearest cousin, I believe you can read my mind."

Joan rode between them along the rutted lanes of *Ville-neuve-le-hardi*. Since her arrival, the number of tents, sheds and cotes doubled, along with the stench. She covered her nose until they passed the worst of it.

"Tell me, Edward, are the rumors I hear true? About the French relieving the siege?"

"Yes. King Philippe is mustering troops."

"Well, he cannot continue to do naught," Will scoffed.

"According to the reports, the French nobles are press—"

"Philippe must march if he is to save face," Will said. "The Calais garrison cannot hold out much longer." With a lift of his chin, he added, "We are more than ready for a fight, are we not, Edward?"

"Indeed, our king is eager to hand Philippe another defeat."

Joan untangled her palfrey's mane. "Mayhap the garrison commander ought to surrender, ending the need for a battle."

"And after de Vienne yields, we will all return home." Will tugged Joan's cloak and leaned closer. "Then, it will be as you promised. We will visit the Salisbury estates and you may decide which you prefer. It is long past time we settled."

Joan stiffened. "Visit your family estates? What do you mean? What promise?"

"The one you made to my lady mother."

Joan knitted her brows. "I do not recall any such promise."

"We discussed it at the queen's welcome celebration."

"My word, so many months ago? I do not recall any such accord." A vague memory surfaced, an incident when Thomas Holland had sauntered back into her life and she was totally distracted.

"My mother was so pleased." Will grinned. "And I shall hold you to it, lady wife."

Edward widened his eyes at Joan.

She wanted nothing to do with visiting the Salisbury estates, nor choose one in which to suffer Will's presence. The thought of sharing a marriage bed with him made her want to retch. She must find a way to cry off, some excuse to escape.

Leaving the ramshackle camp behind, the windswept beach stretched before them. Seabirds sailed in the salt air, their squawks a sharp contrast to the day's gentle waves lapping the shore. Hoofbeats ground behind them. Edward glanced over his shoulder and halted.

Sand caught on the wind as Chandos reined in. "It has taken some time to catch up with you, my lords." He dipped his head. "Lady Joan."

Will's eyes sparked with annoyance. "For what reason do you intrude?"

Chandos lowered his eyes and spoke in a servile tone. "Your pardon, lord. I bear a message from the king. He sent me and bids you meet him at the Nieulay bridge."

Joan adjusted her skirt to shield her surreptitious glance at Chandos. Why was he acting in such a deferential manner?

Will scowled. "When?"

"Now. He asks for you to ride with me."

"I beg your pardon, my lady," Will said. "I shall be unable to accompany you after all. I do hope you consent to ride with me another time." He collected his reins, glared at Chandos, then said, "I bid you good day, lady wife." He heeled his horse and cantered away.

Joan sighed, content to see the back of him. Chandos remained for a moment, a curious glance passing between him and her cousin before Chandos raced off. She and Edward shared a smile; no words were needed.

They rode on. The breeze off the sea lifted the odours of wet sand and seaweed. Far into the horizon, beyond the cliffs, the sky and sea danced a duet of deep grey-green and blue.

With Will's departure and the wind in her face, a sense of freedom swept through Joan. The wet, hard-packed sand near the water's edge beckoned. She squeezed her legs and gave her gelding his head. "Race me, Edward!" She leaned low over her chestnut's neck, and with a nudge of her heels, he charged down the beach. Her laughter overflowed as if she were a carefree child again. The sound rippled over the surf.

Edward raced behind her. "You cheated!"

The beach south of Sangatte gave way to high cliffs rising above a lagoon, with the town of Wissant a few miles farther south. Joan's horse began to labour, so she slowed and halted near the base of the highest peak, raising her eyes to its heights. "Does it have a name?" Birds soared around the chalk face and circled a jagged point, resembling a nose.

"*Cap Blanc Nez.*"

"How fit—"

Hooves pounded the sand. A rider galloped toward them from the eastern end of the shoreline. Joan groaned. Not another messenger to call Edward away.

Her breath caught. The rider…*Blessed Virgin!*

Thomas Holland slid his winded horse to a stop; his one eye

locked on her. After a few heartbeats, he said, "You did not make it easy to catch up!"

Joan gasped. "Edward, you…you contrived this!"

Edward chuckled, a wide grin on his face. "Delivered as promised, Thomas. Jeanette is all yours."

Thomas inclined his head. "No words can convey my gratitude, lord. Once again, I am in your debt. Thank you, for *everything* you have done."

Edward's expression grew serious. "See you make Joan happy. That is all the thanks I require." With a wink and a dip of his head, Edward spun his horse and cantered off.

The tears welling in Joan's eyes blurred the retreating figure of her stalwart friend. When he disappeared, she reined around and walked on. Seabirds keened plaintive cries above the waves.

Thomas Holland. What was she to make of him?

He moved alongside with his good eye toward Joan.

She focused straight ahead. "You left without word," she said, her tone as stiff as her body. "Again." Teeth clenched, she drew in a breath. Would she ever know this man? "You have nothing to say?"

"Did not your cousin explain my reason for returning to England? Pressing affairs required my attention."

The same words Edward had used. "Thomas, do not put me off."

"Do not jump to conclusions," he bit back.

The wind gusted Joan's scarf across her face, hiding her scowl. She tamped down her anger. If she restrained her tongue, mayhap the perturbing man would enlighten her. She reined in and untangled her scarf.

Thomas halted beside her. "You know of Count d'Eu's ransom owed me?"

"Yes."

"A few weeks ago, King Edward offered to advance me one-third." Thomas held up his hand to forestall her. "Let me finish. The amount is enough to initiate action for our union to be recognized and maintain a suitable household until the balance is paid."

"What?" Joan could barely breathe.

"With the king's permission, I returned to England to secure legal counsel and file a petition with the Church as soon as King Edward authorizes the transfer of the payment."

"Oh, Thomas!" Relief and joy overwhelmed her. "Does this mean we can finally be together?"

He legged his horse beside hers, leaned over, and drew her to him. "Yes, dearest love, it is long past time."

Joan melted against him, his lips claiming hers—*his dearest love*. The Lord answered her prayers at last. She clung to Thomas, to her husband, wanting the moment to last forever.

Thomas released her, yet held tight to her hand. "I wish, most ardently, to share a long life with you, and watch our children grow."

Children.

"We will face obstacles ahead. Once the suit is filed, my sweet, there is no turning back."

"The Church will rule in our favour. It must!"

Thomas' expression clouded. "The legal proceedings are one matter, Montagu is another. You know what he is like."

"Yes, he views me as his. His possession."

"He is not wont to give you up—not without a fight." Thomas tugged her to him again and whispered, "Nor will I."

25 June 1347 - Calais

An onshore wind gusted off the sea, snapping the tent guylines and spitting sand against the king's silk pavilion. While seabirds screeched above its billowing canopy, King Edward reread the waterlogged message, tilting the soggy parchment to catch the light. The ink had bled, yet it was possible to make out the garrison commander's words.

King Edward lowered the salvaged letter. When de Vienne's desperate plea for aid, so vividly expressed, reached Philippe and became known, how could the Valois fail to take action? After a ten-month stand-off, the letter would force the French imposter to take to the field to relieve the fortress. The ensuing battle would secure England's ultimate triumph over France. King Edward had laboured long, expended immense sums, and now, a second victory was within reach. He could not suppress his pleasure, a warmth spreading within his chest and a smile across his cheeks.

Footsteps ground in the sand—his son, Warwick, and Admiral Mauny in response to his summons. "*Bon.* Join me." He forestalled their bows with a gesture at the stools positioned around the table assembled by his servants.

"Admiral, you are to be congratulated on your capture of the French galley. Should its attempt to break through the blockade been successful…well, let us say, you saved us from another ten months encamped in this wasteland. Though, it goes without saying, I expected no less from you."

Mauny dipped his head. "I am honoured by your praise, sire."

"Did I hear the captain tossed an item overboard as you were about to board?"

"Yes, but whatever it was sank before we were able to recover it," Warwick said.

King Edward inclined his head toward a water-stained leather courier pouch on the table and chuckled at their reactions. "It washed ashore." He held up the once sodden, now dried and puckered parchment. "Look what we have here. Governor de Vienne's plea to Philippe for relief. He relates the garrison has exhausted every edible morsel, save human flesh."

His heir grimaced. "*Jesu!*"

Warwick shuddered. "A rather revolting circumstance to contemplate."

"*Mes amis*, let us not surrender all hope for de Vienne and his men." The king placed the letter on the table. "Philippe may yet march to save them after such an eloquent entreaty from his countryman."

Mauny raised his eyes. "But with the governor's plea intercepted, it will never reach Philippe."

King Edward tapped a finger to his lips. "True, the letter has come into my hands, but what say you to aiding the loyal governor by sending his missive on its way? Affixed with my seal, of course."

The Earl and admiral took his meaning, expressing a guffaw or two. His son bore a look of consternation. Following a brief discussion, his three visitors rose to leave. The king laid a hand on his son's arm. "Remain a moment."

Edward sat down again and the king waited while Mauny and the Earl slogged through the deep sand until they were a distance away. "*Mon fils,*" the king paused until his son met his eyes. "If my reaction to de Vienne's plight appears callous, do not be fooled. *En vérité,* I recoil from this grisly affair." The king searched his son's face for any sign of charity in spirit. "Sadly, brutality is ofttimes forced upon those who rule, and a king must possess some vein of ruthlessness, or he will not remain king for long."

27 July 1347 - Sangatte

King Edward touched heels to his horse's flanks and cantered away from the residence courtyard. With his guard before him, and his heir beside him, they clattered through the twisted lanes of *Villeneuve le Hardi*. Once in the open, they galloped across the lowlands to the palisade at the approach to town, pausing to inspect the earthwork and the array of archers and men-at-arms posted there.

They continued beyond the guard station, to where the land rose to a high ridge. The king reined in. Atop the heights, French soldiers appeared in silhouette against the lowering sun. "A wondrous sight, is it not? Philippe has rallied his army to meet our challenge and relieve the siege."

"You forced his hand. Philippe must have raged when he learned the supply barges he sent to aid de Vienne were captured."

"The report of that event likely included details of our defences here and knowledge of the forces in Flanders readying to march on my orders."

Edward nodded. "Philippe might be aware of the reinforcements, but his army is here now; he cannot fail to attack."

The king arched his brows. "You believe so?" He shook his head. "While I want nothing more, I fear the Valois will not dare a battle. His reign will not survive another defeat."

"Despite all we have done to bring him to the field?"

"Even so."

The sun dipped behind the lime and sandstone cliff as he and Edward rode back to town. Dusk settled over the soldiers gathering around bonfires, as energized as a hive of bees now that word spread of an imminent battle. Drink flowed, along with raucous banter and laughter.

Upon reaching the residence, King Edward dismounted, and a groom took his reins. As Edward leapt down, the royal chamberlain hastened toward them.

"Lord King." The man bowed. "Two cardinals await you inside."

King Edward's temple throbbed. "It appears, Edward, the Pope's red birds of peace have come to roost."

July 1347 - Calais

Candlelight flickered on the panelled walls of the king's chamber where Edward joined Reginald Cobham, Bishop Burghersh, Admiral Mauny and the earls of Lancaster and Northampton, to hear of their audience with the pontiff's peace delegation. The king paced, his shadow dogging his harried steps. He paused occasionally to aim a dark look at whoever was speaking. Edward 's insides churned, yet his vexation was likely nothing to that of his father.

Bishop Burghersh steeped his fingers. "For four days, we listened to the Pope's two red robes and Philippe's noble lapdogs prattle. Four days! I say, lord, we bade them as polite a farewell as we could muster, but if our courtesy lagged, we beg your indulgence."

"Indeed, sire." Northampton put down his cup. "We commend your largesse in receiving the envoy at all. It is not as if they offer anything of substance."

Edward shared the Earl's opinion. Courtesy might demand the king listen to their pleas but, in Edward's experience, the Pope's delegates never put forth anything of merit. A knock sounded, and his father's steward hastened to respond. A few mumbled words, too low for Edward to hear, were exchanged, then the steward closed the door and returned holding a parchment.

Edward rose and claimed the scroll tied with French royal ribbons of azure and gold. "From the Valois himself."

His father's eyes hardened. "Read it." His jaw set in a hard line.

Edward broke the seal, unrolled the parchment, and skimmed it. "Oh, ho! This is unbelievable. Philippe challenges you to combat."

The men laughed.

"Does he?" King Edward stood, his feet braced apart.

Philippe specifies four knights to represent each side on an open field, any time of your choosing, between this day and Friday."

Every eye in the room fixed on King Edward. He beamed and stretched his arms wide. "My dearest wish. What say you gentlemen? Thursday? What weapons and rules shall we decree?" The king turned to his steward. "Send for my scribe. The sooner my acceptance and safe conducts are conveyed, the better."

3 August 1347 - Calais

Thursday dawned grey with a dark band of clouds hugging the coast. England's standard fluttered above the king astride his white destrier, overlooking the French encampment.

Deserted!

The king clenched his jaw so tight, it ached. The French camp lay smouldering. "God rot that snake, Philippe!"

From beside him, Edward said, "I cannot believe it. Just as you predicted, the imposter king and his army have slithered away."

The king's belly burned hotter than the still-glowing embers from French fires criss-crossing the field.

"Sire, you have won."

The king twisted in his saddle and glared at Calais's ancient stone ramparts.

"Father?" his son's voice rose in pitch.

"Governor de Vienne defied me for eleven months but he held out in vain." King Edward shook with rage. "In the end, Philippe proved himself the coward he is. He abandoned de Vienne and what is left of his garrison." He paused to take a breath to calm himself. "Though we defeated Philippe at Crécy, it was not enough. To end France's attacks on our lands once and for all, I needed to hand Philippe a second crushing blow. "Now," he waved a hand at the charred field, "he has denied me the battle."

"*Us*, Father, *us*. Protecting England is no less my duty, than yours."

"Mark me, Edward, someone will bear the consequences for the cost to my realm this siege has wrought. You may lay wager my terms of surrender to de Vienne will be less than generous." He wheeled his horse. "I am in no humour to offer terms at all!"

Later, while the king dictated responses to affairs in London, Admiral Mauny appeared at his chamber requesting an audience. The king nodded permission to his steward. Mauny entered, swept off his hat and knelt.

"Blessings upon you, lord."

The king waved Mauny to a seat.

"So, Admiral," he said, gesturing a servant for wine, you have returned from a visit with our friend in the citadel. Tell me, how fares de Vienne?" The king spoke not without smugness, then picked up his cup and sipped. With a flick of his eyes, he signalled his steward to leave.

Mauny drank the wine poured for him in one go. "The governor and the few knights and townsmen with him are naught but skeletons, my lord."

"They deserve no less."

Mauny flinched. "Yes, well, with all due respect, sire, de Vienne impressed me. He bade me speak for him. He says, those who loyally served their liege lord, as you would have your men do, have suffered much. He pleads for mercy."

"Mercy? In return for his defiance?" An exasperated grunt escaped the king. "They must submit without conditions."

"Lord, I mean no disrespect, yet implore you to consider." Mauny rubbed his jaw while he appeared to gather his thoughts. "Your own vassals, who loyally obey you, may find themselves in a similar situation. Should you condemn these French to death, you set an example of how such loyalty may be treated. The men of your affinity may hesitate in future, not quite as willing to remain steadfast."

How dare Mauny imply any blame in this matter to him? He stood, forcing Mauny to spring to his feet. With a hardened gaze and steely tone, the king said, "You, Admiral, will inform the governor he is to surrender the fortress and those within it on the morrow. He will kneel to me, before all, and present the keys to the town and stronghold." The king paced a few steps, weighing his desire for retribution against Mauny's entreaty.

"Natheless, I am not so unyielding as to disregard your arguments in the garrison's favour. You may tell de Vienne I shall extend him this much grace…he and five of the town's principal citizens are to march out from the gates barefooted and bareheaded with ropes around their necks. These men will kneel before me, at my pleasure to do as I see fit. As for the rest, I grant them pardons."

Mauny dipped his head, murmuring, "As you wish, sire." The door chinked shut behind him.

King Edward sipped, seeming to chew his wine. God rot the Valois dog. Philippe would pay a price for denying him. What if the English, under Edward's command, were let loose to further ravage Philippe's lands? The Valois could do little to stop them and the plunder would do much to replenish English coffers. Imagining the scenes lessoned the sting of being cheated another victory.

4 August 1347 - Calais

Bells tolled across the barren reaches below the citadel's ramparts where the king and queen sat side by side upon the hastily constructed dais. Edward stood behind them. A golden, gem-studded crown rested upon his father's head.

Rank upon rank of soldiers and inhabitants of the king's Brave New Town, thousands, assembled to bear witness to the French garrison's surrender. The army's Constable, Marshal, and commanders formed a row at the front of the crowd.

The bells stopped, the crowd hushed, and the stronghold's gates swung wide. Drums tapped while a single file of six skeletal men, shuffled forth, shoulders slumped and heads bowed. Nooses dangled from their necks.

Gasps and low mutterings rumbled through the crowd.

The Frenchmen, little more than corpses, stumbled forward. Edward cringed inside, though he did not look away.

A grey-haired man, in the lead, teetered and pitched to his knees. Most likely Governor de Vienne.

"Fetch a horse!" Admiral Mauny called.

With Mauny's help, the man climbed to his feet, and shook his head 'no'. He raised his eyes, and stared fixedly at the king. Without breaking his gaze, de Vienne straightened his back, lifted his chin ever so slightly, and trudged forward.

Edward admired de Vienne. Though the Frenchman lost all else, his courage remained undiminished. Did the king, in his wrath, intend to end the life of one possessed of such valour? Did sacrificing a life mean so little to his father? Montagu's allegation invaded Edward's thoughts. Had his father been willing to sacrifice Edward at Crécy?

"Bring forth the block." The king's order rang out.

Queen Philippa gasped.

Edward gazed down at his mother. White-faced, she placed a forestalling hand on the king's arm. "*Non*, my lord. You must not."

His father stiffened, cold to her plea.

The executioner stepped forward, his axe catching the sun. One by one, the six men fell to their knees and bowed their heads. A low grumbling coursed through the crowd

"Mercy, lord," de Vienne pleaded, not a yard from the king's feet. The other five men collapsed, sprawling prone, arms outstretched in supplication.

Mauny stepped forward. "Lord King, it is entirely within your authority to do as you wish with these men, yet I implore you to spare them. They have done naught save what their liege asked of them."

“Enough, Admiral!” The king cut him off.

“Sire,” Edward entreated, though he dared not openly defy his king. “Father….”

“No more! Sufficient words have been spoken.” The king waved two guards forward.

“Not him, not the governor.” The king motioned to the second man.

Did his father intend to force de Vienne to witness the deaths of his loyal men? What of honour? Of mercy? The guards hauled the second captive to his feet. Edward’s stomach rolled.

Suddenly, the queen rose. All sounds from the crowd ceased.

Slowly, she faced the king and kneeled at his feet, her pale rose-colored gown pooling around her. She reached her beringed hands for the king’s and clasped them tightly.

“Lord King, my devotion as your loyal consort remains constant, yet knowing you as I do, this retribution, this malice, is not befitting of the king I esteem, for he, most dear to me, is virtuous, honourable and fine.” The queen pleaded with her words and her eyes while the gulls overhead cried.

Edward’s throat tightened. Few men in de Vienne’s position would have remained as steadfast to their lord.

“Beloved husband, I implore you to relent. Bestow upon these men the mercy and grace which signify your person. I beseech you, my lord, spare them.” A single tear slipped down his mother’s cheek. Edward held his breath. A man of such bravery warranted mercy.

The king rose, his movements slow and deliberate. Amidst the restless murmurs of the crowd, he clasped his wife’s trembling hands. He paused, holding the queen’s gaze, seeming to consider her ardent appeal and weigh his decision. He pivoted, his eyes resting on the hostages. “Rise all. Admiral, lend assistance to de Vienne.”

Turning back to his queen, the king spoke in a loud voice so it would carry. “As you, my loyal consort have stood beside me these many years and asked so little, I grant you this boon.”

The queen's eyes glistened. "Thank you, lord."

The king had relented, and though the decision robbed him of revenge, Edward believed his *father* would not regret his choice.

The king smiled at his wife and murmured, *"Merci, mon coeur."*

Edward breathed in relief. Sparing these men's lives conveyed a powerful image of England's lion king. Poets would write of his mother's compassion, of his father's charity, the tale told and re-told, their repute burgeoning over the weeks, months, and years to come, like the golden hue of a new dawn spreading over the land. What would they write of Edward? How did he wish to be remembered? It was time he secure his future.

September 1347 – Calais

With the siege ended, vessels of all sorts plied the port of Calais, some arriving and offloading people and goods, some preparing to sail on the next tide. The sailors and workmen shouted ship to dock, dock to ship, and ship to ship, while heavily load-ed carts rumbled along the wooden planks and seabirds wheeled above.

Edward escorted Joan up the ramp to the king's flagship rocking gently in the quay. She hopped from the ramp to the weatherworn deck, turned and waved to the man looking up from the jetty. Joan sniffled back the tears welling in her eyes, as crystalline blue as the morning sky.

"Bon voyage," Holland called, backing up slowly, then turning away, his thoughts most likely already shifting from Joan to his all-important, career-advancing assignment.

"À bientôt!" she called. "Oh, Edward," she sighed his name. "I cannot believe the war is finally ended and we are returning home."

"Yes, I look forward to setting my feet firmly on English soil again." He shared his cousin's joy at thoughts of home, yet he did not share her sentiment about the war being resolved. King Philippe was cowed for now, but wily as the Valois was, he was likely to come at England again. Only time would tell.

Joan tracked Holland's retreating figure. "Did I tell you how pleased Thomas was, and surprised, to be so honoured by your father's appointment? Such a noteworthy sign of the king's confidence in him." She dabbed the last of her tears. "Though I do so wish I could remain here with him."

"Believe me Jeanette, until the final peace terms are agreed, every minute of Holland's time will be spent securing my father's demands."

"No doubt you are right and though I might wish to remain, it is out of the question given my marital status as Will's wife."

"This is an important opportunity for Thomas. May he make the most of it." He squeezed Joan's hand. For her sake, he wished Holland success.

"I have waited so long to be with him," Joan said, "I shall manage a few months more."

Edward hoped the Church would rule quickly in Holland's favour for Joan deserved a happier future than those of years past.

After the last passengers boarded, two of the crew scrambled to remove the boarding ramp. Others hauled on the anchor chain, its rattle prompting the captain's, "Cast off!" Several of the crew unfurled the sails and as the canvas filled, the ship slipped from the harbor toward open water.

Thinking of Joan's future, triggered thoughts of his own. Recently, more often than not, the king engaged him in crown matters and, over the last months they had grown closer, though Montagu's vitriol about Crécy occasionally crept into Edward's mind.

The wind freshened, sending the royal colours atop the ship's mainmast thrashing, adding its rhythmic rapping to the crash of the hull into the sea, and the seabirds' squawks. Edward threaded Joan's arm through his. "Come, let us join my parents."

At their approach, the king scowled. "I see you left it to the last moments to board."

Joan curtsied. "Your pardon, Lord King…my lady."

Queen Philippa threw a sharp glance at the king and held out a hand to Joan. "Come, stand beside me. What my lord husband means is he hoped you would join us sooner. For some reason, his manner today might be likened to a Tower lion a keeper forgot to feed." She patted Joan's arm. "Now you are here and we are cast off, I am certain the king's mood is bound to lighten."

"Only if the weather holds fair for the crossing," the king muttered. "Pay me no mind, Jeanette."

At his father's apology, Edward raised his brows at this mother, a tribute to her skill in managing the king's moods. Despite his parent's arranged marriage, contracted for the purpose of raising an army, somehow his mother and father managed to forge a deep and abiding bond. Such political unions offered little chance of more than mutual tolerance and begetting children. He prayed he might share a future, similar to that of his parents, with his consort, whoever she might be.

"Now, husband, might you tell us what ruffles you so on a day as fine as this?"

"Must I explain myself? *D'accord.* I am aggrieved at leaving with business unfinished, breaking my commitment to Parliament. I promised to finish this conflict with Philippe once and for all, and to do so I needed him to suffer a second defeat at my hands."

"Yet, remaining here would serve no purpose." Edward adjusted his stance with the lift and roll of the ship with the sea's gently undulating swells.

The king stroked his beard. "Philippe's rule is crippled and he is no fool; another defeat would likely end him. The Valois is nothing if not shrewd enough not to chance it."

For more than two years, he and his father had laboured to end Philippe's aggression. Would the peace last? Edward hoped— prayed— it would.

Joan sighed. "England is safe thanks to your efforts, lord king."

"Philippe, the caitiff, knew better than to meet me on the field again, not after his disasterous command at Crécy."

"Husband, need I remind you our son played no small part in your victory?"

Leave it to his mother to acknowledge Edward's feat of arms. It seemed his father never would. Edward came too close to losing his life, no thanks to his father. Montagu's allegation niggled; Edward snuffed it before it took root, reminding himself it was nothing more than evidence of Montagu's green-eyed malice.

His mother entwined her fingers with the king's. "I dare say Philippe's support of the Scots is ended, too?"

The king's eyes twinkled. "Wait until Philippe learns my treaty terms—nothing less than total recompense for our efforts. He is likely to spew blood!"

"No doubt your mediators are well versed with your demands," Joan said.

"Indeed." The king cast a sideways glance at Joan. "I thought to appoint Thomas Holland as one of them. Though Holland may be from humbled circumstance, he displays initiative and is eager to prove his mettle."

Joan's reaction, a slow blink, was imperceptible to anyone who did not know her as well as Edward did. The king's comment surprised him for Edward never knew his father to mention Holland in Joan's presence, never given any hint he was aware of her clandestine marriage, though, of course, he was.

"To be certain, Holland will not shrink from pressing your case," Edward said. "With Derby and Northampton adding their persuasion, the French will capitulate in no time."

A salt-laden breeze whipped across the bow as the ship rose from a trough. In the distance, Dover's white cliffs beckoned. The king brushed his hair from his face. "Let us look forward," he said, "to the future."

Joan repositioned her hand on the rail. "Sage advice, my lord."

"So, what of our Edward's future?" Queen Philippa asked. "He has proven himself an able commander, and is of an age to sire an heir. Is it not time to secure a union?"

The king brushed a kiss upon Philippa's fingers. "Indeed, *mon coeur*, we must inspire our reluctant pontiff to grant the required dispensation. Edward must began to prepare for his future, for when he rules, and for those who will reign after him."

Begin to prepare? Begin? A red hot heat flared in Edward. He dared not look at his father. How could he suggest Edward begin preparing for the future? When had he not been preparing? The future dominated his entire life. Duty drilled into him from the time he could walk!

Thank goodness Joan and his mother talked of seeing family and friends again, for their chatter provided cover for Edward's silence. He thought of the boy, so in awe of his father and determined to exceed the king's every expectation. While the luck of Edward's birth marked him as heir, proving he was worthy to rule drove him.

Throughout his youth, he honed his skills, mastering sword and lance, and recently tutored by the earls of Warwick and Northampton, he molded himself into a respected commander in his own right. Over the course of the campaign, he did his duty, proven his ability to instill loyalty, to command, and yes, to eventually rule. He put his life on the line at Caen and Crécy. What more could be asked of him?

Edward breathed in to calm himself and rested his arms on the rail. Happily would he turn his attention to fulfilling his other duty—one more pleasant to contemplate—of securing a wife and siring a son. The birth of a son would secure *his* line—the unbroken reign of Plantagenet kings.

Author's Note

My exploration into Edward of Woodstock's life came as a result of my interest in the Wars of the Roses, sometimes known as the Cousin's War, the bloody English civil war between the noble Houses of Lancaster and York. (For *Game of Thrones* fans, read Lannisters and Starks.)

For over thirty years, from 1455-1487, the cousins killed each other on, and off, the battlefields. I wanted to know why. Finding answers propelled me back three+ generations to the reign King Edward III (1327-1387) and his prolific marriage with Philippa of Hainault. Their marriage was arranged by Edward's mother, trading Edward's marriage to the Count of Hainault's daughter for an army to depose Edward's father. (*Really, you can't make this stuff up.*)

Despite the union's inauspicious start, let's just say the teenagers hit it off. The proof? Thirteen children. Of those who lived to adulthood, five were sons: Edward, Lionel, John, Edmund, and Thomas, with a twenty-five year gap between the eldest and the youngest!

King Edward III died in 1377 and his grandson, Richard of Bordeaux, succeeded him as King Richard II. So, if Edward of Woodstock was the king's eldest son, why didn't he succeed his father? Simply because he died in 1376, a year before King Edward III.

If Edward had lived and succeeded to the throne, would the Wars of the Roses, the deaths of all those cousins, have happened? To answer that, I needed to know more about Edward.

As I began my research into his life, I discovered he is known in history as the Black Prince. Why? The more I delved into his life, the more questions arose. How did he become known as the Black Prince? Why was he given that moniker more than two hundred years after he died?

Although Edward was considered the 'catch' of his time, he didn't marry until he was thirty-one—unheard of for a prince of the realm. Why? When he did marry, whom did he marry? And why her? A widow almost two years older with four children under the age of ten. A woman with a scandalous past. Married bigamously for over five years! *(Really, you can't make this stuff up.)*

The questions kept coming and my curiosity grew, but not about the cardboard character—the greatest warrior prince of the Middle Ages as Edward was portrayed in history books—but rather about the man beneath the legend. What was Edward truly like? What made him tick?

This novel, and the ones that follow, portray Edward, the heart and soul of the man, as I understand him.

Writing a historical fiction novel requires a combination of imagination and extensive research. My journey began with a timeline of documented historical events. However, many accounts often disagreed for two main reasons: the accounts were based on hearsay and/or the accounts were written years, decades, and sometimes centuries after the events occurred. With that in mind, I tried to be as accurate as possible in creating a plausible story from, at best, some sketchy sources.

Two particular issues impacted the development of my story in a significant manner. Both relate to Joan of Kent and her marriages to Thomas Holland and William Montagu. First, it is an unknown fact whether Joan told anyone about her clandestine marriage to Thomas Holland. The second issue concerns Joan's life in the years between her marriage to Montagu and Holland's petition to the Pope to recognize his marriage to Joan. According to Joan's biographer, Penny Lawne, the historical rolls during that time period contain no mention of Joan, so it is difficult to know where she was or with whom she lived.

Despite this gap in Joan's history, some biographers state that Joan lived with Montagu, and some suggest that she and Holland concocted the story of their secret marriage during the time Holland supposedly served as Montagu's steward. These biographers reference *The Clandestine Marriages of the Fair Maid of Kent*, by Karl Wentersdorf as their source, and Wentersdorf cites the

Hardyng Chronicle as his source. Hardyng's rhyming tome covered events from the earliest period of English history through the reign of King Edward IV, and Hardyng completed it in 1457.

Hardyng's mention of Joan and Holland seems dubious to me. It consists of approximately four, difficult-to-decipher lines contained within two rhyming stanzas of Middle English, written more than one hundred years after the events occurred. For modern biographers—professional historians—to base their presumptions about Joan and Holland on the *Hardyng Chronicle* is, in my opinion, absurd.

Not only is there no record of Joan ever living with Montagu, there is no record of Holland ever serving as Montagu's steward, not according to Michael Stansfield's Corpus Christi College PhD dissertation, *The Holland Family, Dukes of Kent and Exeter, Earls of Huntingdon 1352-1475.*

For purposes of my novel, I allowed that Joan confessed her secret marriage to her mother, Lady Margaret, and confided her secret to her cousin, Edward. In addition, I opted for Joan to reside in Queen Philippa's household, as one of her ladies, from the time of her marriages until Holland's petition to the Pope was resolved. One might imagine the scandal that erupted when Holland's suit and Joan's bigamy became public. (See Appendix for excerpt from *Aged in Valour.*)

The public backlash may have surpassed the outrage over King Edward VIII's abdication and marriage to Wallace Simpson in 1936 or the affront caused by Harry and Meghan's controversial exodus from the royal family in 2020.

Inspiration for characters and plot lines may be derived from many sources. In the case of *Valiant Son,* several relatively minor references contained in historical biographies propelled my story in directions I never originally imagined. One such, if I remember correctly, was a minute reference in Ian Mortimer's biography of King Edward III, *The Perfect King.* Although the Earl of

Salisbury, William Montagu (the elder), was Edward III's close friend and staunch supporter, it is said the king never took a liking to Montagu's son, Will. That led me to imagine Will with a character flaw—one of entitlement, thus creating a nemesis for Edward.

Another item, whether true or not, concerns a statement attributed to King Edward at the Battle of Crécy. When requested to send aid to his son, overwhelmed by the French, it is claimed King Edward replied, "Let him earn his spurs." Does that not give the impression King Edward was willing to sacrifice his son? Might that statement be construed as a betrayal?

One event during the chevauchee through France in 1346 remains a mystery. King Edward halted his army's march to meet with the Pope's peace delegation. That meeting lasted a day and a half and significantly hampered the English army's advance—jeopardizing the entire campaign. What might have prompted the shrewd King Edward to take such a risk? I believe the reason I invented is not only plausible but adds dramatic impact to my story, and might have been the reason for the king's decision.

A few other items deserving mention:

1) So many people during the Middle Ages seemed to have the same names. For example, there are nine Johns, three Joans, four Elizabeths, and three Isabellas in my novel(s). Finding ways of differentiating them was challenging.

2) During the Middle Ages, contractions commonly used today did not exist then. Therefore, I chose not to use contractions in my writing.

3) Forms of address, like Your Majesty and the like, were not in use. The nobility were simply addressed as Lord, Lord King, Sir, or Sire. Even Edward was not addressed as Prince Edward.

4) When William of Normandy invaded England in 1066, he brought with him the Norman/French language. England's nobility thus spoke Norman French rather than English during the years in which Valiant Son is set, hence the French words and phrases sprinkled throughout the dialogue.

It Takes a Village

In the early stages of my novel writing, I didn't know what I didn't know. Numerous organizations and individuals helped me learn the craft, and I'd like to formally thank them, for without their help, I doubt *Valiant Son* would have come to fruition.

Many thanks to Alicia Rasley, author of *The Power of Point of View*, who provided coaching and sorted out me and my story when I had lost my way. In addition, her dialogue class was the best $50 I ever spent.

When I delved deeper into the life of Joan of Kent, Penny Lawne's biography of Joan became an instrumental tool. Discussions with Ms. Lawne, and a collaboration with her on an article published in the Richard III Society's *Bulletin*, provided much-needed and appreciated insight.

Next, I want to thank the online writing support community, *Scribofile.com*, particularly members James McLeod, Max Drayton, and David Nielson, whose candid feedback was essential and inspirational for my writing.

I owe a debt of gratitude to several generous and talented friends:

• Mary Borrelli shares my passion for Plantagenet history and was a tried and true voice of reason for my story.

• Maureen O'Neill Batik, an avid reader of medieval historical fiction, provided invaluable feedback.

• Kris Spinning, whose creativity and artistic talent made publishing *Valiant Son* possible.

• Last but not least, I am forever indebted to my muse, Ami Beatty Johnson Janes, who held my hand and acted as my ever-evolving ideas sounding board from beginning to end. Ami passed tragically, and not a day goes by that I don't think of her.

May she rest in peace.

If you enjoyed *Valiant Son*, I hope you recommend it to friends. Please post a review on amazon.com and consider submitting a request to your local library to purchase a copy. Follow me at substack.com/@plantagenetjunkie

Bibliography

Ayton, Andrew, *Knights and Warhorses*, Woodbridge, The Boydell Press, 1994

Barber, Richard, *Edward, Prince of Wales and Aquitaine*, New York, Charles Scribner's Sons, 1978.

Barber, Richard, *Life and Campaign of the Black Prince*, UK, The Boydell Press, 1979.

Barber, Richard, *The Knight and Chivalry*, UK, The Boydell Press, 2000.

Barker, Juliet, *The Tournament in England*: 1100-1400, Woodbridge, The Boydell Press,
1986.

Belloc, Hilaire, *Warfare in England*, LA, Cavalier Books, 2018.

Burne, Lt-Col Alfred H., *The Crécy War*, Hertfordshire, Wordsworth Editions Ltd., 1999.

Costain, Thomas B., *The Three Edwards*, New York, Doubleday & Company, Ltd., 1958.

Cushway, Graham, *Edward III and the War at Sea*, Woodbridge, The Boydell Press, 2011.

Emerson, Barbara, *The Black Prince*, London, Weidenfeld and Nicolson, 1976.

Fallows, Noel, *Jousting in Medieval and Renaissance Iberia*, The Boydell Press, 2010.

Given-Wilson, Chris, & Curteis, Alice, *The Royal Bastards of Medieval England*, London & Boston, Routledge & Kegan Paul, 1984.

Goodman, Anthony, *The Fair Maid of Kent*, UK, The Boydell Press., 2017.

Green, David, *Edward the Black Prince: Power in Medieval Europe*, London & New York, Routledge, 2023.

Hardyng Chronicle, ch clxxxv, 1543

Hoskins, Peter, & Barber, Richard, *Crécy 1346, A Tourists' Guide, Great Britain*, Pen & Sword, 2016.

Hoskins, Peter, *In the Footsteps of the Black Prince*, Woodbridge, The Boydell Press, 2012.

Jones, Dan, *The Plantagenets*, New York, Penguin Books, 2012

Jones, Michael, *The Black Prince*, London, Head of Zeus, 2018.

Lawne, Penny, *Joan of Kent: The First Princess of Wales*, Gloucester, Amberley Publishing, 2015

Livingstone, Marilyn, & Witzel, Morgen, *The Road to Crécy*, Routledge, London & Boston, 2004.

Mortimer, Ian, *The Perfect King*, London, Vintage/Random House, 2006

Mortimer, Ian, *The Time Traveler's Guide to Medieval England*, New York, Touchstone/Simon & Schuster, Inc, 2008

Oggins, Robin, *Castles and Fortresses*, New York, Metro Books/ Henry Holt, 2000.

Omrod, Mark, *Edward III*, New Haven, Yale University Press, 2013

Orme, Nicholas, *From Childhood to Chivalry*, London & Boston, Routledge, 2017

Phillips, Kim M., *Medieval Maidens*, Manchester, Manchester University Press, 2003.

Reid, Peter, *Medieval Warfare*, Philadelphia & London, Running Press, 2007-2008.

Rogers, Clifford J., *War Cruel and Sharp*, Woodbridge, The Boydell Press, 2000.

Sedgwick, Henry Dwight, *The Life of Edward The Black Prince*, Indianapolis, IN, The Bobs-Merrill Co., 1932.

Seward, Desmond, *The 100 Years War:The English in France 1337-1453*, London & New York, Penguin Books, 1999.

Stansfield, Michael, *The Holland Family, Dukes of Kent and Exeter, Earls of Huntingdon, 1352-1475*, Corpus Christi College, 1987.

Sumption, Jonathan, *Trial by Battle*, UK, Faber & Faber,1999

Sumption, Jonathan, *Trial by Fire*, UK, Faber & Faber, 2001.

Underhill, Frances A., *For Her Good Estate: The Life of Elizabeth de Burgh*, Basingstoke, UK, Palgrave McMillian, 2000.

Warner, Kathryn, *Philippa of Hainault*, Gloucester, Amberley Publishing, 2019

Weir, Alison, *Britain's Royal Families*, New York, Vintage UK, 2008

Wentersdorf, Karl P., *The Clandestine Marriages of the Fair Maid of Kent*, Journal of Medieval History, 5:3, 203-231, North Holland Publishing Company, 2012.

E.
E
P
ICH DIEN
P.

Image Attributions

Duchy of Aquitaine
Used under Creative Commons License - Image Title: Map of
France in 1154. Creator: Reigen - Own work Sources: Image:-
France 1154 Eng.jpg by Lotroo under copyleft france_1154_1184.
jpg from the Historical Atlas by William R. Shepherd, 1911.
Description: English map of the growth of the Plantagenet Empire,
from 1144 to 1166. No changes made.
Full link: https://en.wikipedia.org/wiki/Duke_of_Aquitaine#/media/
File:France_1154-en.svg

Low Countries
Permission for use courtesy of David Cenzer, creator.

1346 English Army Invasion Route
This image is licensed under the Creative Commons Attribution -
Share Alike 4.0 International license. Creator: Goran tek-en File:-
Map of the route of Edward III's chevauchée of 1346.svg Created:
6 March 2019, Uploaded: 3 February 2022. No changes made.
Full link: https://en.wikipedia.org/wiki/Battle_of_Crécy#/media/
File:Map_of_the_route_of_Edward_III's_chevauchée_of_1346.svg

Somme Estuary at Blanchetaque
Project Gutenberg License: The Project Gutenberg eBook of Crécy,
by Hilaire Belloc

Terrain of the Crécy Battlefield
Project Gutenberg License: The Project Gutenberg eBook of Crécy,
by Hilaire Belloc

Battlefield at Crécy
Used under Creative Commons Licence - Public Domain
Wikipedia: File: Battle of Crécy, 26 August 1346.png, Uploaded: 10
November 2007. No changes made.. Full link: https://en.wikipedia.
org/wiki/Battle_of_Crécy#/media/File:Battle_of_Crécy,_26_Au-
gust_1346.png

Badge of Prince Edward
Used under Creative Commons Licence - Public Domain
Wikipedia: Original publication: John Leland, Genethliacon
(London, 1543) Full link: https://commons.wikimedia.org/wiki/
File:Badge_of_Prince_Edward_1543.jpg

AGED IN VALOUR

R. Jay Brenner

CHAPTER ONE

December 1347 - Donyatt Manor, Somerset, England

By the time the last guests bid their farewells, Joan breathed a sigh of relief; her head ached after hours of obligatory gaiety required by the charade of her marriage. Will obviously enjoyed playing lord of the manor as his speech was slurred by the end of the evening. Throughout the festivities, Will's mother watched Joan's every move, her scrutiny somewhat of a puzzle.

The family gathered near the hearth while servants doused the wall sconces. Serving maids cleared the remnants of the feast from the tables where a few tapers still guttered in the candle trees.

Joan's mother linked an arm companionably with Will's mother. "A delightful gathering, Lady Catherine. My compliments on your arrangements. Not a detail was left to chance, nor a servant's foot set wrong." She gestured around the hall and inclined her head toward Joan. "A very warm welcome accorded to my daughter."

Joan glanced sidelong at her mother. When had she and Will's mother become so chummy? "Indeed, Lady Catherine, the meal and entertainments were delightful."

Lady Catherine raised her chin and nodded. "Yes, everyone seemed well pleased, especially by Will's presence."

"His custom means a great deal to the townsfolk for their livelihoods depend upon the estate and the future earl's goodwill," Will's grandmother said.

"We expect King Edward to grant Will the Salisbury title before he reaches his majority," Lady Catherine said, "in recognition of Will's military service in France."

Will struck an unsteady pose before the hearth. "Many of our guests expressed a desire, and hope, that my lady wife and I might take up residence here." He looked pointedly at Joan.

She offered a weak smile. Despite her persistent spurns, Will continued to delude himself, believing that flaunting his noble rank would entice her to accept their union. If anything, his entitled behaviour disgusted her no less now than when they were children. Though he may want her, she wanted no part of him.

Lady Catherine continued, "Though my late husband and I resided at many of the estates bestowed upon him by King Edward, Will was born and raised here for the most part. Indeed, Donyatt makes a splendid family home." Lady Catherine aimed a glance full of meaning at Joan.

Will's grandmother rose. "These old bones are crying for rest. I bid you all a good night."

"If you will excuse me, I believe it is time for me to retire as well," Lady Catherine said.

"And I, my lord," Joan's mother said. "I shall accompany your lady mother upstairs.

Good night, lord… and you, daughter." The ladies departed, their footsteps soon fading completely.

Joan turned to follow. "I bid you good—"

Will caught her hand. "Stay." A malodor of spiced wine wafted from him.

Joan hesitated. Although Will had never mistreated her, given the quantity of wine he had imbibed, should his anger be aroused, he might attempt to force himself upon her. It might be best to humor him.

"Perhaps…" She perched upon a nearby bench.

The few candles still burning cast flickering light onto the paneled walls. The Yule block smoldered in the fireplace, its red embers emitting an occasional spark into the silence. Joan stretched her neck as she kept wary company with the man who was once a childhood playmate, a part of her cousin Edward's royal household.

Will sat on a stool, his head resting against the wall, his eyes closed and his breathing rhythmic.

The mingled scents of woodsmoke, pine, and beeswax kindled nostalgic memories of holidays Joan spent as part of the royal family. She wished she were with them now. In her cousin Edward's recent letter, he related the king was to host a tournament at Bury St. Edmunds in January. Would Thomas return from Calais to compete? She longed to see him and prayed the Church would rule quickly on his petition to recognize their marriage.

As long minutes passed, the heat from the log dwindled and fingers of cold air crept into the silent room. Joan shivered. Her satin gown rustled as she rose to leave.

Will's voice knifed the quiet. "I shall escort you."

"Oh! I thought you were asleep. Please, I have no wish to disturb you."

Will stood with a stagger and offered his arm. The thought of his touch discomfited her, yet she dared not refuse. "Th-thank you."

Their breathing paired with their footfalls as they climbed the stairs. Joan's legs trembled as they neared her bed-chamber door. She dared not open it. Her back to the door, she faced Will. Not a foot separated them.

He grasped her elbows and stepped even closer. "Joan... lady wife, it is time you accept we are wed."

Joan's pulse skittered and her brain raced; how might she put off Will without raising his ire?

He leaned in. "I have been more than patient, allowing you time to adjust, yet you are mine." He pressed eager lips upon hers.

Lord no! She stiffened and wedged her arms between them. "No, Will." She pushed away, her back bumping against the door.

"No?" His breath reeked of soured wine.

"We have been all through this. No." She spoke with a strength she did not feel. Will loosened his grip enough not to cause bruising. Her heartbeat warned of danger. She tried to appease him. "I am sorry, Will... truly."

Misery washed his face, prompting Joan to free a hand from his grip and cup his bearded jaw. "Five years ago my mother forced me to marry you and we both have suffered from that union's falsity."

His eyes narrowed. "Forced?" He grabbed her wrist and yanked her hand from his face.

"Lest you forget, before turning fourteen I could have renounced our marriage. I did not."

"No… but that changes nothing. You knew when we wed that I had pledged holy vows with another before you. You knew."

Will grabbed her upper arms again. "I never believed that absurd tale!" He pulled her against him, pressed so tight she could barely breathe.

"No, instead you fooled yourself into believing my mother's lie… that my marriage to Thomas was not valid. No matter what I said, you all dismissed me, my rantings those of a…mindless child. But I was not mindless then, and am not now."

"Listen to me. I could have anyone, Joan. Anyone. I chose you… then, and I want you now."

Contrary to the conciliatory tone of his voice, a primal hunger flashed in Will's eyes. A predator closing in. Her breathing came hard as she struggled to free herself. Failing, she lifted her chin and poured determination into her eyes, pinning him.

"Do not try to disarm me, Will. Lest you forget I know you… the real you." Joan stared into eyes just inches from hers. "You chose me? More like you believe you bought me. You want me? Oh, yes! You want my royal blood just like the bloodlines in a broodmare you take a fancy to."

Will's grip tightened. "It is not like that!"

"No? Do not blame me for your pent-up frustration!" Joan's chest heaved. "I told you the truth…that I pledged holy, sacramental vows with Thomas. You would not listen."

"You listen." His voice shook. "Our vows are real… ours made in a house of God, before a priest ordained by God, in front of hundreds of witnesses. How can you deny we are wed?"

Shaking, Joan drew a deep breath. "I will say this one last time. Our vows were spoken falsely for I was already a wife to another… in all ways, Will. All ways. Do you take my meaning?

She paused and armed her voice. "To lay with any but my husband is a mortal sin. I refused to lie with you when we pledged false vows, expediently excused by my mother due to our young ages. Since then, I have kept myself from you, safe within the queen's household by serving as one of her ladies. Understand me. I will refuse to be a wife to you until my dying breath!"

The heat in Will's eyes transformed to hardened ice.

Joan's breath seized. She pushed too far. *Lord help me.* Softening her voice, she said, "Please, Will, I am tired and you are hurting me. Please, let me go." Long moments passed and finally, Will released her with a shove, her head banging the door. "You think poor Thomas Holland's suit will win over mine?" His face twisted. "A lowly nobody against the power of the Salisbury earldom? We will see… "Wife." He backed away, then over his shoulder he said, "I am leaving in the morn, but I will return. You can count on it, dearest Joan. All is not over between us."

Will's footsteps receded down the passage. Not until his chamber door latched shut did she dare open hers. Her hands shook when she shut the door, threw the latch, and slumped against it on the floor. *Blessed Virgin!* She soughed for air. What had she done? Will's patience was already at its breaking point, and now she had scalded his pride. Somehow, she must find a way out… of Donyatt… Somerset…far out of Will's reach.